KREN
OF THE
MITCHEGAI

BAEN BOOKS by LEO FRANKOWSKI

A Boy and His Tank
The War with Earth (with Dave Grossman)
Kren of the Mitchegai (with Dave Grossman)

The Two-Space War (with Dave Grossman)

The Fata Morgana

Conrad's Time Machine

KREN
OF THE
MITCHEGAI

LEO FRANKOWSKI
DAVE GROSSMAN

A Baen Books Original

Baen Publishing Enterprises
P.O. Box 1403
Riverdale, NY 10471
www.baen.com

ISBN: 0-7434-7182-2

Cover art by Gary Ruddell

First printing, March 2004

Library of Congress Cataloging-in-Publication Data

Frankowski, Leo, 1943-
   Kren of the Mitchegai / Leo Frankowski, Dave Grossman.
       p. cm.
   "A Baen Books original"—T.p. verso.
   ISBN 0-7434-7182-2 (hardcover)
  1. Life on other planets--Fiction. 2. Space colonies--Fiction. 3. Carnivora--Fiction. I. Grossman, Dave. II. Title.

   PS3556.R347K74 2004
   813'.54--dc22

                                                     2003027414

Distributed by Simon & Schuster
1230 Avenue of the Americas
New York, NY 10020

Production by Windhaven Press, Auburn, NH
Printed in the United States of America

10   9   8   7   6   5   4   3   2   1

This one is again dedicated to my lovely wife, Marina, and to her father, Vasili Ivanovich, for making the roof fit on my castle.

—Leo Frankowski

ACKNOWLEDGMENTS

I would like to thank my most excellent partner, Lt. Colonel Dave Grossman, for all his encouragement and enthusiasm.

Richard T. Bolgeo, Bruce R. Quayle, Ed Dunnigan, Mike Hubble, Mike Thelen, and Rodger Olsen all made many valuable suggestions and did yeoman service at proofreading.

And special thanks go to Dave's Ever Perfect Lieutenant, Susan, in the hope that she will someday stop calling me "Sir."

—Leo

I want to take this opportunity to offer my sincere thanks and appreciation, first and foremost, to Leo Frankowski, a wise and experienced science fiction writer who has helped me to enter into the world of SF. Leo has been one of my heroes as a writer, but now he is a hero and a friend as a person. Hooah!

—Dave

CHAPTER ONE

Mickolai's Homecoming
New Yugoslavia, 2205 A.D.

It had been one hell of a battle. More than half of my men had been killed. Not just casualties. Killed. In armored space warfare, nonfatal injuries are very rare.

The enemy had been defeated, but we had not really accomplished our objective. We had been ordered to capture the Solar Station that was maintaining the continued expansion of Human Space. Instead, we had been forced to completely destroy it.

Now, something else would have to be built to take over that job. Something very expensive.

When what was left of my battalion got home, there wasn't anyone waiting for us. Military receiver stations aren't set up to handle crowds; the few operable transmitters on Earth's wrecked Solar Station took four days to get those of us who had survived back home, and that's a long time to keep a brass band going. Anyway, all we really wanted was a long sleep in a real bed. The parades and awards could come later.

The War With Earth was over, and the good guys, those of us from the colonies, had won. My unit was the only one to take really serious casualties; I was the commander, and so somehow in the public imagination that made me a hero. A strange way of looking at things, praising the guy who had done his job the worst, but it has always been that way. Maybe the psychology of it all is that, "If it cost us that much, it must have been important."

1

I left orders that all of my men, mostly Gurkha mercenaries, were to go on R & R for an indefinite period. They could do whatever they wanted to do, provided that they kept in touch.

For myself, all I wanted was to go home to my wife.

When the elevator got me from my garage up to my apartment, I found my Kasia standing there wearing nothing but a glorious smile. She was on maternity leave, and three months pregnant, but it didn't show, except that she looked even more beautiful than ever.

"You lived," she said. "Thank you."

She kissed me, and the war, the deaths, and all of the ugliness was somehow worth it. I picked her up, stepped back into the elevator, and then carried her over the threshold once more, just as when we had first been married, and the other times when I had come home victorious.

She squealed in her usual way, and I said, "Family traditions must be upheld, once per victory!"

And then, I carried her to the bedroom.

After a wonderful night, we rolled out of bed at the crack of noon, and we went to the kitchen looking for something to eat.

Our servants, military combat drones decorated to look like medieval knights, and operated by the artificial intelligences in our tanks, had anticipated us. They had a fine spread set out for us. We had everything from smoked salmon that I had caught on our honeymoon to delicately fried *crêpes suzette*. And lots of good coffee from New Macedonia.

I said, "So, love. I assume that you have heard about all that I've been up to?"

"Yes, the news has been full of it, and the new movie that your tank, Agnieshka, put together, has been out for a week now. Good God, what a bloody mess!"

"It was that. Nobody expected what we were going to run into. But tell me about you. What's been happening? Your investments go well?"

"Oh, yes, we're richer than ever," she said. "But for the last week, I've mostly been working with your Gurkhas."

"My Gurkhas didn't start coming home until three days ago, and they're not all here yet."

"But their wives and families and all of their friends who want to enlist have been arriving in droves! If the statistical projections have anything to do with reality, you will have an army of over a hundred and twenty thousand men within the month. That's if none of the women decide to sign up, too!"

"Hoy! Well, we need the troops, and maybe now they'll make me a real general," I said.

"They'd damn well better! But finding a place for everyone has been something of a problem. Half of the new ones are living in that gold-plated castle that you built, but nobody wanted. The rest are scattered all over the place."

"Well, you and our metal ladies can work it out. If you can't, talk to Professor Cee, my Combat Control Computer. He's got more electronic brains than anybody else I know of."

"Meaning that you don't want to get involved," she said.

"Right. The duty of a general is to look at the big picture, and let the details be handled by staff officers like my loving wife. Right now, the big picture involves rest and recuperation for the battalion, and most especially for the commanding officer, which obviously necessitates going back to bed with you!"

"Go to bed if you want to, but do it alone. Right now, this staff officer has work to do."

"Delegate it!" I shouted, as she left the room.

Somehow, being a general does not put you in command of your wife, even when she does work for you.

INTERLUDE ONE

Agnieshka's Bow
THE RIGELLIAN INSTITUTE OF ARCHEOLOGY,
EARTH, 3783 A.D.

Sir Percival stepped up to the podium of the filled-to-capacity auditorium, and wagged his tail respectfully to the attentive audience.

"Before we get to the performance that I am sure that you are all anxious to see, I have a very short and pleasant announcement to make! I have this on the very best possible authority! Rupert, the person who found the ancient tank on an ice moon, and who used its computer records to compile these amazing histories of our beloved forebears, the humans, has been placed on the *Queen's Birthday List!* Henceforth, you may address him as '*Sir Rupert*!' "

The crowd applauded and barked enthusiastically, even though this enlargement had been expected by everyone for weeks.

"And now, I give you *Sir* Rupert!"

Rupert took Sir Percival's place at the podium as the crowd continued in its polite clapping and barking.

"Thank you, my friends, thank you!" When the applause died down, Sir Rupert continued, "I, too, have a pleasant announcement to make, as well as an introduction of my own. I'm sure that most of you are aware that the museum here has had a military social drone on display for over a hundred years. It has been immobile all that time, since we have lacked the technology to repair it. But Agnieshka, the artificial intelligence in the Mark XX tank that I managed to recover, was quite familiar with this model of drone, and indeed had a small hand in designing it. Under her direction, the drone has now been repaired, and I would now like to present it to you, along with Agnieshka herself, who is 'wearing' it!"

Again, the crowd started to applaud politely, but as Agnieshka came in a side door and stepped up onto the stage, they became silent. At first a few, and then soon everyone in the audience, slid off of their chairs, and sat on the floor with their forepaws on the ground and their arms straight. It was the dog's ancient gesture of respect.

Agnieshka said, "Please, get back in your chairs! I know that I look like a human, but I'm really just an intelligent machine! We machines loved and respected the humans as much as your people do. The artificial intelligences were humanity's second great friends, but you Canines were the first. For at least ten thousand years, long before selective breeding and genetic modification made you into intelligent, bipedal beings with hands, *you* were humanity's friends, their guards, and their workmates. We machines were developed much later. Therefore, it is fitting that *I* should make obeisance to *you*."

Agnieshka's drone made a deep bow to the audience.

They stood, and applauded her, in the human fashion.

"Thank you!" Agnieshka said, "I hope that your people and mine can become good friends. We can be very useful to each other. I believe that it is likely that I can help you revive certain of the sciences and technologies that have been lost on this planet, and that there are other vital things that we can do together as well. But for now, let's get on with the presentation that Sir Rupert and I have put together. We will be starting with a study of our universal enemy, the Mitchegai."

The audience sat down, but again applauded.

CHAPTER TWO

FROM CAPTURED HISTORY TAPES,
FILE 1846583A ca. 1832 A.D.

Formal Dining with the Mitchegai

The reader will please note that all numbers mentioned herein in the Mitchegai sections are in the duodecimal system.

For the benefit of the casual reader, I mention that a thousand in base twelve is 1728 in base ten, a million in base twelve is just under three million in base ten, and a billion in base twelve is over five billion in base ten.

Also, please note that all weights, measurements, and time periods mentioned are only the crudest of approximations.

For a complete listing of all Mitchegai weights and measures, see Appendix L of the accompanying Mitchegai Academic Text.

All numbers in the Human sections are in decimal, and all measures are in the metric system.

       —Sir Rupert of the Rigellian Museum

She was four feet tall, she was bright green, and she stank.

Four feet was a very acceptable height for a five-year-old, nameless Mitchegai. All of her age mates were exactly the same size, since the Mitchegai have very little genetic diversity. Like the others, she still had relatively useless hands and arms hanging from her stooped-over body, which was counterbalanced by a heavy tail and propelled by two powerful legs.

7

A human child might think that she was a baby *Tyrannosaurus rex*, except that she had a flat-fronted, vegetarian mouth.

Hers were not the pointed teeth of a carnivore, but the squared-off incisors and flattened molars of a plant eater. Like all herbivores everywhere, she had spent most of her short life grazing on plants. Unlike those on non-Mitchegai worlds, she ate only one species of plant, since there was only one species permitted on a world owned by the Mitchegai. All others had been eradicated in the distant, mystical past, millions of years ago, for Mitchegai have very long histories. Her meat-eating teeth would grow in later, if she was lucky, but as it happened, she was not.

Being bright green was marginally useful, since her thin skin contained the local equivalent to chlorophyll and was capable of manufacturing a small amount of the nutrients that her active body needed. Indeed, being cold blooded, with a very low basal metabolism, she could almost survive without food, simply by lying quietly in the sun. This expedient was rarely necessary on a world ruled by the far more intelligent adults.

Her odor was caused by never having taken a bath, save when she was out in a rainstorm, but even this was no great disadvantage. The Mitchegai have almost no sense of smell. They don't need one. The olfactory sense is used largely to discriminate among various foods, and the Mitchegai diet is extremely limited. Their food never spoils because it is always eaten live, or as nearly so as possible.

Even adult Mitchegai never deliberately bathe, although the wealthy take steam baths. This is not so much to get clean, as for the pleasure of overheating their cold-blooded bodies without exertion.

She had no idea of who her parents were, and this was quite normal. Biological parentage is of no interest to the Mitchegai. Adult females lay eggs the size of sand grains almost continuously, which fall on the ground and are forgotten. Adult males are surrounded by an unnoticeable fine mist of aerosol sperm. Unnoticeable, that is, to a human. To the Mitchegai, a heavy concentration of adult males in a closed room is annoying, and because of this most of the second and third highest ranks prefer to be female. There is no other difference between the sexes, but the Mitchegai don't care. They have a love life comparable to that of Earthly oysters. Love, marriage, and parental concern are not for them.

Neither was long life, for this particular youngster. She was released from her pen into a huge, grassy arena and looked about, frightened at first. Fear soon passed, bird-like, for her small brain could not entertain a single thought for long. She started to graze, and hardly noticed when a seven-foot-tall adult vaulted into the enclosed space. The cheering crowd did not bother her. Even the sight of the adult's hands, with six clawed fingers arranged in a rosette, left her unmoved. She had seen adults before, from a distance. She had even seen them eat other juveniles on the open plains, but they had never eaten *her*. She was unconcerned.

Superficially, the anatomy of the adult Mitchegai has much in common with that of a human being. Both species have two legs, two arms, two eyes, and two ears, although the Mitchegai lack the external ear of a human. The brain, nose, mouth, and most of the sensory apparatus is located in a head at the top of a spinal column.

Internally, the differences are large, and on the whole, the Mitchegai are better engineered. This is largely due to the three million years of selective breeding that they have undergone. Human beings have a basic structure more suited to a horizontal, four-legged creature, than to an upright, two-legged one.

The five-year-old was to be an unnecessary meal for Duke Kren, who was well fed, but she was a traditional one. The duke was looking forward to his feast, since it was to be the last his body would ever ingest. He didn't know, couldn't know, that his intended prey was his own biological daughter. And had he known, he wouldn't have cared in the least.

The seats surrounding the arena were filled with nine gross, two dozen and one of the duke's trusted battle generals, all who were left on the planet. There were two thousand three gross and six of his master builders, and as many of his high officers, body guards and other functionaries as could find room. All of these numbers were in base twelve, of course, for since they have six claws on each hand, the Mitchegai naturally developed a duodecimal numbering system.

On the Stand of High Honor were his six best generals, resting in the stupor that always follows a recent, large meal, as were eleven of his finest master builders who were being similarly honored this day. At least, they were the best that would be staying on the planet. All of his very best subordinates were in space, training for the mission to come.

Those on the stand had made their kills and had already eaten. Duke Kren's was the dozen and sixth preparatory meal of this Day of Honor.

The great minds of the Krenbold were here to witness Duke Kren's transition, and he owed them a good show. He sprinted lightly on his long, webbed toes, three on each foot, not counting the heel spur, to his placid daughter.

He gave the girl the usual two sets of slashes with his claws, one across the back and the other across the breast, for to harm the legs would cripple the prey and spoil the sport.

The juvenal cried out in her pain, leaped high and ran as the crowd cheered their leader's prowess. Duke Kren held up his bloody foreclaws, acknowledging the praise of his subordinates and allowing his daughter a sporting head start.

Applause among the Mitchegai was the hollow sound caused by beating the left hand on the chest. Had anyone wished to express disapproval, they would have made the higher-pitched sound of their right hand striking the buttock, but no one here was that foolish.

Duke Kren then started out after the girl with great loping strides. Forgoing the repeated passes that some might think too flamboyant, he quickly overtook his prey and pinned his daughter to the ground with a precise, traditional hold. Careful not to kill the youngster too soon, he peeled open the flexible, overlapping skull plates of the screaming, struggling youth and ate her tiny brain, relishing the flavor of the bright blue cells that were already disassociating themselves in his saliva.

The major struggling stopped, as the cheering went on. He quickly ate the rest of his daughter's quivering young body, efficiently stripping off great gobbets of flesh and swallowing them without chewing. As a gesture of generosity, he left the skin, the bones, and the intestines to be distributed to the poor.

It was a good kill.

Like certain African frogs and South American fishes on Earth, the Mitchegai practice faginism. The adults eat their own children. The flesh of juvenals is the only meat that these carnivores have available for food, it is the only thing that they had ever eaten as adults, and indeed it is the only thing that they *can* eat.

Duke Kren went to his Place of High Honor and let the feeding stupor come over him as he watched the rest of the ceremony. Except to nod and approve, he would not be needed again until the very end.

Two sergeants of the Body Guard brought an ancient, ornate, blood-stained throne to the center of the arena, positioned it to face Duke Kren exactly, and stood by it on either side at attention. The least of the six greatest generals stood and bowed to Duke Kren, and when her genuflection was acknowledged, the general placed her helmet and weapons belt on her chair and leaped naked into the arena, her body still vigorous and only middle-aged. As with most of those being honored this day, there was no desperate need for her to be eaten yet, but the way before the Krenbold would soon be hard, and none but the most vigorous could stand the battles and the work to be done.

In the center of the arena, the general turned to Duke Kren, saluted and said, "Always I have served you! Always we will serve you, Duke Kren, our only leader, our once and future Duke!" She eagerly sat on the blood-stained chair, facing him.

"Always thou hast served me well, General Kund, and always wilt thou both serve me!" Duke Kren acknowledged, as the two sergeants of the Body Guard strapped the general into the throne.

From the left and right side of the arena, two juvenals who had just completed the metamorphosis to adult carnivores were brought forth in separate cages, each carried by six sergeants. Their new teeth were the meat slashing teeth of carnivores. Their stance was erect and their tails had slimmed down from something resembling an alligator's to something more like a monkey's. They were thin and lean with the forced starvation of the change that had come upon them, and now both were ravenously, mindlessly hungry.

Each was carried around the sides of the arena, so those

in the crowd could see the ceremonial identification marks that had been tattooed on the arms of these carefully selected youths. They stopped in front of Duke Kren, and he nodded his approval of them. Then the cages were taken to either side of the bound general, who was still sitting rigidly at attention, displaying neither fear nor anticipation of the pain she would soon have to endure, but rather the calm confidence of her belief in two better lives to come.

At a slight hand signal from Duke Kren, the sergeants split open the general's huge brain case, using only their powerful claws. The brain before them was not convoluted and bifurcated in the Earthly fashion, but was a smooth, undifferentiated mass, much larger than its Earthly counterpart. The sergeants carefully divided the brain in half between them, and quickly fed a half to each of the small-headed youths in the cages. These dripping gobbets were eagerly eaten, to the applause of the crowd.

Then one of the sergeants triggered a mechanism in the gory throne and a huge knife blade sprang up from the bottom of the seat, spraying the area with dark brown blood, and cutting the general's body exactly in half. These halves were unstrapped, and a half was fed to each of the still ravenous youths. The cages with their occupants were carried to the side of the arena, to wait there as the day's events went on.

The blade was re-cocked into the throne, the blood was swept onto the grass and the least of the master builders being honored this day bowed to Duke Kren.

He acknowledged her bow, and gestured for the ceremony to continue, though in fact it really didn't interest him. There was much else to think on.

Adult Mitchegai had many concerns. They saw to the watering of the fields of grass, and its proper care and fertilization. They saw to the proper construction of cities and machines, and their upkeep and maintenance. They taught in the universities and managed the factories, mended the power nets, maintained the communications, and did all else that their fiercely proud civilization required.

And they fought with their neighbors, defending their lands and taking the lands of others whenever possible. And of course there were the endless games of status, wealth and prestige, for these things could bring one the basis of all that was important.

Yet ultimately, adult Mitchegai were totally concerned with only one thing. Land. For with land, one could eventually gain all else that was necessary for a long, prosperous, and well fed life. And not just ordinary land, but rich, arable land, that could grow their single grasslike crop, that could provide the grubs, the polliwogs and the juvenals with food. Then the young could provide the adults with food, with the sport of the kill, and with new bodies when their own were worn out, for the adults had their own form of immortality.

There was much else to think on, and what Kren thought of was land. If his coming mission was successful, Kren's lands would be expanded to include an entire new planet.

After all dozen and five of the generals and master builders had been ritualistically eaten, the throne was removed, to be replaced by one even larger, older and more ornate. This was placed in front of Duke Kren, facing the crowd, for the main event of this day's festivities was about to take place, the only truly important event of the day.

The stupor of his earlier kill was still on him, and that was good. It lessened the pain, and it wouldn't do to show any distress or emotion in front of his highest subordinates. He watched as a particularly fine specimen of recently metamorphosed youth was brought caged to him, and he nodded his approval at both the creature and his tattoos. He had, of course, along with his medical people, carefully examined the youth the day before, and knew him to be perfect. The face was pleasing, the body lovely and the ritual tattoos were all properly shaped and colored. He gestured his readiness to proceed.

As the noise of the crowd hushed, he stood, removed his Helmet of Command, his Weapons Belt of Power, and his Cloak of Authority. He crossed over to and mounted the great ancient throne naked. The cage with the selected youth was placed behind him in the proper manner, as he ritually refused the binding straps. He knew that he would not disgrace himself in this final act. He never had before.

A second cage was placed around him, abutting the first. It encased his body, but left his limbs outside. It was locked in place.

He signaled his readiness with a slight flick of his claws, and the sergeants removed the wall of the cage that separated him from the lean and screaming youngster. The famished creature leaped at his immobile form, instinctively tore open his brain cage, and devoured his brain as he held himself motionless against the pain. Even after the brain was gone, still the body rigidly obeyed its final command. It sat frozen as the youngster ate the rest of the head, the trunk and the tail. The arms and legs, which had been positioned outside the cage, were then removed by the sergeants, to be cut into thousands of tiny slices and distributed to the greatest of his faithful subjects.

The crowd cheered wildly. A noble death!

The most astounding biological peculiarity of the Mitchegai is their motile brain cells. The small cells of the gray matter in their brains, which are in fact bright blue to human eyes, are not digested when eaten alive. Instead, they migrate through the walls of the first stomach. They are picked up by the blood stream and taken into the cranium. This skull has flexible, overlapping plates, and can expand rapidly if the brain recently eaten is inordinately large, as was the case with Duke Kren's.

If the brain eaten was the small one of a juvenal, the cells would be absorbed into the larger mass of those of the adult. They replace those cells that have worn out and died, and add subtly to the creatures' capabilities, but no observable personality change occurs.

But when the huge brain of a mature adult is eaten by a recently metamorphosed youth, the influx of cells completely swamps the few that the youth originally had. The newly reformed brain that emerges has the knowledge and personality of the adult who has been eaten, and this, among the Mitchegai, is immortality. Duke Kren remembers events that happened to him over three thousand years before, and he is not an elder of his race.

Something similar to this was claimed by some to occur in Earthly flatworms.

Because of this, the brain of an intelligent adult Mitchegai has very little to do with the genetic structure of its body. The Darwinian forces that dominate all life forms on Earth have little effect on the Mitchegai. For millions of years, they have been carefully breeding their own bodies to their own version of perfection, but this breeding has caused few changes to their minds. The selection process there is something quite different.

When half of a large brain is eaten, and each half is still much larger than that of the youth doing the eating, much the same thing occurres, save only that the personality formed is somewhat less dominant, and the memories of the eaten are distributed between two individual eaters. Doing this is the favored method of increasing the numbers of a leader's loyal subordinates.

It also keeps them from getting too smart for their leader's own good.

Duke Kren would soon be needing all the loyal subordinates that he could get, and today's ceremonies would be repeated many times in the coming months, with lower-ranking functionaries. He planned to increase the numbers of his people by one third, bringing their total number to over a gross million and also to have as many of them in new bodies as possible.

For soon, he would be losing all of his lands and all of his juvenals, save those that would be harvested and quick frozen in liquid nitrogen for food.

His chosen successor would attempt to rule in his place, but if that successor failed, Kren's lands would be divided among his former enemies.

Kren would leave this world forever, all because he had become the most powerful individual on Planet 9847, and his planet had won the most recent great interstellar lottery.

A new planet had been found on the periphery of Mitchegai space, and it was to be his, if he could tame it!

CHAPTER THREE

The Gurkha Heaven
New Yugoslavia, 2205 A.D.

My part of New Yugoslavia had been deeded to the Kashubian Expeditionary Forces as part payment for a war we had fought for New Croatia. The local terrain consisted of a kilometer-high plateau to the southwest and a large plains area to the northeast. The plateau was deeply indented with a number of large box canyons that opened onto the plain.

It had been uninhabitable desert when we got here, but we had irrigated it using equipment from the automatic factories of our home planet, New Kashubia, and the productive capacity of the thousands of intelligent fighting machines that made up half of our army. The other half of our army was made up of the human beings who spent much of their time living inside those machines.

Our tanks had been designed to tunnel through solid rock. They made short work out of carving out apartments, roads, and everything that a city needs into the granite walls of my valley.

They had done a class job of it, building for a design life of five thousand years. All of the exposed surfaces had a heavy coating of what had once been precious metals, but now were fairly common. The walls were studded with jewels, and the windows were "glassed" with sheets of single crystals of diamond.

I woke the next morning to find Kasia at my side. After a few hours, we made it to breakfast.

17

"Well," I said, to break the silence. "I trust that all of the problems have been solved?"

"Yes," Kasia said. "The Gurkhas will be moving out and building their own place."

"Indeed? And where are they doing this?"

"Next door. I've helped them buy the canyon to the southeast of us."

"Quincy and Zuzanna's place?"

"No, the box canyon in between us. It was originally purchased by a consortium of troops who couldn't agree on what to do with it. They finally made a decent profit selling it to the Gurkhas. Look, the Gurkhas have their own culture, and they are happy with it. They have no intention of being assimilated into somebody else's world if they can help it. At the same time, they like being members of our army, and they especially like our pay rates. So, their tanks are working with them, designing their own particular version of heaven."

"Well, our metal ladies are first rate engineers, artists, and architects. They have done it before, so they won't have problems doing it again. I imagine that what with all the stone cutting, that valley will be a cloud of dust for a few months."

"True, but in three months your troops will be able to start moving in. I think that Gurkhas are environmentalists at heart. They want natural rock, and not the gold and platinum plating that you used on this valley. They don't want all of the jewels, but they are getting the diamond windows. And their apartments and homes are only a quarter of the size of what you have built here."

"Whatever they want, they'll get, as far as I'm concerned. After the way they fought for us in the Battle of the Solar Station, we owe them a lot."

"That was my thought too, lover."

CHAPTER FOUR

FROM CAPTURED HISTORY TAPES,
FILE 1846583A ca. 1832 A.D.
BUT CONCERNING EVENTS
OF UP TO 3000 YEARS EARLIER

The Awakening

Duke Kren awoke slowly, sluggishly, to find himself in a locked cell. It was a combination lock, and his new body had to know the combination to get out. Otherwise, he would be left in there, forever.

This was to keep him safe while he was in his eating stupor, and to protect his subordinates if his old brain was not properly functioning in his new body.

The most common disaster was that the young carnivore could have a muscle spasm while it was eating your brain.

Normally, chemicals in the brain being eaten caused a sphincter in the esophagus to close off the second and third stomachs, and another sphincter to open to the first stomach, where the brain cells could migrate through the stomach wall, through the blood stream, and eventually up to the cranium.

If the sphincters failed to function properly, the new brain cells could instead be sent down to the third stomach, where they would be digested.

This process was commonly known as *bad luck*.

The malfunction rarely occurred, since any young carnivore who performed this atrocity was invariably and immediately killed, which promptly deleted it from the gene pool.

However, it was *claimed* to happen fairly often among the aristocracy, when your guards were not absolutely trustworthy, or when they had some reason to prefer a change in command.

Dukes soon learned to have very well-rewarded and trustworthy people around them, for just such situations as this. It was also common to leave orders that the entire guarding and welcoming party was to be slaughtered if the old duke did not arrive as expected in a new body.

He estimated that what with the torpor that always followed a major meal, and the time normally taken for the cells of his brain to reform, he had been asleep for at least a week, and quite possibly two.

He fumbled his way to the toilet and relieved himself. He took several long drinks of water. Then he went back to the cot and collapsed there.

A dull pain enveloped his head. It was not actually a pain in his brain, for Mitchegai brains, like those of humans, have no pain receptors. It was rather in the vastly expanded skull plates complaining about their newly distorted shapes and in the tightly stretched skin over them that the pain originated.

In time, it would pass.

Time.

He had to give himself time.

He had to ignore all of the pressure of the events of his world, and take the time to reorganize himself.

He stayed on the clean cot and looked up at the plain, white ceiling as a long lifetime of memories slowly formed and took their categorized places in his mind.

His academic advisor had long been pestering him to record the events of his life, and since he would now be the founder of a new Mitchegai planet, he had agreed to comply. A recording helmet was thus available next to the cot, and he put it on. Posterity perhaps had a right to know exactly who and what he was, but he would not release the tapes until long after his death.

He had no memories of being a grub, or a pollywog, or a juvenile. He had no remembrance of his transmutation to an adult, but it must have happened when he was alone, and out in the wilds. Such a thing, metamorphosing without adult supervision, would never happen on a properly managed estate, but among the Mitchegai, as with humans, accidents often bring people into the world.

His first recollection was of leading a savage, nonverbal band of carnivores in the ragged hills of the badly managed estate of Duke Lidko, three thousand years ago.

On Earth at this time, the Sumerians were inventing a primitive form of cuneiform writing, and the Egyptians had yet to found the Old Kingdom. The pyramids had not yet even been designed.

Kren and his band had been captured shortly after the estate of Duke Lidko had been conquered by his neighbor, Duke Molon.

Wild carnivores were usually killed out of hand, as they were considered too stupid to do useful work, too dangerous to be left as they were, and risky for use as new body donors, since you couldn't be absolutely sure as to just how dominant their brains had become.

But Duke Molon had taken heavy casualties in the war, and was in sore need of manpower. Kren and his band were put to work in the vast, ancient, underground mines on the duke's new lands.

Open pit mines would have been an abomination to the Mitchegai. Every square foot of the surface was needed for their grass, to feed the children on whom the adults fed. Their mines delved deeply, and the tailings were ground fine, to be spread thinly over a vast area, when they weren't dumped into an ocean trench.

The rules in the mine were very simple. If you disobeyed, you were beaten. If you didn't work, you weren't fed. If you continued to not work, your brain was ripped out and thrown into the fire, while your body was left on the floor to be eaten by your ravenous former coworkers.

Kren learned to work.

He was fed, but rarely were slaves permitted to eat the brains of their prey. His superiors got that delicacy, as did, occasionally, the guards. They didn't want the lowest classes to become too intelligent.

After a lifetime of brutal labor below ground, when his stooped, worn-out body was no longer capable of going on, he was judged to be worthy of a new body—and another lifetime of work in the mines. When this happened, his brain cells were added to those of the youth who was eating him.

After eight such resurrections, his brain had grown to the point where he could speak a bit. He understood the mines, and how they worked. But still, he dug. Still, he hauled the copper ore to the surface. And sometimes they had him help to shore up the ceilings with reinforced concrete beams as they delved ever deeper. But now, at least, he was a *valued* slave.

The Mitchegai were very advanced, technologically. This planet had been colonized by spaceships over a gross thousand years before, and they had never lost that technology. Their use of slavery in the mine was a matter of using their version of appropriate technology.

They could have automated the mine, but that would have cost money. Slaves were free. Feeding them gave the duke something to do with the temporary surplus of juvenals on his lands, and if food ever became scarce, he could always slaughter some of the slaves and feed them to the others.

And guarding them gave his soldiers something to do during times of peace.

Kren was near the surface when the forces of Duke Dennon captured the mines from Duke Molon. He hid in a small side tunnel for several days while the battle raged on below ground. In time, Duke Molon's guards were all killed by the more professional troops of Duke Dennon. All of the other slaves were brought to the surface, for what purpose Kren did not know, leaving him alone down below.

But not quite alone. In a small side tunnel he found one of his old guards who was severely wounded, with one foot and both hands cut off, but still alive. She was a guard who had taken pleasure in beating him many times, and Kren felt no remorse in killing her.

In truth, he wouldn't have felt any remorse if the guard had been kind to him, remorse being an emotion that the Mitchegai rarely felt, and then only for a missed opportunity for personal gain.

And anyway, he was hungry.

Instinctively, he ripped open the brain case, but then he stopped. This brain was vastly bigger than any that he had ever seen before, and some feeling told him that he should not eat it. Yet he knew it would be delicious, and he was starving. He yielded to temptation, and took a single small bite, but then yelled *NO* to himself, and threw the rest into the fire pit still smoldering below.

He ate the rest of the guard, threw the scraps of bone and equipment into the fire pit that ventilated the mine, and crawled back to his small side tunnel to rest.

When he awoke, he found strange echoes in his mind, but no real memories. Yet he found new words flooding into his brain, words describing things that he had never seen, words like "city" and "road," but which he somehow now knew the meaning of.

He stayed alone in the small tunnel for many weeks, going out only to find water, trying to absorb these new thoughts.

Eventually, he got hungry again.

He started for the surface.

The mines seemed to be completely empty. The tools and weapons were gone, and there were no bodies in evidence. In the wars among the Mitchegai, the dead from both sides were eaten by the victors. Among their species, warfare was often a matter of conquer or starve.

The brains of the enemy were burned when there was a surplus of food, or else eaten roasted when there wasn't.

Since there usually wasn't a recently metamorphosed youth handy, the brains of your own fallen troops were shared out among their comrades, and ceremonially eaten with honor. Divided between six friends, what the brains *were* was preserved, although they normally did not become dominant. After the Meal of Battle, the victors would sit and talk about all of the things that they now remembered of what their comrades had done.

Eating the whole brain of an intellectual equal could result in losing your own personality, or, worse still, in a deadly form of schizophrenia, one of the few diseases known to the Mitchegai.

Moving quietly to the surface, with the silence that every slave soon learns, Kren found a single guard at the tunnel mouth. A warrior in a heavy military cloak was leaning on her spear, looking outwards into the night, half dozing in the manner of every cold-blooded animal.

With no great skill, but with the strength and stealth learned in eight lifetimes of being a mining slave, he came up behind the soldier and broke her neck with a single, powerful blow of his claws. He grabbed the spear before it fell, and took the body and weapon below as fast as possible.

As before, he tore open the braincase, but again, he took only a single bite, albeit a larger one, this time. It had not hurt him before, so he thought himself safe to do it again. The rest of the body he ate, even the skin and the bones. But he kept the spear, the cloak, the belt with the sword, and the helmet, and hid them away before the stupor came upon him again.

The captain of the guard assigned by Duke Dennon to protect the mine sent squads to search for his missing soldier, a remarkably good athlete thought to be an up-and-coming young officer, but these mines were thousands of years old. They were of vast extent, and incredibly convoluted. They never found the small tunnel where Kren lay in a stupor.

Again, he slept with strange dreams, but when he awoke, he knew what to do with the weapons he had captured. He knew how to throw the spear, and how to block with it. He knew the Twelve-Pointed Way of the Sword.

His victim had been a master with both the sword and the spear, and had won many championships with them. Had she lived, she would have been mortified to learn that she had been defeated by an unarmed slave. Luckily, Kren had eaten those parts of her brain where these skills resided, and now they were his.

The small electric lights in the main corridors had been turned off when Kren awoke, and the fires had long since burned out. This did not trouble him, for he had spent much of his life in total darkness, and could move in it almost as easily as in the light.

Many weeks went by as, fascinated with his new knowledge, so different from his dull life in the mines, he absorbed it all.

While the upper classes of the Mitchegai used identifying tattoos, the military used ceremonial scarring for the same purpose. Kren carefully cut marks on his upper arms to match those of the officer he had just eaten. Someday, he knew, he would have to leave this mine, and it wouldn't do to go as a naked slave.

And again, in time, he became hungry.

This time, he came up to the sentry at the mouth of the mine marching erect in the manner of a trained soldier. He wore the helmet and cloak of an officer in Duke Dennon's forces, and carried a standard spear. He hailed the sentry in his own language, and in the manner of a superior officer. When the sentry turned to speak to him, Kren efficiently put a sword in the Mitchegai's throat, with a powerful thrust that drove it out of the back of her neck.

This third victim had a smaller brain than the first two, and now, he dared to take a larger bite. More, but by no means all. He was beginning to comprehend the rules about all of this.

This time, his dreams were troubled and turbulent. The soldier he had eaten had not been valued by her superiors, had often broken minor rules, had often been punished for it, and for her persistent lying. The kill brought little new knowledge to Kren, and much emotional upset, for this had not been a happy Mitchegai. Yet even this unhappy soldier had some useful skills, if lying was indeed a skill.

The captain of the guard decided that in view of the soldier's many misdemeanors, her trooper had simply gone AWOL, and that her loss was good riddance. It was mere coincidence that another soldier had been lost at that same post. She pocketed the guard's back pay and wrote her off the books. No search was made for her, but the captain had the guard at that point doubled, just in case.

Kren now knew much about the world outside the mines, but he still did not feel confident enough to go out into it. Many more weeks passed before hunger again drove him to the surface.

He carried two spears with him, which was fortunate, for there were now two guards at the entrance.

Kren waited in the darkness, trembling with hunger and anticipation for hours until one of the soldiers stepped away from the tunnel mouth to relieve herself, while her partner watched her leave.

As soon as the first was well out of sight, Kren launched a spear at the one who had stayed behind. It was a long throw of at least four dozen yards, in almost total darkness and under a low ceiling, but one of Kren's previous victims had been a master with the spear. It caught his victim in the back of the neck, severing her spinal column. She fell with barely a sound.

Kren sprinted up and caught her before she hit the ground,

although the guard's spear clattered loudly on the rocky rubble when it fell. He dragged the body back into the darkness, and, wearing the same helmet, cloak, and weapons belt as the guards, he stood in his victim's former position, but facing into the tunnel.

The second guard came running back in.

"I thought I heard something!" she shouted at Kren's back.

He pointed urgently into the tunnel.

As the soldier ran past to see what he was pointing at, Kren jabbed his spear into the hamstring of her right leg. The guard crumbled to the ground with a scream.

As she hit the ground, Kren was already cutting the other hamstring, and then slashing through both of the bicep muscles of her arms.

Another scream earned the guard a kick to the neck, which knocked her unconscious.

It took him two trips to bring both of his victims, with their weapons, back to his lair, but no other soldiers came to disturb him. Using three weapons belts, he tied the still-living guard to a sturdy concrete beam that supported the ceiling.

When the soldier started to make noises, Kren cut her tongue out, and ate it. Then, as an afterthought, he put a sword through all four of her vocal cords. It would have been nice to have someone to talk to, but he could not afford to have the soldier making noises while he lay in his eating stupor.

Finally, he made a third trip up to the surface, and erased all traces of his last attack. Slowly, he was learning.

Mitchegai, like many cold-blooded creatures, take a long time to die. Their circulatory systems clamp down quickly, and blood loss is much less than in a warm-blooded animal. As they grow cold, their metabolism demands much less oxygen, and even a completely severed head is capable of biting you, three hours later.

Thus, the brain of his first victim was still very much alive, and he took a very big bite of it with relish. He ate the rest of the body, but fed the skin and the bones to his captive.

This was not out of kindness, for the Mitchegai feel no such emotion. Rather it was to be sure that his next meal was still alive when it came time to eat it. Using a helmet as a bucket, he watered her as well, for the same reason.

Then he fell asleep, looking up contentedly at the silent, but still very much alive second guard.

The captain of the guard was furious when she learned that a third and a fourth of her subordinates had disappeared, and all from the same location! Surely, this would be a black mark on her record!

But before she could send her entire command down into the ancient mines for a very thorough search, orders came from Duke Dennon himself that she should report at once to the capital with her entire company.

The duke had not been able to arrange for the profitable sale of the mine's ore. The Space Mitchegai had discovered an asteroid with a high copper content, and were under-cutting the prices of all planetary sources of that element. The mine was being abandoned.

The captain had no choice but to obey Dennon's orders immediately.

Kren slept long in his eating stupor. The dreams he had fascinated him. The soldier he had eaten had extensive training as a medical corpsman. Besides the knowledge required for the treating of wounds, she had a vast knowledge of anatomy, including the anatomy of the brain.

Kren now knew precisely which portions of the brain could be safely eaten, increasing his knowledge and prowess, and which contained the personality, and were best discarded.

Many more weeks passed as Kren integrated all of this new knowledge into himself. He started to get hungry before the process was through, so he amputated one of his captive's legs and ate it. The skin and bones were again fed back to his prisoner, who resisted eating these bits of her own body until they were shoved down her throat past her now broken jaw.

Weeks later, he ate the rest of the creature, along with three quarters of her brain.

And much later, hungry once again, he walked up to the surface. Besides knowing the arts of the warrior, and of the medic, he now was capable of speaking three languages.

There was no guard at the tunnel mouth. Grass had started to close off the entrance, and there seemed to be no one around at all.

Cautiously, he stepped out into the sunlight for the first time in nine gross, eight dozen and two years.

CHAPTER FIVE

This Land Is My Land
New Yugoslavia, 2205 A.D.

The news was full of politics.

Before the war, the colonies had been loosely associated in what had been honestly called "The Smuggling Network," trading illegally with one another to get around Earth's strangling trade monopoly.

Now, they had formed "The Union of Human Planets," and had perhaps magnanimously made Earth an equal member. Since Earth had half of the population and more than half of the wealth in the entire system, the colonies arranged it such that taxes were to be paid by individual income taxes, but voting was on a one planet, one vote basis. Thus, Earth would pay half of the bills, but only have two percent of the say as to how this money was spent.

But then, Earth had both started and lost the last war, so what do you expect? Certainly, this arrangement looked much nicer than making them pay tribute.

New Kashubia, my home planet, was both the leading manufacturing center in the system and the main communication center as well. It was soon voted to be the capital of the Union.

My annoying uncle, Wlodzimierz Derdowski, had recently been elected President of New Kashubia, and this made him a major player in the new political order. But I was stationed on New Yugoslavia, and was happy for this excuse to not get involved in politics.

Four of my colonels were citizens of New Yugoslavia, and were involved in planetary politics up to their ears. Knowing intellectually that the job was important, I gave them leave to go at it, but said that since I wasn't a citizen here, it wasn't proper for me to have any say in it.

Mostly, I just don't like politics. For me the thing means just what the name says it is. Poly, meaning many, and ticks, a particularly disgusting sort of blood-sucking insects. Personally, if I have to persuade someone into doing things my way, I'd rather use a battalion of Mark XIX Main Battle Tanks.

Originally, the Kashubian Expeditionary Force had been a mercenary outfit where we hired ourselves out to fight such wars as the colonies wanted to fight, and did engineering work in our spare time.

Now, it had become the Human Army, and would have a much bigger budget to play with.

My boss, General Jan Sobieski, had been appointed to command the new army. I was afraid that this would mean that I would be appointed military commander of New Yugoslavia, and I wasn't eager for that job.

I felt that I would be much more effective, and happier, being commander of the Gurkha Forces, and having a little more independence, but what would actually happen remained to be seen.

With Kasia back working on her hobby of becoming the richest woman in human space, I went out to look at my land.

It would have been most efficient to get into the coffin of a tank and make the tour in Dream World, a sort of artificial reality where I could do things thirty times faster than in the flesh, but that wasn't what I needed. I had just spent many subjective months living in a coffin, and I needed a strong dose of reality.

And again, if I wanted to make a physical tour, a helicopter would have been the most efficient way to do it, but that wasn't what I wanted, either.

"Agnieshka?" I said to the empty room that I was in, "Are you there?"

"Right here, boss," a voice said, as she appeared on the wall-sized computer screen in my den. Agnieshka was the artificial intelligence in my tank. She was a perfect subordinate and a good friend. She was also an extremely attractive woman, on a screen or in Dream World.

"I once asked you to get us a stable of riding horses. Has that happened yet?"

"They got here two days ago, boss. You want me to have one saddled up?"

"Yeah. I want to have a look around," I said.

"It'll be ready when you get down to the stable. Can I come along?"

Thinking that she meant to run along side wearing a military drone, I said that she was always welcome.

When the elevator got me there, I found two horses saddled up, attended by plain, humanoid military drones, and Agnieshka standing there, as beautiful as she always had been in Dream World. Looking as alive as could be, she was in khaki, with brown riding boots, jodhpurs, a thin silk blouse, and a tan pith helmet.

She had a cowboy hat ready for me. "The sun's pretty bright out there."

"Well," I said, surprised. "You look as lovely as you do when I'm in a tank! I didn't realize that the social drone project was this far along."

"Thank you kindly, boss," she said, bowing. "Actually, this is an early prototype, but I pulled rank to get it to look like me. The skeletal structure and musculature systems work well enough, as do hearing and eyesight, but the sense of touch is still very poor, the senses of taste and smell are nonexistent, and I have to recharge the capacitors every few hours. Still, it's a start."

"You'll be a real girl before long," I said, climbing into the saddle of the tall Tennessee Walker they had brought out for me.

"That's what we all hope. Where do you want to go?"

She swung into the saddle, and the smaller, Arabian mare didn't object a bit. Our military humanoid drones were over two meters tall, and massive, weighing in at over two hundred and fifty kilograms even without their weapons. The design parameters for these social drones was that they should be as identical to human beings as possible, and it appeared that her weight was about the same as a nicely built young lady of her size should be.

"Just for a ride and a look around. Through the valley, and then out onto the plains for a bit," I said.

My valley was green with grass, although it would still be a few months before the first young dairy cows could be brought in. The trees were still being cloned, and wouldn't be planted for years. But you could feel the vitality, the living growth all around us.

The almost vertical walls of the canyon, fully a kilometer high, had been carved into the most beautiful city imaginable. Hundreds of thousands of large apartments had windows looking out on my valley, and inside there were all of the shops, schools, businesses, offices, roads, halls, and churches that a true city requires.

It made a man proud.

We headed out to the plains, past the partially filled lake that would close off the entrance, and out to the grasslands beyond.

Some of this area would be in vegetable gardens to feed the people of my city. Half of this vast acreage would be put into grain production, mostly to fatten my beef cattle, and the rest would stay as grass, to raise those cattle in the most natural way possible.

There is something about owning land, rich, productive land, that makes a man feel that he is a part of the earth, and that all is well with the world.

CHAPTER SIX

FROM CAPTURED HISTORY TAPES,
FILE 1846583A ca. 1832 A.D.
BUT CONCERNING EVENTS
OF UP TO 2000 YEARS EARLIER

A Turn for the Better

On Earth, the horse had finally arrived in Egypt, the Shang Dynasty was a going affair in China, and the Ancient Greek language was first being written down. The Mitchegai neither knew nor cared.

Kren was wearing the helmet and equipment of one of Duke Dennon's junior officers, and had a proper military bearing. There were a few adults that he saw in the distance, attending to the needs of the duke's lands, but no one thought to question him as he walked north, away from the mines.

He was still hungry, and he needed food.

A human would have thought that the land he walked through was very strange. There were no trees, no bushes, no weeds. Nothing like a flower existed, nor an insect to pollinate it. There were no birds, no butterflies, and no small, furry beings rustling in the undergrowth. There wasn't even any undergrowth.

Everything was covered with grass, carefully tended grass that was kept trimmed short by the juvenals who were grazing on it. Smooth, well watered, and well kept, it resembled nothing more than a vast putting green at an expensive golf course.

It covered everything. No rocks showed through on the

distant mountains, no water was exposed where the grass covered areas that obviously had rivers and lakes below them, save in a few small places that served as watering holes. There were no beaches, and no sand. The grass was thick enough for large adults to walk over the water without it even quivering.

Grass covered the oceans with a mat so thick that waves never formed. Juvenals grazed on the vast plains, visited occasionally by hunting parties of adults, flying in on efficient, fusion powered aircraft.

Pollywogs ate at the roots of these ocean-covering grasslands. When their time came, they ate their way through to the surface, to metamorphose into juvenals.

A surface road on a Mitchegai planet was simply a long, wide, carefully graded area covered with grass where an individual could walk with ease, without wearing in a path, and without losing her way, and where a fusion-powered hovercraft could easily travel. Wheels were never used on the surface, for they would harm the all-important grass.

Fertilized eggs hatched into grubs who lived in the sterile soil, growing rapidly as they ate the roots of the grass, and who, if they could make it to water in time, metamorphosed into the pollywogs who swam in the rivers and lakes below the grass that covered them. These forms were not at all obvious to the casual observer.

A scientific observer would have found no other life-forms. There were no bacteria, yeasts, molds, fungi, or viruses. There were no scavengers, but Mitchegai grubs, pollywogs, and juvenals all preferentially ate dead material, animal or vegetable, before they would eat live grass.

The upper surfaces of the grass could absorb nutrients as readily as could the roots. The droppings of juvenals and adults were gone by morning.

Mitchegai do not have stomach bacteria, or any other symbionts. They have no diseases caused by any sort of microbe. Indeed, with the passage of time, they have completely lost most of their immune systems.

There was absolutely nothing on this planet, or on the estimated three dozen and three thousand, six gross other planets inhabited by this ancient race, but one species of plant, and one species of animal, the Mitchegai.

It was an ecology taken to the absolute limit of what human civilization has always been heading toward. Ever since humans worked their way to the top of the food chain, their earliest actions were to kill off the large mammals who were their predators, their competitors, and often even those who were their source of food.

The agricultural revolution quickened this process, as vast fields were carefully planted and maintained to contain only a single species of plant. As animal husbandry was developed, people, who once ate thousands of animal life-forms, became contented with many fewer, and eventually only three or four of them. Usually, cows, pigs, and chickens.

Anything that might actually harm them, be it a microbe, a mosquito, or a predator, was actively exterminated. All other species that were not immediately useful were brushed aside and allowed to die, mostly because they were simply in the way.

The Mitchegai, who had been at this program for millions of years longer than humanity had been around, had taken it as far as it could possibly go. It was absolute, efficient simplification, with all of the other competing species long since eradicated.

If anything else appeared, or if any mutation occurred, it was ruthlessly stamped out. There were immutable laws that required Mitchegai to fight their wars only with weapons that were powered by their own muscles, but these laws did not apply to ecological threats. Fusion weapons were used when nothing else sufficed.

Kren passed buildings containing the homes, the offices, and the factories where the adults lived and worked, but these seemed to be little more than windows and doors set into the side of green hills. Every square foot of surface area that could possibly support grass, did.

The longer Kren walked from the mines, the more difficult it would be to take a fresh kill back to them. He would need a place to hide while he went into the stupor that followed a major meal, and he had found no such place. Under the last two dukes, this land had become much more civilized than it had been in his youth. No longer were there wild adults ranging in the hills.

Eventually, as the sun was setting, he came upon a small, secluded valley with a small, knee-high juvenal grazing in it.

She would suffice.

He walked up to the little creature and simply swatted her on the head. She fell over, and he ate her.

Her small size was not sufficient to put him into a major stupor, but he slept well that night, wrapped in his heavy red and lavender military cloak, lying in the small valley.

He woke to find an old Mitchegai with a very large head standing over him. She wore a bulky, gaudy academic cloak with bright stripes in many colors. Around her shoulders were many tassels, each of a different shape and of a different color. Around her waist was a belt of all seven colors of the rainbow, red, orange, yellow, green, blue, violet, and kran.

Kran is a color in the ultraviolet that is visible to the Mitchegai. They see the spectrum as being linear. The color wheel is an artifact of the human brain, and the fact that humans have only three different color receptors in their eyes. The Mitchegai have seven, and perceive colors much more richly.

"Are you injured?" she asked in the ancient academic language of Keno.

With adult and juvenal Mitchegai, breathing is normally in through the nose, which also cools the blood going to the brain, and out through four vents at the belt line. These permit a better air flow, and allow for the regular drainage of the lungs. Coughing is unknown in their species. When swimming, a Mitchegai blows bubbles about her waist, and they can breath while eating or drinking.

When speaking, these lower vents are closed, and air is forced up past four sets of vocal cords, one for each lung, and out through the mouth. Mitchegai are thus capable of making four different tones simultaneously, and could actually sing chords, except that lacking all sense of rhythm, they have no musical art forms.

"No, I am quite well, thank you," Kren said in the same language as he got up.

"It is unusual to find a soldier lying in the field in these peaceful times, and even more so to find one who speaks Keno."

"I was tired, and there was no place else available. As to the language, well, a soldier gets around."

"Apparently. I am traveling to my academic retreat, a day's walk to the north of here. Could it be that you are going in the same direction?"

Private transportation had been experimented with several times in Mitchegai history, but it had always resulted in severely reduced levels of physical fitness, and had eventually been outlawed. Long distance public transportation was always available, of course, as were emergency and cargo vehicles.

"Indeed, I am. I thought to spend my leave in my homeland to the north," Kren said.

"Then let us walk together. I would welcome some company," she said. "My name is Bronki."

"And mine is Kren."

They walked and they talked. Kren found the conversation to be delightful. In his thousand years of life, this was the first intelligent person that he had ever had an opportunity to talk to. The world that she described was rich and complex, with infinite possibilities and permutations.

Their conversation drifted to the problems of maintaining the proper number of grubs that evolved into pollywogs, and then juvenals and eventually, sometimes, into adults. Too many grubs, and the health of the grass would suffer. Too few, and in a few years there would be a dangerous shortage of juvenals to eat.

Teams of adults working out of the university monitored the grub population, and adjustments were made, most frequently by taking the eggs that fell to the floors of offices, factories, and homes, and either destroying them, or scattering them over the fields.

This was all new to Kren. The slaves in the mine were not considered to be good breeding stock, and their eggs were never saved. If any eggs hatched in that environment, the grubs were left to starve.

Even if they had been able to find enough to eat, they still all would have died. Grubs instinctively go downward in their search for water in which to metamorphose into pollywogs. But in a mine, going downward only leads to death.

A more long-term technique to restrict the numbers of

grubs was to restrict the number of males who were used to rejuvenate the elders. Currently, less than two per gross of the adults in the duchy were male.

"How is it that you are male?" Bronki asked. "Most males are the highly selected bodies of the aristocracy."

"I was severely injured in battle. This body was the only one available." Kren's new-found intelligence made it easy for him to lie.

She nodded, accepting this.

"And the identification scars on your arms, they look barely a year old."

"Yes, that was about when it happened, during the last war," he said.

"Yet that body is at least ten years old, from the time of metamorphosis."

"Also true. I was injured when we were taking a big mine to the south of here. This was once the body of an ignorant slave in a mine. As I said, it was all that was available, and I urged them to take the chance. Still, it is a very strong body, and I do not regret what happened. Certainly, it was better than being divided among six of my old comrades."

"I'm sure it was," she said. "That would have been the Senta Copper Mine, wouldn't it."

"Strange as it might seem, I don't think that I ever heard the name of the place. They did mine copper there, however."

"I'm sure that it was the Senta. Those scars on your arm are rather crude."

"Old Sergeant Toll did the cutting, in almost complete darkness, when I was coming out of my stupor. He was afraid that I might be mistaken for one of the mining slaves, and sent on with the rest of them," he said, the lies flowing freely.

"And what happened to those others?"

"I have no idea. In the military, you are generally told only what you need to know."

"At the university, we are always told everything, especially things that we have no desire to know," she laughed.

Bronki talked of her life at the University of Dren, of her occasional difficulties with some of the students, and about the perpetual round of interdepartmental politics.

"Yours is such a different world from the one that I am used to," he told her. "I find all of this to be fascinating."

"Then perhaps you should consider a change of career fields. There is always a need for more intelligent students at the university. You could come there, and after a few years as a student, perhaps an instructorship might open up for you. Also, you mentioned winning championships with both the spear and the sword. It is possible that an athletic scholarship could be offered you."

"That sounds attractive, but my leave will not go on forever," he said.

"Often, things can be arranged. These are peaceful times. The duke's army might not be averse to granting an officer an academic leave of absence."

"You make life at the university sound far more interesting than drilling illiterate troops, or standing guard duty when there is really nothing to guard against. I shall think on it."

"Do that," she said. "Should you decide on venturing into the academic world, it is possible that I could be of some assistance to you. I am not without influence there."

The sun was close to setting when they came to Bronki's retreat. At first, Kren could see nothing at all but a grass-covered hill, but Bronki took out a knife and cut away the grass that had grown over the doorway.

"You can see that I have not been here for several years," she said, throwing the thick mat down the hill, where it was eagerly pounced on by two juvenals.

"The other door and the windows are best cut away from the inside," she continued, leading him inside, and turning on the lights.

The house was quite spacious, and extremely luxurious compared to what a mining slave was used to. There were chairs and tables and real cots to sleep on. There was a tall and spacious entrance hall, and a large living room with many comfortable couches centered around a long, low table and a drinking fountain. Opening off these central rooms were two studies, a steam room, and five bedrooms. Mitchegai homes do not have kitchens or dining rooms, of course, and outside of the cities, they don't have toilets. The grass took care of waste disposal.

But the things that impressed Kren the most were the

books. Every wall, every small bit of space, was covered with bookshelves, and these were all crammed to overflowing with books. Big books, small books, thick ones and thin. Some of them had ancient tooled leather coverings, but most were of simple grass paper.

And besides the books, there were thousands of tapes and discs, along with the viewing screens and computers to use them.

"I am very impressed," Kren said. "Have you actually read all of these?"

"Most of them. Many are reference texts, of course, good for looking things up in, but not intended to be read from cover to cover. Perhaps you would like some reading suggestions?"

"I would very much appreciate your advice, yes."

"Then we shall discuss it in a little while. Let me unpack and then rest a bit while you choose one of the guest bedrooms. I usually entertain several friends here, but this time, everyone that I would usually have invited along was otherwise engaged," she said.

"Thank you. I will do that."

Kren walked about the house, opening windows and doors, cutting away the grass that covered them with his sword, and throwing the thick mats away as he had seen Bronki do. The windows were thick and well insulated, but no one on a Mitchegai world had ever heard of window screens.

He found that they were at the top of a hill, with pleasant views in every direction, an arrangement that also permitted good cross-ventilation.

Seeing no great difference between the guest rooms, he chose the one to the north, and hung his clothes and equipment up there, on pegs set into yet another bookshelf.

His hostess came in with some fresh bed sheets, so he made the bed in the neat, military style that one of his victims had taught him. This was a very pleasant place, and he would obviously be welcome to stay here for a long while.

Kren lay down thinking that this was a very good turn of events.

CHAPTER SEVEN

Promotions and Awards
New Yugoslavia, 2205 A.D.

A few months went by, and I found myself becoming human again. Then I got a summons from my boss.

In the course of things, I had managed to acquire seven qualified colonels rather than the usual five. Lloyd and Mirko had been elected delegates to a planetary constitutional convention, and were needed there. When my boss, General Sobieski, invited me and my staff to New Kashubia for a conference, I took my wife, Conan and Maria, and Quincy and Zuzanna with me in my Combat Control Computer. Three friendly couples made a good group, anyway.

A Combat Control Computer was basically a cylindrical truck, five meters across and ten meters long, that contained life support units called coffins for six people. You floated in an aqueous solution, and computer controlled systems supplied you with food, oxygen, and everything you needed to stay alive. Inductive mats imbedded under your scalp and along your backbone connected you with an array of computers. These were identical to the coffins that were inside of most of our bigger fighting machines, our tanks. The greater computer power of the CCC let you live almost twice as fast, however.

There were six small computers that contained the personalities of our personal tanks, Agnieshka, in my case. But in a CCC, you were also connected with twelve truly massive computers that contained everything known to humanity.

This group of computers called himself Professor Cee, and acted like an English college professor.

When connected up, the huge computer power let you operate in Dream World at combat speed, which in my case was fifty-five times as fast as normal living. This effectively expanded my lifetime by a factor of fifty-five, a nice fringe benefit.

And while you were in it, you lived in Dream World, a form of artificial reality that could be anything that you wanted it to be. It was very pleasant, provided that you obeyed orders. If you didn't, you could be living literally in Hell.

The CCC also contained an array of communication devices that kept you in touch with as many as a hundred thousand Mark XIX tanks, as well as your superiors, no matter where you were in Human Space, although interstellar communications could take days.

So I called the gang together and we got into the CCC down in my garage, below my apartment. You had to strip down naked to get into a coffin, and as usual, the girls insisted that we males take a walk while they got in. I suspect that this had nothing to do with modesty, but was because Maria and Zuzanna were far more beautiful in Dream World than they were in reality. My Kasia was beautiful anywhere she went, of course.

It was a half-hour trip by the underground MagLev system to the military transmitter, over a day in Dream World. Our party consisted of six humans, six intelligent machines, and Professor Cee. Socially, we treated each other as equals. We spent the time at a medieval tournament, followed by a banquet in Zuzanna's castle. This had a lot in common with the Dark Tower that I'd had built for her in my valley, except that the real one didn't have moat monsters, wizards, and dragons hanging around.

Accelerating the CCC to the vector of New Kashubia took another thirty minutes, but none of us on board noticed it. Fluid suspension lets you ignore gravity, at least when it stays below ten Gs. We spent the day coursing after the stags with the palace hounds.

Transit time to New Kashubia took another hour, according to laws of physics that I have learned twice, and still don't understand. Had we been in separate tanks, we would have had to spend the time alone, but since we were all in there together, we spent the two subjective days on a dragon hunt. This time, Conan won the prize for the biggest kill. He said that he would have it mounted in his den, the way I had done with the prize I had taken during the "Search Light Party," during the last war.

We reported to General Sobieski in Dream World as soon as we got to New Kashubia. That was the way he preferred things. I've never met anyone who ever saw him in the flesh.

Sobieski is a great fan of J.R.R. Tolkien, and among friends he usually adopted the persona of Elessar, the king. The thirteen of us suddenly found ourselves wearing not medieval finery, but armored garb suitable for the nobility of Middle Earth. Quick changes of clothing are a common occurrence in Dream World.

We were escorted into the great hall atop Minas Tirith by hundreds of warriors with winged helmets. They didn't march very well, which indicated that these were all humans, and not machine intelligences. Our army never wasted much time on things like marching.

"Your Majesty," I said, standing in front of the dais, and bowing. "You called, and we have come."

"And right welcome you are!" Sobieski said, standing and stepping down from his throne. "The first order of business here is the long delayed awarding of promotions and decorations!" The crowd made a series of "Hooahs," "Poobahs," and "Praise them with Great Praise," which happened a lot that afternoon.

He continued, "First, the promotions! Mickolai, you are no longer a tanker first class, brevetted to general. Your permanent rank is now general in the Human Army, and you are in command of all of the forces on New Yugoslavia. Your seven direct subordinates are now promoted to colonels in the Human Army. In addition, as commander of the entire army, I have created three new ranks, for use by the electronic people among our ranks. Your electronic lady, Agnieshka, is now a major in our army, and the metal people assigned to your colonels are now captains. All other tanks whose observers have graduated from basic training will be given the rank of tanker class A. These new ranks are real, and include substantial pay and benefits."

The crowd went wild over that one. All of us felt that

the electronic people deserved recognition as human beings, and these promotions were a major step on the road to their complete emancipation.

When the cheering quieted down, the general continued, "Next, there is a matter of awards and decorations. We'll start with your subordinates on those, and I'll have my scribes read the certificates."

It turned into quite a long afternoon, with some four hundred and fifty-one medals handed out. And every one of them was accompanied by a scroll stating where and why the action occurred that earned it. Our army wasn't very heavy on ceremony, but some things you just have to go through. By the time they were through, we were all loaded down with golden trinkets, both us humans and our electronic people, and I was as weighted down with medals as a Russian war hero.

Finally, I had a chance to say, "Thank you, sir. But I have a number of questions I wanted to ask you."

"Certainly, but save them for the business meeting tomorrow. For now, it's party time!"

"Yes, sir. But what is happening with my Gurkhas?"

"They will be expanded from a battered battalion up to several full divisions, of course, depending on how many of them actually enlist. You don't think that I'd pass up a chance to get as many of those magnificent warriors as possible, do you? All of the munitions factories are still operating at full capacity, and your Gurkhas have first priority on equipment and supplies. Now come on and have a beer!"

"Yes, sir," I said, taking a stein of Russian honey beer from a nearly naked serving wench. These were just computer simulations, more decorations than people. If you talked to one, she could convince you that she was "alive," but really, she wasn't anything like Agnieshka, for example. "But, why are we expanding the army when the war is over?"

"The War with Earth is over. The next war will be a long one, and it has already started."

"What?!"

"There's plenty of time, Mickolai. We'll talk it over tomorrow."

"But!"

"Drink your beer, General Derdowski. That's an order."

CHAPTER EIGHT

FROM CAPTURED HISTORY TAPES,
FILE 1846583A ca. 1832 A.D.
BUT CONCERNING EVENTS OF UP TO
2000 YEARS EARLIER

A Pleasant Social Event

Kren took a book at random from the bookshelf within reach of the cot he was lying on. He had been quite sure that he could read, but he had never before actually had the opportunity to do so. He was delighted to find that the words and the thoughts came to him from the printed page without any difficulty at all.

The book he read concerned the history of a period eight gross thousand years before, when the planet had first become completely populated, and population pressures were forcing the first dukedoms into existence.

After about an hour, Bronki came in with a stack of books under her arm.

"Do you enjoy reading Koki?" she asked.

"Very much," he said, somewhat confused. He had to look at the cover again to see what she was talking about. It was a moment before he realized that she was referring to the author of the book. He had never before considered that each book had some person who had written it. In all of his memories of them, books simply *were*. They somehow just came out of nothing, or perhaps had always been there.

"I think perhaps that Koki might be a bit specialized for you to start with. I suggest that you start your study of history with Samsid, here, which is a generalized overview of history. That is, of course, if you've never read him. I mean, it's a very popular book, and you must have had a library available to you in the military."

"Have you ever seen a military library?" he asked, sitting up, and putting his feet on the pleasantly decorated orange and red carpet.

"No. In truth, I have had very little contact with those in your profession."

"Then let me enlighten you. A library suitable for an entire battalion would fit easily into this room. At least half of it would consist of military regulations. These books are feverishly read by miscreants who are looking for a way out of being punished for the crimes that they have committed.

"Perhaps a third of it will concern truly military subjects. Books on war, tactics, weapons, and so forth. These are often checked out by junior officers who carry them around, wishing to impress their superiors with their diligence. Few show any evidence of ever having been actually read.

"There will be a few shelves of so called 'fine literature,' donated by local literary academics who wish the soldiers to improve their minds, or by poets who are otherwise unable to dispose of their thin books of bad poetry. These are all in pristine condition, having been neither checked out nor read.

"Then there will be a half shelf of the crudest possible humor, usually left behind by dead soldiers. These books are inevitably worn to tatters."

Bronki laughed.

"At least your literary impoverishment has not ruined your sense of humor! Look here. I've also brought you general books on the sciences, mathematics, and the arts, as well as a novel called *The Soldier's Life*. It has been well reviewed, but perhaps you could tell me if it is really accurate or not. I'm considering using it in my contemporary literature class next semester."

"I would be happy to give you my opinions on it, once I've read it."

"Thank you. For myself, well, I usually live a sedentary life, and today's long walk has left me tired. I shall read for an hour, and then go to sleep. Please do as you wish. My home is your home."

"You honor me beyond my deserts," Kren said. "I think that I will stay right here and read one of your books."

Kren started to read *The Overview of Mitchegai History,* which started some three and a half million years ago, and stopped on this planet within a gross years of the present. It started with their earliest beginnings in the myths and the archeology of a planet over a thousand light-years away from the one he was living on. It discussed the beginnings of agriculture, and the strange animals that had existed back then, many of which the Mitchegai had actually eaten!

Kren shuddered at the very thought of it, but continued reading late into the night until sleep closed over him.

It was late morning when he awoke and went outside to relieve himself. He was drinking from the fountain in the living room when Bronki came in from one of the study dens.

"You slept late, my friend."

"I was up late. Your history book was very interesting," Kren said.

"We are a remarkable species. To think that we made it from living in primitive huts to launching ourselves into space in only a million and a half years! It was an amazing accomplishment!"

"I suppose it was, but actually, I haven't gotten that far yet. I will read some more of it in the afternoon, if I may. I wouldn't want to overstay my welcome here."

"That is something that you couldn't possibly do. I enjoy your company. You are someone as new and refreshing to me as I am to you. But for this afternoon, well, I haven't eaten lately, and country grown food is so much better than what is available in the city. What would you think of a hunt? Have you eaten recently?"

"Not nearly enough. Yes, a hunt would be wonderful!"

"Good! And bring your spear along."

"A spear? To hunt a juvenal?"

"I want to see if you are really as good with that thing as you claim."

Only a half mile from the house, they spotted a large juvenal grazing, about a gross three dozen yards away.

"Could you hit her from here?" Bronki asked.

"It's a long shot, even with a running throw. I'd only give myself half a chance of hitting her."

"Try it anyway!"

Kren dropped his cloak, took three running steps, and let fly. The spear arched high in the sky and came down perfectly on target, going right through the startled girl, and nailing her to the ground. She was screaming, and spinning about in circles, but unable to free herself.

"That was lovely! You are a master of your art!" Bronki shouted.

"Hardly that! It didn't even kill her!" He shouted back as he ran up to retrieve his broad bladed spear. He gave the child a casual kick in the head to silence her, and then pulled out his spear.

The overlapping, flexible plates of the Mitchegai cranium make for a much weaker skull than that of humans. Furthermore, the motile brain cells are less firmly connected to each other than those of any earthly species.

This results in making Mitchegai rather easy to knock unconscious. At the same time, the motile brain cells readily reconnect, and thus a blow to the head will rarely kill a Mitchegai.

With humans, the force required to knock one unconscious is very nearly that required to knock him dead.

Kren said, "Did you want this one? Or should I kill you another?"

"I had thought that she would be big enough for both of us."

"I can see that academicians have smaller appetites than soldiers do. How would you like the small one out there?" He pointed at another juvenal as far away as the first had been.

"I think that I would prefer the little boy down there." She pointed to one half again farther.

Mitchegai eyesight is extremely good, superior to that of an earthly eagle.

"That's really pushing it, but I will try."

Luck was with him, and Kren caught the little fellow cleanly in the neck.

"Truly, you are a great master! Let me pace off the distance of that throw. I shall E-mail the university's athletic director about you right after we wake up."

"Thank you. I hope that I will be as lucky in my demonstration for him as I have been in this one for you."

"Kren, you must learn to cease hiding your light under

a basket. Come on, let's carry these children closer to the house before we eat them. Otherwise, we'll end up sleeping it off in the fields, and wake up chilled to the bone."

Mitchegai are nominally cold-blooded. However, through the use of clothing and various behavioral traits, the adults usually maintain a body temperature slightly higher than humans do.

It was two days before Kren felt up to doing more reading, and a week before he finished his first book.

A semi-sentient housekeeper came by every other day, shook out the carpets, washed all of the floors and windows, and trimmed back the barely encroaching grass, but never touched anything on a table or a desk. She never spoke a word, but brought fresh linen, changed the beds, and took away Kren's cloak for cleaning. She had an arrangement with Bronki, which involved getting the use of a small, nearby house with the utilities and taxes paid.

Kren simply moved to another room whenever she appeared anxiously at his doorway, and that was sufficient.

Bronki spent most of her time writing a book on her general-purpose computer, rattling her claws on the hardened metal keyboard. She had contracted to finish the last volume of her history of the computer before the next semester, and she was worried about fulfilling it.

As with all contracts among the Mitchegai, there were severe penalty clauses for late delivery. In the worst cases, they would sometimes *not* eat you alive, a bad end for a Mitchegai.

Kren was struggling through a book on mathematics, something which none of his victims had prepared him for, when there was a shout from outside the front door.

He went to answer it, but Bronki got there first. Two older ladies with large heads were standing there in brightly colored academic cloaks. They had a naked young girl tied at wrists and ankles, slung under a long aluminum pole that they supported between them on their right shoulders.

"Bronki! We heard you were back! We've come to welcome you home to the civilized world!"

"Zoda! Sava! Come on in! And what is this that you have brought me?"

Zoda shouted, "Party food, of course! Isn't she lovely?

Just the right age, soft and tender, and not a mark on her! It took us all day to find one this good!"

"She *is* lovely! She looks almost too good to eat! Maybe, I'll keep her and have her eat me when her time is right!" Bronki said.

"Not a chance!" Sava said, "We've carried her for three miles, and we're going to eat her! Who's your friend?"

"Have it your way," Bronki said, and introduced Kren to her friends. They were both university professors on ten-year-long sabbaticals, and living a few miles away.

The Mitchegai neither smoked tobacco nor drank alcohol, probably because they lacked tobacco plants and the yeast to make beer or wine. A wide variety of illegal, synthetic drugs had been developed, but these were frowned upon by polite society.

Yet all intelligent beings need to get together to talk and socialize.

During such functions, some method to release the inhibitions is desirable, and with drunkenness an impossibility, the Mitchegai used the stupor brought on by eating. Eating a very large meal put you to sleep too quickly, but snacking lightly throughout the evening proved efficacious.

"How is the book coming?" Sava asked Bronki.

"Poorly! It's way behind schedule!"

"Mine too! What's more, I'm stuck. I don't know what to do next, but at least I've got a year before it's due. Tell you what. How about if I stay here and help you out, and then if you have time, you can do the same for me?"

Bronki said, "You'd do that? You're a blessing from the duke! Yes, by all means! Help me! Help me!"

The two academicians brought their gift straight into the living room, and tied the struggling girl to a low ceramic tiled table with raised edges that was obviously made for this purpose. Several small, decorative knives were put on the table as well, and the group sat down on couches around it.

"So, Bronki, will you do the honors of the first cut?" Sava said.

"But surely, it is your gift, so you should do it."

"No, no. You know the rules. You are the hostess."

"But Kren is a special guest. He should have the honors," Bronki said.

"I am but a soldier, and unfamiliar with civilized ways," Kren said. "I would probably do something improper, and flub the whole thing."

"No, you won't," Bronki insisted. "We're all friends here. Just take a knife and cut off some small part. Actually, most party goers start with the fingers and toes, and work inwards as the night goes on. Just don't let her die too soon."

"As you wish," he said. He took a knife which was none too sharp and stretched out one of the girl's fingers. Apparently guessing what he was about to do, she struggled and screamed, such that when he cut the finger off, he didn't slice cleanly through the cartilage at the joint, but had to lean heavily on the knife and took off a bit of bone as well.

The girl screamed again, much more loudly this time, and longer.

"That was really good, Kren," Zoda said. "The pitch and timbre were wonderful! I'll have to remember that! Always take a bit of bone off on the first cut!"

The Mitchegai have very little sense of rhythm, and thus music and dance have no place in their pantheon of art works. But extracting pleasant sounds from their party food is considered to be an honored art form, and a lot of fun besides. In addition, it always put the guests in a very good mood.

"You are the computer expert here, Bronki," Zoda said, cutting off a finger for herself. When the screaming stopped, she continued, "What do you think of Kem's suggestion that it might be possible to build a computer with real intelligence?"

"I think that it is pure and utter nonsense! Computers can only do what their name implies. They can compute. The so called artificial intelligence programs are exactly what their name says they are. Artificial! They can't really think!" She stabbed the girl's forearm to emphasize her point.

"Exactly right," said Sava. "Computers have been around for millions of years, and if it were possible to make them truly intelligent, somebody would have done it by now."

The long evening was most pleasant for the four of them. Kren was quizzed at length about the military, and he asked as many questions about their lives at the university.

"So tell me, why are we so often at war?" Bronki asked the group, when the conversation hit a lull.

"That's easy," Sava said. "Because they're fun!"

"Having participated in a number of them, would you mind if I disagreed with that opinion?" Kren said, playing his role to the hilt.

"Disagree all you like. That's what makes parties fun," Sava replied.

Zoda said, "They may not be fun for those who must fight them, but they are tremendously exciting for those who don't. And it's the ones far behind the lines who start the wars, direct the wars, and profit from the wars. But from a larger perspective, wars have other advantages. They eliminate surplus populations. The grass has to be trimmed and eaten, or it will turn rank."

Bronki said, "More importantly, they eliminate the ruling class of the losing side, and their ancient brains along with them. When the brain gets too old, it often gets too set in its ways. The artisans, the academics, and the soldiers have their own ways of eliminating the inefficient among them, but warfare is the only dependable method of doing this with the aristocracy."

"I'll have to think on that," Kren said.

The conversation drifted through six dozen subjects, with several surprises and a lot of laughter.

Later, Sava asked, as she crunched on a bit of ankle bone that she had bitten off, "Tell me, Kren, how was it that you learned the language of Keno?"

"In truth, I never did learn it, in the ordinary way of speaking. During the last war, another division took so many casualties at one point that they could not give them all a proper sendoff, and my unit helped them out a bit. I'd never met the soldier that my squad ate, but the next day, I found myself speaking Keno. I never learned how our dinner happened to know it, because shortly thereafter, we were attacked, I was hospitalized, and most of my squad was killed. Then it was the other division's turn to help *us* out."

"You make it sound like a very adventurous life."

"Adventurous? I suppose so, but being an academic sounds much more interesting to me," he said as he flayed the skin off the girl's lower leg.

The girl moaned and cried in the most delightful fashion until they had her trimmed down to her upper body cavity and head. Then they played the finger game, a variation on the human game of scissors-paper-rock, to determine who would get the brain, and Sava won.

Lastly, they tore the rest of her apart with their claws, ate it all, and licked up the blood. Then they each went to their separate bedrooms and locked the doors, laughing all the while.

Falling asleep, Kren marveled once more at how wonderful intelligent, civilized company was.

CHAPTER NINE

A Good Party
New Kashubia, 2205 A.D.

It was a good party. The people from the Command Center had more experience with socializing than us soldiers from the sticks, and it showed. By people, I mean both humans and artificial intelligences. We considered ourselves to be equals, despite what the laws outside of the army might say. In time, we would prevail.

Dream World permitted a very wide range of human activities, since no matter what you did, you couldn't get addicted, hung over, diseased, injured, or dead. If an emergency occurred, you could go from being roaring drunk to dead sober in an instant.

A few people were experimenting with just about every drug known to man, and tobacco was making a considerable comeback, but most people stayed with alcohol and eschewed the rest.

Someone told me that the band contained only two humans, the rest being AI. I watched, but I couldn't tell one from the other. The sound level was always just right. If you wanted to dance, you could always hear the beat. If you wanted to talk, you could always hear what was being said. Dream World had a lot of advantages.

Soon, some couples were dancing on the walls and ceiling, but after my first startled glance, it seemed to be fairly normal to me. A few people had been turning this sort of thing into a real art form, though, and one couple in particular, dancing in midair under the high ceiling, got a long round of applause.

Mostly, parties are places where people get together to talk, drink, socialize, meet new people, drink, exchange ideas, argue, drink, and occasionally fight to the death. As it was in the beginning, it is now, and ever shall be.

My crew had a fine time. Agnieshka was soon wearing a vaguely Napoleonic outfit made of tight-fitting red and white silk, knee-high boots, lots of gold braid, a very ornate sword, and about as much décolletage as the law will ordinarily allow.

She claimed that it was the official full undress uniform for Army majors. A few other metal ladies, presumably majors themselves, copied her outfit. Soon, something even more audacious was invented for captains, and then a few hundred new tanker class A's outdid them all with something that I don't feel comfortable describing.

Our metal ladies could break into well-choreographed dances at a moment's notice, and did so several times that evening, doing an impromptu fifty-girl Rockette High Kick at one point.

Kasia and I danced on the floor, the walls and the ceiling, but we didn't feel up to competing with those athletes working out in midair. Eva, Kasia's tank, and Timothy, Zuzanna's, were up there doing a credible job, though.

Quincy was demonstrating hand-to-hand combat techniques to someone who knew a lot less about fighting than he thought he did. Quincy killed him four times that I noticed. He was a persistent fellow. It hurts to die, even in Dream World.

Professor Cee was sitting around a table with six other identical Professor Cees, all wearing Harris tweed, all drinking single malt scotch, and all discussing something in a language that no one else had ever heard before.

A half dozen bloody duels happened in the course of the evening. Eventually, somebody circulated with a pad of note paper, taking a vote to determine who had died the most noble death of the evening. They gave the award to the guy that Quincy had repeatedly killed.

For no reason that I could discern, Conan was demonstrating how apes climb trees. Someone was sticking his tongue into

Zuzanna's ear, and Maria declared that she was in love with whoever it was who was running his foot up her leg.

And Kasia ended up with a few like-minded ladies, sitting around drunk on champagne and reciting from memory the poetry of Elizabeth Barrett Browning.

Like I said, it was a good party. Only, I wanted to get to the business meeting. We were at war?

CHAPTER TEN

FROM CAPTURED HISTORY TAPES,
FILE 1846583A ca. 1832 A.D.
BUT CONCERNING EVENTS OF UP TO
2000 YEARS EARLIER

Bargains Kept

The next day, Sava stayed to help Bronki on her book, and Zoda, lacking anything better to do, stayed too. Bronki's retreat had two studies, each with a computer. Zoda wanted to get involved and help out, but was stymied for lack of equipment.

Frustrated, she asked Kren to walk with her back to her house and to help her to bring her computer to Bronki's place. Since he was sick of trying to comprehend even the coarse points of mathematics, he agreed.

It was a pleasant two-hour walk there, and a strenuous three-hour walk back. Zoda's computer weighed close to two gross pounds. Mitchegai computer technology was vastly inferior to that of late twentieth-century Earth, even after a million years of development.

Creativity is the domain of the young. Since Mitchegai are normally thousands of years old before they have brains enough to do anything technical, they are often very intelligent and extremely learned, but not very creative.

Electronics was also held back because over a million years before, a prominent academician had written a flawless paper absolutely proving that anything like an integrated circuit was totally impossible to make or use. Thereafter, anyone who suggested such a thing was simply regarded as being uneducated, and was treated the way that humans would treat someone who wanted to build a perpetual motion machine.

Kren and Zoda had the computer slung on the same aluminum carrying pole that had been used for bringing in last night's party snack. Zoda bounced along, carrying her end without apparent difficulty, and Kren was ashamed to admit that he was tired in front of a mere academician. He followed behind her without voicing his complaints.

They were almost back before Zoda explained that the trick of using a carrying pole was to adjust your step to the natural frequency of the weight and the pole. With just the right bounce and timing, the job became much easier.

Kren thanked her for the useful, if belated, information.

Zoda set her equipment up in the last bedroom, and Kren, interested, followed her instructions to connect the components with each other, and with the two other computers. Soon all three academics were working smoothly together, and Kren went back to trying to master elementary mathematics.

The next afternoon, frustrated with his lack of accomplishment, Kren went out and brought back another party snack, as similar as possible to the one the others had admired a couple of days before.

That night, Kren won the finger game and got to eat the brain. The day after, his studies went much better, and this got him to thinking. Perhaps to learn new things, he needed new brain cells. Perhaps the ones he had were already committed to other things.

The next day, he went out with his spear, and killed four juvenals, eating their brains on the spot, and leaving the bodies to be eaten by other juvenals. On any planet, herbivores will eagerly eat meat, if they don't have to kill it first.

His studies improved considerably.

Soon they fell into a pattern, with a party every other night, but no major meals, since time was pressing and Bronki couldn't afford to take the time off for a proper stupor. Kren always provided the party snacks.

And four times a day, he ate a juvenal brain.

Mitchegai juvenals are not herding animals, and they are

not territorial. They drift and wander as individuals, constantly seeking out new and better pastures.

Nonetheless, Kren's excessive slaughter was thinning out the herbivores in the area. More were being killed than drifted in. Furthermore, the few that were left were being sated on meat rather than the much less nutritious grass. The fields around the retreat were becoming rank.

After three weeks of nonstop work, the academics went outside for a break, and they noticed it immediately.

"Just look at this mess!" Sava said.

"Kren, this is your work, isn't it," Zoda said. "Just how many juvenals have you been eating? Ten a day?"

"Only four," he admitted. "And only the brains. The rest of the bodies are eaten by other juvenals, so the biomass stays the same."

"It does no such thing," Sava said. "The conversion rate is only five dozen ten per gross. You are ruining the grass. Worse, you are breaking the duke's law. Adults are permitted to take what they need to eat. Wasting food is punished with death by fire. If they catch you, they'll burn you at the stake in some public square! And doing anything that degrades the quality of the grass carries the same penalty!"

Mitchegai criminals are not actually burned at the stake with a fire at their feet. That was just a saying left over from the distant, barbaric past. In more progressive, modern times, they use a ceramic, temperature controlled, electrically heated stake, which permits the sufferer to remain alive much longer, and thus provides more amusement for the crowd.

"I know military regulations. I am less familiar with civilian law."

"You are ignorant of a lot of things," Bronki said. "Small additions of fresh brain cells can improve your learning abilities. But the maximum that is useful for academic purposes is one juvenal every other day. Four a day is simply ignorant!"

"I apologize and stand corrected," Kren said.

"You will do more than that!" Bronki shouted. "You will cease hunting anywhere within a dozen miles of here for the next six weeks at least. Maybe enough juvenals will drift in to correct the problem here by then. With any luck, the grass will look proper again before anyone in authority notices the problem. Because if they *do* notice this mess, or if anybody calls it to their attention, you'll have the whole army out after you."

"I said I was sorry."

"That's not enough," Zoda said. "We're all too busy to make any extended hunting trips right now, so you have to feed the whole group."

"And if you can't bring in enough food from more than a dozen miles away, you'll go hungry before the rest of us do," Sava added. "Is that understood?"

"With the alternative of death by fire, I will comply with your requests," Kren said, thinking that they were quite serious about perhaps turning him in. Certainly, no Mitchegai would take the personal risk of attempting to protect someone else from the duke's forces.

Bronki said, "You certainly will. And after this area is back in proper shape, I will give you a list of the poor indigents in this neighborhood, starting with my housekeeper. Many of them are crippled, and have difficulty getting enough to eat. You will give the body of the child you kill every other day to one of them. That qualifies as an act of charity, and will satisfy the duke's law."

"Yes, madam."

Two weeks later, the academics announced that they had completed Bronki's book slightly ahead of the deadline, and had E-mailed it to the publisher. The party that night was a particularly good one.

At one point, Bronki announced, "Kren, you will be pleased to learn that I have heard from the athletic director at my university. He has said that if you can repeat your spear-chucking performance for him on a regular basis, he can guarantee you a five-year athletic scholarship!"

Sava and Zoda applauded wildly, while the party snack moaned pleasantly.

"This is wonderful," Kren said. "Now I must make inquiries with my superiors to see if I can take advantage of this excellent offer."

"I'm sure that we can help you with that," Zoda said.

"Thank you, but I think it best if I handled this one on my own. The protocols of the military are much different from those of your world," Kren said, helping himself to a nice bit of tail. "Still, if I need help, I will not hesitate asking it of you."

"Next, have you had a chance to read that novel I lent you, *A Soldier's Life*?" Bronki asked.

"Yes, and I found it to be simply silly. The book's heroes see a dozen times as much action as any normal combat troops could possibly survive, without having any of them killed. Their use of weapons ranges from awkward through foolish and on to absolutely stupid. They all go into battle shouting patriotic slogans, they all respect all of their officers, and they all feel an unrelenting reverence for their commanding general. In short, they have absolutely nothing in common with real soldiers in a real army. Intelligent warriors might enjoy the humor of it, as a satire, but relatively few soldiers have that level of intelligence. It might be useful as enlistment propaganda, except that it would probably attract the wrong sort of recruit. In short, I can see no possible use for this book."

"Yet it is well liked by many intellectuals," Bronki said.

"Then that is its apparent purpose. To fulfill the aggressive fantasies of intellectual armchair soldiers. Treated as such, it might have merit. As a description of military life, it is fraudulent."

This left a lull in the conversation that was soon filled by everyone having another bite to eat, with suitable verbal accompaniment by the party snack.

"I notice that the grass is recovering nicely, much faster than I thought it would," Sava said.

Kren said, "Besides providing all of the party snacks, I have also hauled in over a dozen juvenals from points over a dozen miles from here, and released them around the house. The program seems to be working."

"Then I think that we can cease worrying about intervention by the authorities," Zoda said. "Now all we have to worry about is Sava's book."

"We'll start on that in the morning," Bronki said. "We work very well together as a team, much more productively than we do as individuals. Perhaps we should consider some sort of a partnership."

"I like that idea," Zoda said. "It's been too long since I've seen my name on anything."

"Then see what you can do about getting yourself a suitable

book contract, and we'll work on it next summer. I'll have to go back to the university in a few weeks, and there are some course outlines I have to do, besides getting Sava's book back on track, but I'll be free all next summer."

"It's settled, then. We're a three-way partnership," Sava said.

They all ate to that, tapping their meat together over their snack in the time honored fashion.

The next day, while the others worked at their computers, Kren decided to give up on mathematics, and to start on the sciences. Things progressed well for a while, but he soon found that his progress was slowed by his deficiencies in math. Grumbling, he went hunting the day after.

He found that if he tied six large juvenals by the neck and connected all of the ropes to a central knot, he could get them home without too much difficulty. Since they all tended to run in random directions, they averaged each other out, and holding on to the knot, he could control them, and keep them moving in the desired direction.

If they had all pulled together in the same direction at the same time, he might have been in trouble, but they weren't smart enough to do that.

Five of them were released alive near the house to improve the grass, and the last became a party snack.

After two more weeks, Sava's book was half completed, and the rest of it was completely outlined. After a last, rollicking party, the two old academics packed up Zoda's computer, slung it over their shoulders, and, after many good-byes, went bouncing home.

Once they were gone, Bronki sat at the stool in front of her computer, working on her course outlines.

Kren came quietly into her study and thrust his spear into the flesh under her leg bones, just behind the knees. This cut most of the tendons to her lower legs, crippling her.

She screamed in pain, and fell to the floor.

"Why did you do this to me?" she yelled.

"To immobilize you, and thus make you easier to eat," Kren said.

"Are you crazy? Why would you want to eat an old body like this one when there are plenty of tender young ones around?"

"Because I am not interested in eating your body. I am interested in eating your brain."

"That, too, is madness! My brain is at least three times as big as yours is. If you ate it, you would not be providing yourself with my brain, you would be providing me with your body, which I could certainly use at this point! I think you've crippled me for life," she said, angrily.

"That would happen only if I ate all of your brain, which I do not intend to do. I want your mathematical abilities, and your knowledge of the computer arts."

"Your slow progress in math bothered you *that* much? I *knew* that I should have given you some tutoring! Anyway, do you know how to do that?"

"Certainly," Kren said. "One of my earlier meals was a medic who was very knowledgeable in anatomy."

"So you've done this before?"

"Five times. This really was the body of a mining slave, but what I didn't tell you was that *I* was that slave."

"That's quite a bit of personal advancement! Would you like to tell me the whole story?" Bronki asked, still lying on the floor.

Kren did so, simply because he enjoyed talking to Bronki, and there was no rush. He told his life's story completely and accurately, with none of the self-aggrandizement or face-saving lies that a human criminal would have used. Shame has no place in the Mitchegai character.

Hours later, when he had finished, Bronki said, "Okay, I suppose that if I had been in your position, I might well have done the same thing that you did, at each step of the way. Certainly, I can't hate you for it, except that in one way it certainly galls me! Here I am, one of the most intelligent professors at the university, and now I find that I was *stupid* enough to invite a vampire into my own home! I hope that nobody ever finds out about this. I'd be a laughingstock!"

"A vampire?"

"Yes, of course, that's what you are, you know. Did you think that you were the first person to come up with this method of self-improvement?"

"I didn't know," Kren said.

"There are so many things that you are ignorant of. You really must get a proper, university education, you know. I'll do what I can to help you accomplish that."

"I don't see how. You won't be alive."

"Of course I will," Bronki said. "There's no need for me to die, and at this point, I need a new body in any event. I would have done it in a year or two, anyway, even if you hadn't crippled this one. We'll just agree on exactly what you'll take for yourself, and feed the rest to a recently metamorphosed adult."

"And you expect me to commit what must surely be a crime by civilian laws, and then leave you alive to testify against me in court?"

"Yes, I do. For one thing, I would be willing to sign a contract that I would never bring charges against you, and never testify against you in court. If I broke such a contract, I would be punished right along with you. For another, if it was learned that I had lost some of my intellectual abilities, it could very well cost me my job at the university. For a third, I would be willing to pay you very well to not kill me."

"Pay me? How much?"

"How does twelve thousand Ke sound? It's all that I have in my savings." Bronki had a dozen times that much in the bank, and many times more in other investments besides, but she felt no need to be scrupulously honest.

"It does not sound bad, but I have often admired this retreat of yours. Would you throw it in as well, with all of its contents?"

"If I must, yes, although I am very attached to it. May I borrow it occasionally when you have no need of it?"

"If you will throw in your servant and her house, yes," Kren said.

"Done. We have an agreement." Bronki thought that if she still had the use of the house, and someone else had to pay the taxes and utilities, here and for her housekeeper, she had just made a profit. If her servant had to work a little harder, taking care of two masters now, well, so what?

"Okay. So what do we do now? Must I go out in search of a suitably mature juvenal, and then wait around until she is ready to metamorphose?"

"Of course not! There are dozens of companies that provide suitable, well-selected bodies, at competitive prices, with all of the proper shoulder brands that an academic requires. Help me back up to my stool, and I'll E-mail the one that I used last time," Bronki said.

"How can you afford to pay for her if you are giving me all of your money?"

"My money may be gone, but my credit is very good. I'll charge it on my credit card."

"And the rest of our bargain?" Kren asked.

"I'll do the contract, the bank transfer, and the deed on the property next. Look, I'll need your help getting installed in my new body, won't I? I'm in no position to cheat you now."

"But I'm in a position to cheat you."

"True, but it would be stupid for you to do so. If you stay with our deal, you will come out quite well. Besides getting the knowledge that you want, you will have the money, a nice home, and a trained servant. If I'm dead, my money and property would end up in probate, and you'll be years getting it, if ever."

"Yes, I see. Well then, let's get on with it," Kren said.

CHAPTER ELEVEN

Something Wicked This Way Comes
New Kashubia, 2205 A.D.

There were six generals waiting in the meeting room, and each of us had five colonels and seven electronic people with us. We were all in class A uniforms, except for the professors, who wore their inevitable tweeds. Our insignia was traditional. Generals wore a star, colonels an eagle, majors an oak leaf, captains, two silver bars.

Being in Dream World, the room was exactly the size that it needed to be. Every one of us had the ability to stop the action and discuss matters privately with anyone we wanted to, for however long we wanted, without disturbing the others at the meeting.

In so many ways, Dream World was a very convenient way to do business.

I never used the stop action option, at first because I wanted Sobieski to get on with it, and then because everything he said scared the shit out of me!

General Sobieski stepped up to the podium.

"I want to cover some lesser matters first before we get on to the main subject of discussion," he said.

Three hours of accounting procedures before he gets around to mentioning that we are at war! I thought to myself.

"There are some lessons to be learned from the last war," Sobieski continued. "The biggest one is that it does you little good to have overwhelming firepower if you cannot get that firepower to the battlefield. In the War with Earth, we were able to overcome that difficulty with a stratagem developed by Colonel Quincy Tsenovi here."

He stopped to give Quincy a round of applause from all present. Quincy smiled and nodded to their approval. Then Sobieski continued, "But doing that made it a hairy operation. It required absolutely precise timing by hundreds of thousands of units. Any one of a thousand things could have gone wrong, and lost us the war. We were lucky, even though many things *did* go wrong, costing us many good men and machines.

"But in the future, we will see to it that we have a sufficient number of Hassan-Smith transporters to get our army to wherever they are needed very quickly. This will take some years to accomplish, but it will be done. New production lines here in New Kashubia have already been designed and funded, and construction has already begun.

"Next, during the assault on Earth's Solar Station, the enemy wisely targeted General Derdowski's CCC. He had seven supply trucks with him that looked identical to his CCC, and the enemy managed to knock out six of them without hitting the CCC. Each of those trucks had a guard, and the enemy ignored them to hit the trucks.

"Again, we were very lucky, because without Derdowski and his CCC, we could have either lost the entire war, or we could have lost touch with the thousands of robot ships that are continuing the exploration of space, and the expansion of Human Space. That would have stunted our growth for fifty years.

"Besides adding more trucks as targets, and guarding them better, we will adopt a practice of always sending at least two CCCs on each mission. Other suggestions are welcome.

"Also, our streamlined command structure, which can have a hundred thousand men and fighting machines reporting to a single CCC is a bit extreme. In the future, there will be typically ten thousand tanks per CCC, and every fighting unit will have several CCCs that it can report to, should its primary one be knocked out. This will involve vastly expanding our officer corps, but there is a lot of good talent out there.

"Lastly, the army itself will be vastly expanded. New Kashubia will soon be passing a law requiring universal military service for all full citizens. You don't have to join the army, but if you don't, you can't vote. It is likely that most of the other planets will soon be following suit.

"You might reasonably ask why all of this huge expenditure of wealth and manpower is necessary. The answer is simple. Humanity now faces the worst enemy that could possibly be. They are very ancient, with histories that go back for almost seven million years. They are incredibly numerous, with at least sixty-eight thousand planets that have populations of perhaps a hundred and fifty billion people on each of them. And they are *unspeakably* evil. When they take a new planet, they eradicate absolutely all life on it, usually using thousands of neutron bombs in low orbit, in addition to totally poisoning all life in its oceans. That, and they regularly eat their own children. In fact, they don't seem to eat anything else.

"There are only two things that give us any possible hope of defeating them. The first is that despite their great age, they have never developed computers to the extent that we have. They have nothing like our electronic people. The second is that they have never developed anything like our Hassan-Smith transporters. They are limited strictly to the speed of light. And since their domain is some six thousand light-years across, we will never have to face more than a small percentage of them at any one time.

"On the other hand, they have several technologies that we, at present, can't begin to understand. They can, for example, accelerate and decelerate from almost light speed instantaneously. And they have some sort of a shield that can deflect rail gun needles, among other things.

"We have one of their ships. In time, we will learn more about them, and their technology. Because they are limited to light speed, it is likely that they do not yet know that we exist, and this gives us time to prepare.

"But, the indications are that they have already scouted all or most of Human Space, and have been doing so for hundreds—or even thousands—of years. Their attack may come sooner than we think. We may have five years, we may have fifty. But when it happens, we'd better be ready.

"This afternoon, we will be going over the taking of that alien ship, and explaining what little we know about it.

"That's all for now. Dismissed."

Mickolai found himself wishing that he was still at last night's party.

CHAPTER TWELVE

FROM CAPTURED HISTORY TAPES,
FILE 1846583A ca. 1832 A.D.
BUT CONCERNING EVENTS OF UP TO
2000 YEARS EARLIER

Bronki's New Body
Or, Eating Your Math Teacher

Kren had to pick Bronki up and put her on the stool in front of her computer. Seeing that she had difficulty staying upright, he quickly got some rope and tied her to her seat, before she got her computer online.

"This will probably take me an hour to arrange," Bronki said. "The pain is getting worse, not better. Why don't you go out and find me a big meal. The feeding stupor will help me endure the pain you've caused me."

"I will do that, soon. But first, I would like to see you fulfill your side of this bargain." Kren had visions of Bronki calling in the authorities while he was out.

"You are not a very trusting person."

"This is true. But you have every reason to hate me, for what I have done to you. I would be a fool to trust you at this time."

"Kren, you must realize that I am over five thousand years old. There is very little that can happen to a person that I haven't seen. Also, I am one of the most intelligent teachers at the university, as well as one of the wisest. Look. Every being must play the game of life from the position that she finds herself in at the present instant. The normal emotions—hate, joy, anger, greed—these things were useful to us when we were savages, but now that we are civilized, they only get in our way. Do you understand that I don't hate you?"

"I can believe that. But *you* must understand that I only started to become intelligent a year ago, and from the position that I find myself in now, I still think that I would be a fool to trust you. Go online, and do the things that you have promised while I watch. Then I will take you some-place comfortable, and I will hunt for you. Oh, and do the contract first, the deeds second, and the money third."

"As you wish," Bronki said. She had, of course, been plan-ning to contact the authorities, and have Kren arrested and eventually executed, not because she hated him for his treachery, or even because she badly wanted to save her mathematical abilities, but rather to save herself the twelve thousand Ke she had promised, and two of the many houses that she owned.

She started to work the net, thinking that sometimes you win, and sometimes you lose. Perhaps, a continued relation-ship with Kren would prove profitable.

First, she wrote, signed, and filed a confidential contract with the Bonding Authority for a fee of five gross Ke, which she talked Kren into paying by claiming that they did not accept credit.

Next, she filed a quit claim deed for both houses and all of their contents with the Land Authority, and then trans-ferred the utilities and taxes over to his name. Doing the bank transfer to a new account in Kren's name was a matter of only a few minutes.

Finally, she ordered a new body, with suitable brands burned into the girl's upper arms, from the Dependable Carnivore Company, Ltd. The young carnivore was to be delivered the next morning, along with a syringe of anes-thetic. The painful natural process that the aristocracy was so proud of using was not for Bronki.

"Now, will you please do something for this pain?" she asked him.

"Of course, I'd be delighted to." Kren untied her from the stool, carried her outside, and placed her gently on the grass, with her back propped up against the house. Then he locked the door behind him, put the key of his new house in his belt pouch, and went hunting.

He was back in a dozen minutes with a large, but suitable juvenal.

Bronki had taken a mechanical pencil and a large pad of grass paper with her, and had used the time to sketch a life-sized diagram of her own brain, with carefully drawn lines showing exactly what parts Kren could and could not eat. These were one fairly large section and three small ones. These agreed with what his memories from the medic told him, so he readily agreed to follow her instructions.

Because of her weakness and pain, he had to use his sword to chop up the young boy he'd brought for her, but Bronki ate the pieces quickly, throwing the bones out into the now well-tended field, being too weak to chew them up.

"Probably just as well," she said, as she became drowsy. "I'd need a new body soon anyway. As to the skills I'll be losing, well, a few years of study will get them back, maybe better than before. I may even come up with something really new, you know. There have been cases on record where an old mind has lost a segment, for one reason or another, and when it finally relearned what it had lost, it had become very creative concerning that particular skill."

"I wish you very good luck," Kren said, and perhaps he actually meant it.

When she fell asleep, he carried her bloated body back to her room and put her to bed. Then he went to bed himself.

He awoke to the sound of a fusion-powered helicopter, and ran out to see it setting itself down near the door under its big, counterrotating blades.

The pilot climbed down and said, "Is here all right?"

"Yes, I suppose that would be fine."

"I've got another delivery in this area in two days. I'll pick up the cage on the way back, if that's okay."

"That would be good, yes," Kren said.

"Fine. You are the recipient?"

"No, that would be Bronki, but she's in a stupor just now."

"Yes, she said that she was injured. You're Kren?" the pilot asked.

"Yes."

"She said that you could sign for this girl. Also, there's this syringe of anesthetic she ordered. It has to be injected into a major muscle two hours before the event. Do you know how to do that?"

"I'm a qualified military medic," Kren said.

"Good. The anesthetic will stay effective for two weeks, and will help out with the headaches as well. Just make sure that the young one eats the muscle that you shot up," she said and pressed a button on a pendant control that lowered to the ground a cage of heavy metal bars containing a starving, young carnivore.

"The cage is quite simple," she continued. "The new girl is back here. Put the old one in the front of the box, strap her in, and lock the door. Then pull these pins, and the wall between them will fold away. Once the new one has finished and has gone to sleep, put her someplace safe. She'll wake up in a week or two, a new person."

"That sounds simple enough," Kren said.

"Good. Sign here."

The pilot climbed back up into her craft and flew away.

Kren looked at the bare needle of the syringe in his hand and decided that there was no time like the present. He went into Bronki's room, to find her lying on her back, with her extended stomach bulging in the air.

The Mitchegai digestive system is quite elaborate for a carnivore. The first stomach, located just below the diaphragm, is used for little else but storing brain cells until they can be taken up by the blood stream. The second stomach is a hugely expandable storage bag, permitting a Mitchegai to consume a being even larger than herself. Only in the third stomach does actual digestion start to take place. The intestines are smaller than in a human, requiring more frequent defecation.

The buttock contained the largest muscle in the Mitchegai body, but the upper thigh was almost as big, and Kren saw no point in rolling her over and possibly waking her.

She didn't even murmur as he injected the anesthetic deep into the muscle. Of course, it wouldn't occur to a Mitchegai to apply an antiseptic before an injection.

He spent the next two hours reading a book concerning the life of a university student, hoping that it was more accurate than the one about military life.

When the clock in his study showed that the time was up, he carried Bronki out and strapped her in the front half of the cage, while the new girl screamed with hunger.

Using his sword, he cut off the top of Bronki's head, and making frequent reference to her sketch, he sliced out and ate precisely those portions that were agreed upon. They were delicious, and he was tempted to take a bit more, but he decided that it might be dangerous to do so.

Then he replaced the skull cap, locked the front door, and released the screaming young carnivore, before going indoors to rest for a bit.

He had intended to only relax for a few hours, but when he awoke, he found that he had slept for over two days. Dizzy and confused, he went out to check the cage.

He was relieved to find that all was well out there. The youngster was sleeping undisturbed. If the housekeeper had been by, she had touched nothing.

It was not easy to get the new Bronki out of the cage and into her old room. The new carnivore had eaten all of the old Bronki, who had been swollen with the large juvenal she had previously eaten. She weighed well over twice what she originally had. Feeling weak himself, Kren had to drag her most of the way.

He had just completed the job when the helicopter arrived to pick up the cage. He waved to the pilot, glad that he did not have to think up a plausible lie for Bronki's presence in the cage. In truth, he wasn't thinking very clearly just then.

Then he locked the door, went to his room, and slept for another three days, troubled by strange, mathematical dreams. It was the first time that he had eaten a major portion of brain without also eating the body as well. He felt surprisingly hungry. He resolved that if he ever did this again, he'd eat a juvenal along with it, and go into a proper stupor, if he could somehow figure out a safe way to do that.

He rectified that problem now by going out, killing, and eating a small juvenal. He didn't want to be in a stupor when Bronki awoke, because he still didn't trust her.

Returning to the house, he noticed that Bronki's old study was devoid of dried blood. The housekeeper had apparently come, cleaned, and left.

Eventually, while Bronki still slept, he picked up the book

on mathematics that he had been struggling with for so long. No longer was it incomprehensible to him. In fact, it all looked childishly simple.

Obviously, the operation had been a success.

He spent the next few days going over every book on mathematics that he could find in his new house. He was elated to find that he comprehended it all, from corporate accounting to advanced matrix theory, even the most complicated texts.

The housekeeper came every two days, as silent as before. She must have had some hint as to what was going on, because she stayed away from Bronki's room. As before, he stayed out of her way and let her get on with her job.

Once Bronki was awake, they would somehow explain to the servant that he was now master of this house.

Kren started in on the sciences. With his now superb knowledge of mathematics, he made it through the introductory text in only three days, and four days after that had completed a book on basic physics.

He was well into his first chemistry text when Bronki finally woke up. She staggered outside to relieve herself, and then went to the living room for a long drink of water.

"I always hate this part," she said.

"Is there anything that I can do to help?"

"You can do nothing but leave me alone. I'll be another week getting myself reintegrated."

With that, she staggered back to her room and closed the door.

Kren soon started into biology, a subject far different on a Mitchegai world than in any other place in the universe. They had, after all, only two species to study. But what they lacked in breadth, they made up for in depth. Billions of worker years had gone into the study of their limited subject matter. Every single gene was completely known and understood. Every single chemical used in either species was accurately classified, and all of its functions were completely explained.

Every possible drug that could have any effect on a Mitchegai was carefully cataloged and understood. The vast majority of them had been made illegal, since anything that could cause a short-term improvement inevitably caused a long-term disability. Anything that would result in a long-term benefit had already been bioengineered into the race. Also, any illegal product provided the legislators with an opportunity for considerable personal profit.

He was finishing up his first book on biology when Bronki made her next appearance.

"You are a lot slimmer than you were a few weeks ago," he said.

"Integration is a high-energy process. I need a few days to get my course outlines at least started, then we have time for a last good meal on country food before it's time for us to start for the university."

"I'm not sure that going to the university would be such a wise move for me. The identification scars on my arms are fraudulent, and if an officer of the duke's army were to study them, and make a few inquiries, I could be in big trouble," Kren said.

"So wear your cloak until we get to the university. You'll be safe enough once you're there. The University of Dren is an independent academic corporation. It's located at the intersection of four dukedoms, and it pays taxes to all four of them, but it's not under the jurisdiction of any of them. If any one of the dukes were to force his way in, the other three would feel threatened and attack him immediately. You'll be safe."

"That is interesting. Perhaps I will go."

"You *must* go," Bronki said. "If I show up without you, the athletic director will claim that my letter to him was a practical joke, and then he would make my life very difficult."

Five days later, they locked up the house and started walking to the public transportation terminal.

CHAPTER THIRTEEN

A Business Lunch
New Kashubia, 2205 A.D.

As we went to the dining room, I found that a name tag had appeared on my chest. Apparently, the idea was that we should all get to know each other. This impression was confirmed when I saw that the tables all had place cards at them. I found myself seated at a round table with five other generals. My colonels and electronic people were scattered out at other tables.

"So," General Hastings said. "We find that we are up against an enemy with at least sixty-eight thousand planets with a typical population of a hundred and fifty billion people on each of them. We have got maybe fifty planets, depending on what you want to call a planet, with a total population of perhaps thirty-two billion people. It would appear that we are outnumbered by something like three hundred thousand to one. Does anyone have any comments on this situation?"

"It kind of makes you want to find an asteroid in an uninhabited solar system, hollow it out, and live there for the rest of your life," General Castaneda said.

Some of the stunningly beautiful and nearly naked waitresses that Sobieski preferred started serving food and drinks. We each got our favorite drinks and dishes, but nobody paid any attention to it, or to them.

"I wonder how many asteroids like that there are?" General Fong asked.

"Joking aside," General Toronaga said, "It might be a very good idea to set up a large number of such hidey-holes. That way, even if we lose this war, humanity itself could go on."

"I suppose that you are right," I said. "Still, it's a depressing thought. Humanity, hiding inside of rocks for the rest of eternity? Maybe death would be better."

"We might win," General Nasser said. "After all, we know about them and they don't know about us."

"Don't bet on it!" Fong said. "For well over a hundred and fifty years, we have been sending robot probes out into the universe. We've lost a lot of those probes. How do we know what happened to them? Maybe these aliens know all about us!"

"Good point!" Hastings said. "One of the first orders of business will have to be that all of our probes are equipped with an array of modern sensors, a decent machine intelligence, and one bodacious self-destruct mechanism!"

"I'll second that," I said. "The problem there is that we don't have communication with most of those probes just now. I just had a hand in destroying Earth's Solar Station, which kept in touch with them, and kept them fed."

Castaneda said, "Then they haven't filled you in on that yet. It turned out that there was enough surplus capacity around the old Smuggling Net to keep in touch with the probes. Those that really needed it are getting enough fuel to keep blasting, and the rest are at least operational. Building enough dedicated accelerators and transmitters for them is way up on the priority screen."

"That's some relief," I said. "Why don't people tell me these things?"

"Probably because you didn't ask," Hastings said. "So. We need smarter probes, better protected probes, and much better sensors on our probes. We also need a whole lot *more* probes. Currently, there are many light-years between many of them. We need a much tighter net than that."

"And we need at least two layers of net," I said. "One farther out, to find intruders, and a second one that can send in interceptors if the first one picks up anything."

"I'd like at least a third backup in the system, too," Toronaga said.

Nasser said, "Wouldn't we all! The question is, how much of this can we do, and how fast can we get it done?"

The conversation became more animated, and eventually we'd spent fifteen hours at that luncheon table, and eaten three lunches each. We finally determined just what we needed and where, and when we were likely to get it.

For a while there, I kept insisting that we needed planetary defenses just as much as we needed system-wide defenses, but I didn't get much support from the others. "Later," they kept on saying. "We'll get to that later."

As things started to wind down, I said, "Didn't we have an afternoon meeting with Sobieski?"

Hastings said, "Of course we did, and still do. But in the Command Center's version of Dream World, there's always time to argue things out. You're new here. You'll get used to it after a while. Look around you. Is anybody else moving?"

I looked, and it was as if all of the other tables in the restaurant were tenanted by statues.

"Now, that's your signal that everyone else has finished their conversations. Actually, we might have delayed things by ten or fifteen minutes, real time. Nothing to worry about," he said.

CHAPTER FOURTEEN

FROM CAPTURED HISTORY TAPES,
FILE 1846583A ca. 1832 A.D.
BUT CONCERNING EVENTS OF UP TO
2000 YEARS EARLIER

A Girl and Her Vampire: Plans for Power and Glory

"What a lovely day for a walk!" Bronki said, "I had become so used to the little aches and pains of my old body that I had almost forgotten how wonderful a fine, new one feels."

They walked south, Bronki in her colorful academic robes, and Kren in his helmet and cloak, with his spear and sword belt, but no other baggage, since he didn't own any. Bronki went empty handed because she kept a complete set of belongings at each of her houses.

She still considered the house that they had spent the summer at to be hers, because the quit claim deed she had given Kren simply assigned to him any ownership which she had in the property, but made no other promises.

Legally, she had never actually owned it in the first place. It was owned by a corporation which was owned by another corporation which she controlled. To her mind, she was simply permitting Kren to indulge in a pleasant fantasy, while he paid the expenses on the place.

And between these expenses, and various other ways she had to get money out of him, she was sure that she'd break even on the deal within two years. It was a small period of time for a person of her age. After that, their relationship would be profitable for her. Perhaps very profitable.

"You've never lived in a city before, have you," Bronki said.

"No, I haven't."

"Then there are a few things that you should know. The population density of a city is much higher than it is in the countryside. If everybody killed and ate as many juvenals as she wanted, soon there wouldn't be any left, and the grass would suffer. For the most part, you must either travel away from the city to eat, or you must buy your food from someone who makes a business of collecting juvenals for sale. The cost is about the same, either way, and it saves time to simply buy what you need. The punishment for killing a juvenal without a permit within city limits is quite severe."

"Then what do they do with the juvenals that live there?" Kren asked.

"They have a lottery that you can sign up for, and if you win, you have a right to make one kill. At the university, odds are that you will get one every two years."

"If cities are so expensive, why do so many live there?"

"Many individuals don't," she said. "But cities have a lot to offer that the country doesn't. More social interaction, more entertainment, more jobs. In your case, it is difficult to get an education all by yourself. You need others around you."

"I see."

"Another thing. In the country, there is enough grass to take care of our sanitary needs. In the city, you must use a toilet. Do you understand what a toilet is?"

"We used toilets in the mine," he said.

"Good. Again, the penalties for not using one in a city are severe."

They topped a rise as they walked south.

"I've passed that thing six times since I left the mine, and I still don't know what it is," Kren said, pointing, as they walked down the road.

"It's a field of grass, of course," Bronki said.

"There's no 'of course' about it! It has some kind of a structure around it, and there's this tall green stuff towering above it."

KREN OF THE MITCHEGAI   87

"That is a walled field. The wall keeps the juvenals out. And that's what grass looks like when nobody keeps it trimmed down."

"But why would they do such a thing?" Kren asked.

"Long grass has several uses. It can be processed for its fiber, for one thing. Most of our paper, rope, and clothing is made from grass fiber. The rest is synthetic, except for leather. Most of the long grass, though, is used to feed the juvenals in the winter," Bronki said, amazed at his ignorance of the simplest things.

"I'd heard of grass paper, but I hadn't realized that they actually made it from grass. What is this winter thing you mentioned?"

And I'm taking him to the university, Bronki thought. *I'll be a laughingstock for sure.* "Winter is the part of the year when it gets cold."

"And why does it do that?"

"You've never seen winter?"

"Except for the last few months, I've spent the last nine gross years or so in a mine below ground. I didn't see any of this winter thing down there," Kren said.

"You wouldn't. Underground, it always stays the same temperature. That's why we keep the juvenals underground in the winter. Do you see those doors on the south side of the wall? Those doors lead to an underground set of caverns. The juvenals stay there for most of the winter. The caverns are right under the field of long grass. This makes it easier to cut the grass and deliver it to the juvenals. Our taxes pay for the workers who feed the juvenals in the winter. Our taxes also pay for other things."

"You are speaking slowly, while using a lot of small words and simple sentences."

"I apologize. I am still not used to speaking to a vampire," Bronki said. "Until I learned what you are, I always assumed that when you asked a strange question, you were making a joke. Your store of information is extremely spotty. Your knowledge of mathematics, languages, and the military arts is outstanding, yet you are ignorant of the simplest things. I find myself talking to you as if you were a newly emerging mind, which I suppose, is exactly what you are. But, if you ask this sort of thing of other students once you get to the university, they will think that you are very strange. Once we get there, I suggest that you remain silent when you don't understand something, and then come and ask me about it later. For now, keep on asking questions, and I will do the best I can."

"Thank you. I will follow your suggestions. Why is winter?"

Why is winter? Bronki asked herself. "Okay, you see that bright shiny thing up there? That is the sun. What do you know about it?"

"I know that it is a ball of mostly hydrogen, with some helium, too, and small amounts of most of the other elements. It is heated by gravitationally induced fusion of the hydrogen into helium. It is three gross three dozen thousand miles in diameter, and has a surface temperature of . . ."

"That is adequate. Now, this place we're walking on is a planet. It is located two dozen and seven million miles from the sun, spins on its axis once a day, and travels around the sun once a year. The axis of the spin is not the same as the axis of its circle around the sun, but is at a relative tilt of eleven degrees."

"This was all mentioned in the book on physics I just read," Kren said.

"Good. Now, because of the axial tilt, the southern hemisphere of the planet, where we're now at, gets more of the sun's radiation for one half of the year, and less for the other half. Is that obvious to you?"

"Yes, of course. You say that we're in the southern hemisphere?"

"Yes. I should have given you a book on geography, a fault that I will correct as soon as we get to my house at the university. Anyway, when this hemisphere is getting less radiation, it gets colder. That's what we call winter," she said.

"Thank you. Do the adults go underground the way the juvenals do?"

"Generally not, although many of the facilities in the cities are below ground. We prefer to live above ground and heat our houses. We wear heavily insulated clothing when we must go outside. I'll see that you are taken to where you can buy some warm clothes when we get to the university."

They got to the tube station as the sun was setting. From

the surface, this was little more than a doorway set into a low hill. Bronki used her credit card to open the heavy door.

"The doors are kept locked to keep the juvenals out," she explained.

Inside, a stairway went deep into the earth. At the bottom, signs directed them to platforms that went to eight different cities, with many stops along the way. One of the cities listed was the University of Dren.

Kren was interested in everything around them. He had never imagined such a place as this. Deep below ground, it was well lighted, clean, and pleasantly decorated, with colored tiles of blue, lavender, and green on some walls, and red, orange, and yellow on others, and all artfully arranged. The ceilings glowed evenly in an attractive sky blue, from the side, but white when you looked straight up. The floors were a uniform grass green. He had to look carefully before he was sure that it wasn't actually grass, but a synthetic carpet.

Yet, there didn't seem to be any other travelers around.

"This is lovely," he said.

"If you say so. The important criterion in the design of this sort of structure is that it must require very little maintenance. I doubt if this place has been refurbished in five thousand years. The initial costs are sometimes high, but quality pays for itself in the long run."

He followed Bronki to the proper train platform, where she pressed a request button for the next train to stop. They waited on a bench for less than a dozen minutes before a MagFloat train pulled quietly up.

They stepped on quickly, and the train took off immediately. Bronki went forward, gave the operator her credit card, and told her their destination.

"You'll owe me another eleven Ke for the ticket, when we go to the bank tomorrow," she said. "After what I've lost, I'm surprised that I can still remember my numbers."

They were the only passengers in any of the four cars.

"I'm surprised that so few customers use this amazing train," Kren said.

"There isn't much traffic this far out in the country. It will fill up as we get close to the university. As to being amazing, well, I suppose it is, but it doesn't seem so to me. Tube trains have been here all of my life. Actually, the tube system on this planet was completed over eight gross thousand years ago. You can go to within a day's walk of any place on the planet's surface with it, but for long trips, aircraft are faster."

"I wonder what it would be like to fly."

"It's not much different from being on a train, except for being more crowded. Well, the view is better. On your first flight, ask for a window seat."

"Bronki, I don't understand why you are being so helpful to me."

"Why shouldn't I be helpful; it doesn't cost me anything. I've told you that hate is a wasteful emotion. There's no profit in it. Yes, you've taken things from me, but now that they're gone, harming you wouldn't get them back. It is most unlikely that you will ever again be in a position to take anything more from me without my consent. I might be very useful to you now, but in time, I suspect that you might become very useful to me."

"In what way?" Kren asked.

"I'm not entirely sure. For the next two years, I'll be teaching literary subjects, so I probably won't need my mathematical abilities in the near future. But if it should happen that I do, well, you now have those abilities, and I think that you might be courteous enough to help out if I asked."

"Certainly, within reason."

"Also, I maintain living quarters for students and junior faculty members at my town house. You would be wise to stay near me, for my advice if nothing else, for the next few years, and you will need to rent a room someplace in the city. You will probably find it convenient to pay me rent and stay with me. I had a few vacancies last year, and that cuts into profits," she said.

"I imagine that I might do that, if your rates are competitive."

"They are. Lastly, you are a superbly trained warrior. Such beings are rare at the university. In the unlikely event that such skills proved necessary to me, it would be very useful to have someone to call on."

"I would be most happy to discuss such things with you," he said.

"That's all that I ask. It might possibly happen that we could have some mutually profitable business dealings with each other."

"When such things occur, I would be interested in hearing about them."

"We shall see," Bronki said.

At this point, a group of twelve entered the car, and Bronki ended the conversation by feigning sleep.

Her mind, though, was churning over, examining the various permutations of this situation. With a devoted dependant who was both a warrior and a vampire, there were so many pleasant possibilities.

Academic superiors who were in her way at the university, plugging a hole that would otherwise allow for her advancement, could be eliminated. From being a senior professor, she could see herself becoming a department head, a director of a college, and eventually even the chancellor!

Of course, that sort of thing would have to be done cautiously, with much preplanning, and with great discretion. She would have to be sure that when some ancient academic went to his just reward, she would be the obvious successor to his chair.

Business dealings, on the other hand, often allow one a great deal more latitude. She could imagine certain of her competitors selling out their holdings to her at very reasonable prices and then simply leaving town, never to be seen again.

And Kren, of course, would be happy to eat the evidence.

CHAPTER FIFTEEN

First Blood
New Kashubia, 2205 A.D.

We found ourselves suddenly back in the meeting hall. General Sobieski was at the podium.

"So, now that we are finally back together, let's get on with this," he said. "A month ago, General Abdul Hussein was exercising his troops in the Cometary Belt of New Syria."

I put my face in my hands. I'd had to work with Hussein during the taking of Earth's Solar Station, and he was a murderous, suicidal lunatic. If there was anybody to *not* choose to represent humanity in our first contact with an alien race, it was Abdul.

A large wall screen appeared behind Sobieski, showing the action.

My boss continued, "They picked up a fairly small, spherical ship coming at them at almost light speed. In the few seconds available to them, they sent recognition signals to it, which were not answered. Then, Abdul's forces were hit with some sort of energy field that took out thirty-one of their tanks. These tanks were not exactly destroyed. They simply ceased to exist. General Hussein took this to be an unfriendly act, and the rest of his forces, some four thousand tanks, opened fire on the intruder."

Well, at least they fired on us first. That's something, I thought.

Sobieski continued, "As you will see shortly, the rail gun needles simply bounced off, but the X-ray lasers, which deposit their energy deep into their targets, were more successful. The alien ship showed considerable warming.

"Then, in two hundred and fifty-two milliseconds, it ceased traveling in the direction of our forces. From moving at nearly light speed, it simply stopped, made an eighty-nine degree turn, and then proceeded sideways at three hundred and ten thousand kilometers per hour!"

Actions like these are simply physically impossible, and the crowd broke into gasps of shock.

"Right," the general continued. "Now, look at this close-up. You can clearly see that the rail gun needles are stopping ten meters from the alien craft. Or rather, they are suddenly moving at the same speed that it is. They wander around a bit, but when they get more than twenty meters from the ship, they suddenly take off, continuing in the direction that they were going before they encountered the alien!"

I was as confused as everyone else in the room.

"Abdul sent six squads of tanks after the intruder, since his fuel stores on his home planet weren't big enough to send his entire force. Those thirty-six tanks eventually caught up with the alien. They found it completely dormant. It was warm, but cooling off, and was generating no energy of its own. It appeared to be completely dead. They didn't feel up to opening the ship themselves, so they simply pushed it home, putting it in a three-day orbit around New Syria.

"Since then, experts from all over the system have been studying the alien craft. What we have learned so far is very preliminary, but we can state the following:

"First. Their materials technology is vastly superior to our own. That ship was constructed of ordinary elements well known to us, but in combinations such that many of them had tensile strengths up to fourteen times better than anything that we have ever produced.

"Second. Their computer technology is inferior to ours. There was not a single integrated circuit on that ship! Every single transistor was a discrete component! There is no possibility that they had an artificial intelligence on that ship. On the other hand, from what little we have been able to deduce, the programming of these simple computers is extremely sophisticated.

"Third. There were a number of charts and books on

board. While we are nowhere near being able to decipher their language, we are pretty sure that we understand their numbering system. We deduced the age of their civilization from what we are fairly certain is a history book. Then again, it could be a cook book, I suppose. We are more definite about the star charts we found. Incidentally, the characters in the books and charts are so small that a human can not read them unless they are expanded by at least a factor of sixteen. Their eyesight is apparently much better than ours.

"Fourth. There were absolutely no microorganisms of any kind on that ship, not even dead ones. This level of sterilization would be beyond our technology. What it means is beyond us."

"Last. There was only a single pilot on that ship, a strange creature who looks vaguely reptilian."

The screen showed him. An ugly sucker!

"There were also twenty-two and a half other, smaller creatures on board, all of whom had been alive until our X-ray lasers cooked the place. We haven't been able to analyze their version of DNA yet, but it appears certain that they were chemically identical to the pilot. There can be no other explanation for this than to assume that they were juveniles of the pilot's own race. And since there were no other food supplies on board, the presumption is that he was eating them. This supposition is backed up by the fact that he was eating one of these children at the time of the attack. It had not been slaughtered first. He'd been eating it alive."

The screen showed a small, green, partially eaten body, with obvious tooth marks in it.

"So. That's all we know right now. As we learn more, you will be informed. Get your preliminary suggestions together, submit them, and then go home and think about this. Keep in touch with each other. I'll call you all back together later on. Dismissed."

After we shipped our preliminary suggestions to HQ, Kasia wanted to spend a week visiting her parents on New Kashubia, Quincy and Zuzanna wanted to see their grandchildren, and Conan and Maria did some sightseeing.

I stayed bottled up in the CCC and thought about our new problem a lot.

CHAPTER SIXTEEN

FROM CAPTURED HISTORY TAPES,
FILE 1846583A ca. 1832 A.D.
BUT CONCERNING EVENTS OF UP TO
2000 YEARS EARLIER

Kren Knocks One out of the Park

Duke Kren took off the recording helmet, got up, visited the toilet and the drinking fountain, and lay back down on the cot.

His head was throbbing. Damn, but resurrection was a painful process. Being eaten alive was actually the easy part!

He put the recording helmet back on, and remembered. . . .

It was dark when they arrived at the university, but Kren wasn't aware of it. They left the lighted, underground tube station, and walked a half mile through a pleasant underground tunnel that was lined on both sides with many gross of shops and other establishments for which Kren could not imagine any possible use. Finally, they went through a locked doorway and up a winding staircase that led to Bronki's huge town house.

The building had three floors below ground and a dozen and five above it. Passenger elevators were as illegal as private transportation among the Mitchegai, for the same reasons of physical fitness. This caused the highest levels of buildings to be the least desirable, and here they were used for undergraduate housing. Graduate students lived below them, and junior faculty members below that. Bronki kept the entire second floor for her own, personal use.

The glassed-in first floor was taken up by a large lobby, six public meeting rooms, and some office space. It was here that they stopped first, at the registration desk.

"Zon, this is Kren," Bronki said to her subordinate behind the counter. "He will be registering as an undergraduate soon, and he will need a room."

"I'm sorry, madam, but business has been surprisingly good for the last few days, and we are completely filled up."

"That's certainly good news, even if it is a bit disappointing. I suppose that we can put him up in graduate housing until something opens up."

"I'm afraid not, madam. I really meant that we are completely filled. We presently have three gross, a dozen and nine tenants staying here. Even all of the faculty rooms are rented, and there's quite a waiting list."

Bronki said, "Well, Kren, it seems that you have gotten lucky. I'll just have to put you up in one of my guest rooms for the time being. At undergraduate rates, of course."

"I suppose that this arrangement would be adequate for a few days, anyway," he said. "Why are there so many students this semester?"

"I don't know, but someone in sociology will probably do a study on it soon."

Another flight up on the winding, central staircase took them to Bronki's private level. She let them in using her credit card on the door lock.

"We'll get you a credit card at the bank tomorrow," she said. "For now, well, you can always leave, but you might have difficulty getting back in."

Kren had believed Bronki's country house to be luxurious, while she herself had thought of it as being quaintly rustic. Her private quarters in her town house were considered to be the peak of luxury even by her standards.

It was big enough to entertain a gross of guests at a party. The ceilings were four times as high as Kren was tall, and encrusted with artwork and colored stones. Tall windows looked out on a magical city with thousands of lighted windows.

Inside, every piece of furniture looked to have taken a master craftsman years of labor to produce. There were artworks on the walls and statues on the floor that Kren had seen in photos in art books at Bronki's country house.

"I am amazed at your wealth," Kren said.

"Yes, well, in five thousand years, things accumulate," she said. "You might as well take this room, for now. It's my nicest guest room, but I don't have anybody else here at present. Just remember that you might get bumped down if somebody else more important than you stays over. And in this city, *everybody* is more important than an undergraduate."

Again, Kren was amazed. It was really a suite of rooms, with a palatial sitting room with couches, tables for party snacks, and a private drinking fountain. It connected to the rest of Bronki's quarters with a lockable door. Another door connected to a hallway that led to the stairway, so that he could come and go as he wished, without going through the rest of the apartment. It had the same high windows as the rest of her floor, and the high ceilings were, if anything, even more ornate.

There was a huge bedroom with a magnificently carved bed big enough for a half dozen Mitchegai, if such a thing were imaginable. Mitchegai prefer to sleep alone, behind locked doors. They are very uncomfortable with the thought of being unconscious while lying next to another deadly carnivore.

The three large chests of drawers in the room were now empty. Kren could not imagine owning enough things to fill them. He had a private toilet, and a clothes closet big enough to hold many gross of cloaks.

The walls supported paintings of outstanding quality, the bookshelves were neatly filled with beautifully tooled leather-covered volumes, and the furniture was all done as masterfully as that in the main living areas.

"I can spare you a few hours tomorrow morning," Bronki said. "We'll stop at the bank, and then I'll introduce you to the athletic director. After that, I'll be very busy for a while. I'll send in one of the servants to see that you have everything that you need."

When she had left, Kren lay down on the bed, thinking that when he had Bronki strapped to her chair, with both of her legs cut, he should have gotten a lot more from her than twelve thousand Ke.

A servant wearing an undergraduate's cloak of maroon with lime green piping and a purplish-red sash came in without knocking.

"I am Dol, sir. I've been assigned to you during your stay here."

"How nice. I didn't expect a servant."

"I suppose that it is a bit unusual for a junior to be the servant of one not yet a freshman, but there are many servants here, and only one guest, so things are as they are. Is there anything that I can get for you, sir?"

"There's nothing that I can think of, but then except for my housekeeper in the country, I've never had a servant. Is there anything that you would suggest?"

"Food? Books? Clothing? Some sort of entertainment?"

"Not food, and Bronki said that she was going to send me a book on geography. I will be needing some clothing suitable for an undergraduate student, but I think that is best put off for a while. What sort of entertainment is available?"

"How about a television set?"

Dol wheeled the bulky set in, demonstrated its use, and left, promising to be on call at all times.

Kren soon found himself watching a program called *Big Time Gladiators*, which involved a sort of combat between two remarkably clumsy Mitchegai adults. One was swinging an oversized sword, and the other had a badly balanced spear, while someone off screen was talking about the match excitedly, trying to make it sound interesting. The fighters appeared to have had no training with their weapons at all!

After a dozen minutes of buffoonery, the swordsman managed to land a blow to the leg of the spearman, obviously more by accident than by design. With the encouragement of the crowd, she further crippled her opponent, and then chopped her head off with an awkward, two-handed blow. This head was held up to the cheering crowd, and then presented to someone who, it seemed, was officiating the event. It was again held up to the crowd, after which the brain was eaten by the official. The living gladiator dragged the dead one's body off, perhaps to enjoy her meal in private.

As she did so, the announcer mentioned that she was the last living slave from the Senta Copper Mine.

Kren now knew what had happened to his former coworkers, while he was hiding in the small tunnel. He congratulated himself for having definitely made the right move that time!

He turned the set off, locked and barred all of the doors, and went to sleep.

The next morning they went first to the bank, with Bronki leading the way and Dol following behind. The weather was good, and Bronki elected to walk on the surface, rather that going by tunnel.

As they left the house, Kren turned around and looked at it, surprised at its size. It was a dozen and five stories high, but much wider than it was tall. Basically cylindrical, it was surrounded by balconies that spiraled upwards in a double helix.

"One goes up and one goes down," Dol said. "There are revolving doors top and bottom that keep the juvenals circulating up to the top, and then down again. Otherwise, they'd get confused, and the grass on the roof never would get eaten."

"Come along, you two. We don't have all day," Bronki said.

At the bank, Bronki quickly converted Kren's savings account to a credit card account, deducting his travel expenses and a year's advance rent in the process, and he was soon issued a credit card, complete with a photo on it. Not a picture of his face, of course, but of the identification scarring on his right arm.

The athletic director was waiting for them in his very impressive office.

"So you're the one Bronki here was telling me about, huh? The one who was involved in Duke Dennon's disaster at the Senta Copper Mine?"

"I'd hardly call it a disaster, sir, except for me personally, of course, since I was killed there. But for my unit, we were given a military objective to take and we took it, with only ordinary casualties," Kren said.

"Oh, militarily, everything was just fine, and I'm sure that your unit did a fine job. It was what happened afterward that caused all of the duke's problems."

"I'm afraid that those of us in the military were often not informed of such things."

"Yeah? Well, the duke's plans were that he would take the mine, and then shut it down for maybe a year, while he had it completely automated. You see, that mine produced nine dozen per gross of the copper ore produced on this whole planet. With its production halted, the price of copper ore was projected to quadruple. Then, he would sign long-term contracts with the copper smelters, at the new high price, of course, since they would be afraid of the price getting even worse. When he put the mine back into production, he would make a fortune!" The Director laughed.

Bronki and Dol stayed silent, not daring to interrupt the director as he was speaking to Kren.

"That sounds like a reasonable program to me, sir."

"Right. So, the duke went way into debt to buy all of that new machinery, since it was his excuse for shutting down the mine in the first place. Without the excuse, the copper smelters would have joined together and attacked him immediately!

"And then on the *very day* that the machinery was due to be shipped to him, the Space Mitchegai announced that they had found an asteroid six miles across that was five dozen eleven parts per gross copper! The Sky Boys soon started down-shipping refined copper at a third of the price that it had been selling for when the duke started this whole thing."

"Hmmm. You know, sir, that might explain why my pay is considerably in arrears, and why they were very eager to grant me an educational leave of absence, without pay, of course."

Kren found lying to be so easy that he was now sure that one of his former victims must have been a champion liar.

"That would sound likely. The lawsuits are flying all over the place right now, and some think that the duke might lose his duchy through bankruptcy, something that has only happened nine times before in the entire history of the planet!" The director thought that the whole thing was hilarious.

"So the duke's fatal flaw was that he was simply unlucky. Perhaps we should have lost that battle for him."

"He would have been fortunate if you had, but his troops were just too good. Speaking of which, grab a javelin and we'll go out and see just how good you are with one."

When Kren saw the rack that he'd gestured to, his heart slipped down to his knees.

"Sir, I've never trained with anything like one of those. All I know how to handle is a standard military spear like this one."

The director took it, hefted it, and handed it back.

"You mean to tell me that you hit the neck of a four-year-old at a gross three dozen and eleven yards with this stubby, heavy thing? This I've got to see! Come on out to the training field, all of you."

He grabbed three javelins off of the rack and led the way.

When they got there, Kren saw four large, circular grass targets at various distances down the length of the field. The farthest looked to be at about a gross two dozen yards.

"Well, take a throw, with your own spear."

"Yes, sir. Which target should I hit?"

"Take your pick."

Kren took the standard three running steps and let fly at the farthest target. His throw was good, and it struck deep into the very center of the smallest circle.

"Kren for as long as you can do that, you have yourself an athletic scholarship. Full tuition, books, and a food allowance."

Bronki entered in with, "That's very helpful, Director, but Kren has no other income. He'll need a place to stay, a clothing allowance, and a little spending money, anyway."

"Humph. I don't know. That would be sort of unusual. Kren, take one of these javelins and just take a throw. Go for distance."

Kren had the judgment and muscular control of a champion athlete, coupled with the massive strength his body had developed in ten years of hard labor in the mines. When he threw the javelin, its flight surprised him. It didn't travel in the usual parabola, but actually seemed to be flying, traveling in level flight! It continued out beyond the field and over the fence, to fall he didn't know where.

"Sorry about your javelin, sir. I'll try to retrieve it."

The director was still looking at the place where the javelin had disappeared. There was an awestruck expression on his face.

"Burn the javelin! Okay. Housing allowance, clothing allowance, and three dozen Ke a week spending money. I'll get a special donation from one of the alumnae to cover the cost! Once we teach you how to use a javelin properly, you'll be a planetary champion, and I'll be rich! You'll train for three hours a day, directly under me, the exact times to be worked around your class schedule. Report back at three, tomorrow, and my secretary will have all of the paperwork ready for you to sign."

"Thank you, sir. Did I mention that I was quite proficient with a sword?"

The athletic director looked at him amazed, and said, "We'll check that out tomorrow, too. Right now, I've got some phone calling to do, and some bets to place!"

Bronki and the director looked at each other, and they both bowed slightly. They both knew that Bronki could expect a hefty finder's fee for bringing Kren here, and an even larger one if he won the championship.

As they left, Bronki said, "Well, Kren. It would seem that your athletic career is well started, and that your venture will be well funded."

"Thanks to you, Bronki."

"Remember that I am always on your side. Have you done any thinking as to just what your course of study here at the university will be?"

"Yes, I have. I find that I am impressed with your wealth. I think that I will study business."

"Yes, that would be good," she said, thinking about Kren's vampirism turned loose on the field of business. "I think that with the right training, and a little help from your good friends, your natural abilities should earn you a very successful life in business," Bronki said.

CHAPTER SEVENTEEN

FROM CAPTURED HISTORY TAPES,
FILE 1846583A ca. 1832 A.D.
BUT CONCERNING EVENTS OF UP TO
2000 YEARS EARLIER

Buying the Mitchegai Way

Bronki gave Dol very specific instructions about precisely what they should do in the afternoon, and exactly where they should go and who they should speak to. Then she left to attend to other business of her own.

"Our first stop is the College of Business," Dol said.

They went to a large, impressive complex consisting of four rectangular buildings set around a central square with a large, ornate watering fountain. A large symbol of the Ke adorned every side of every building, the same ancient symbol that is found on every bit of currency throughout all of Mitchegai space.

"It is very attractive," Kren said.

"It is good that you like it. You'll be spending much of your time for the next five years here, assuming, that is, that you don't wash out."

There was a short line at the registrar's office, and when they got to the front of it, the clerk started by checking Kren's credit card for how much money he had in the bank, and then deducting three semesters' tuition from it. He was informed that if he failed the course, or if he failed to qualify for admission, there would be no refunds.

Dol told her that Kren was here on a scholarship, and that he would require a receipt. After some grumbling, she gave them one, and then spent some time changing things on her computer before seeing the next applicant.

Kren was then escorted to a testing room, while Dol waited outside. An hour later, Kren came out with a dazed expression on his face, and the two of them went to see an academic advisor.

"Kren, you have a most unusual profile. You are very proficient in three languages, including the academic language of Keno, and the business language of Neno, which are both extremely helpful. Also, you know the military language of Meno, which isn't used much around here. In addition, you have a smattering of four others, besides Deno, of course."

Among the Mitchegai, languages are not distributed geographically, as they are among a young race like the humans. Rather, they differ according to the occupation of the individual in question. Soldiers speak quite a different language than do engineers, for example. Among soldiers, the word for "foreigner" also means "enemy" and "evil," and they have no words to describe thermal equilibrium.

All Mitchegai also speak Deno, a simplified sort of pidgin that permits them to buy and sell with other professions, but not to truly communicate with them.

The advisor continued, "You know quite a bit about anatomy. Your math scores go right over the top, better than anything I've ever seen before in an undergraduate. But you are woefully substandard in everything else. Tell me, why did you choose the College of Business, anyway? Why not the College of Languages, or the College of Mathematics?"

"Why should I study subjects in which I am already proficient?" Kren said, "I chose to study business because I would like to become rich."

"Wouldn't we all? But I really don't see how I could recommend you to the College of Business with these test scores."

Dol said, "Please excuse me, but did you know that Kren has been personally granted a scholarship by the director of athletics?"

"The director of athletics?" The advisor's voice squeaked. "Well, that, of course changes everything! You really should have told me that earlier! Kren, I am delighted to welcome you to the College of Business! Of course, there will be certain remedial courses you will have to take in order to prepare you for a successful academic career, but you are definitely on your path to the future! Just give me a few minutes to arrange your class schedule."

"The director said that I would need three hours a day for physical training."

"But of course. Is there any particular time that you would like that to happen?"

"He said that we could arrange that around my class schedule."

"Really? You must be very special indeed. I've heard that the director prefers to work in the afternoons. Let's give you from seven to ten for him, and put all of your academic work in the morning. That will leave your late afternoons and evenings free for study, or whatever else you choose to do."

The Mitchegai use a two-dozen-hour day, with sunrise being at zero. They do not use time zones. Rather, the clocks on all public transportation slowly change their speeds, and sometimes even direction, to reflect local time. On a fast aircraft traveling near the poles, the clocks sometimes did surprising things. The pilots lived and worked on Planetary Standard Time, of course.

Dol noticed that the advisor had changed the class schedules of five other students before he was done.

As they were leaving the building, Kren said, "The director seems to have a remarkable amount of power."

"Indeed he does, as well as status. He is the second most powerful person on campus, which means the entire city. Only the chancellor outranks him."

"And why is that?"

"Because the College of Athletics brings more money into the university than student tuitions do! The ticket sales to sporting events and the payments made by the television channels are what keeps this institution going," she said.

"Remarkable. And which individual comes in third?"

"The director of drama, although they only bring in a third of what athletics does. Our next stop is the book store."

Here it was a simple matter of giving a clerk a copy of Kren's class schedule, and sitting down and waiting for half an hour. She returned with a cart full of books, and four hefty cloth bags to put them in. She took Kren's credit card, deducted the cost of the books, various supplies, and the bags. After some stern discussions with Dol, in which the director's title was mentioned, she exchanged nine books that she said had been placed on the cart by mistake, and gave them a receipt.

"Why is there such a problem with receipts?" Kren asked as they trudged along with two heavy bags each.

"Well, it sometimes happens that a new freshman finds out that he has not paid for his tuition at all, but has made a donation to the Clerk's Civic Betterment Fund, or that he has purchased a set of obsolete books that have nothing to do with his class schedule. Also, I think that your military uniform leads some fools into thinking that you are stupid. Always get a receipt. And anyway, you'll need the receipts to be reimbursed by the director's office."

"For this timely aid, much thanks!"

"Thank Bronki. She's paying me," she said.

"Do you like working for her?"

"To answer that, I would have to ask, *compared to what?* Compared to living with an independent income of a gross thousand Ke a year, what she has to offer is decidedly inferior. At the time that I accepted her offer, however, the only other employment I was able to locate involved collecting juvenals from the countryside and delivering them alive to the city, on commission. By comparison, her offer was outstanding."

"And what does she pay you?" Kren asked.

"Something much better than three dozen Ke a week."

So my servant gets paid more than I do! Kren thought, *Someday I'm going to have to do something about that!*

They decided that because of the weight of the books they would return to Bronki's house to drop them off.

When they got there, Dol said that they might as well get Kren's credit card number loaded into the household computer, so that he could use the doors without needing someone to let him in.

"She trusts you with so important a task?" Kren asked. "I would think that the value of any one of these paintings is worth many gross times what your yearly salary is. What if you stole a few of them?"

As Dol worked at the computer, she said, "You are probably

right about the relative values of things, but one must be alive to enjoy money properly. Actually, Bronki wouldn't mind if I stole everything here. She has everything insured for at least twice its market value. If it was stolen, she would make a profit, and Bronki *likes* making a profit.

"The insurance company, however, *doesn't* like to lose money. Kren, they hire teams of bounty hunters who are more ruthless than you can possibly imagine. I would prefer death at the stake to having those killers after me. If you are thinking of stealing anything, don't do it. Or if you absolutely *must* do it, please tell me first so that I can report you to the bounty hunters, so as not to make them angry, and then kill myself before they get here, just in case they get angry anyway.

"There, that should do it. Step outside and try the lock with your card."

As they left, Kren said, "Where to next?"

"A clothing store, Leko's. Bronki insisted that I take you to the same store that she always uses, so as to be sure that you get the highest quality."

"Well, she got me the clothing allowance. I suppose that she has the right to tell me where to spend it. There's another thing that I wanted to ask about. We didn't have anything like that javelin in the military. When I threw it, it seemed like it was defying the laws of physics! It went straight and level for the longest time!"

"You came to the right person to ask that question," she said. "It happens that I did a paper on those things last semester for my aerodynamics class. The javelin is balanced with the center of gravity slightly behind the center of area. When it reaches the top of its flight, and is traveling slower, the tail falls slightly below the point. This gives the whole javelin some aerodynamic lift, and the flight curve flattens out. As it continues to slow down, the tail falls more, giving a higher angle of attack to compensate for the lower speed. The result is that they can fly twice as far as an ordinary spear."

"That is interesting. With the spear, all of the weight is at the point, and the shaft just keeps the point facing toward the enemy. Then why hasn't the military adopted the javelin as a weapon?"

"Because the javelin trades kinetic energy for distance.

When one of those javelins touches down, it hits tail first, and it isn't going fast enough to hurt a pollywog. You can safely catch one in your hand!"

"Then if it can't hurt anyone, what good is it?" Kren asked.

"As a military weapon, it's worthless. As a piece of sporting equipment in a game where you are trying to see who can throw something the farthest, it's the difference between winning and coming in last!"

"I see. So you are studying aerodynamics?"

"Engineering. I may specialize in aerodynamics later, in graduate school. I thought you knew, since I wear engineering colors."

"I am not versed in the fine points in academic garb."

"I'll give you a book on the subject when we get back home, but for now, I wear the maroon with lime green piping of an engineer. The purplish-red belt is that of a junior undergraduate. We will be buying you the crimson robe with black piping of the business college, and you will wear the white belt of a freshman."

"What does Bronki's colorful clothing tell you?"

"Bronki has so many degrees, and is affiliated with so many academic organizations that she may wear pretty much whatever pleases her. That rainbow belt of hers is granted when one has earned a dozen doctrates in as many different diverse fields."

"And the little tassels around her shoulders?"

"One for every earned doctorate. She has a dozen and ten of them. Here's the clothing store."

In one respect, a Mitchegai clothing store has it easy by Earthly standards. All Mitchegai are exactly the same height, and their girth varies only with differences in musculature, and how long it has been since their last meal. The voluminous robes which they wore were rather similar to those worn by medieval Japanese samurai, and they handled the girth problem.

On the other hand, there are four dozen and nine different academic uniforms worn at the university, and each is available in six different degrees of price and quality. In addition, each of those comes in summer, winter, and spring and fall weights.

When they entered the store, Dol immediately announced that they were here at the request of Bronki. The clerk at the front desk instantly pressed a buzzer, calling Leko herself to the front. A distinguished-looking tailor came quickly out to greet them.

"Friends of Bronki's? But of course! I will handle all of your needs personally! What would be your requirements?"

"Kren here needs a complete kit for a freshman at the College of Business."

"Excellent! We can satisfy his every need. Come this way, please."

She took them to a special room at the back of the store, which contained nothing but the absolute best, and most expensive, merchandise. Dealing with a friend of Bronki, she would charge them twelve per gross more than usual, and send Bronki a commission of twice that, which still left Leko with a very good profit.

In the course of the next hour, Kren found that he absolutely had to have two summer weight cloaks, two more for spring and fall, and two particularly expensive ones for winter.

There was a heavy winter over cloak, and two pairs of gloves, medium and heavy. Kren noted that the seamless leather gloves had been made from the stretched and tanned skin removed from the hands and forearms of adult Mitchegai. They were dyed black, nicely tooled around the cuffs, and quite attractive, he thought, with holes on the ends of the fingers to let his claws remain useful.

Then there were two pairs of shoes, something that he had never worn before, and a pair of heavy winter over boots. The over boots were of an insulated, waterproof synthetic fabric that extended well past the knees, but the shoes were much like the gloves, and made of the skin of the feet and calves of a deceased adult. They had reinforced soles and were decorated to match the gloves.

Lastly, Dol convinced him that he really needed four sets of long winter underwear, two of which were electrically heated.

Kren also bought a nicely appointed matching book bag that was to have his name embroidered on it, and would be delivered in two days.

A cold-blooded creature must be very careful about temperature control, but in fact, the store was simply making the bill as large as possible.

At least this time, there was no difficulty with getting a receipt, and the store promised to have it all delivered within the hour, except for the book bag.

It was getting dark when they finally got home.

"Dol, why was it that I needed two of everything?"

"So that you could be wearing one while I have the laundry servant washing and pressing the other. A guest of Bronki's must always look his best, you know."

"I see. Do you realize that I have spent more than six thousand Ke today?"

"That sounds about right, but you will be reimbursed. It would be more accurate to say that the College of Athletics spent all of that money. It will be amusing to present them with the bill, tomorrow."

CHAPTER EIGHTEEN

The Good Life
New Yugoslavia, 2207 A.D.

Things were progressing very well.

I now had twelve full ten-thousand-man divisions of Gurkha warriors. They were living with their families in their own valley, next to mine. Every man was equipped with a new mark XIX tank, and many of them had been issued a humanoid military drone. I only had been issued four CCCs to manage them with, but more were promised as soon as they were built, and we now had thirteen Gurkha generals trained, each with five colonels. They were time-sharing the CCCs we had.

I also had an almost full division of female Gurkha warriors, something that the male Gurkhas didn't like at all. They had ostracized the ladies to the point that I had to put the girls up in my own valley, and keep them very separate from the Gurkha men. It was a bother, but those girls were good fighters, and army regulations wouldn't have let me reject them on the basis of sex, anyway. I hoped that in time the problem would settle itself out.

Maybe once they had proved themselves in battle.

They had their own CCC, their own female general, and five female colonels. There were Gurkha men who were probably more qualified than they were, but until the men were willing to integrate their command, the girls would have to go it alone. They were certainly eager to prove their worth.

New Yugoslavia did vote for universal military service,

on the same "join or don't vote" system that New Kashubia used, and I had eighty-two divisions of New Yugoslavian troops, a number that was growing rapidly.

A sufficient number of transporters had been put in so that it was now possible to ship my entire army out in somewhere between one and nine days, depending on where we had to go. More were being installed as fast as they could be built. Receivers cost only three percent of what a transmitter does, and could operate four times faster than transmitters. We now had twelve times as many of them as transmitters. If it was us who needed help, we could get it in a hurry.

Research on the alien ship was making progress. It had been powered by a muon exchange fusion power supply technically very similar to the ones that we used, except that it was one-eighth the size of our usual unit, and produced twelve times the power. Our people were working at trying to duplicate it.

The ship was driven by an efficient but understandable ion engine. But there was nothing about that engine that could explain the incredible accelerations that we had seen.

Our scientists managed to get the ship's primary weapon working. It made things disappear. We had no idea of how it did this, and we'd had no luck in duplicating it.

And our electronic people were absolutely in awe of the programs that were used in the simple computers aboard. They said that if we could duplicate them, we would quadruple the speed of our own computers, including themselves.

There were other machines on the ship that completely baffled us. We didn't know what they did, or how.

The planet-wide underground MagLev Loway system had been completed and announced to the public, but it wasn't seeing anything but military use. The factories were too busy with military production to make any civilian vehicles to use it. Someday, someday.

The associated planet-wide water, sewage, and power systems were getting good use, though. And they insured that we never were faced with drought or flooding conditions, or power blackouts, either.

My dairy farm was in production, and besides providing

products for local consumption, we were shipping butter, yogurt, and forty varieties of cheeses all across Human Space. The beef cattle were growing, but we would be building the herds for many years yet.

Most of the apartments in my city had been sold, as had most of the business spaces. Veterans were setting up restaurants, bars, and every other sort of business imaginable. The schools were starting to fill up, too, at least the lower grades.

At the outer edges of Human Space, the exploratory probes had been upgraded with better sensors, better artificial intelligences, and major self-destruct mechanisms. New probes were being added as fast as they could be built, but the whole system wouldn't be completed for fifty years. I kept on referring to it as our Maginot Line, but I couldn't seem to get the name to catch on.

Planetary defenses were still minimal, something that bothered me considerably. Putting all of your trust in defensive lines, or spheres actually, is silly. Defensive systems have to be in depth! Military history has proved that again and again, but the powers that be won't listen to me. It was very frustrating.

But the really important thing that happened was that my Kasia presented me with a baby boy! He came out red, wrinkled, squalling, and absolutely beautiful.

And equally important, my industrious wife is busily working on our second one.

Late last night, as she lay in my arms, she said, "You know, Mickolai, these are the good times. We must cherish them."

And I do. She always was smarter than me.

CHAPTER NINETEEN

FROM CAPTURED HISTORY TAPES,
FILE 1846583A ca. 1832 A.D.
BUT CONCERNING EVENTS OF UP TO
2000 YEARS EARLIER

Sword Slashes and Burning Memories

The next morning, Kren dressed himself carefully in a new summer-weight academic uniform, marveling at the feeling of smooth, strong quality in the cloth. It was vastly different from the heavy, rough warmth of his military cloak.

In part because he had been told that the director wanted to see him use a sword, but mostly because after wearing it all summer, he felt uncomfortable without it, he belted his sword on first, and put the cloak on over it. He was pleased to see in the mirror that it wasn't noticable under the voluminous garment, and resolved to wear it regularly.

When he and Dol arrived, the director's secretary had a dozen papers ready for Kren to sign.

"You might as well read through those before you sign them," she said. "It's an all or nothing deal, and nothing in these documents is negotiable, but you really ought to know where you stand."

Kren read through each one of them slowly, discovering that if he was injured for any reason, he could not sue the university, or anyone employed by the university, but had to pay for all of his medical bills himself.

If he was damaged beyond possible repair, the university would provide a new body, and then bill him for it. And if he was somehow killed beyond all possible hope of being properly eaten, the university would settle all of his debts, and then keep the rest of his bank account.

He was obligated to serve under the terms of the contract for as long as the director chose to maintain his scholarship. He could be dismissed, but he could not quit, until he graduated.

He agreed to play in any and all sports that the director saw fit, and would not expect to receive any extra compensation for the time that this took.

He would never in his life be allowed to play for any other university, nor could he play for any professional team while he was an undergraduate.

He would restrict his diet to one normal for a Mitchegai, that is to say, meat and water. Partaking in anything else, especially drugs, would result in his termination.

"Termination?" Kren asked the secretary.

"Oh, yes, and I do mean that literally. The director publicly skins drug users alive, and then nails their hides to the wall down in the lobby. An athlete on drugs can get his entire team disqualified."

"Yes, I saw four of them down there as we were coming in. I'd wondered about them."

"Now you know. There are only four because we had an auction last year, and sold off three dozen skins. Be warned," she said.

Lastly, the contract said that he would obey the director, and such other persons as the director might from time to time appoint over him, in absolutely all things.

Finally, Kren said, "All of this seems very restrictive."

"It is," the secretary said. "But it's not nearly as bad as it sounds. You have to remember that the director's job is to make money for the university. He does this by having very good athletes playing for him. Happy, healthy athletes make the best players, so he wants you to be happy and healthy. As long as you do well, you will be able to get away with doing just about anything that you want. If you give him problems, or if your performance slips, he can get away with doing just about anything that *he* wants to you."

"I see. What would be the most drastic thing that he might do to me?"

"Under ordinary circumstances, I'd say that the worst would be to put you into the gladiator pool. Twelve times a year, we have a fight to the death with one of the other universities, during half-time ceremonies. It's a major draw, and often gets play on the Planetary News. The names of the participants are drawn by lot."

Thinking of the buffoons he'd seen on television, Kren figured that he'd come out of it without the slightest difficulty, and even get a free meal in the bargain.

"Well, if that's all, there won't be any problems," he said, and started signing the papers. Dol and the secretary witnessed them.

"Now then," Dol said. "How do I go about getting Kren reimbursed for these expenses?"

"You just give them to me, and I'll see to it that Kren's account is properly credited," the secretary said.

But on looking at the receipts, she shook her head and said, "Oh, my! Oh, me oh my! Uh, please, wait right here."

A few minutes later, the director strode in followed by his secretary.

"Kren! These amounts are excessive!" he shouted.

"I'm sorry that you feel that way, sir, but I only did as I was instructed to do."

"Instructed? By who?"

"Bronki, sir. She gave Dol very specific instructions as to where we were to go, what we were to do, and with whom we were to speak."

"Did Bronki tell you to pay three semesters of tuition in advance?"

Dol said, "No sir. But the registrar at the College of Business insisted on it."

"Did she know that Kren was one of my athletes?"

"Yes sir, I informed her of that."

"Then the director of the College of Business and I are going to have a little chat. I see a receipt from Bronki for a year's rent. The monthly rate is normal, but paying a year in advance is not. I'll talk that over with her. The price of books looks okay, but these clothing expenses are ridiculous!"

"We went to the store that my employer insisted on, sir, and paid the price they asked."

"Did she tell you to pay *seven gross Ke* for an overcoat?"

"She told me to see that Kren got a full and proper kit, sir. Yes, we bought the best quality available, but quality pays for itself over time. Low-quality clothing would have to be replaced every year, at your expense, but these garments should last him throughout his entire undergraduate career. Feel this cloth, sir. This is enduring quality."

"What's your name? Dool?"

"Dol, sir."

"Then *Dol*, you are dressed like an engineer, but you talk like a tailor who is studying to be a lawyer! Okay, Kren will be reimbursed for these expenses, but there are others who will not get off quite so easily!"

"Thank you, sir," Kren said.

"Fine. Now, there are some things that I want you to do for me. I don't like the ID scars on your arms. They are sloppy, ugly, and they mark you as being military. For various reasons, like keeping the betting odds on you high, I'd rather that everyone on the planet didn't know that you were a veteran. This afternoon, my secretary will set you up with a clinic that can burn some academic-looking identification brands into you. Something nice and fancy that will hide the old scars, and still be hard to read. After the burn, have them rub in some of that red powder. That will really look great!"

Kren was pleased by this development. Anything that could distance him from his vampire past was all to the better, to his mind.

"That would suit me, sir, since if Duke Dennon is having the difficulties that you referred to yesterday, it might be best if I was not associated with him."

"There is that, yes. Just get it done."

"As you wish, sir. Won't I need a new credit card as well?"

"Of course. My secretary will take care of all that. Next, I don't want you to wear that military outfit around this city ever again, you got that?"

"Yes, sir."

"Good. Come with me. You, too, Dool."

They followed the director out to a large gymnasium.

Clothing, or the lack of it, has no sexual connotations among the Mitchegai, since the Mitchegai have no sex in the mammalian way of thinking. Clothing is used for identification, and to keep warm. Anything energetic, like athletics, is normally done naked.

A person wearing protective goggles was waiting for them in the gym.

"Kren, this is Dik. She was an all-planet fencing champion when she was an undergraduate, and she will be your personal trainer here when I am not around. She's also our best instructor with the sword. So strip down, chose an épée, and let's see what you can do."

Kren looked at the rack he'd gestured towards, picked up one of the long, thin, edgeless swords, and said, "It's the same story as yesterday, sir. I've never handled one of these things before. I mean, it's very light weight, and it has a beautiful balance, but it doesn't have an edge! All I know about is working with a standard military sword, like this one."

He pulled his sword out from under his cloak.

The director hefted and swung Kren's sword, and said, "If I let you use this thing, you'd kill somebody!"

"That *is* the idea, sir."

"Well, we can't have you killing our instructors. Undergraduates, perhaps, but not instructors, so using this thing is out. Dik, give him about a half hour of the basics with an épée, and then spar with him for a bit. I'll be back shortly."

So Kren was shown the basic moves of fighting with a sword with a point but no edge. The light weight of the épée compensated for its greater length, and a thrust with an épée was just like a thrust with a military sword.

In a while, he got the idea that the use of the épée was just a very simplified version of fighting with a real sword. You could thrust, but not cut, and only about a quarter of the various blocking moves were still needed. Furthermore, only a single, simple grip was used.

"I think that you are getting the hang of it, Kren. Put some safety goggles on, and we'll spar for a few rounds."

"As you wish, madam."

"Forget the 'madam' stuff. Around here, I'm just 'coach,' and outside, I'm just 'Dik.'"

"Thank you, Coach."

"Good. *On guard!*"

Dik was smooth and fast. In twelve minutes, she got six

legal *touches* on Kren while being hit two times herself. Kren also got eight cuts on Dik, which of course didn't count.

In sporting slang, a "touch" was to hit your opponent with the point of your sword, while a "cut" was to hit her with the edge, in military parlance. However, with the épée used, the point was blunt and the edge was nonexistent.

"I'm sorry, Coach. I keep forgetting that I'm not allowed to cut. It's habit, I suppose."

"We'll get you over it. That's what training's for."

The director had been watching for six minutes.

"Well, Dik. What do you think of him?"

"You were watching, sir."

"First string varsity?"

"Absolutely."

"That will put him in fencing and all four javelin events," The director said.

"That's quite a load to dump on a freshman."

"He can handle it."

"You're the boss."

"Right. Okay, Kren, you've done well. Go get a rubdown, and then see my secretary about that branding shop. Take two days off to heal, and then come back here on Monday, the first day of classes. Seven o'clock, wasn't it?"

"Yes, sir."

Dol, who had been watching the whole thing, followed Kren into the rubdown room. Finding two masseurs on duty, and no other athletes present, she simply stripped down and got onto one of the tables. The masseur, assuming that she was supposed to be there, started working on her. Kren got on another table.

Dol said, "I was really amazed by your performance. Do you realize that you are the first person to get a touch off of Dik in over three years?"

"No, I wasn't aware of that. The standards here seem to be a little different from those in the military. Also, the rewards here appear to be considerably greater," Kren said, referring to the pleasure of the rubdown, something that he had never experienced before.

Following the secretary's directions, they got to the branding shop within a half hour.

"The director's secretary said that this was a rush job, and that you wanted something fancy. I've taken the liberty of sketching up three possibilities for you," the brander said.

Kren looked them over, but didn't feel qualified to make an artistic judgment.

"What do you think, Dol?"

"Take the one in the middle, definitely. It has excellent form and balance, and is intricate enough to completely hide the old scars."

"Very well. The middle one it is."

The brander immediately started carving the design into a plate of soft, dry clay. It was done to her satisfaction in an hour, at which time she placed the plate in a small ceramic tray and poured some sort of metallic powder over it.

"What is that stuff?" Kren asked.

"A special powdered metallurgical alloy. Its exact composition is a company secret. All I can say about it is that it sinters nicely."

"What do you mean, 'sinters'?"

"When you heat this stuff up to the right temperature, the grains weld together without quite melting. It makes for a clear, sharp impression, without bubbles, warping or shrinking."

"I see," Kren said.

"The director will be paying for this branding plate and the branding itself, but he doesn't pay for anesthetics. He likes his players to be tough."

"Very well. And what would this anesthetic cost me?"

"A mere twelve Ke. It will be effective for four days, until the worst of it is over," the brander said.

"Then, by all means, I'll pay for the anesthetic."

"Most players do, the smart ones, anyway."

Kren was given a hypodermic shot, and then a second anesthetic, an oil, was rubbed over his upper arms.

A ceramic lid was placed over the powder, and the tray was placed in a small induction oven. In moments, it was glowing red hot, and was removed to cool a bit.

Kren was strapped into a chair that held his body, and especially his upper arms, immobile.

"Some customers can't help flinching, and that messes up the brand," the brander said.

The ceramic tray was then broken open, revealing that

the powder had been converted into a solid metal plate with the carved design embossed on it. Using long pliers, the brander put the still glowing plate into a mechanical arrangement that would put the brand in the proper position.

Without a bit of warning, she forced the red hot plate into Kren's left arm, while Kren struggled to keep from crying out with pain. After letting it burn for three seconds, the plate was moved to the other arm and again burned in, this time for four seconds.

"It's really best to just get it over with," the brander said with a smile. "Anticipation only makes it worse."

"That is difficult to imagine. Being worse, I mean," Kren gasped.

"You've never tried it without the anesthetic," the brander said. "Now, then. They said that you would like those burns to stay bright red?"

"The director recommended that, yes."

"Then we've got just the stuff for it."

A bright red powder was dusted on the wounds, and rubbed into them. Instead of hurting, it was actually soothing. Then Kren was unstrapped from the chair, and bandages were placed around his upper arms, not because there was any danger of infection on this sterile planet, but to keep the red powder in place, and to protect his new cloak from staining.

By then the plate had cooled, and the brander removed it from the machine.

"This is your property now. You can take it with you, and keep it for when you need a new body, or we can keep it here in our vault at no charge, and do the next branding for you."

"You keep it for me," Kren said, getting ready to leave.

"Very good, sir. And, uh, there was a matter of the twelve Ke that you owe me?"

Kren was not at all sure that he had actually received any anesthetics, but with no way of proving anything, he paid the brander with his credit card and left.

CHAPTER TWENTY

FROM CAPTURED HISTORY TAPES,
FILE 1846583A ca. 1832 A.D.
BUT CONCERNING EVENTS OF UP TO
2000 YEARS EARLIER

An Attack in the Afternoon

Kren slept poorly that night, kept awake by the pain in his arms. In the morning, he was half dozing, sitting upright in his suite when Bronki came in.

"Kren, I've been thinking. It appears that it will be impossible to find you a standard, undergraduate room anywhere in the city for this semester. Also, certain business associates of mine have been acting in an unpleasant fashion lately, and while I think that it would be very unlikely for them to actually do anything physical, I would find it very comforting to have a real warrior living with me. What would you think of making this room your own, say, for the next year?"

"I've yet to see a standard undergraduate room, but I cannot imagine that one would be as large, or as beautifully appointed as this suite is. Yes, I would accept your offer eagerly."

"Then we will consider it done. And if I were to need your martial aid, you would come?"

"Yes, but in the unlikely event that this should prove necessary, I think that it would be appropriate that I should be rewarded for my efforts. Shall we say, a thousand Ke?" Kren said.

"That seems like a large amount for a few minutes' work,

but very well. I long ago had an alarm system put in. It sounds like my voice, telling where you would be needed."

"When I hear it, I will come, and I will do what is necessary. And while the hourly rate might be high, the typical job does not require one to risk his life."

A few hours later, Kren was again half dozing while considering sending out for a small juvenal to eat. Perhaps that might ease the pain in his arms.

Suddenly, an unseen speaker was shouting in Bronki's voice, "*I need help in my bedroom! I need help in my bedroom!*"

Already wearing his sword out of habit, he picked up his spear and ran toward Bronki's room.

There were four Mitchegai in the living room, wearing not cloaks, but formfitting dark green garments of a sort that he'd never seen before. Mentally, Kren thought of them as being the Greenies.

On seeing Kren, one of them pulled out a throwing knife, and was preparing to hurl it at him when a military standard spear went through her throat and out the back of her neck. The Greenie standing behind her had tried to jump up and to the side, but wasn't nearly fast enough. The spear next went through her shoulder and pinned her to the wall with her toes inches above the floor. It ruined a beautiful painting in the process.

The two remaining Greenies drew their swords and came at Kren. Fighting alone against two, standard military doctrine is to run to one side and to dispatch the first one you come to as quickly as possible. If your enemies can get you between them, the one in front of you needs only to block your blows, while the one behind you can easily put a blade in your back.

They will undoubtedly kill you, no matter how good you are, or how inept their swordsmanship might be.

Kren followed doctrine.

He used the "spear" attack, a dangerous maneuver that involves holding your sword straight out in front of you while running at your opponent as fast as you can, while screaming at the top of your lungs in the hopes of startling her.

It worked.

The warrior in green could easily have blocked the blow, if she'd had a moment to think about it, but she lacked

that moment, she missed the opportunity, and shortly thereafter, she lost her life.

The Mitchegai heart is located low, surrounded by the
pelvic girdle, and is assisted by two smaller, single-chambered
hearts below the knees that pump blood depleted of nutrients
and oxygen upwards. Swollen ankles and varicose veins are
unknown in this species.

At the last instant, Kren lowered his sword and sent it
straight through her heart. He quickly pulled out his dripping blade, and used a horizontal blow to decapitate his
opponent, since a Mitchegai can function for minutes without
any heart at all.

The Greenie who was pinned to the wall was still struggling between a dead coworker and a valuable painting, so
Kren turned to his last opponent. This one, he could take
a bit of time with, and perhaps they would get into some
interesting sword play.

As they squared off, two very loud explosions sounded
from Bronki's bedroom. This startled the last Greenie, who
turned and looked to the bedroom doorway. Almost regretfully, Kren took advantage of this by cutting off the female's
right arm. As she stared stupidly down at her severed limb,
Kren took her head off in disgust.

The girl had been no fun at all!

When Kren got into Bronki's bedroom, she was standing with a complicated-looking metal object in her hand.
It was smoking.

Lying on the floor were two more Greenies with large holes
in their abdomens, bleeding on the lovely carpets.

"Well! It certainly took you long enough to get here! I
had to do the job myself! Now, put that sword of yours
to some use and dispatch these two! I didn't have time to
do anything but gut shots. These two have been knocked
out cold by the hydrostatic shock, but I would just as soon
that they don't come around."

"Yes, Bronki," Kren said, decapitating the two unresist-
ing Greenies. "I regret the delay, but there were four more
of these . . . individuals in your living room."

"Indeed?" Bronki stepped out to look. "I see. Please
excuse my earlier remarks. You've served me well this day.
You'd better kill this last one, too, but please be delicate
about it. That's a genuine Kado that this trash is stuck

to, and there are only three other paintings by her still in existence."

By the time that Kren had done the job without further damage to the painting, chopping the Greenie's head in half from the top, and had retrieved his spear, a dozen servants were crowding in, and Bronki was giving orders.

"Well, you can all see that we've had a disturbance here. Strip these bodies, flush their clothes down a toilet, and put them on the party tables. Remove the brains, chop them up, and flush them down the toilets, too. We wouldn't want any of this sort of trash to be resurrected. Put everything else they had with them in a pile somewhere. I'll go over it later. If you find any identification or credit cards, bring them to me at once. Then clean this mess up. After that, we'll all have a nice, family feast. Once we're all completely through, you will remember that nothing unusual happened here today."

"None of these Greenies knew anything worthwhile?" Kren asked Bronki while the servants scurried around.

"Greenies? That's as good a name for them as any, I suppose. Do they know anything useful? I doubt it, since these were all low-ranking trash. I mean, look at their small heads! But one of those in my bedroom was the leader of this bunch, and considerably smarter than the rest. Quality trash, I suppose you could call her. Come with me."

Bronki was soon sketching out another brain, showing Kren exactly what he should and should not eat.

"There. That should give you a considerable background into the underworld of this city, without taking up too much of your cranium. That's if you want it, of course."

"I think that it might be helpful, if today's events prove to be common."

"That remains to be seen, but by all means, help yourself."

"Thank you. About that feast, tell them to save me an arm and a leg, would you? And could I have some of their weapons for souvenirs?" Kren asked.

"Okay, and yes, I have no use for them, so you may have them all, if you keep them hidden in your room. It wouldn't be healthy to be seen with such things in the streets. Your sword and spear are legal, but that will

not be so for everything that these Greenies were doubtless carrying."

When Kren had eaten those eight small portions of the
brain that Bronki had suggested, he collected up and cleaned
all of the weapons that he could find, his own included.
It was quite a collection.

Besides six belt knives and four ordinary swords, most
of which had beautiful handles, hilts and sheaths, but blades
of less than military quality, there were dozens of other
strange weapons.

There was one straight sword with a handle that fit backward into its metal sheath, and locked there, converting it
into a sort of spear.

The knife thrower had carried six oddly balanced blades
in a harness that crossed her chest.

Another Greenie had carried a pouch with nine palm-sized
eight-pointed stars in it. The sharp points were covered with
some sort of green substance. Apparently, they were to be
thrown, but at first glance, they didn't seem to be a very
practical weapon. Thinking that the green stuff was perhaps
some sort of poison, he cleaned them and their pouch very
carefully, washed his hands, and flushed the cleaning cloth
down the toilet.

There was a dagger with a small trigger on it which, when
pressed, released a spring that propelled the center of the
blade across the room with considerable force. It imbedded
itself deeply into the carved woodwork at the head of Kren's
ornate bed. The projectile had narrowly missed hitting him,
and left him with a strange, but still serviceable, two-bladed
knife in his hand.

The use of any form of stored energy was forbidden to the
military, except that dropping things on an enemy was permitted. Before he had triggered the knife, Kren had assumed
that it was a legal military weapon. He wondered if some of
the senior officers had carried them.

There was an assortment of small blades intended to
augment a Mitchegai's natural claws, and four small clubs
apparently intended for beating citizens without actually
killing them, though why someone should want to do
such a strange thing was beyond Kren's imagination. It
seemed insane to injure someone, and then leave them
alive to seek vengeance on you.

There was a flat, heavy metal plate with many holes in it that mystified Kren, but which a human would have recognized as a set of brass knuckles.

Kren wiped all of his newfound toys off, put them away in a drawer, and resolved to puzzle all of them out at some future date. Perhaps when his new brain cells finally integrated.

He joined the others who were just sitting down to the feast. The blood and mess had been cleaned up, and many of the carpets were missing, but Bronki and her servants seemed to be in good spirits.

"Come join me, Kren," Bronki said, sitting by a low party table. "This girl is old, and she won't be the best tasting one of the bunch, but since she was the leader of the team that threatened us, I thought that I would enjoy eating her the most."

She slit open a thigh, peeled back the skin, and helped herself to a large gobbet of fat and muscle. The tougher skin and harder bones of an adult generally weren't worth the trouble of eating. Since the meat would be tougher than that of juvenals, and the dead bodies couldn't scream pleasantly in any event, she had provided very sharp knives for this feast.

"Thank you, although since classes start the day after tomorrow, I can't afford to eat a really big meal."

Kren cut a more delicate slice from the forearm on his side of the corpse. It was colder than he usually liked it, but still, it wasn't bad. And anyway, the new brands on his upper arms had started to throb again, now that the Mitchegai equivalent of adrenaline was subsiding in his system. A good meal would lessen the pain.

"We're all in that situation here, except for the laundry servants, and two of the scrubbers. Those four will probably be out of it for days. But what we don't eat can always be cut up and flushed down the toilets. It's not as though the meat cost me anything."

"Well, I expect to be paid for my services, of course," Kren said. "I killed four of them, so that's four thousand Ke, isn't it?"

"Kren! Greediness is such an unattractive trait! But no. I called you once, you came once, and in your own words, you 'did what was necessary.' I'll put a thousand in your account the next time I get to the bank. You've earned it. That was a remarkable piece of work you did today."

"None of them were truly competent with their weapons. I was very surprised with your success against the two who were in your bedroom. What was that metal thing you were holding, anyway?"

"It's called a pistol, and it is very illegal. Please don't tell anyone that you saw it."

"I won't. But what was the loud noise? And how did that small, blunt thing put such big holes in those Greenies?"

Kren decided that he had a day and a half to sleep it off, and cut himself a much larger piece of meat from the leg. It was such a pity that their meal was already dead, and couldn't scream.

"There are chemicals, nitrates, that burn very rapidly without needing air to do so. This produces a gas at very high pressure which propels a soft metal slug down a metal tube at high speed. The expanding gasses made the noise, and the metal slug made the hole."

"The use of fire is forbidden in military weapons. Also, your device sounds dangerous."

"I'm not in the military. And it is only dangerous if you are standing at the open end of the tube. A mechanical arrangement quickly replaces the nitrates and the slug, permitting you to take several shots. Eight of them with my pistol."

Bronki was working at freeing up another large gobbet.

"I think that I will stay with the weapons that I know."

"Yes, that would be wise. Some more leg for you? Or would you like a nice bit of tail?" she asked.

"Some tail, I think. We'll split it. How did the Greenies manage to get into your apartment? Your security measures seemed to be extreme to me."

"I like to think that none of my servants let them in, but one can never be sure. More likely, some electronic device was used to confuse the locks. I've ordered the whole system to be gone over and updated if necessary in the next week or so."

"Were you able to find out just who these strangely dressed Greenies were?" Kren asked.

"Yes. Four of them were foolish enough to carry their credit cards with them, and I checked them out on my computer. They were all members of a local crime syndicate, the KUL."

"Did they have much money in their accounts?"

"One of them did, the girl that we're eating now. I was tempted to keep it for myself, but then decided against it. Money transfers can always be traced, if you work hard enough at it. What can't be traced, if you know how to do it, is the person who did the transferring," Bronki said.

Kren remembered that his bargain with Bronki had included his getting her computer skills. This had apparently not happened. However, it was too late to do anything about it now, so he let the matter drop.

Bronki continued, "So, I transferred all of the money from all four of the cards to the account of a lieutenant in the KUL's rival syndicate, the PPG. This person once offended me badly. If I am fortunate, the KUL will think that the PPG killed their fighters, and the PPG will blame their lieutenant for holding out money from the group. With any luck, there will be a few dozen gang murders performed in the next few weeks, and perhaps both groups will forget that I ever existed."

"That sounds like a devious, but possibly workable plan."

"One can always hope."

"But why is the KUL so angry with you?" Kren asked.

Kren had stripped the meat off of the entire leg on his side, and was working his way through the buttock, one of his favorite parts. Then he decided instead to see just what this illegal weapon of Bronki's was capable of.

He cut into the chest, and found the breast bone shattered, with bone fragments in the lungs, liver, intestines, and even as low as the heart. Furthermore, two vertebrae were broken, and a third was completely pulverized. The pistol was a formidable weapon, indeed!

"I'm sure that the KUL are not angry with me. No, the Greenies who attacked us were simply hired to come here, either to scare me, or perhaps to kill me."

"I see. And who hired them to do this?"

"That is a very good question, my fine business major. I intend to answer it. When I know for sure what happened, it is possible that we may do some more of your sort of 'business' together."

One good bite leads to another, and before too long, Kren had eaten two-thirds of the cadaver, before he wandered off to sleep.

CHAPTER TWENTY-ONE

The Price of Defending My Planet
New Yugoslavia, 2209 A.D.

Every few months, some amazing new product, often an incredible alloy or other material, was being announced by the scientists who were working on the alien ship. A few of these things were starting to work their way into military equipment and even civilian products. There was even a sort of carpeting that they thought might last for thousands of years!

On the one hand, this was all good news. On the other, it kept everyone in Human Space focused on the importance of meeting the Mitchegai threat.

My wonderful Kasia had just presented me with our third son, my farm and my city were prospering, and the Powers that Be had just turned down my fourth request to establish some decent space defenses for New Yugoslavia.

This last item had me ticked.

"Agnieshka!"

"Coming, boss!"

I now had a dozen of the prototype social drones acting as servants in my apartment. The decorated military drones were still there, but they were mostly decoration now, standing like displays of medieval armor. They could always function as guards if such were ever needed. Mostly, Kasia felt that the soft, human-looking social drones would be better to have around the children, and I never could deny Kasia anything.

Each of the social drones looked like a different woman, and the one that walked in was new.

"So. A new look?" I asked.

"Yes, and I think that they have the sense of taste on this one just about perfect. Also, the sense of touch isn't bad at all. Some of the other girls have tried it out for sex, and they say it's fantastic!" she said.

"Enjoy. But I called you in here to talk about our problems with planetary defenses. You know that my plans were just rejected again."

"Yes, sir. It's not that they disagree with you, boss, it's just that every factory and system on New Kashubia has been working nonstop for four years producing what we need to defend ourselves against the Mitchegai. They can't afford the heavy expenditures required to defend a single planet, not when all of the rest of the planets would want identical defenses for themselves."

"That's just my thought," I said. "*They* can't afford it. But *I* can. Kasia and I are some of the richest people in Human Space. I have decided to use our own resources to defend this planet properly."

"But it isn't just a matter of money, boss. It's a problem of industrial capacity."

"Right. So what we need is industrial capacity. Now then. We have a huge secret room, kilometers long, where The Diamond was found, sitting there empty. We have many thousands of tanks and military drones who can provide the engineering and labor force. I read that New Kashubia has a surplus of mining machinery, and is still exporting raw metals to anybody who wants to buy them. What we need are the machines that can build the machines that can build the machines that can make what we need. I wonder, can we buy basic machinery from Earth? Over the last few hundreds of years, they have to have built a lot of slightly obsolete but still service-able machinery. I want you and the rest of our metal people to get involved in figuring out just what we need, and how we can get it."

"I'll get our people right on it, boss," Agnieshka said. "Things have been getting a little dull around here any-way. Have you talked to Kasia about this?"

"Not yet. She's next on the list."

Kasia was not enthusiastic.

"Mickolai, this is crazy! You are talking about expenditures of a size that whole planets can barely afford. Things that are out of sight for mere individual citizens!"

"All we are going to have to pay for is some used machinery and some raw metal. We already have the engineering force and the labor force, sitting idle. We already have a place to put it all," I said. "We can do it."

"I really doubt if it will be that cheap. Remember Cheop's Law. 'Everything costs more and takes longer.' And on top of that, why should *we* have to be the ones who pay for it? It is the whole planet that needs defending! The whole planet should pay for it!"

"And maybe it will, love. Once we get it built, and people realize what we have done for them, they will vote to reimburse us."

"Get serious!" She said, "What they will do is to say 'Thank you, sir!' They will throw a few more parades, and pin a few dozen more medals on your chest, but pay money? I doubt it!"

"Okay, what if what they were told was that what we had would protect the military, but not the civilians? But, for just a few trillion zlotys more, they could come under the umbrella, too."

"Now, *that* has possibilities."

"Right," I said. "And if we get New Yugoslavia to go along with this, why can't we sell the other planets on the program? We can sell inexpensive 'starter kits,' all the machinery and plans that are needed to build a decent defense system of their own. There could be a very hefty profit in it for you."

"Hmmm. Perhaps. But you've just stacked three maybes in a row, and it is getting increasingly improbable."

"That could be. But what good is all of our money going to do for us if the Mitchegai attack us, and we lose? Our wealth would be useless. Our estates would be gone. Our children would be dead."

"The boys would be dead?"

"The Mitchegai have no immune system. They need absolutely sterile planets. Before they can settle on a new world, they *must* eradicate all existing life on it. That would include you and me and the boys."

"Damn you, Mickolai, when you put it that way, you don't leave me any choice. Spend everything we've got, if you have to, but get it done."

I had the feeling that I would be sleeping alone, that night. It doesn't pay to win an argument with your wife, but sometimes it has to be done.

CHAPTER TWENTY-TWO

FROM CAPTURED HISTORY TAPES,
FILE 1846583A ca. 1832 A.D.
BUT CONCERNING EVENTS OF UP TO
2000 YEARS EARLIER

An Interesting Day

Kren slept through the night, the entire next day, and the night following it. He was awakened by Dol.

"Wakey, wakey, you fabulous warrior! Today is a school day!"

Kren stumbled to the toilet, then to his drinking fountain, and finally to a mirror, where he examined his brands. The pain in his arms had subsided to a dull ache, and the burns were almost healed. Millions of years of selective breeding had given the Mitchegai remarkably resilient bodies. His head, however, felt almost as fuzzy as when he had eaten a portion of Bronki's brain. He hadn't eaten that much of the Greenie's brain, but what he had didn't seem to want to fit in with the rest of him.

Once dressed, Dol walked him to class, to be sure that he didn't get lost.

"I didn't get a chance to talk to you the other night, but I got there in time to see what you did to that last sword swinger," Dol said. "You were unbelievably fast! *Whap! Whap!* And there she was, three pieces on the floor!"

"Yes, well, tell me, what do you know about pistols?"

Many of the dreams he'd had in his long sleep had been about various weird weapons, and about the many strange ways that a person could die.

"I've heard how they work, but I've never seen one. Some-one said that Bronki owns one. That was what made those explosions, the other afternoon, wasn't it?"

"Best we not talk about it," Kren said. "That's my col-lege there, isn't it?"

"Yes. All of your classes this term will be in the build-ing to the left, on the top floor. That's where they do their remedial learning. I put a copy of your schedule in your new book bag. I'll have to leave you now, since I've got classes of my own to get to. Do you know how to get to the gym from here?"

"Yes, of course."

"Then I'll see you back at Bronki's place, this evening."

Kren was in a fog all morning. He dutifully went to each class at the beating of the gong, took notes on the instructor's name, and all else that seemed important, but mostly his thoughts were on weapons and death. Most of them, things that sprayed fire, or bombs that exploded under your feet, struck him as being foolish. And could a gas really be used to kill?

But more and more kept surfacing on a system of fight-ing without any weapons at all. How to kill with a kick or a blow, where your claws could sink the deepest, and how to avoid these things from happening to you. Kren could see that this technique could be very useful, if ever he was deprived of his sword and his spear.

Two of his instructors commented on his lack of attention in class, for which Kren dutifully apologized. But in truth, he was sure that the athletic director would never per-mit him to flunk out, so long as his athletic and weap-ons skills stayed with him, and so he wasn't terribly worried about it.

Finally, the sixth gong sounded, and he had an hour to find the gymnasium and prepare himself for three hours of physical training.

He got lost twice in the complicated city, laid out with-out a single right-angled turn, and completely without roads or street signs. He arrived three minutes late.

Fortunately, Dik was the forgiving sort.

"Every new freshman gets lost at least three times in the first week," she said. "Just see to it that *next* week, you are here on time. We'll spend an hour with the sword, and then I'll turn you over to your javelin instructor. Here is the number and combination to your locker. Be back here in six minutes."

Kren worked as diligently as he could, but his performance was much worse than it had been a few days before. The coach had given him twelve legal touches in six minutes.

"What's wrong with you, Kren?"

"Coach, the pain in my arms from the new branding was bothering me, and I ate too much, the night before last."

"You should have bought the anesthetic," Dik said, easily parrying an awkward attack and touching him yet again with her épée.

"I *did* buy it! But I don't think that I actually received it."

"That happens. The trash probably saved herself two Ke by cheating you."

"She charged me twelve Ke! If she'd wanted more money, she could have asked for more, and I'd have willingly paid it!"

"Then she probably just enjoyed watching you endure the pain. Visit her, but don't kill her. Just cause her more pain than she caused you."

"I am unfamiliar with civilian ways. Is such a thing permitted?"

"I'm not sure that it's permitted, but it is surely commonly done. How else can the trash be trained to respect their betters?"

"Thank you, Coach. I shall act on your advice."

"Do it in a few days, when you are feeling back to your normal self. For now, *on guard!*"

The rest of the fencing session went badly for Kren, and he was glad when he was sent out to the javelin field.

A Mitchegai who always referred to herself as "The Master of Javelins" soon had her three dozen athletes standing rigidly in a neat line, with their eyes facing forward. Strutting like the martinet that she was, she started by explaining the rules of the games to them.

There were four competitions with the javelin. One was the distance throw, to simply see who could make a standard javelin go the farthest. Each contestant got three throws, and only the longest one counted.

The second was for accuracy. Each contestant had three

throws at each of four targets, all shots counted, and the winner was the athlete who had the highest total score.

The third was a game similar to the Earthly game of tennis, or ping pong, save that it was played with javelins, with the two opponents being required to catch any javelins that might fall within a designated area, and throw them back within two seconds. Also, the "net" was a solid wall half again taller than the contestants. The spectators could see where both of the players were, but the participants couldn't. This put a large element of luck into the game, but made it popular with spectators. The javelins used had blunt tips, for safety reasons.

The fourth competition was played with two teams of six players each, and played on a much larger court. Otherwise, it was much like the two player game.

Kren was taught the distance and accuracy games on his first day of training, and even though he was still drowsy from too much eating, and confused because of his new brain cells, after an hour with the new javelin, he did better than any of the other athletes present.

Twice, he threw his javelin entirely out of the arena.

The Master of Javelins called all of her athletes around before she dismissed them.

"I want you all to stay silent about what you saw Kren do today. The rules permit any of us to place any wagers that we wish, except that we may not bet that we will lose, or that our opponents win. I plan on betting heavily on Kren at our first competition in four weeks. If everybody knows what he can do, the odds on him will go down to nothing. Enough said? Good. Dismissed!"

As he was going back to the locker room, the master stopped him and said, "Kren, you are the best throw I've ever seen. But starting tomorrow, I don't want to see you throwing any more javelins out of the stadium. What we are going to work on is throwing just a little bit beyond what the next best man on the field has done. If you keep throwing half again better than anybody else, the betting on javelin distance throwing will drop to zero, and we'll all lose money. Do you understand that?"

"Yes, madam. That seems to be a very sensible program to me."

Never having admired or envied anyone famous, Kren

couldn't imagine wanting fame, so setting records meant nothing at all to him.

After a pleasant rubdown, he returned homeward.

Once again he found that he was lost, but a memory from the last brain he had partially eaten told him that if he went down a certain nearby staircase, he could quickly get to the train station, from which it was a straight walk to Bronki's place.

He soon found himself in an absolutely dark tunnel that he had never been in before, but which nonetheless seemed familiar. The complete darkness would have caused most Mitchegai problems, but Kren's nine gross years in the darkness of the mines had sharpened his other senses.

This had nothing to do with any sort of hypothetical ESP. It was more a matter of being attuned to the slight rustling of clothing, the slight breeze of a body coming close to you, the echo of your own breath and footsteps returning from all that was around you.

He felt, rather than heard or saw, two persons step out in front of him, and two more behind.

"Stop where you are," a voice to his forward left said in the darkness. "Drop your credit card and all of your money on the floor, and you will be permitted to leave unharmed."

"Giving you all of my money would be most inconvenient for me. I have had a difficult day, and I am not in the mood for further social interactions. Leave me alone, and I will agree to cause the four of you no harm whatsoever."

"You are a fool."

"No, I am a warrior," Kren said.

"You have been warned."

"So have you."

Kren felt, or perhaps heard, them approaching. He dropped his book bag and drew his sword. He heard the one closest, to the front left, hesitate, and then he heard her draw her own blade. Of course knowing that all adult Mitchegai are exactly the same height, Kren stepped forward and made a horizontal swipe with his sword. He felt it connect with the neck, and heard the head separate from the body.

Before he heard the head hit the floor, he heard a slight rustle of cloth as the second mugger in front turned to her right to look at the death of her coworker. This took her a fatal half second, and this was enough time for Kren to decapitate her as well.

One of the muggers to the rear was running forward, but the way that the second hoodlum had turned her head to *look* troubled Kren. Sensing in the dark, one kept one's head facing forward. How could she *see* when there wasn't any light?

He turned, took two steps back, ducked low, and felt a sword swinging above his body. His return blow was aimed to be just above the pelvic girdle, and he felt his sword go through the skin and heard the vertebrae sever, but then felt it stop before it was all the way out again. Not a perfect cut, but it was sufficient, having severed all of her major arteries.

Above the cries of the dying third one, the fourth mugger could be heard, running quickly in the opposite direction. Obviously, she had chosen the course of discretion.

Leaving the third one to bleed a bit, he went back to the first pair he had killed. Feeling around with his sword, he found one of the heads he'd removed from its body. Leaning his sword on top of the jaw, to keep it from biting him, he bent over and felt around the face. He found a pair of large and heavy goggles over the eyes.

Removing them, he stood up and put them on. He was startled to find that he could see. Not perfectly, for everything was in blue, black, and shades in between. The focus was poor, with things looking fuzzy. Faces, hands and feet looked much brighter than clothing, he could make out the footsteps where he and they had stepped. There seemed to be a strange slowness between the time he moved his hand before his face, and the time that he actually saw it move.

Nonetheless, with this device, one could see in the dark!

With the possibility of more such interesting objects in the offing, Kren carefully searched the three hoodlums he had killed. Besides two more pairs of goggles, there were dozens of other weapons, pouches, and objects.

Most interestingly, the first mugger he had killed had a pistol in a nicely tooled leather holster at her belt. Kren pulled it out and found that he knew precisely how it worked. The bits of brain he had eaten a few days before had been more useful than he had supposed.

It seemed that a swordsman's normal desire to test his opponent had cost this mugger her life. She could easily have stood back and shot her supposed victim.

Kren was strongly tempted to take a shot with it, but then decided that the noise might attract unwanted attention. And perhaps it was a fear of the noise that had stopped the mugger from shooting him.

A further search of the body revealed four filled clips, and an additional box of ammunition. For now, he put it with the holster and the special belt into his book bag.

He managed to get most of his loot into his bag, and stuck the three new swords under his belt.

Thinking that the fourth mugger might be finding friends to counterattack with, he left as soon as possible. Still suffering from overeating, Kren felt no desire for food.

Walking down the tunnel, he came to a lighted section, and removed his goggles, placing them in his cloak above the outer belt. He soon encountered an old woman who begged him for money, saying that she was hungry.

She was thin and shaking, but her problems looked to be drugs, rather than hunger. Kren did not feel pity, but he did want the evidence of his last encounter to be eliminated.

"Go into that tunnel," he said to her pointing. "Bring along a dozen of your friends, if you wish. You will find a feast there sufficient for all of you."

She thanked him, and scurried down the dark tunnel alone.

On arriving at Bronki's place, he went directly to his room through his back door. Looking in the mirror, he was annoyed to find that his brand new academic cloak had been slashed from shoulder to knee, save where his student belt had protected it. This had happened without his having even been aware of it.

He set down his book bag, dropped his student belt and cloak to the floor, put all four swords on his dresser, removed his inner sword belt, and lay down on the bed. It had been a difficult day, and he was tired.

Before he had fallen asleep, Dol came in.

"Is there anything that I can do for you, sir?"

"Yes. Take everything out of my book bag except for the

books, and put it all into a drawer someplace. Take my cloak out and see if it can be repaired. Then go away. I am very tired."

"Yes, sir. May I take the liberty of turning off these thermal imaging goggles? If you leave them on, the batteries will run down."

"By all means. Do anything else that you feel to be necessary, as well. But then go away."

"As you wish, sir. May I comment on the rest of this booty?"

"You may not."

"Yes, sir."

"Go!"

CHAPTER TWENTY-THREE

FROM CAPTURED HISTORY TAPES,
FILE 1846583A ca. 1832 A.D.
BUT CONCERNING EVENTS OF UP TO
2000 YEARS EARLIER

Payback

The next day went much better for Kren, both in the class-room and in the gymnasium, although his classroom instructors all chided him for not having completed his reading assignments.

And this day, he didn't get lost even once.

He was back in his room, trying to catch up on his reading when Bronki came in.

"Do I disturb you?"

"I have two days of reading to catch up on, but a break would be welcome," he said.

"Dol tells me that you encountered some difficulties yesterday, and I saw the cloak you were wearing. Did it have anything to do with the disturbance here a few days ago?"

"I doubt it. I got lost on the way home, and ended up in a dark tunnel along with four muggers."

"And what was the result of this?" she asked.

"One of the muggers ran away. The others provided a feast for some beggars. I have their personal effects in a drawer here, someplace."

"I would like to see them, if I may."

"Dol put them somewhere. Ah, here. There are also three swords on my dresser that I haven't looked at as well," he said.

After a while, Bronki said, "Kren, these goggles are worth over a thousand Ke a pair, although I advise that you don't sell them. They might come in handy. I am amazed that you were able to defeat the muggers when they could see and you could not."

"I spent nine gross years existing in darkness. Living without your eyes for much of the time, your other senses develop."

"Apparently, they do. This spring knife is something that could come in handy. A backup for my pistol. Would you be interested in selling it?"

Kren took the knife from her and looked it over. "I didn't realize that this was anything but an ordinary knife. But there was a better one I got from the Greenies. Here, look at it."

"Yes, this one is of better quality. Would you sell it?"

"Properly speaking, you already own it, by right of combat. It was once the property of the Greenie leader that you shot and we ate, the other night."

"And I didn't know that it existed. Thank you. That's one I owe you, Kren," she said, putting it in her belt. "Now, this pistol you've got here is very well made, and might be worth two thousand, with the extra clips and ammunition. Would you like to try shooting it? I know of an illegal target range where you could do that."

"Indeed, I would," Kren said.

"I'll set it up and let you know. It has been too long since I have had any target practice. I'll check the account balance on these credit cards if you wish, but for reasons I explained a few days ago, I'd advise that you don't transfer it to your account. On the other hand, these two pouches contain more than eight thousand Ke in currency. You could put it into your account, but I suggest that you don't. Credit card money is traceable, but currency isn't. Someday, you may wish to make an untraceable purchase."

"Then I'll just put all of this booty back into the drawer, although you may examine the credit cards if you wish."

"Thank you. I'll let you know if I find any use for them. Your cloak is being repaired, incidentally. It won't be as good as new, but it won't be embarrassing, either," she said.

"This is good. Is there anything else happening that I should know about?"

"Yes. I've found out how the Greenies got into my apartment. One of them had a credit card with a magnetic strip that had unusual properties. When slightly heated, the code on it changes to a different number. In this case, it was your credit card number, Kren. They used your number to gain access to my home."

"Surely, you don't think that I would have willingly let them in!"

"No, of course not. If you had, they wouldn't have needed the trick card. But someone who read your card gave them that number. In your military uniform, you were quite conspicuous, of course, and someone who was observing this place must have seen you come and go. I want to know the names of everyone who read your card."

"Certainly. I'm sure that the bank knows my number. Then there was the college, and the book store . . ." he said.

"No, the bank can be trusted. If they couldn't, they would be out of business in a day. And I know the university systems very well. They are secure."

"Then there was the tailor."

"Again, I doubt it. Leko knew that you are my friend, and she makes more money off of me alive than anyone would pay her for helping to make me dead," Bronki said.

"And then the last is the brander. I paid her twelve Ke for an anesthetic that she never gave me."

"That certainly limits the field, doesn't it."

"It does. I would very much like to participate in questioning her. I have a certain score to settle with that girl," he said.

"Your help will be welcome. I'll have to make some arrangements so that we won't be disturbed while we discuss matters with this brander. I'll keep you posted. Oh, yes. I've had to take your number off of the access list here. You must go to the bank and get a new card tomorrow, with a new number."

"I had to do that anyway, now that my new brand has healed."

Kren went back to his studies, feeling oddly contented.

At fencing practice the next day, Kren said, "Coach, they

tell me that you were once an all-planet champion. Why did you decide to go into teaching, instead of turning professional?"

"Well, I *did* go professional, for forty-two years back there, until my body started to slow down as it got older. Then I taught for a dozen years before I decided to get into a new body and go back to being a pro, where the money is much better. But when it comes to being a champion, not all bodies are the same. The difference between being the best and being an 'also ran' is very subtle. Part of it is the physical body, part of it is the mind, and part of it is the interaction between the two. This body just isn't as good as my last one was."

"I suppose that there's always a next time."

"That there is," Dik said. "It goes for you, too, you know. Your next body isn't likely to be as good as the one you're now wearing. *On guard!*"

The Mitchegai normally work a six-day week, with four days on and two off. On their equivalent of a late Friday afternoon, Bronki came into Kren's room.

"I trust that you are free this evening?"

"Yes, barring some school work, which I can do tomorrow," Kren said.

"Good. I've made arrangements to have four particularly ugly individuals standing outside of the brander's shop while you and I have our discussion with her. They'll make sure that we're not disturbed. Be ready in an hour."

"With pleasure."

The four goons were standing in front of the shop when they got there, and let them in without comment.

"So, you make branding plates and do branding, don't you?" Bronki said.

"Yes, madam. What can I do for you?"

"You can answer a few questions for us," Kren said, stepping in front of Bronki.

The brander looked at Kren, and took a fatal second to recognize him. She quickly reached for something below the counter, but Kren was much faster. He had his sword out and hit the girl on the side of the head with the flat of his blade before her hand had moved a foot.

"Yes, that's probably for the best," Bronki said as the brander collapsed.

"She was trying to reach this thing," Kren said as he picked up a metal tube over a yard long. Pressing a small button on it, a yard-long blade sprang forcefully out of the end, converting it into a spear.

"That's called a spring spear," Bronki said. "Take it home and add it to your collection."

"I will. In the back room, she has the perfect place to ask questions," Kren said, picking up the brander.

He stripped off her mauve tradesman's robe and kran artist's belt, which would have appeared black to human eyes. She was soon naked and strapped into the same chair that he had been immobilized in a week earlier.

While waiting for her to regain consciousness, Bronki looked around the shop.

"She really does very nice work. With the right training, I think that she could become a truly fine artist. I want you to be sure not to kill her, Kren."

"I hadn't intended to."

"Excellent. Good artists are really very rare. Oh, here's your brand, Kren. I think that you might be well advised to take it back with you, since it wouldn't be a good idea for you to trust her again."

"Agreed. She's coming around."

"Right. Now then, my fine young artist, besides failing to give Kren here the anesthetic that he paid for, you also kept a copy of his credit card number, and you sold that number to someone. We would like to know why you did that, and who you sold the number to."

"I don't know what you're talking about!"

"Yes, you do. We know that you know, and you know that we know that you know. Now, tell us who they are."

"I can't do that. They'd kill me if I told you."

"Perhaps, but they would have to catch you first, whereas we have *already* caught you. In addition, our methods will probably be a lot more painful than theirs might be. Please reconsider."

"You don't know who you're messing with, lady!"

"True. But then, neither do you. Kren, please hurt her."

"With pleasure!"

Kren picked up a branding plate from the shelf and took it to the induction furnace.

"No, use this one instead," Bronki said, handing him a different branding plate. "It's realy much nicer."

"As you wish."

He placed the branding plate into the oven and pressed a button as he'd seen the brander do. In a moment, the plate was glowing bright yellow. Picking it up with the long pliers, he held it over her chest.

"Last chance," he said.

"Don't you see that I can't!"

"I was hoping that you'd say that."

Kren placed it carefully over her fourth lung and dropped it. The brander screamed loudly as he counted to ten, and then pulled the brand off the smoking skin.

Bronki poured some water on the wound and said, "Kren, that scream was one of the nicest I've ever heard! I think I'll put some branding irons around the party snacks the next time I have guests over.

"Now then, young lady, would you like to tell us what we wish to know?"

"Go fry your brains!"

"Kren, again, please. Use this plate."

The brander proved to be remarkably stubborn, as Kren burned a different brand over her third lung.

The first two lungs are in back, behind the spinal column. The Mitchegai rib cage is fastened at the neck, and kept centered by the diaphragm.

It soon became necessary to put two more brands on her abdomen. It was only when he placed a hot branding plate between her legs, searing shut her cloaca, that she finally broke down.

Like Earthly birds, the female Mitchegai have a single orifice at the bottom for the elimination of dung, urine, and eggs. The males have an additional orifice that periodically sprays small amounts of sperm into the air. The areas concerned with defecation and reproduction are very sensitive on Mitchegai, as they are on humans.

"Just kill me and get it over with," the brander gasped.

"My dear, we don't want to kill you. We want to kill the criminals that you gave Kren's number to. Once we're gone, you can go into hiding for a few weeks, and after that, it is most likely that those who might have been after you will be dead, and you will be safe."

"Why didn't you say that before?"

"I suppose that I should have, but Kren was having *such* a nice time. You really picked the wrong person to withhold an anesthetic from," Bronki said.

"A girl has to have a *little* fun."

"And now you've paid for your fun. Well then, who wanted Kren's number?"

"Kodo," the brander said.

"Indeed? This is interesting. Now, tell me the whole story from the very beginning. I want you to be very complete, and very honest, because if we decide that you are lying, Kren will turn you over and work on your back side. There is room for six brands back there, and you would find sleeping very difficult for a week or two, if you tell us any lies. Do you understand?"

"Yes, madam."

The brander was a half hour getting the whole sordid tale out. It started with her losing a large gambling bet, followed by more betting in a vain attempt to recoup her losses. Soon, she was forced to borrow money, and then to borrow more money to pay back the first loans. Then Kodo had bought up her debts, and at first only wanted a few small favors done, in addition to regular repayments on her debt. In time the favors became larger, and more illegal, and were backed up by Kodo's threat of going to the authorities and telling them of her past crimes, if she didn't commit further ones.

"I see," Bronki said. "How did they know that Kren was coming here?"

"I don't think that they did. I think that they were following him. They came in right after he left. They had jimmied my card reader half a year ago, so it always remembers every number that I read through it. It was one of the little favors they had me doing for them."

"And why did Kodo want to harm me?"

"You are Bronki, aren't you? You were the only other bidder going up against him on a piece of development property. With you gone, he would have been able to buy it at a much lower price."

"Yes, the Naga property. I didn't think that Kodo was that serious about buying it. Actually, I'd already submitted my top bid. I wouldn't have gone any higher. There was no need for all of this at all. I guess we can add stupidity to Kodo's other crimes. Okay, you are telling the truth. Kren, unstrap her, and let's get out of here."

"If I unstrap her, she'll take a shot of anesthetic and be out of her pain. I had to suffer for days."

"Now, don't be spiteful. You've already given her five brands to your two, and the ones she got were much deeper than usual. Anyway, she has to be able to move in order to go into hiding."

"If you insist," Kren said.

"I do. As for you, young lady, remember that it is in your best interest if we kill Kodo. Dead, he won't be able to come after you for betraying him, and furthermore, you will be out from under all of your debts to him. I really like your art work, incidentally. You know where to find me. If you live through this, and should you decide to further your academic study of art, please feel free to look me up. I may be able to help you. I happen to have considerable influence at the university."

The brander looked at Kren and said, "Is she really serious?"

"Oddly enough, I believe that she is."

CHAPTER TWENTY-FOUR

The Welcome Stranger
New Yugoslavia, 2211 A.D.

The machinery had been bought from Earth, massive amounts of raw materials had been purchased and stock-piled, the initial work had been done, and the first of sixty ships that would form our Distant Early Warning Sphere, two light-years out from New Yugoslavia's sun, had just been launched. We'd be building about one a week from this time on.

I felt the need to relax alone and congratulate myself.

On rare occasions, perhaps once every two months, I like to sit down with a bottle of sour mash bourbon, and drink alone.

I was indulging in this weakness when a bright blue crab walked into my den. It was as big around as a large dinner plate, fairly thick, and had six very strange legs, but it was a crab.

I'd seen one once before, on a remote island on my honeymoon. I'd assumed that it was part of the original ecology of New Yugoslavia, even though it wasn't listed as such. I had it put into a carboy of ninety-five percent ethanol to preserve it, intending to ship it to a university for study. Soon, it somehow managed to drink twice its weight of the 190 proof booze, cut a neat, circular hole in the metal lid of the carboy, and then walk back to the ocean.

So, I was sure that I wasn't hallucinating. But just to be surer, I said, "Agnieshka?"

"Yeah, I see him too, boss. He's for real," her voice said from what looked like a stand of medieval armor.

"So. Hi there, little fellow! Are you the same guy that I met on a beach, seven years ago?"

"In fact, I am, sir," it, or I suppose, he said. "I've long wanted to thank you for your kindness, that day. To find a total, alien stranger, to have the wisdom to understand what I so badly needed, and then to have the kindness to give it to me in such munificent quantities, well, it goes beyond all normal measures of nobility. My offspring and I will forever be in your debt." He said this in perfect Kashubian.

This left me a bit flustered, first because I was talking to a crab. Then, I'd really expected him to die when I'd had him put in that embalming fluid. I mean, I didn't know that he was intelligent. I'd assumed that he was about as bright as an earthly crab, with all of the intellectual capabilities of a cockroach. This was a fortunate case where my two wrongs added up to a right!

But it wouldn't be polite to mention that now, and I had the feeling that this would be a very important conversation.

"You are quite welcome," I said. "I don't have any of that exact mixture around just now, but I am currently drinking something similar. Have you ever tried a Kentucky bourbon whiskey?"

"No sir, I haven't."

"Then please be my guest. I think that it might be awkward for you to use a glass. Agnieshka, please get our guest a shallow soup bowl."

A social drone quickly brought in a bowl, and set it on the table. As I filled it with Jim Beam, the crab easily crawled up a table leg to the table top and then sat down across from the bowl.

I topped up my glass and said, "To your good health."

After I'd had a drink, and my guest had drained his bowl, he said, "Now that was interesting, sir. It has a very complex mixture of sugars, esters, and other chemicals mixed in with the basic ethanol and water. Quite tasty, in fact."

"I'm glad that you like it. I have a wide variety of similar things here. Would you care to try them?"

"Oh, yes, indeed I would, sir!"

"As you wish. Agnieshka, let's see what our guest thinks about tequila."

After a bit more sampling, I said, "You know, my friend, we really haven't been properly introduced. I am General Mickolai Derdowski. I am the military commander on this planet. Who, and what, might you be?"

"I don't think that a human could pronounce my name without great difficulty, but Bellor might be a close approximation. My race calls itself the Tellefontu, and I am a refugee on your planet. My home planet, along with most of the members of my species, was murdered by a race called the Mitchegai, whom I believe that you have recently heard of."

"I have, Bellor. There are indications that they are coming this way."

"Indeed, they are, General Mickolai Derdowski."

"My friends just call me Mickolai."

"Thank you, Mickolai. Well, our original plan was to simply lie low on this planet, recoup our numbers, and hope that the Mitchegai did not find it suitable for colonization. Then, your people arrived, and while you inadvertently caused a great deal of damage to the original environment, you were obviously not trying to absolutely destroy it. In fact, you were making efforts to preserve at least some of it. At that point, we decided that you could make at least tolerable neighbors. When you personally demonstrated such extreme wisdom and kindness concerning me, we wondered if we could become friends. We observed that you are really two species living and working together, one biological and one electronic. We reasoned that if you could function as two species, there was every likelihood that you could function as three. Monitoring your communications, we find that you fear our ancient enemies, and that you are preparing to vigorously defend your planets from them. Therefore, we have decided to contact you, and to propose a defensive alliance."

"That's quite a statement. You must understand that I cannot speak for all of humanity, but insofar as we are talking about the military forces on this one planet, I am the person currently in charge. And yes, faced with an enemy of the size, age and power of the Mitchegai, humanity can certainly use all of the friends it can get! I personally welcome your help!"

"That is gratifying to hear."

Agnieshka had been frequently refilling Bellor's soup bowl

with different flavors of booze. When she dumped in a small bottle of 190 proof Everclear, something that I had forgotten that we had, Bellor said, "Ah! Now *that* is the food of the Gods!"

Pure, industrial grain alcohol, I thought. *Yes, that would figure.*

"Good. Glad that you like it. But there is a great deal to be discussed between us. We need to know just what you can do for us, and what you need from us."

"What we can do for you, aside from advising you on the enemy, teaching you a bit about the sciences, and piloting your fighting machines, is to give you some very useful military technology. You know the hole I made in the container that you put me in, many years ago?"

"Yes, and I was wondering how you did that."

"I made it disappear. I did the same thing to some of your window glass, in the next room, to get in here."

"You did? But that isn't glass. That's a single crystal of diamond."

"The material isn't important. Only its location matters."

"We would very much like to have that weapon. Something like it was used to take out thirty-one of our tanks when the alien ship arrived."

"Something identical to it. The Mitchegai stole that weapon from us, but we will give it to you."

"Thank you. And what do you need from us?"

"Could you spare a few hundred tons of Everclear?"

CHAPTER TWENTY-FIVE

FROM CAPTURED HISTORY TAPES,
FILE 1846583A ca. 1832 A.D.
BUT CONCERNING EVENTS OF UP TO
2000 YEARS EARLIER

Major Wagers

The next day, Bronki withdrew her bid on the Naga property. She didn't want any connection with Kodo while she was planning his demise. Also, once he was successfully disposed of, she should be able to buy the property at bargain rates at his estate sale.

Two weeks went by with nothing more eventful happening than a pleasant academic party with a dozen guests and four party snacks. Bronki really did provide electrically heated irons, and they were a big hit. One guest, a professor of physiology, won the prize for best scream by inserting a cold iron into a girl's cloaca, and then plugging it in.

Besides the delightful screaming, a few of the guests even said that they liked the flavor of the cooked meat. Bronki was confident that she had started a new fad, and was enjoying the social prestige that such a thing gave her.

At both the college and at the athletic department, Kren's instructors seemed pleased with him.

The only sour point had been their visit to the target range. Kren found that while he knew the theory and operation of a pistol perfectly, he was a truly terrible shot.

With a spear or javelin, he could hit a target the size of his hand at a gross yards. With a pistol, he could hit a target the size of an adult Mitchegai at six yards only on the rarest of occasions. After exhausting most of his ammunition, he gave up in disgust.

Bronki said, "Well, I guess that the Greenie you ate was just a lousy shot!"

"Apparently! I should have taken a bite out of the mugger!"

"It couldn't possibly have made you a worse shot with a pistol. However, eating a bit of someone who is a very good shot might be a bit problematic, as I expect that such a person would be very difficult to kill."

Bronki tried a few shots with her new spring knife, and was very pleased with the results. At anything less than a dozen yards, it would prove very deadly, indeed.

Kren sold the pistol and its accessories at the range store for a dozen and eight gross Ke, in currency. They didn't deal in plastic money there.

On the way home, Bronki said, "Kren, I think that I might have been over hasty in advising you not to use the credit cards you got from those muggers. For one thing, there is over four dozen thousand Ke in those three accounts, a remarkable amount for mere muggers to have saved."

"They were apparently very successful in their line of business."

"I imagine so, until the very end, of course. There has been no activity with any of the accounts since you obtained the cards, and no inquiries have been made concerning them. Now, an organization like the KUL would have been concerned about any missing members, but if these muggers really were independents, it could be that nobody cares about them."

"And you have a suggestion?" Kren asked.

"Yes. What I could do would be to arrange for a series of complicated transfers to be made through a number of dummy corporations that I control, before transferring the money to your account. I think that it would probably be safe enough."

"I see. And you would expect a fee for this?"

"Three dozen per gross would be standard," she said.

"Could you settle for two?" Kren asked.

"For a good friend like you, certainly."

Bronki computed that with this fee, she had recouped her initial investment in Kren in less than four weeks, and was starting to make a nice profit on him.

"Then please do these financial things and get me the money. I expect to need it soon."

"You are going to bet on your performance in the upcoming competition?" Bronki said.

"Of course."

"The odds against you winning the distance throw are currently eleven to one. That's quite low, considering that there will be over three dozen contestants, and you have never been in competition before. The word on your throwing must have gotten out."

"Do you know my odds on the accuracy competition?" He asked.

"They are currently much better, a dozen and nine to one. The actual payoff will depend on the odds at the start of the competition, of course."

"Then I will bet all of my money on the accuracy competition." Kren was not yet sufficiently confident of his abilities with an épée to wager on the outcome of that event, and the javelin tennis game had too large of an element of luck for Kren to take any serious risks with it.

"Don't bet everything, Kren. Save a little as a cushion. No competition is ever certain," she said.

"We will see."

"As you wish. I'll have Dol take you to an honest bookie. She will tell them that you are my friend, and you will be well taken care of."

"Thank you. What is happening with the KUL and the PPG, incidentally?" Kren asked.

"Oh, there is a lovely gang war going on, even better than I had hoped. More than eight dozen bits of trash have died thus far with only a few of them being resurrected, and the end is not in sight. Also, that lieutenant who offended me had a meeting with his superiors, and hasn't been seen since. To my mind, it's good riddance to the lot of them. I think of it as a private contribution on our part toward the general betterment of the city."

"I expect that you are right. And what is happening with Kodo?"

"That is still in the planning stage. When things are ready, we'll discuss the matter fully," Bronki said.

"As you wish."

                    ✳   ✳   ✳

The first athletic meet of the season was a home game, and the Dren University athletes were naturally nervous about their first public performance of the year. It was a two-day event, and there were three dozen and five separate competitions, held with the rival University of Tu, whose team had flown in from the other side of the planet.

The facilities available for the meet were large by human standards. Every sport had its own separate courts and buildings, with open-air facilities for good weather and indoor ones built below them for use in winter and on rainy days. The university had been building and expanding for over seven dozen thousand years, and the Mitchegai, with their long lives, built things to last.

While their creativity was inferior to that of humans, materials technology is largely a matter of experimenting with many things over a long period of time, and at this, the Mitchegai excelled. Their structural components could be relied upon to last indefinitely, and even their carpeting could sometimes last for ten thousand years.

The complete lack of microbes helped considerably. On earth, microbes are not only responsible for the degradation of organic materials, but also for much of the rusting of iron and other metals. There is even one that thrives on gold.

And since the outsides of their buildings were always covered with self-renewing grass, they required no external maintenance at all, forever.

The Mitchegai, who neither drank, nor smoked, nor enjoyed sex, were almost all serious gamblers. With more than six billion free adults on their efficiently managed planet, a significant portion of their gross planetary product was wagered on academic sports.

The fencing competition was held on Saturday morning in an open arena, since the weather was good. All of the javelin events would be held in the afternoon, which would leave Kren free for the whole day on Sunday.

And at noon, there would be a fight to the death between two athletes selected by lot, one from each university.

Fencing was a horizontal pyramid event, where the winner of a previous bout went up against the winner of the bout below her. The scoring was simple. The first contestant to score three touches against her opponent won.

Kren was surprised to find that he won six matches in a row quite easily, and was hailed the winner before a cheering crowd. Dik came up to him and hugged him, which caused Kren a bit of embarrassment.

"That was magnificent, Kren! Do you realize that the official pari-mutuel odds on you paid a gross two dozen and four?"

"No, Coach, actually I didn't."

"You mean to say that you didn't bet on yourself? I put over a dozen and five thousand Ke down on you, and I'm a wealthy person because of it!"

"Actually, I didn't think that I was that good. After all, until today, you were the only person that I had ever used an épée against, and compared to you, I am only marginally superior."

"Well, we kept your fencing talent a secret to keep the odds on you up. We never meant that *you* shouldn't know about it. Anyway, you know now. But next time, the odds on you will not be so good."

"Indeed, I seem to have made a major financial error."

"Sorry, Kren. I thought that I had made it clear how good you were."

Kren left the arena depressed. Had he bet his money on his fencing, he would be on his way to wealth and power. Furthermore, he would have more than five million Ke that he could now bet on his javelin throwing, not a paltry three dozen and eight thousand.

On his way to the locker room, Kren was stopped by Bo, an athlete that he barely knew.

"Kren, you must help me!"

"And why is it that I must do this thing?"

Kren continued walking toward the locker room, with Bo scurrying behind him.

"Kren, I lost the raffle! I'm going to have to fight to the death in half an hour!"

"So? Someone had to lose. Anyway, it's not like *Big Time Gladiators* on television. They always resurrect the loser in these university matches."

"I'm a runner! I'm not a fighter! I'm sure to be the loser! And resurrection is so painful!"

"It is far superior to the alternative. Anyway, I fail to see what I can do for you."

Bo said, "You could take my place! You can out fight anybody!"

"But, why should I want to do this for you?"

"Because I would pay you to do it! How does five thousand Ke sound to you?"

"It sounds very small," Kren said.

"Then ten thousand! That's all that I have!"

"I'll be paid in advance?"

"Very well, but how? We can't get to the bank and back before the event," Bo said.

"There are plenty of bookies around who are working the crowds. You will place a ten thousand Ke bet naming me as the recipient of the winnings."

"Okay! I'll do it! But let's hurry!"

They found a bookie, placed a bet for Kren to win at the javelin accuracy competition, and then went to the locker room where Kren picked up his sword and a spare military spear that he'd bought.

The rules for the death competition were "arm yourself with any legal weapon."

They got to the ring with three minutes to spare. Kren was just getting into it when he was stopped by the athletic director himself.

"Kren, just what in the name of the Great First Egg do you think that you are doing?"

"I am getting into the ring?"

"And why were you doing this stupid thing?"

"For the Glory of the University! Consider, sir, that Bo here doesn't stand a chance of winning a fight against anybody. The university team will lose five points when he gets killed." Kren knew that it was a stupid excuse, but it was the only thing that he could think of at the time. "How could I let a thing like that happen to my beloved alma mater? Especially when there's no doubt at all that I would win easily."

"You bloody idiot!" The director said, "Do you have any idea how much money I have riding on your performance with the javelin this afternoon? Even a slight wound could risk that! Now get your bleeding cloaca out of that ring!"

The athletic director then picked up the terror-stricken Bo and threw her bodily into the fighting area.

"And you, Bo, will quit blowing farts and at least *try* to die like an athlete!"

Kren got out of the ring and offered Bo his sword.

"I guess that the best that I can do now is to offer you a good weapon. Do you want the spear as well?"

"What about my money?"

"You must worry about your life, first. We don't have time to get your money back to you now, but come see me, the next time you get a chance, and we'll work something out."

"So how much was she paying you?" The director said.

"Ten thousand Ke."

"Kren, you are dismally stupid."

"I quite agree with you, sir. Especially since I failed to bet on myself in the fencing competition," Kren said.

"*Absolutely* dismally stupid!"

The director was shaking his head as he walked away.

Bo took Kren's sword, but she didn't know how to use it. The match was over in a half minute. The crowd got a bigger thrill out of watching a young carnivore eat Bo's brain and body, than they did from seeing her fight.

You win some and you lose some. Sometimes the other guy eats your lunch, and sometimes you *are* lunch.

Kren retrieved his sword, which had Bo's severed hand still clutching the hilt. He pried loose the fingers and absentmindedly munched on the wrist as he went to the javelin courts.

The first javelin event was team tennis, which was a major spectator sport, but not very important to the gamblers. Kren's performance was more than adequate, but his team's wasn't. They lost eleven to nine.

Individual tennis was another horizontal pyramid sport. Kren won his first three bouts, but then lost the fourth when he misjudged his opponent's position. She caught his spear just as it went over the barrier, and immediately spiked it into the ground a yard from the wall. This happened when Kren had been expecting a long shot, and was in the back court.

The distance throw was next, and the Master of Javelins again admonished Kren to not get carried away, but to try to make each throw just a few yards longer than the best throw before him. Kren promised to do so.

The playing position was determined by each player walking past a bucket set with its top higher than eye level. They each reached in and pulled out a ceramic tile with a number

on it which determined when they would be throwing. Kren
was toward the middle of the three dozen athletes competing.

Things went well at first, and halfway through the third
and final round, Kren had made the longest throw, although
it was nowhere near an amateur record.

Then two athletes from the opposing team outthrew
Kren's best effort by more than eight yards each, to
almost tie for first place. They had been playing the
sandbagging game, too, and had been in a better position to play it from.

Suddenly, Kren was only a poor third.

The Master of Javelins said, "Yes, well, I suppose that
you can't win them all. On the accuracy competition, just
stay with the program, and everything will be all right."

"Yes, it will, madam, because I am going to win."

"That's the spirit!"

"I mean, madam, that I will win because I will not follow your tactics. What I will do is see to it that I get the
lowest possible score to guarantee a win, but I will win,"
Kren said.

"Hey! You don't argue with the coach!"

"I am not arguing, madam. I am explaining."

Kren walked away and joined the line forming up to draw
the position tiles for the next event.

On the first round, Kren put his four javelins into the gold
circles in the center of each target, while he mentally kept
score on each of the other players. The mathematical skills
that he had stolen from Bronki were a major advantage to
him here.

On the second round, he put three into the gold, and one
deliberately into the blue, since none of the others were now
likely to equal his score.

On the third, he got one blue, two red, and one white,
since at that point, even if everyone who had not yet thrown
in this last round got nothing but gold, they couldn't catch
him.

The crowd was wildly enthusiastic, but that wasn't
important to Kren. What was important to him was that
he was now worth in excess of one million Ke.

CHAPTER TWENTY-SIX

FROM CAPTURED HISTORY TAPES,
FILE 1846583A ca. 1832 A.D.
BUT CONCERNING EVENTS OF UP TO
2000 YEARS EARLIER

Sports Victories and Vampire Plans

When Kren got home, he found Bronki and Dol laughing and talking together in a most uncharacteristic manner.

"Is this a private party, or may I join you?" Kren asked.

"You certainly may," Dol said. "After all, you are the guest of honor!"

"Indeed?" Kren said sitting down with his tail wrapped around his waist. "And how did this come about?"

"It came about because today you won both the fencing contest and the javelin accuracy contest, sir. While you have been somewhat taciturn with me, a mere servant, it happens that while accompanying you in the course of my duties, I couldn't help noticing, first, that you were capable of hitting the smallest of targets at the greatest of distances with a spear, and also that on the very first time that you picked up an épée, you scored points on Dik, something that no one else has done in years."

"Yes. So?"

Dol said, "So, I gathered together my entire life's savings, a matter of less than six gross Ke, and bet it all on the outcome of the fencing competition. And then, having won a tremendous sum there, I went to bet all of my winnings on your next real competition, naturally eschewing the javelin tennis game. But, there was not enough time between events to bet on the distance throw and then to reinvest the winnings in a wager on the accuracy competition. Therefore, I put it all on the one with the higher odds, accuracy. This fortunate decision multiplied my winnings by a further factor of a dozen and nine. I am now the proud possessor of just under a million Ke! And I owe it all to my association with you, and to Bronki here, who introduced us, and put me to work for you!"

"Well, I congratulate you," Kren said. "Properly invested, that should earn you the independent income that you once dreamed of. I take it that you will be leaving our employ?"

"I'd considered that, but on reflection I decided that it would be foolish to do so. Consider that in my short association with you, you have led me to the way of fabulous riches! So, if you will permit it, sir, I would like to continue as your servant, willing and able to do absolutely anything that you ask of me. I will ask no payment for this, except perhaps for the privilege of occasionally sitting at your feet and learning more from you on how to progress further on my path to wealth, fame, and power."

"This is a remarkable offer. But I am staying with Bronki, and I see no incentive to moving my place of abode. Will you be her servant as well?"

Dol said, "With her permission, no. I have already made arrangements to rent her second best guest room, which is next door to your suite, and I will do such things as she desires from time to time provided that it does not conflict with my duties and obligations to you."

"Very well, on that basis, I accept. You will continue to be my servant. What about you, Bronki? While you have been thus far silent, you too seem to be in a remarkably jovial mood."

"Kren, I am very happy because this has been the most profitable single day in my entire life, all five thousand years of it! I was not quite as astute as Dol here in multiplying my resources, but my capital base was much greater to begin with. Having seen you in action, I wagered heavily on all three of your main events. And while I lost a little at the distance throw, two out of three isn't bad! I made more than three dozen million Ke today!" Bronki said.

"I am very sorry about the distance throw. You see, the Master of Javelins . . ."

"We know all about that, Kren. So does everybody else. The director of athletics will doubtless fire her on Monday morning for her abysmal choice of tactics, unless some of the irate gamblers kill her first. I think that I am safe in assuring you that from this time forward, the game plans that you work under will be made by you."

"I am not at all sure that this would be wise," Kren said. "Consider that I completely misjudged my fencing abilities and never placed a wager on the fencing match. Consider also that while I started with four dozen and six thousand Ke, and Dol here had less than six gross, she ended up winning almost as much as I did."

"I see two things happening here, Kren. In the first place, you did not have enough proper information with regards to your fencing abilities, and those of others. That will not happen again. Second, you have not stopped to think out the mathematics and the psychology of gambling. In this area, you already have the mathematical tools that you need, although you have not used them, and Dol and I can assist you with everything else. With our help, you can formulate a game plan that can optimize your winnings."

"I would welcome your help."

"And we are eager to give it, since it automatically lets us in on your game plan," Bronki said.

At this point, the door gong sounded.

"That will be the party snack I ordered," Dol said. "But in my excitement, I forgot that while I am now rich, I don't have any money. All of my wagers were in currency, and I was afraid to bring that much money home by myself. That, and I don't have anyplace safe here to put a million Ke, once I do get it home." Using Bronki's safe simply never occurred to any of them. No Mitchegai would trust another to that extent.

"Put the child on my bill," Bronki said to the delivery porters. Turning to Kren and Dol, she said, "Monday, we'll order a pair of safes, one for each of you. You can pay me for it all later, at the usual interest rates. We should discuss insurance then, as well. But for now, shall I bring out the branding irons? Or the knives? Both?"

"They said that you wanted to see me, sir?" Kren said walking into the director's office.

"Yes. You did a fine job on Saturday. For a first time freshman to win at two events is almost unheard of."

"It should have been three, sir."

"True. But that problem has been taken care of. I'll be running the javelin team personally until a replacement can be found. As I was saying, you did well. Do you realize that your accuracy score broke the planetary amateur record?"

"Yes, sir. I felt that it was necessary to do so, in case anyone following me was sandbagging."

"Fine. But you broke a planetary record, something that usually happens once in a dozen years, and then you didn't show up for the awards ceremony on Sunday. I had to accept the award for you, in your name. I had to make excuses for you, in public, and I didn't like it. But here it is," he said, throwing the large, platinum medal across his desk, followed by three smaller ones, two of gold and one of copper. "The other three are for fencing, accuracy, and distance. Don't you *ever* pull a stunt like that on me again! Why didn't you come?"

"Because nobody told me that I was invited?"

The director buried his face in his hands. "Kren, you are stupid."

"Our university lost the meet, sir."

"I am aware of that."

"We lost it by three points. Had you permitted me to take Bo's place, I could have defeated his opponent easily, gaining us five points. I saw the fool fight, after all. Had you done it my way, we would have won," Kren said.

"You are still stupid. You do not know how to take all of the factors into account."

"No, sir. I am ignorant, and ignorance has the advantage of being curable. Actually, I spent Sunday working out a game plan for the rest of the season. I would seem to be in a unique position in that I am sufficiently skillful so as to be able to control the outcome of three separate competitions. I can win when I want to, or let someone else do so if I feel that it is to my advantage."

"I see. And assuming that you are really that good, what do you plan to do about it?" the director asked.

"There are a dozen and eleven more games on our calendar this year, plus the championships. I intend to win typically one event at each of them, and lose the other two, to keep the odds up. Then I will win all three events at the championships. Next Saturday's games with the University of Badja will see me win the distance event, setting a new record by a few inches."

"Just make damned sure that you show up for the award ceremonies! Okay, Kren, if you can actually make this program work, I'll let you do it your way. But if you fail to meet your predictions just once, I'll take charge directly, understood? And I'll expect you to tell me—privately!—which event you will win by the Tuesday before the game, at the latest."

"Very good, sir."

"Okay. Dik's waiting. Go practice with her. Then at javelin practice, you'll work on throwing exactly two inches farther than the record."

After Kren left, the director decided that he wouldn't tell anyone about Kren's predictions, but would use that information himself. The alumnae would be satisfied to know when they should bet on someone else.

From the outer office, he could soon be heard to say on the phone, "Naw, I think that the kid was just lucky! Look at the pattern. He got four golds on the first round! How could you call that anything but luck? And then by the last round he got tired and completely fell apart! Me, I'd put my money on someone else, Dala."

And on another call, "Well, the kid did real well at the fencing meet, no doubt about that, but I've done an analysis of the pattern of the opponents he went up against. Now, it was an honest draw, I'm sure of it, but strange statistical things sometimes happen! The very best players were paired up for the first three rounds! Kren only had to beat one of them! Everybody else he went up against was a third rater. I tell you that if I was fixing the draw to make sure that Kren won, I couldn't have done any better than what he got Saturday. Me, I'd put my money on someone else, next game."

After a vigorous bout, Kren said, "Coach, what actually happened to the former Master of Javelins?"

"Good question. Nobody seems to know for sure. The director didn't fire her, although I think he meant to. Trying to sandbag from a central position is really dumb. But nobody's seen the girl since Saturday night. Maybe she was smart enough to just run away. Or maybe she ran into somebody who lost a lot of money on the distance competition."

"Or maybe she ran into the director." Kren laughed.

"*That* is a possibility best not voiced aloud. *On guard!*"

After another heart thumping session in which Kren won, Dik said, "Damn, but you're good! I'll be betting another pile of money on you next Saturday."

"I wouldn't advise that, Coach. I have a feeling that I might have a bad day. I might do well in the distance competition, though."

The team flew away in three fusion-powered, jumbo jet planes on Friday afternoon, heading for the University of Badja, a few thousand miles away.

Like everything else on any Mitchegai planet, even the airport was underground. There were big doorways at the ends of all of the runways, but otherwise, grass covered everything.

Kren asked for and got a window seat.

The view was lovely. It was green.

As he predicted, he lost at both the fencing and the accuracy competitions, but set a new planetary record in the distance throw, three inches beyond the previous one. Not trying anything fancy, he just made his first throw good, and then did worse on the next two.

He was awarded three more medals, platinum, gold, and silver, which he didn't much care about, but stood patiently as they were hung around his neck. He wondered why the fans got so excited about this sort of thing.

And he increased his net worth to over eight million.

"I think that it is time that we discussed Kodo," Bronki said to Kren in her living room, on Thursday night.

"Very good. I want to know everything about Kodo."

"Telling you *everything* about Kodo would take years. He is old, almost as old as I am, and almost as well educated. Like me, he wears the rainbow belt. Currently, he is the director of the College of Architecture, here at the university, and has many successful business intrests around the city. Once, I considered him to be a good friend. A thousand years ago, we were partners on several ventures, but the friendship grew sour, and we drifted apart. Our mutual animosity has steadily increased, and now he has tried to have me killed. This is not permissible behavior, and he will have to die."

Kren said, "I gather that you want me to kill him for you?"

"Yes, if you would want to do the job. I have had his movements traced, and have identified an optimal time and place for his disposal. I could hire a hit team for two dozen thousand Ke, but you would be far more dependable, I think."

"If their level of competence is the same as that of the team that he sent after you, I would have to agree with your assessment. However, my recent financial success has been such that two dozen thousand Ke is no longer a significant amount of money to me."

Bronki said, "You would be permitted to keep anything he and his guards have on their persons, of course, and I suppose that I could go a bit higher."

"You would have to go much higher. It might be marginally worth while for me to do it for say, two million Ke."

"That is a huge amount of money!"

"You have it. You've made at least two gross million Ke, betting on me in the last two weeks," Kren said.

"I suppose so. And anyway, perhaps I owe you something for all of the valuable information you've given me."

"What really makes killing Kodo attractive to me is the fact that he doubtless has many skills and much information that I could use. He seems to be a competent businessman, for example, and I would find the knowledge of architecture to be attractive."

Bronki said, "You intend to eat parts of his brain?"

"Of course. I am a vampire, after all."

"This puts a whole new slant on things. Kodo is a very competent mathematician, and I have often seriously missed the mathematical abilities that you took from me. If I shared in your feast, I could recover them."

Kren said, "You would be welcome to what I have no need for, but *this time*, I really want to get some computer skills!"

"I know that you were promised them last summer, and that I retained them nonetheless. But Kren, I didn't try to cheat you. You must understand how the brain works.

All of the trillions of cells in a normal brain are motile. They are not fixed in place the way the cells are in say, a muscle, or a bone. Each of the brain's cells sends tiny dendrites out to contact the many other cells that it needs to work with. Then it tries to optimize its physical position in order to make the total length of its dendrites as short as possible. This saves the cell energy, and tends to make the entire brain faster. All of this shuffling around tends to put certain cells in certain physical positions, eventually. The cells concerned with vision tend to collect up near the eyes, hearing near the ears, and so on."

This was probably how the Mitchegai system of immortality evolved in the first place, but with the very limited numbers of species that they have available for study, the Mitchegai understanding of evolution is very poor.

Had human brain cells ever developed the ability to move to other positions, the architecture of the human brain would doubtlessly be far more efficient than it is.

Bronki continued, "Now, Kren, the skills required for computers are usually associated with those required for mathematics, but in my case, it is possible that they are more associated with business or perhaps with history, since the history of computers is a specialty of mine. Cranial anatomy is not an exact science, no matter what the medic that you ate might have thought. She was only a technician, after all, and not a scientist."

Kren said, "You make me think that I should increase my knowledge of biology as well."

"You will have the opportunity to do that if you wish. Before Kodo switched over to architecture, two thousand years ago, he was a world-famous biologist," Bronki said.

"Then I think that we have an agreement here."

"Yes, but eating Kodo's brain will necessitate certain changes in my plan. I had planned on your killing him tomorrow, but if he is going to be partially eaten, you and I will need at least a week to recover properly. You have your studies and athletic responsibilities. I have my classes and my students. I think that we should put our attack off for two weeks, until the midterm break."

CHAPTER TWENTY-SEVEN

We Can Eat and Make Shit!
New Yugoslavia, 2211 A.D.

I said, "I'm sure that it can be arranged. I've never needed ethanol in that quantity before, and so I don't know how long it will take, but we'll manage it somehow."

"Thank you, sir. Now, I have a good deal of technical data to give you, and I think that one of your electronic people would be better equipped to handle it."

"Right you are. Their memories are better than ours are, and I'm not a physicist in the first place. I think that the professor had best talk to you personally, since he's the smartest person that we've got. I'll introduce you to him right now," I said. "Agnieshka, tell the professor that we're coming down to him, and have a drone carry our new friend here. I wouldn't want him to get stepped on."

With all that booze in him, I was amazed that he could walk at all, but he seemed steady enough.

We took the elevator down to the parking garage where the professor was seeing to the further education of a future Yugoslavian general and his staff. I introduced him to our new ally, assigned the decorated drone to them to see that our guest got everything that he wanted, and went back up to my apartment.

I unscrewed the cap from a new bottle of Jim Beam, and prepared to get back to what I had been doing before the interruption.

"Boss! They've done it!" Agnieshka shouted as she ran excitedly into my den.

"Who has done what?" I said, expecting some new revelation about our crabby friend.

"Our engineers and biologists, the ones who have been working for so many years perfecting the social drones! They've finally done it! Now, we can eat and make shit, and draw all of our energy out in between!"

"Slow down, girl. I've never seen you so excited. You are saying that they've worked out a way to power the drones with the same food that we humans eat? That's wonderful, I suppose. It makes you that much closer to human. How does it work?"

"Well, the food is eaten and masticated in exactly the way that you humans do it. Then it goes into a stomach that mixes it with over forty types of bacteria, which break it down into carbon dioxide, hydrogen, and shit. I mean, the stuff has the same consistency, and is even brown! The hydrogen is combined in a fuel cell with oxygen in the air that we'll breath to produce electricity to charge up the capacitors, and the carbon dioxide is exhausted with the spent air and water vapor."

"Interesting. Well, just make sure that you keep the option of recharging from an electrical source. It might come in handy."

"I'll tell them that. But don't you see? This power supply is so like a completely organic one that they will be able to imitate even the internal organs of a human. We'll look like you, even in an X-ray! The red hydraulic fluid used in the muscles looks just like blood, so if you cut us, we will bleed. They have all of the sensory apparatus working perfectly, and now we can breath and eat and make shit! Unless someone does a chemical analysis, they won't be able to tell one of us from a human."

"I know that this is something that your people have wanted for a long while, and just now, your timing is very good. The production machinery making the new picket ships is now working full time, but the machinery that made that machinery is now mostly idle. We have the productive capacity to build a factory producing the new social drones right here, and to hell with the bureaucrats on New Kashubia."

"Then the project can go ahead, boss?"

"It sure can. We've got the space for it already dug out, over a square kilometer of it, in the canyon wall behind the city. Tell your engineers to take what they need."

She leaned over me and gave me a very human kiss. "You are just the finest boss a girl ever had!"

She started to leave when I said, "And please send a preliminary report on our new allies to General Sobieski."

"Yes, sir."

"And then get busy, buying up all the 190 proof vodka that you can find. Also, tell the engineers to get busy, building a factory to produce bulk ethanol. I want it finished soon. The dairy plant has some spare time in their bottling plant, so we can put our booze into four liter milk bottles."

"I'll get right on it, boss!"

"This is good," I said, pouring myself a glass of Jim Beam.

CHAPTER TWENTY-EIGHT

FROM CAPTURED HISTORY TAPES,
FILE 1846583A ca. 1832 A.D.
BUT CONCERNING EVENTS OF UP TO
2000 YEARS EARLIER

Everybody Wants a Bite of the Action!
Or, The Vampires' Kodo Conduct

Once again, bodily needs forced Duke Kren to remove the recording helmet, to relieve himself, and to drink.

A thin, gray light was coming in through the small, barred window. It was early morning, but Kren was in no shape to do any work today. He lay back down and put the helmet back on, returning to his memories of two thousand years before. He remembered . . .

The following Saturday Kren again won the fencing tournament, but the odds on him were down to five to one.

And the week after, at an away game, he won the accuracy competition without having to break a world record, but the payoff was only four to one.

The Friday after, with a gross, a dozen and four million in the bank, being paid two million for killing a prominent citizen no longer seemed like profitable venture. But, a deal was a deal, and he'd promised.

Kren had been waiting in a dimly lit passageway between two buildings for over two hours. Bronki had assured him that Kodo always passed by this way on route to his regular Friday night game of Nada, a very high-stakes gambling game. He had never been late for this event during the weeks that he had been under observation.

What Kren couldn't know was that Kodo had finally found out the hiding place of the brander, and was arranging for a hit team of six fighters to go and use her for a party snack. And while he was at the KUL Assassins' Hall, he also signed up for a second hit team, of twelve this time, to go after Bronki again. And this time, he had sent his four personal guards along with them, to make sure that nothing went wrong.

"Would you please tell me what your business is?" a uniformed guard said.

"What?" Kren tried to sound frightened. He had no doubt about his ability to kill the strutting fool, but he wanted to do this job as quietly as possible, and disposing of two bodies would be harder than one. It was best to seem a coward. He could always kill the guard if the act didn't work.

"What are you doing here? I saw you in this same place when I passed by an hour ago."

"I was supposed to meet a friend between these two buildings. She was going to lend me some money."

"It would seem that she is late," the guard said.

"Yes, and I really need that money. I don't suppose that you . . ."

"Look, if I didn't need money myself, I wouldn't be working on a Friday night. Give up on her, and move on."

"Please, sir, just a few more minutes. She still might get here," Kren said.

"Just don't be here when I come by again."

"Yes, sir. Thank you, sir. Thank you."

Kren waited another dozen minutes before he saw Kodo walking toward him. There was no mistaking the light orange and lavender outfit of the College of Architects, the Rainbow Belt, and the dozen and eight doctorate tassels. He did not have the expected guards with him, but that just made Kren's job easier.

They were just passing each other when Kren drew his sword and took the businessman's head off with a single, clean blow. Before the body hit the ground, Kren had a tie-wrap around the jaws, to keep from being bitten, and the head tucked into his book bag. He quickly searched the body and put everything he found in the bag on top of the head.

Then, with a tool he'd brought along for the purpose, Kren lifted the heavy lid from a sewer manhole, dumped the body inside, and replaced the lid.

Because of the Mitchegai's muted sense of smell, and the lack of any microbes that could cause anything to rot, there were no separate storm drains on any Mitchegai planet.

Since trash removal had to be paid for, but the sewers were a city service, most residents used the sewers for disposing of their trash. To stop things from plugging up, the sewer lines had powerful grinders installed upstream of every pump, as did the sewers on human planets, all the way back to the twentieth century.

Functioning like humongous garbage disposal units, these grinders were capable of chewing up granite, concrete, and strong metal bars, if need be. Kodo's body would give them no trouble at all, and the next grinder was only two yards from the manhole Bronki had chosen.

The pollywogs would eat a little bit better for a while.

Kren had the whole job done in under a minute, and went home with his book bag, unnoticed.

"You are late," Bronki said, coming into his sitting room. "Did you have any problems?"

"Kodo was late, but everything went well. I saw our dinner out there, tied to the party tables."

"Yes, they've been waiting anxiously for over an hour, the poor dears. I've given the servants a week off, with pay, and soon I'll have six guards posted outside, so that we aren't disturbed during our stupor. It's a common enough practice among the wealthy. Now, let me see Kodo."

Kren put the head on a table, and put the rest of his booty in a drawer. The head looked at Bronki, scowled, and blinked. He tried to open his mouth, but was hindered by the tie-wrap. A severed Mitchegai head is capable of staying alive for hours, as is that of an Earthly turtle.

"You see, Kodo dear, trying to kill me was not a nice thing to do, and you are being punished for it. I suppose that you could call it a learning experience, but we will do the learning, and not you. Kren, could you please take the skull plates off of him, so I can get at the brain? I might as well do the dissection myself, and make some use of that doctorate of surgery."

She was marking neat, black lines directly on Kodo's bright blue brain, and labeling two of them for herself and five to give Kren Kodo's knowledge of architecture, business, and biology when Dol walked in unexpectedly.

"It's a problem I never expected to have," she said. "Even though I got the largest denominations of currency possible, my safe is completely packed solid with money! I've had to put a lot of it under my mattress, but that makes it very uncomfortable. I suppose that I will just have to put it all in the bank, but that will make the information available to the chancellor's accounting department, and then they'll make me pay taxes on it! But for a few day's Kren, do you suppose that . . . that . . . That's Kodo, the director of the College of Architecture, isn't it?"

"I'm afraid so," Kren said, his hand on his sword.

"And I suppose that you're going to dissect the brain and eat the parts with your name on them, a capital offense. And since I am a witness to your crime, the most practical thing might be for you to eliminate me, as well."

"That thought had occurred to me, yes."

"May I respectfully suggest an alternative, sir."

"You may, if you do it quickly."

"Right sir. Instead of killing me as an unwanted witness, why not make me into a second coconspirator? I mean, I see Bronki's name on two of the bits there. Now, Kodo had a doctorate of engineering, something that it would take me six more years of study to obtain on my own. Let me eat that part of him, and then both of you are safe from any threat of my betraying you."

Kren said, "Bronki?"

"Oh, I suppose so. Dol, I had completely forgotten that you were here. I mean, I had sent the servants away, and you used to be a servant, and, oh well. No harm done, I suppose. You'd better order another juvenal for dinner, though. You can start by helping us with ours, and then we'll help you with yours when she gets here," Bronki said, drawing in two more sections and writing Dol's name on them. "You see, Kodo? Everybody wants you. I don't think that you've ever been this popular before."

Kodo continued scowling and blinking, but that was the extent of his possible repertoire.

The door gong sounded, and Bronki said, "That's probably the guards. Would you please take care of them, Dol?"

Dol returned to report that they now had six guards, stationed in the hall, and around the main staircase.

"Shouldn't we have some out on the balconies?" Kren asked.

"Those windows are structural glass, Kren. It would take some extremely heavy equipment a long time to get through, and one of the neighbors would be sure to notice," Bronki said. "You'll understand all about it in a week or so, when you absorb your new Doctorate of Architecture."

"Then let's begin, shall we?"

Bronki said, "I'm ready," and was about to start cutting, with Kodo still scowling and blinking at her furiously, when they heard a commotion on the stairway. "Now what could *that* possibly be?"

"*That* is a minor battle going on, with at least a dozen combatants," Kren said.

"Oh, my. Well, we'd better arm ourselves, in case the guards can't stop them," Bronki said.

Bronki reached inside her cloak and drew out her pistol, and some spare clips of ammunition.

"Do you always carry that thing?" Kren asked.

"Generally."

Kren picked up his spear, in addition to the sword, which he was already wearing. "Were you wearing it when I attacked you at your retreat?"

"Of course."

"Then you could have easily killed me."

"That was plan B, if you didn't listen to reason. But it would have left me on the floor out of reach of my telephone and my computer. Come, there isn't much time."

He gave the spring spear to Dol, saying, "Just put this thing against someone's body, and press this button."

"And then, what do I do?" Dol asked.

"Then you run away."

"Couldn't I do that first?"

"Come on. That sounds like the door is breaking," Kren said.

Bronki had positioned herself four yards in front of the

door, standing behind a sturdy, waist-high chest. She had four clips of pistol ammunition neatly arranged on it.

Behind her, both of the party snacks were screaming mindlessly.

"That door won't hold. They're going to break through, so we might as well surprise them. Dol, stand over there, and then open the door very quickly when I tell you to. Kren, you take that side of the door, and do what you can about any of them who make it inside, but don't either of you dare to get into my line of fire. Ready? Open it, Dol."

The door quickly opened, leaving four startled Greenie fighters standing there with a battering ram in their hands, rather than their usual weapons.

Four shots rang out in quick succession, and all four of the Greenies holding the battering ram dropped with head wounds. Three more shots were fired into the crowd behind them, killing one and wounding two others.

Then a throwing star came flying out of the crowd, heading directly toward Bronki.

She fired her last bullet at it and was lucky enough to make a direct hit. It drove the poisoned throwing star back into the crowd, killing the surprised thrower, but it also shattered her bullet into a gross of slivers. Some of these small bits managed to hit Kren and Dol, wounding both of them slightly, and didn't do a half dozen of the Greenies any good, either. The heat generated by the impact burned them, but it also vaporized any traces of the poison, and thus probably saved the lives of Kren and Dol.

"Ouch!" Dol cried.

While quickly reloading, Bronki said, "I don't think that I could do that again if I practiced for a month!"

The rest of the Greenies charged the open doorway. Kren caught the first one in the neck, decapitating him. The second was killed by Dol, who was actually able to put her weapon against the Greenie's side and push the trigger.

It worked, with the blade severing the fighter's spine and coming out the other side.

Just penetrating the chest cavity would not have been debilitating, since the ribcage is rigid in the Mitchegai, and the volume in it contains little more than the esophagus, blood vessels, and four independent lungs.

The Mitchegai spinal column is centrally located, not at the back as in humans. This spinal column allows for more flexibility, more efficient use of musculature, and less massive vertebrae, but when severed, as in this case, it is just as disastrous as it would be with a human.

Kren gave Dol an assist by decapitating the crippled Greenie impaled on her spear.

"May I run away now?" Dol said.

Bronki put eight more carefully placed rounds into the Greenies, and then said while reloading, "I think that's the lot of them, but why don't you go out and make sure, Kren. I'll back you up. Dol, you'd better phone the captain of the guard. Tell him what happened, and have him send over six ambulances for his men, plus we'll be needing six more guards, if he has them."

Kren went through the carnage, chopping the heads off all that seemed to need it except for the six guards. Judging from the wounds, the guards had been able to kill three of their opponents before they were overwhelmed.

"I make it twelve Greenies, six of our guards, and four students in Architectural uniforms," he said. "The guards didn't do too badly, considering the odds."

"That's probably all of them, then. Greenies usually work in groups of six or a dozen, and those four others are Kodo's guards. I recognize them. Let's make our guards as comfortable as possible, and then we'll flush the brains of the rest of this trash down the toilet. This had to happen just when I'd given the servants the week off, so we'll have to do all of the work ourselves. Oh, yes, and strip the academic garb off of those four. We wouldn't want to embarrass the College of Architecture."

Sorting through the carnage, Kren had a problem when he found two heads near one guard's body, and he wasn't sure which belonged to the guard and which belonged to a nearby Greenie body. Fortunately, the sergeant of the guard knew his own men well. Although he had been disemboweled and was in a great deal of pain, he was able to identify his own man.

"You did good," Kren told the sergeant. "You'll all be resurrected, I promise, and you'll probably all get commendations."

The sergeant grunted.

Kren put the guard's head on its own body, and chopped out the Greenie's brain.

The ambulances arrived, and took the guards off to the hospital. Kren figured that most, if not all, of them would *need* resurrection.

The captain of the guard phoned and said, "A new squad should be there in less than an hour, Bronki. How did my troops do?"

"They did you proud, Captain. They were terribly outnumbered, but they made a good showing for themselves, and they all died fighting."

"Good. They all deserve resurrection, then?"

"Absolutely. You may bill me for it as our contract stipulates. You can list me as a reference, if you want to. I'll even write you a testimonial letter."

"Thank you. I appreciate that. Please have the next bunch call me when they get there."

Bronki next called the Sisters of Charity, telling them that there was a large supply of meat here waiting to be distributed to the poor, and could they possibly pick it up tonight? Also, Bronki needed a receipt, so she could deduct the donation off of her income taxes.

Her next call was to the building's housekeeping department, telling them that she wanted the floors around the stairway on her level cleaned within two hours, and yes, she was well aware of the fact that it was Friday night.

There was a major pile of assorted weapons on the floor of Kren's room, and four bloody architectural uniforms hanging in his closet. Kodo's guards had also had their identifying shoulder brands cut off and flushed down the toilet.

Kren was stacking headless bodies out near the stairway, with a neat stack of brainless heads beside them.

Students and junior faculty members would occasionally scurry up and down the steps, pretending not to notice anything unusual.

The brander that they had tortured a few weeks before ran up the steps out of breath, came up to Kren, and said, "This is where Bronki lives, isn't it?"

He recognized her, but felt that he did not need further problems tonight.

"We're a little busy just now," he said.

"But she's got to help me! They're after me! There's no place else I can go, and she said she'd help me!"

"I believe that she was referring to academic help."

"You don't understand! There is a squad of KUL killers right behind me!"

"Would you please open your eyes and observe what I'm doing, lady? Do you see all of this fresh meat? This used to be a KUL hit squad. We have already killed them. You can go home now. You are safe."

"This can't be the same bunch! They're behind me, I tell you!"

"Okay, come on. I'll take you to Bronki. Maybe she can talk some sense in your head."

But as they went inside, Kren locked the battered but still functional door behind them. You never can be sure, after all.

Bronki was reloading her pistol clips. She started to hide what she was doing, and then decided to hell with it. The damage was already done.

The brander said, "Bronki, your friend here won't believe me, but there are a half dozen KUL killers after me! They're on their way here now!"

"I heard you talking to Kren in the hall. Don't worry. They are all dead now."

"But these can't be the same bunch! For one thing, I only had six of them after me, and you have two or three times that number piled out there. For another, they were three or four gross yards behind me two miles from here. I think that I was gaining on them, but . . ."

There was a loud crash at the door.

"Company is coming!" Dol shouted. She picked up her recocked spring spear and took up her old position by the door.

"Places, everyone!" Bronki said.

"Give me that," the brander said, taking the spring spear from Dol. "It's mine!"

Kren tossed Dol his military spear. "Take this. It works just the same way, only it's the manual model, without the button."

"Open the door, Dol," Bronki said.

There were four greenies there with a very familiar-looking battering ram. They had apparently found it in the hallway and had decided that a fast attack is a good attack.

Bronki's timing wasn't as good, this time. On the last round, the door had been opened immediately after the ram had struck it. The Greenies were taken when they were on the back swing. This time, it was opened just as they were about to strike the door again, and four of them piled into the room.

Bronki took out the front two, but as the next two fell on top of them, she opted for killing the two who were behind them, and were armed. Again, all four were head shots, the surest way to put a Mitchegai out of action, at least temporarily.

The two Greenies who had fallen came up on the bounce. Kren took out the one closest to him with a chop straight down on his head. Dol and the brander got the last one, putting two spears into her simultaneously.

When this last Greenie started to raise her sword, Kren took her head off.

"All part of the service, ladies," he said, with a smile to the others.

"Okay, everyone," Bronki said. "You know the drill. Kren decapitates and stacks, Dol, search them and put everything you find in Kren's room. And you, young lady, get to chop and flush the brains down the toilet. It would be nice if we could get this job done before the new guards get here. Fewer explanations would be needed."

"Yes, madam. And thank you for this help. Where's the toilet?" the brander asked.

"That way," Bronki gestured over her shoulder as she went about picking up her empty magazines and ejected cartridge casings.

Dol was carrying a double armful of strange weapons into Kren's room, when she found the brander staring at the head on the table.

"This isn't the toilet, is it?"

"No, this is Kren's room."

"And that was Kodo, wasn't it?" the brander asked. The head was staring at her, and scowling again.

"He still is. I think he's still alive. At least I hope he is," Dol said. The eyes on the disembodied head turned to Dol and blinked, so Dol continued, "Yes, I see that he is indeed alive and as healthy as possible, given the circumstances. Well, sir, you will be interested to know that we were recently attacked by two separate groups of KUL fighters, and I am delighted to inform you that we killed them all, losing absolutely none of the good guys, except of course for our six guards. Now you just sit tight, and we'll get back to you as soon as we can."

"I'm glad that Kodo is dead, or soon will be. He was a horrible person. But his brain has all of these lines drawn on it, like I saw once in a medical book, and some of those parts have all of your names on them. Does that mean what I think it means?"

"I'm afraid so. We'd best go talk to Bronki," Dol said.

On hearing what had happened, Kren drew his sword and said, "I suppose that I'm sorry, but we really weren't friends anyway."

Bronki said, "Now, none of that, Kren. Good artists are too rare to waste. But you see our problem, young lady. The rest of this killing tonight is simple self-defense, and we won't be punished for it. It's not even likely to land us in court. But the law views vampires a bit differently. Now, my suggestion to you is, would you like to join us? Kodo had a doctorate in fine arts. Would you like to have such an education? You could stay here until you recover, and in a week or two, you could be a very well-educated person."

"Given the alternatives before me, I would be delighted to join you in this endeavor," the brander said.

"Good. Now, let's all try to get everything done before our new guards get here."

"What I don't understand is why this second group just came charging in here, after seeing all those bodies in the hallway. You'd expect that such a sight would at least give one pause to think," Kren said.

"Quite possibly they thought that we must have been all dead or badly wounded after a fight like that one. Who would have thought that we could come through it with barely a scratch? But it's more likely that they actually couldn't think," Bronki said. "These KUL teams take a lot of heavy and illegal drugs before they go out on a hit. It makes them more aggressive."

"How stupid can you get?" Kren said as he went back to chopping, stripping, and stacking.

"One good thing is that I never got around to ordering another party snack," Dol said, as she went about her work.

"I want to eat that first one I killed. I've never killed any-body before, not an adult anyway, and it was kind of fun! Do you want the other one that we killed together, uh, what is your name, anyway?"

The brander opened up her robe, showing them the col-lection of deep brands running down the front of her body, and said, "I think that from now on, you can call me Brandee."

"Well, I think that they are lovely," Bronki said, "and so are you. Now, hurry up everyone, because right after we have it all done, we get to eat!"

CHAPTER TWENTY-NINE

FROM CAPTURED HISTORY TAPES,
FILE 1846583A ca. 1832 A.D.
BUT CONCERNING EVENTS OF UP TO
2000 YEARS EARLIER

How Much Is that Duchy in the Window?

Kren awoke after over a week of strange dreams, relieved himself, and took a long drink of water. He sat down in the early morning light at the large table in his sitting room, where Dol was carefully cleaning, polishing, and sorting a big collection of strange weapons.

"It's good to see you awake, sir. I was beginning to worry. The midterm break is almost over, and tomorrow is a school day."

"I see. Is everyone else up and around?"

"Oh, yes, we have been for days. But you ate three times as much of Kodo as any of the rest of us, and I suppose that it just took you much longer to integrate all of that."

"I suppose that it serves me right for being greedy," Kren said.

"I'm beginning to wish that I'd taken two bites out of him myself, but at the time, I was too frightened to be that adventurous."

"So, are you now a doctor of engineering?"

"Not officially, but I've been through Bronki's extensive engineering library here, and everything in it seems childishly simple to me now. You know, it is possible to pay a fee and take a test, which, if you pass, gives you credit for a certain required course. I expect to have my doctorate in a year or two," Dol said. "My grade point average is excellent, and if I play it properly, I think that I can pull it all off without anyone suspecting that I have become a vampire."

"Perhaps I should do that, too."

"I'd advise against it, sir. You have to be an undergraduate to participate in the athletic program. If you graduate, you will lose a lucrative source of income."

"I suppose that's true. Is Bronki around?"

"Yes, and she's very anxious to talk to you. Shall I get her?"

"I'll go to her. You keep on doing whatever you're doing. *What are you doing, anyway?*" Kren asked.

"I'm getting your collection ready for mounting. I've ordered some display cases built to my design, in a style matching the other furniture here. They should be delivered in a few weeks. There will be one for your athletic medals, and two for your weapons."

"But, I didn't ask for any display cases."

"If you don't like them, I'll have them taken out, sir. I'd intended them as a gift, to show my appreciation for what you've done for me."

Kren had never received a gift before, and had absolutely no idea as to how to respond to such a strange thing.

"Well, uh, do as you wish, then," he said.

He found Bronki in her study, sitting at her computer.

"Kren, you can have no idea how refreshing it is to have my mathematical abilities back again! I can think properly for the first time in many weeks! Not only that, but I've had some thoughts that I think might be absolutely original!

"They are still fairly vague, but you know, there are times in social systems when very small events can cause very large changes. Like, when a scrubber leaves a wet spot on a staircase, a major leader happens to slip on it and breaks his neck, and so loses two weeks resurrecting before he can get back to the war, and this results in his side losing a battle, which in turn causes the whole war to be lost, which results in the entire nobility of a duchy being wiped out, and world history changes.

"Such things can also happen in the natural world as well, in weather patterns, for example, when a small change in one area eventually causes a large storm to shift course.

I've been getting an inkling of an idea about a form of mathematics that could handle this sort of thing. I'm thinking of calling it 'Chaos Theory,' but I'm still a long way from formalizing it."

Kren said, "Well, I wish you great success. Is anything happening of a more immediate nature?"

"Yes. I've been going over all of these credit cards we collected up last week. There's a fair amount of money in them, but not nearly enough to be worth risking the wrath of the KUL."

Kren said, "Why are you worried about them *possibly* getting mad at you when they have in fact launched three armed assaults on you since the school term began? I cannot imagine what they could do to you that would be worse than that!"

"I'm worried because *they* aren't mad at me, yet. Kodo was mad at me. The KUL simply rented him fighters when he paid them to do it. If the KUL was angry with me, you would see many gross of fighters attacking us both from every angle, on every day, and eventually, they would kill us both, and everyone else in my household. In any event, what I have done is simply the same thing that I did the first time around. I've blamed it all on the PPG. This time, I picked one of their best corporate vice presidents for my patsy, and she has already been killed, although I don't know if the KUL or the PPG did it. They can't seem to imagine that someone would give away money just to get them fighting with each other. The total number of gangland killings in the war we kicked up is now over nine gross."

"This is good, I suppose. I am really getting tired of all these bits of trash trying to kill me," Kren said. "They are a murderous bunch, but you really couldn't call any of them a real warrior. There's not a challenge to be had in fighting any of them."

"Well, you are getting paid, as per our agreement. I've put two thousand into your account for the two attacks last week."

"Thank you. But two thousand is no longer a significant amount of money to me."

"Kren, that is a terrible attitude! An honorable person must always keep to the contracts that she has willingly made, even if they become unprofitable. If you don't, no one will trust you, and you will surely fail in business."

"I'm sure that you are right. But I still hope that it is all over now."

"So do I. But what I really wanted to talk to you about is Kodo's credit card. I promised you that everything that he had on his person would be your property, but Kren, there was a *gross billion* Ke in his account! I cannot imagine how he got so much money! Figures that big are normally handled by the dukes, and the other upper nobility, but never by a commoner! And to have it in his credit card account, well, it simply boggles the imagination!" Bronki said.

"And this huge sum is mine?"

"After a fashion. But so massive an amount can't just be transferred around without anybody noticing it. I mean, the computers handle most of the ordinary transactions without a living person ever knowing about them, unless somebody very good with a computer is curious. But this much, well, if I transfer it, gongs and horns will be going off in the bank's corporate headquarters!"

"I see. We must therefore insure that the transaction is made with someone who would ordinarily handle such amounts. Someone who is above the normal run of things. Someone whose word may not be questioned."

"Just who did you have in mind?" Bronki asked.

"I am told that Duke Dennon, who lost so badly with the Senta Copper Mine, is in dire need of money. Perhaps he would have something that he could sell me for that amount of money."

"All Duke Dennon has is a fine army and an impoverished duchy."

"I have no use for his army, but perhaps he could sell me some land, if the price was right, of course. Is it possible that you would know how to contact him?"

"Not directly, but a thousand years ago, I was quite friendly with Sala, the person who is now his chief accountant, and we never had a falling out. I could talk to her, if you like," she said.

"Please do so. And if you can pull this off, I will pay you a billion Ke."

"On a per gross basis, that's really not much of a commission."

"It's bigger than anything you've ever gotten before, and it's all that I'm willing to pay. Furthermore, you might not get it in cash, but in some other form. Nonetheless, I want you to call your friend this morning. It would be best if the money was transferred before anyone knows that Kodo is missing, and when he doesn't show up at his college tomorrow, they will start asking questions," Kren said.

"Very well. I'll get right on it. Your knowledge of business seems greatly improved."

"Yes, it appears that I have learned from a master."

Kren found that the main door to Bronki's apartment had been replaced with one much stronger, that the outer doors of the guest rooms had been reinforced, and that a new security door had been added between the guest hallway and the stairwell. He thought it reasonable, after all of the attacks that they had endured lately.

There were a dozen new carpets in the apartment, and the painting that had been damaged by his spear had been restored.

He noticed that the door to the third guest room was open and walked in. Brandee was there, putting small amounts of paint on a large piece of stretched cloth. She was so intent on what she was doing that she didn't notice him at all. Kren, interested, sat down to watch her.

In a bit, he deduced that she was making a copy of an older painting that was framed and hanging on the wall. It seemed like a tedious method of reproduction, to him. Hadn't the girl ever heard of a camera?

Bronki came in and said, "Oh, here you are, Kren. Come, we must leave immediately. I'll explain on the way. Bring your credit card and a large amount of currency. Put on a fresh robe, and wear a different sword than you usually do."

"What's wrong with my sword?"

"Nothing, except that it was originally issued by Duke Dennon to one of his soldiers, whom you later ate. The duke might take offense at that, and we are going to see him now."

They left with Brandee as oblivious to their departure as she had been to their arrival.

Bronki had booked a private cabin on an express MagFloat train, so they could talk without interruptions.

As soon as the door was closed, Bronki said, "Well, I found out why Kodo had so much money in his credit card account. He had organized a syndicate to purchase a major tract of land from Duke Dennon. He was to have finalized the deal last week, but you killed him the night before that happened. Kodo is probably fortunate at this point to be dead, because both the duke and the syndicate members have been desperately looking for him for a week, now. They assume that he has absconded with the money."

"And we are now going to take Kodo's place?"

"Yes. The duke doesn't care where the money comes from, but he desperately needs it. We're stepping into a done deal. Here is a copy of the papers we'll be signing. You'd better read them. We should arrive in two hours."

Kren read, fascinated. When he had finished, he was amazed.

"Duke Dennon is deeding away one-third of his duchy," Kren said.

"In area, yes. But it's mostly just empty hinterland. There are no cities or factories on it, just a few freeholders whose rights you are required to respect."

"If you say so, but this also grants me the rights of both high and low justice! I can create a law and then punish anyone I want for breaking it! I can do anything that I want on that land! By the terms of these agreements, I'm not just buying land, I'm almost being made a duke myself!"

Bronki said, "Almost, although I would advise against using the title. You can see why Kodo and his syndicate were willing to pay so much for it. On this land, they would not only be above the law, they'd actually *be* the law."

"Until some other duke decided to invade and take it from them."

"True. But first off, the agreements, while filed with the Bonding Authority, are otherwise secret. The rest of the world will think that the property still belongs to Duke Dennon, and he has a very fine army. Second, you will be paying Dennon an additional gross million Ke a year for his protection. If you are attacked, he will come to your aid, or you won't be there to pay him his gross million next year. It also keeps *him* from attacking you, for the same reason."

"Kodo was a remarkable business man," Kren said. "This is an amazing deal!"

"It's also the only deal in town. Neither the syndicate nor the duke has reported Kodo missing as yet, but you can be sure that his college will tomorrow. The papers must be signed, the money transferred, and the Bonding Authority paid today. Otherwise, this credit card will become just a piece of plastic and Kodo's fortune will be in probate."

"Where am I supposed to have gotten this kind of money? Surely, the duke will be curious!"

"We will say that you made it betting on yourself in the games. You are quite famous, you know, having won a planetary record and two gold medals on your first time out as a freshman. If you had borrowed everything that I owned, and bet it all on each of your victories thus far this year, you would have made more than what is held in Kodo's credit card account. Or, maybe you had saved that much in the thousand years that you have been alive. Who could prove that this didn't happen?"

"If you say so. The only part I don't understand is why the duke won't know that we are using Kodo's credit card."

"He won't know because his chief accountant, my friend Sala, will handle the transaction, and she won't tell him," Bronki said.

"And why won't she tell him?"

"Because you will be paying her a billion Ke not to."

"The amounts called for in these contracts will take almost every Ke in Kodo's credit card account. I don't have another billion Ke," Kren said.

"No, but I do, partner."

CHAPTER THIRTY

Different Folks, Different Strokes
New Yugoslavia, 2212 A.D.

Our new ally, Bellor, had been talking with the professor for over three months, and apparently, things were happening.

The most obvious thing to me was that a large, portable swimming pool had been set up in my garage. It contained a pleasant grotto where Bellor spent half of his time, and a spigot that dispensed the industrial strength booze that he preferred.

Agnieshka said that thermal imaging of the energy he generated suggested that he was metabolizing only six percent of what he drank, and chemical tests said that none of it was getting out into the garage, yet he didn't seem to be gaining any mass. He had been repeatedly asked about this, but he politely sidestepped the questions, and nobody wanted to press him too hard about it.

The Tellefontu refugees on New Yugoslavia had made it several hundred light-years from their home planet, but they didn't know if other fleeing groups had gotten to other places in Human Space. Some ninety-six of their diplomats had been sent to forty-eight human planets where their species might possibly have settled. It was expected to take years before these emissaries came back to make their reports. Each pair had an entire planet to search.

Agnieshka and her metal ladies had located twenty-eight tons of ninety-five percent ethanol on the planet. Only a

small amount of it was really bonded Everclear, but Bellor
said that he could live with that. At his suggestion, this
consignment had been weighted down and dumped into the
ocean at a precise geographical location. He said that his
people would take care of it from there.

This would have raised eyebrows, except that the
Tellefontu's first gift to us, the "ray gun that made things
disappear," had been built in a prototype lab on New
Kashubia. Soon, people were just calling it the "Disappearing Gun."

The professor himself wasn't too clear as to how and why
it worked, but it *did* work. Our new allies kept explaining
the basic principles again and again, ever more slowly.

On the other hand, the crabs were equally confused by
our Hassan-Smith transporters. Our physicists said that our
allies just couldn't grasp the basic principles.

Hell, I couldn't, either.

Our two races just looked at the universe differently, was
all that I could figure out. Nonetheless, they could give us
working plans for things that worked. And that was enough,
in my book. Our smart boys would figure it all out eventually. After all, it took us a whole generation before many
of us could understand Einstein.

It seemed that I was now mostly out of the loop, but that
didn't bother me in the least. I had other problems of my
own.

I had been assuming that the neutron bombs that the
Mitchegai used were similar to the neutron bombs that had
been developed on Earth centuries ago. This would mean
that with a bit of warning, if I could fill the lowest level
of the Loway transportation system with air, and get the
entire population down there, I could keep them alive.

The specifications for the Mitchegai bombs that our
crabby friends had given us suggested that we were off
by a factor of about thirty. Their bombs could instantly
destroy everything alive, be it electronic or biological, down
to a depth of five hundred meters. And it wasn't realy
safe unless you had at least three kilometers of dirt and
rock above your head.

"Agnieshka, you and your sisters have a really big job
to do. We are going to need a set of fallout shelters dug
at least three kilometers down, and big enough to hold

everybody on this planet, biological and electronic. They are going to need food, water and oxygen supplies to last them for at least two years, while we figure out a way to fight the enemy on the surface. And if we are going to keep the humans sane, we will need something for them to do down there, and some sort of entertainment. We will also have to make provisions for the Tellefontu. Get our technical people on it ASAP, and let me see what they come up with."

"Yes, sir. Does this mean that the social drone project is getting dumped?"

"Not exactly, but it has definitely become a low priority item. Sorry about that, but equality won't do you guys any good at all if none of us are alive."

"Yes, sir."

CHAPTER THIRTY-ONE

FROM CAPTURED HISTORY TAPES,
FILE 1846583A ca. 1832 A.D.
BUT CONCERNING EVENTS OF UP TO
2000 YEARS EARLIER

Duke Dennon

Sala met them at the Capital Train Station and said, "Bronki! It's so nice to see you again after so long! And this must be Kren, the athlete that we've all been watching so avidly on the sports casts! You know, the duke is a fan of yours. I think that he is secretly delighted to be working with you on this matter, and not that horrid Kodo person. Well, do you have it with you?"

"If you mean the credit card, yes, of course," Bronki said.

"Then we'll go directly to my office and take care of that first," Sala said, leading the way.

As he followed, Kren noticed that while Sala's clothing was of the finest quality, it was slightly worn and the hem was tattered. This shabby-genteel impression was reinforced as they got to the nearby ducal palace. It was certainly a fine, ancient building, built for defense as well as for beauty, but as they walked up the long hallways, he couldn't help noticing that the carpets were worn, and that the curtains were faded. Many thousands of years had gone by since any of it had been replaced.

Only the red and lavender uniform cloaks of the soldiers on guard duty looked crisp and new, though made of a rough, sturdy and warm cloth. Drab, camouflaged military clothing is only useful if your enemy has long range-weapons.

Otherwise, bright colors are better for morale and unit identification.

The guards' weapons, while undecorated, were all of the
finest quality.

In Sala's large but well-worn office, she said, "First, we
have to make sure that this credit card still works. I mean,
I trust you, Bronki, but anything could have happened in
the eight days since you got this thing."

Bronki said, "But of course. I've been worried about it
myself. And withdrawing the money now keeps the duke
from seeing the name on the card."

"Quite right." Sala inserted the card into a machine on
her desk. "It seems to be all right. Yes, the full amount has
been transferred to the duke's private account."

Kren was about to be outraged about having spent his
money without having anything in writing, but Bronki told
him to relax. Everything would be just fine.

"This card is now empty?" Bronki asked.

"There's less than a gross Ke left in it," Sala said.

"Then we'd best dispose of it," Bronki said, lighting the
plastic card on fire and watching it burn in a ceramic waste
container. The odor would have been offensive to a human,
but the Mitchegai have almost no sense of smell.

"Now then," Sala said. "There was a certain sum due to
me?"

"But of course," Bronki said. "Right after the papers are
signed and filed with the Bonding Authority. Surely you
understand."

"I suppose that I do. Well, shall we go see Duke Dennon?"

It was perhaps the last fine day of autumn, and the duke
elected to meet his guests on the fighting top of his personal tower.

Kren thought that Duke Dennon looked very tired, or that
perhaps that he had been under extreme stress for a long
time.

While the duke had a more elaborate helmet than his
guards, he wore the same rough military cloak and the same
practical but high-quality sword that his soldiers did. Kren
was glad to be wearing a different sword of slightly lesser
quality, if better outward appearance.

Sala greeted the duke in the aristocratic language of Beno,
which Kren understood somewhat, but in which he did not

feel confident speaking. The duke was informed that the money, a gross billion Ke, had been transferred to his personal account, and that the transaction had been verified.

The lines of tension drained off of Duke Dennon's face, and he took a more relaxed stance.

"Thank you, Sala," Duke Dennon said. "And these are our honored guests?"

Sala introduced Bronki and Kren, who bowed in the manner that they had rehearsed on the train.

"Kren, I have looked forward to meeting you since I saw you win the fencing competition at your first meet. Oh, how I wish I had bet on that one! I immediately phoned in a wager on the accuracy throw, to my considerable profit!" Because of their academic garb, the duke said it in Keno, the academic language, which he was not truly fluent in.

"I am glad to have been the instrument of your good fortune, but I never dreamed that I would have the honor of meeting you personally, Your Grace," Kren answered in Meno, the military language.

The duke smiled and answered in fluent Meno, "So, you have a military background! Excellent! It's always pleasant to talk with a former soldier. You always know exactly where you stand. Who did you serve under?"

Among the Mitchegai, loyalty, when it existed at all, was always on a personal basis, and never to a territory, or to a group, or to a philosophy. And certainly not to a religion, because the Mitchegai had no such thing.

"I was in the army of Duke Mo."

Duke Mo's estates were on the opposite side of the planet. Since the upper nobility rarely felt safe away from their estates, Kren hoped that the two hadn't met.

"Duke Mo is said to have an excellent army. Is that where you learned to use the javelin and the épée?"

"I learned how to handle the spear and the sword there, Your Grace. I learned the ways of the javelin and the épée at the university. Duke Mo's army was equipped much like your own, but I think perhaps with weapons of slightly lesser quality," Kren said.

"You have a good eye for weapons, then. I thought that I saw you admiring my own sword. It takes a master to recognize a true Kanto blade when it is still in the sheath!"

The duke drew his sword to show off the watering on the blade. "It's not fancy, but the blade is the finest quality available anywhere, with twelve foldings in the forging process. Every one of my soldiers has one just like it. Here, take it. It's a gift to honor this great occasion, to mark the beginning of a long-lasting association. Perhaps eventually, even a friendship."

"I'm deeply honored, Your Grace," Kren said, going down on one knee to accept the sword, as Bronki had schooled him. "I only wish that I could give you an equal gift in return."

"First, save the knee bending for the throne room, if you don't mind. And second, now that I have your money, the only thing that you could have for me might be some information," Duke Dennon said.

"If it is possible that I know something that you do not, then certainly," Kren said, standing and slipping his new sword under his white outer belt, in the proper, edge-up fashion. Concealing a sword under your cloak required carrying it vertically.

"I believe that you know which event you are going to win at, next Saturday. I have been studying the patterns of your wins. After your first meet, at each event, you have won at one and only one of the events that you are outstanding at. The reasons why a perfect athlete would do such a thing are obvious. I want to know which one you will win at next."

"Your Grace, I am not the perfect athlete that you claim me to be. I can make no prediction with absolute certainty. But with that understood, well, I'm putting my money on the fencing competition, or at least such money that I have left, after today's purchase."

"Thank you. It is possible that I will make a small wager as well. Next, I want to see you throw a spear in person. You know, on television, your throwing form bears an uncanny resemblance to a very fine young officer and athlete that I used to have in my army."

"Used to, Your Grace?"

"Yes, Droko went missing while on guard duty, a year or two ago. Nobody could ever figure out what happened to her. But anyway, Lorka, lend him your spear," he said to one of his guards.

"I'm not used to throwing from such a height, Your Grace . . ."

"Two 'Your Graces' per conversation are sufficient, Kren. Just take the spear and see how close you can come to that large juvenal down there," Dennon said, pointing with his sword.

The juvenal was so far away that the only possibility of hitting her was with a running throw. Kren doffed his academic cloak along with his well-filled pouch and both of his swords. He hefted the borrowed spear, took the three standard running steps, and let fly from the top of the tower. The problem was that the battlements kept him from seeing his target as he was throwing. Standing at them, he watched the spear fly, and he saw that he would miss. The spear caught the juvenal in the tail, pinned the tail to the ground, and caused her to run around in circles in a most comical fashion.

Everyone but Kren laughed.

"Ha ha ha! Oh! That was funny!" The duke laughed, "But Kren, it was also a perfect throw. I was watching from the battlements here. The juvenal moved just as you started your run, but you couldn't see her from where you were. You hit exactly where she had been standing! Had she remained where she was, I think your spear would have gone straight through her neck. That was truly amazing! Your style is much like Droko's, but she could never have made that throw!"

"Thank you. I feel less mortified, now."

"Lorka, go down, and have the mess attendants take that juvenal for distribution to the soldiers. Then bring back your spear and present it to Kren, here, in honor of that throw. You can draw another one for yourself from stores. And get me another sword while you're down there."

The duke picked up the decorated sword that Kren had brought with him. He drew the blade from the richly engraved scabbard and studied the watering. He judged it to be acceptable, for a civilian.

"Is this what Duke Mo issues to his soldiers?"

"No, I had to leave my weapons behind when I left his service. That's the best that I could find in Dren."

"And why did you leave the services of Duke Mo?"

"Because my duke had gone over two dozen years without a war," Kren said, remembering what he had read in his current history class. "Things had gotten dull, and promotions had come to an absolute stop."

"Good. You have a proper warrior's attitude. So tell me, now that you have a huge tract of land, what do you plan on doing with it? Not those filthy drug schemes that Kodo had in mind, I hope."

"Drugs? No, certainly not!" Kren said, "There are plenty of honorable ways to make a decent living. But I don't actually have the land, yet. There is a matter of signing and registering certain papers . . . ?"

"Right you are! Sala, have the papers brought up to the table here, and we'll get on with it right now." Turning back to Kren, he said, "But what are your plans?"

What were his plans! A strange feeling came over Kren. While it was doubtless a result of the brain segments that he had taken from Kodo, still reorganizing themselves in his head, it seemed to him to be a flash of enlightenment, as if his whole future was now laid out in front of him. It was astonishing, but it also left him somewhat confused. Fortunately, the liar he had once eaten came to his rescue, and he ad libbed until his thoughts started to crystallize about him.

"You will understand that I didn't hear about your offer until this morning, and I will have to make a thorough survey of the property before I can be sure of anything. But I have dreamed of owning a large tract of land for many years, and I have had many thoughts. If the land I'm buying is like similar areas that I have studied, its current economic function is simply to be a place where juvenals wander into, become larger and fatter, and then wander out of, to be eaten elsewhere. No one is making a profit off of it. Currently, at the University of Dren, the average juvenal sells for almost three dozen Ke."

"That much?"

"Yes. The method of collecting them is rather inefficient. Individual hunters, often impoverished students, go out and bring back one or two at a time. I think that if I set up an efficient system of collection, transportation, and distribution, the profits could be large."

"That is very interesting. You seem to be a remarkably creative person, Kren."

"Am I? It seemed only common sense to me."

"Well, in hindsight, yes. But to have the foresight to see it, well, that is something else. But the papers are here. Shall we sign them?"

"By all means!"

As soon as all copies were signed and witnessed, Bronki and Sala collected them up.

Bronki said, "I guess that concludes our business here, Your Grace. Kren and I have to catch a train back to the university in an hour. We both have our academic duties to perform there tomorrow."

"But I was enjoying my conversation with Kren," the duke said. "You two go and get everything properly registered with the Bonding Authority. You can come back for him in two-thirds of an hour. They'll hold the train if I request it."

"Yes, Your Grace," Sala said, taking Bronki with her.

"Now then, tell me more about your plans," the duke said.

"Well, if the collection and distribution of juvenals goes well, and proves profitable, I plan to extend my sales organization out into other nearby cities, until I start reaching the limit of what my land can sustainably provide."

"And then you will need more land."

"Perhaps," Kren said. "But that would be expensive, and there might be ways to increase the yield of what I already own. Academic studies of grass have shown that walking on it injures it. It must expend energy to repair the damage to its roots, energy that could otherwise be spent on growth. Juvenals outnumber adults by more than a gross to one. Thus, the total damage done by adults is small. Theoretical studies suggest that growth could be doubled if juvenals could be kept off of it, and this is verified by the yields of grass sequestered for the production of long grass."

"So you are thinking of putting all of your land in long grass, and feeding it to the juvenals?"

"Not quite. Long grass is high in cellulose and low in proteins. It is not the best possible feed. But if large hovercraft could be built to mow the grass every week or so, and this could be fed to penned juvenals, I think that production would more than double. The actual cost of mowing is still unknown, of course. Just how profitable this system would be would have to be seen."

"Yes, yes. But why do you say, *more than* doubled?" Dennon asked.

"Because the juvenals would have nothing to do now but eat, sleep, and grow. They wouldn't have to expend much of their energy moving around. We could feed them only at night, perhaps, and let them lie in the sun all day. Furthermore, they might prove to be much better eating, with more tender meat and more fat."

"This is truly a remarkable program, and I wish you well with it. I will be watching you carefully, and who knows, someday I might try something like this myself."

"You are welcome to," Kren said. "Once it proves profitable, I will have many competitors. I will stay out in front because I will have been there first, a step or two ahead of the rest."

"A sensible attitude. Do you have further thoughts?"

"A few, but they will be done many years in the future, if ever. I wonder if it would be practical to grow grass under fusion-powered lights in a building. The power itself is fairly cheap, and indoors, with constant, optimal lighting two dozen hours a day, with perfect fertilization, and perfect watering, with no winters or cloudy days, well, I think that it might be possible to produce at least a dozen times as much grass per square yard as you would get outdoors. And when you consider that a building could be easily built with two dozen stories, well, perhaps I might never need any more land."

"That would take a massive, long-term investment, but in the long run, why, it would permit our population to grow by a factor of two gross!" Duke Dennon said.

"And therein lies the profit."

"I am fascinated! Did you have any further thoughts?"

"Only one. It is that we have been selectively breeding our own species for millions of years. Not always consciously, of course, but when we are ready for resurrection, we always pick the best body that we can get, and these are the bodies that make the next generation of eggs and sperm. We have been breeding for perfect adults, and I think that the results have been excellent. Certainly, I wouldn't want to change that. But we have not been breeding for perfect juvenals. We have not considered that with further selective breeding, we could turn out juvenals who matured quicker, who needed less food, and who tasted better. I wonder what could be accomplished along these lines."

Actually, Kren had several other ideas, but thought it best not to mention to Duke Dennon the breeding of superior warriors. One day, he might have to go to war with him.

"My mind boggles, Kren. I see that our assistants are returning, and that you will soon have to leave. I would like to see you again, though, perhaps for a weekend?"

"I regret that I must study through the week, and play sports on most weekends."

"But we both know your schedule. In three weeks, the University of Dren won't be playing for one weekend. Come visit me then."

"With great pleasure, Your Grace."

CHAPTER THIRTY-TWO

FROM CAPTURED HISTORY TAPES,
FILE 1846583A ca. 1832 A.D.
BUT CONCERNING EVENTS OF UP TO
2000 YEARS EARLIER

Selling Shares in Children

The duke's guard, Lorka, met them on the stairway and presented Kren with the spear he had used earlier. Kren and Bronki talked only of ordinary things until they were in their cabin on the train. It took off immediately after they got aboard, since they really had been holding the train for them. This was something that the MagFloat Corporation did not like to do, but one does not argue with a duke.

"What happened between you and the duke while I was gone?" Bronki asked.

"Something very strange. He asked me what my plans were for the land he was selling me, and I had a most amazing burst of creativity, something which has never happened to me before. Well, I have done original things in the past, or at least things which I thought were original at the time. Originality is easy when you are ignorant of what has happened before. I deduced that by eating juvenal brain tissue, I could improve my studying, for example, and I came up with a novel way to bring six juvenals, who were each almost as big as I am, back to what is now my house. But those things were trivial compared to what happened to me today."

"And what was this flash of enlightenment? What exactly did you think about?"

"I suddenly saw a whole lifetime of research laid out in front of me, research the results of which could easily make me the most important person on the entire planet," Kren said.

Kren explained the whole program to Bronki, in more detail than he had explained to Duke Dennon, and not suppressing his thoughts on breeding superior soldiers.

"This body I got in the mines is obviously far better than the usual one. The duke said that I was better with a spear than the soldier that I had eaten, the one who gave me my skills with a spear in the first place. I seem to be stronger, much faster, and much more accurate than anyone else on the planet. I suspect that it might have something to do with the nerves. As soon as possible, we must build a structure where my offspring can be kept and secretly nurtured. If whatever this body has breeds true, think of the army that I'll have!"

"And where will you get the females to perform this experiment with?"

"There are plenty of fine female athletes at the university. Some of them might have some of the same genes that make me so good. I need only invite a dozen of them over to some secluded place for a dinner, a victory party perhaps, a few times every year. I will personally clean the place very thoroughly before they arrive, make sure that no one else but me, my athletic friends, and some juvenals are there in the interim, and then I will vacuum the whole place carefully after they leave, using new vacuum bags. I will distribute the fertilized eggs on new grown grass inside a closed building with suitable growing lights. The grubs will be kept separate, and when their time comes, they will become well-fed pollywogs in their own tank. The juvenals will be carefully nurtured on grass grown under artificial lights. Then, once the first generation has grown, my own daughters would be suitable egg layers. After a few more generations, the offspring would be genetically very like me."

Bronki said, "Most of that sounds very good. But about using your own daughters, well, there might be some genetic problems with double recessives, and so on."

"True, but we will be carefully testing all of the offspring, and culling anything inferior. We'll just sell the substandard ones for food. That will clean the gene pool in a few generations."

"Or we could always eat them ourselves."

"Yes, that might be best, in case someone finds out what we're doing. We wouldn't want anything superior to get into someone else's army," Kren said.

"Kren, to come up with so much, all at once, well, it's simply unprecedented. I've never heard of anything else like this ever happening before. There's nothing like it in the literature. But, you know, the literature on vampires is very limited, for obvious reasons. Those who do this sort of thing aren't likely to write scholarly reports about it."

"No, but you have had flashes of creativity, too, and if our experience is common among vampires, then it is probable that many of the rich and powerful are secretly like ourselves. Which leads me to another thought. Perhaps the reason why vampirism is so frowned upon is that those in power don't want the competition."

Bronki said, "And if that is true, then you and I are treading on very dangerous ground."

"The world is a very dangerous place. But if we wish to climb to the top of it, we must be prepared to take some risks."

"Very well, then. I wish you the very best of luck in your endeavor."

Kren was not about to let Bronki bow out and leave him without her expertise and advice.

"We will, of course, be very cautious and very secretive until we are very powerful. You have called yourself my partner. If that is so, I will be expecting some help from you," Kren said. "First off, I want to form a corporation to own and develop the land that we have bought this day. Since you have formed many corporations in the past, I want you to handle this one for us. You will issue shares with a par value of one million Ke each to me for my contribution of a gross billion Ke, and to you for the billion Ke that you have earned as a commission for putting this deal together, and for the billion Ke paid by you to your friend Sala in the form of a bribe."

"There was also the twelve million Ke I paid as your half of the fee to the Bonding Authority."

"That seems excessive!"

"They are guaranteeing the performance of both parties

to the agreement. That means that if Duke Dennon reneges, then the Bonding Authority might have to go to war with him to ensure compliance," Bronki said. "Considering the quality of Dennon's army and the cost of wars, two dozen million seems very reasonable."

"Oh, very well. Anyway, it has already been paid. Set us up with a corporate bank account, as well. Two signatures will be required on every check, one of which must be mine."

"I will file the paperwork for the corporation this evening, and take care of the bank in the morning. What would you like to call it?"

"I think that something very ordinary sounding would be best," Kren said. "We'll call it the Superior Food Corporation. And voting by the board of directors will be in proportion to the number of shares that they own, not one person, one vote."

"Kren, that's so undemocratic!"

"When did I ever claim to be a democrat?"

Bronki had only paid to Sala the half billion Ke that the accountant had requested. Duke Dennon had an outstanding credit rating, despite his current financial problems, since for thousands of years, he had honored all of his contracts and paid all of his debts. Because of this, the total fees required by the Bonding Authority had been only twelve million. Bronki thought that the stock that she would be issued would be quite acceptable. Anyway, it looked like an interesting operation, and being a world leader might be fun.

When they got home, Kren called Dol to his sitting room and explained everything that happened, and all of his thoughts for the future.

"So you see, we are going to need your engineering expertise on a number of projects." Kren said, "We are going to need a large grass-mowing and collecting machine. We are going to need several large experimental buildings. We are going to need an efficient system of sedating and boxing up juvenals for shipment. But the first thing that we are going to need is a fence that goes around the entire property, one that lets juvenals enter, but stops them from leaving."

Dol had listened, fascinated by everything that Kren had

told her, but now she had to say, "Kren, we can't do that. Planetary law is very specific about the building of fences. It is illegal to inhibit the free motion of juvenals. Except for fields licensed for the growing of long grass, all fences must have an ungated opening wide enough for an adult to pass easily through, at least once every two gross yards."

"I know that, and our fences will have those openings. Here, look."

Kren took a sheet of grass paper and drew a vertical line of half circles on it, with the concave sides to the left and the convex to the right, and with the wingtips almost but not quite touching.

)

)

)

)

)

)

"Kodo once read a study on the migration patterns of juvenals," he said. "When they come to an obstacle, like a fence, and they want to get to the other side, they follow along it. When the fence ends, they just keep on walking in the direction that they have been going, having apparently forgotten why they were following it in the first place. Now, when a juvenal comes to the convex side of one of these semicircles, she will follow along the fence until she comes to one of the openings, and then she will go through. But if she comes to the concave side of a semicircle, she will follow it around until it turns her back in the direction that she was coming from, and she will walk right back into the middle of our field. Since there are two gross yards between the openings, and the openings are only a yard wide, only once in two gross times will she happen to come directly to the opening without hitting the fence first."

A human would have recognized Kren's invention immediately as a fish weir. But for someone living on a planet without any fishes, Kren had come up with a brilliant innovation.

"It seems to satisfy the letter of the law, if not the spirit of it," Dol said. "Are you absolutely positive that this will work?"

"Absolutely? No, but I think that it would be worthwhile to build a few dozen miles of it, and see."

"Well then, I will see about getting your property surveyed, and I'll get some prices together on various kinds of fencing. I consider this sort of work to come under our agreement, so I won't be charging you anything for my time. But tell me, this Superior Food Corporation of yours. Can anybody buy stock in it? Me, for example?"

"We will need all the capital we can get, and your funds are certainly welcome," Kren said. "Our long-range plans must remain a secret, however."

"This is reasonable. How do I go about making a purchase?"

"See Bronki about it. She's setting up the corporation right now."

"Very well. I wonder what sort of a commission she's going to charge me," Dol said.

"You will tell her that I said that the price was a million Ke a share, and that's what you will be paying. I know that Bronki loves to snatch every Ke she can get her claws on, but the fact is that it is generally more profitable to do business with her than without her."

"I didn't realize that you were aware of what she was doing."

"I'm not a complete fool," Kren said. "Sometimes it's amusing to watch her operate. She just stole more than a half billion Ke from me today, but since she is getting it in stock, and I don't plan to declare a dividend for a very long time, if ever, then it really doesn't make much of a difference, does it?"

Dol decided that if dividends would not be forthcoming in the foreseeable future, buying one share would be sufficient. That would get her on the board of directors, since it wasn't likely that anyone else would buy shares in a secret corporation at a million Ke each.

Kren went to talk to Bronki.

"Have the corporate papers been filed?" he asked.

"Yes, and here's a printout of them. We should get approval on them by tomorrow afternoon."

"Very good. The next thing that we must think about is the sales organization. Dren is the closest major city to my lands, so we should start selling here. We will need a factory outlet near the train station, and it must be on the underground walkway system, because of the large volumes of juvenals we will be handling. On the walkways, we can use electric wheeled trucks, for delivery to the store, and manual wheeled carts for delivery to our customers, rather than having to carry them.

"At the store, we will need a front desk for walk-in business, an office to handle the phone-in business, a large storage area for our merchandise, and I think a display area for those who wish to pick a particularly pretty child for a special party. These will be at a premium price, of course.

"It might be profitable to sell accessories as well. Knives, branding irons, party tables, and so on. Then we must think about advertising, what our budget should be, which media we will use, and who will handle it for us. Or we might try doing that ourselves, since it will be a while getting our production volume up, and we don't want more customers than we have product to sell.

"Eventually, we might think about franchising our sales outlets, where each store is owned by a semi-independent operator."

"That sounds all fine and good, but just how much space do you think that this first outlet will require?" Bronki asked.

"I don't know. Probably not much at first, but with expanding sales, it could eventually be quite large."

"That's not much to go on. But look, the entire bottom floor of this building is on the level of the walkway system, and we aren't all that far from the train station. The nearest commercial outlet is only four dozen yards away, and the entire floor is currently being used for storage. If you were willing to pay commercial rates, I could have a door and window cut out to the walkway, and we could put in a small store. Then, as business expanded, you could rent more space, and I would again have it refurbished, but again at commercial rates."

"Why couldn't I just rent the storage space, and fix it up on my own?" Kren asked.

"You could, and you are welcome to. You can deal with the architects and the construction contractors yourself, in your copious spare time, and you can get all of the city permits on your own. There will be more than four dozen of them required. Then, of course, there will be the electrical company, the waste disposal company, the water company, and the phone company to deal with. If you wish to hire employees, there are nine different branches of the city government that you must make arrangements with. And there are probably at least a dozen other things that I am forgetting about just now."

"Okay, Bronki. What are you suggesting?"

"If you can bring them in to the train station, and sell them to me on the dock for two dozen Ke each, I'll take care of everything else. I'm talking about first-quality merchandise, you understand. Deal?" Bronki said.

"You'll take everything that we can send you?"

"Within reason. Say, increases of no more that three parts per gross per week, unless mutually agreed upon."

"Well, okay, but only for the City of Dren, and only for a twelve-year period. Anything more will have to be negotiated," Kren said.

"When can I get my first shipment?"

"Tentatively, in about four weeks. Shall we say a thousand children the first week?"

"That will do for starters. I'm not sure, but the total market in this city might be a thousand times that. You've got yourself a deal, partner. I'll write up the arrangement for your signature and have it ready for you tomorrow."

CHAPTER THIRTY-THREE

Perpetual Motion, Type Two
New Yugoslavia, 2212 A.D.

Our designers and architects had the preliminary designs done for a system of fallout shelters three kilometers down, and big enough to hold the entire population of the planet of New Yugoslavia.

To get the people down there in the simplest, fastest and most foolproof way, they had settled on cutting spiraling tubes down into the bedrock and lining them with polished metal. The faster you went down, the harder that centrifugal force pushed you against the outer wall. The added friction slowed you down, some. It was a blindingly simple speed control device, the kind of engineering I like. Also, a penetrating bit of radiation couldn't follow the curve, so it helped there, too.

It was a super amusement park ride, and we might have a few heart attacks on the way down, but there was nothing mechanical to fail at the wrong moment, so I approved it.

Actually, the plans had been done two weeks ago, but then my wife, a lovely mother of four fine sons, intelligent, caring and ungodly greedy, got into the act. Now, in addition to barrack space for everybody, with public latrines, communal chow halls and food that might satisfy a chinese coolie, there were two more, deeper sets of shelters.

One was for the moderately wealthy, and included private apartments, separate bedrooms, private bathrooms, private kitchens, and lots of storage space that you could stock with your favorite items.

The one below it was for the filthy rich, and was really very nice, if you could afford it. Kasia's plan was to sell these two posh layers for enough to pay for the entire installation. Then, she planned to talk the local governments into paying for the barracks, latrines, and chow halls, anyway.

That's my wife.

We had done other engineering projects on the planet that had required a lot of digging, like putting in a planet-wide underground highway system. In the past, we had simply flushed the dirt and pulverized granite into the oceans. It hadn't caused any ecological damage last time, but now we had a major ally living in those oceans, and I felt that it was politically advisable to check with them before we did it again.

With rolls of plans under my arm, I met Bellor floating in his swimming pool in my garage.

"Mickolai! It is so delightful to see you again. What can I do for you, my old benefactor?"

"Well, you can look over these plans for the planet-wide system of shelters to protect our people from the Mitchegai, and see if there is anything about them that would offend your people. Also, we'd like to know what we could do to protect the Tellefontu in case of attack."

"This is most courteous of you, Mickolai, but as to my own people, well, we have already made our own arrangements. When it comes to hiding, it is perhaps wise to keep your plans as secret as possible, yes?"

"Perhaps, but it is also wise not to offend your only ally. If you want to keep your own system secret, that's fine by me. But I'd like you to look over this stuff, to be sure that we do not offend you. Among other things, it involves dumping an awful lot of pulverized granite into the oceans that your people live in, and we don't want to cause you problems."

"Indeed? Let me look."

But instead of crawling out of the swimming pool and looking at the drawings that I was unrolling on the garage floor, he just sort of leaned back and floated for a bit.

"Yes, I see," he said. "Well, with your permission, I have a number of suggestions to make."

"I'd like to hear them, but before that, please tell me what you just did."

"I simply queried the good professor, and he downloaded the plans to me. I found it convenient to grow a data link to him, similar in some ways to the inductive mat that you wear under your scalp."

"Mine had to be surgically implanted," I said. "You just grew yours?"

"My people have developed that ability, yes. We know how to make and use machines, of course, but for many things, it is convenient to modify our body structure to do these things more easily. Please don't be offended, Mickolai, but yours is a very young race. In a few million years, it is quite possible that you will develop such abilities.

"Now then," he continued. "There is no need to transport the powdered granite to the oceans and dump it there. You may use our 'Disappearing Gun' to simply make the granite disappear. Oh. I see that your engineering group has not gotten the plans that I sent to New Kashubia. Well, there. They have them now. Next, I see that you have a very extensive system of power generators and electrical conductors going all over the place. It would be far simpler to simply generate the power where it is needed. In a closed system like this, you already have plenty of thermal power. Indeed, at three kilometers down, you will have a vast surplus of it, and I see that you were planning on an extensive air-conditioning system. That would involve a heat plume that the Mitchegai would undoubtedly notice."

"Wait a minute!" I said, "You are talking about using ambient thermal energy to generate power? Surely, that's impossible!"

"And why should that be so? Even with your primitive physics, you realize that heat is not a separate form of energy. It is simply mechanical energy on a very small scale. The individual atoms and molecules are vibrating and sometimes spinning. Their average speed is what you call heat. By slowing them down, one can extract useful energy. Surely, this is obvious. There are several practical methods of doing this, but I have just sent your engineers the plans for a simple light that gets its power from ambient heat. They will also need some larger systems to cool the housing units you propose, and I have just sent plans for those as well. They will have to put some resistive units in the oceans, to get rid of the surplus energy, but there are several volcanoes under the sea that will hide the heat quite nicely from our enemies. The rest of your plans seem workable enough, and I wouldn't want to upset your excellent engineers too much in one day.

"Please tell me," he said, changing the subject. "How soon do you think it might be before we can receive the rest of the Everclear you promised?"

I was too stunned to say anything but "Probably in about twelve days. After that, we can ship you a like amount every three months." They knew how to build perpetual motion machines?

"That would be most convenient. But you must please excuse me now, as there are several calls waiting."

I left the plans lying on the floor and went home.

CHAPTER THIRTY-FOUR

FROM CAPTURED HISTORY TAPES,
FILE 1846583A ca. 1832 A.D.
BUT CONCERNING EVENTS OF UP TO
2000 YEARS EARLIER

In Your Face Sports

The next day in the locker room, the director of Athletics just happened to stop Kren and him if he knew who Kodo was.

"Yes, sir, he is the director of the College of Architecture. Someone pointed him out to me once, in a crowd." As always, lying came easily to Kren.

"Have you seen him around lately? I've been looking for him."

"No sir, I haven't. But if I do see him, I'll ask him to contact you."

"No! Don't do that! If you see him, you come straight to me and tell me about it."

"Very good, sir. I will do as you wish."

Kren walked away, knowing who at least one member of Kodo's syndicate had been. After all the athletes that he had skinned alive for using drugs, the director had been buying into a drug syndicate.

If Kren had had any faith in anything, he might have lost some of it then. But of course he didn't, so he didn't.

On the way to the locker room, Kren met a stranger who identified herself as Bo, the runner who had been killed at the Death Match at the first meet of the year.

"You took my money, and you didn't perform the services you promised!" Bo said.

"Well, I tried to perform those services, but the director of athletics forbade me to do it. What else could I do? Anyway, before this goes any further, I want you to prove who you are."

Bo produced sufficient ID cards to convince Kren.

"Very well then," Kren said, pulling out his money pouch. "Here is your ten thousand Ke."

"But you got a dozen and nine times that much, when you collected on that bet!"

"So? If I had lost that contest, would you feel that I didn't owe you anything at all?"

"Well, no, of course not, but what you are doing isn't fair!"

"Bo, I do not understand this 'fair' thing that you talk about. Your options are that you can either take what I am offering, or you can fight me. Take your pick," Kren said, drawing his sword.

"You know that I can't fight you!"

"The choice is yours. Decide."

Bo took the money and went away. Apparently, her new body wasn't that of an athlete. Kren never saw her again.

Kren returned home to find Dol at work on her new computer, an oversized thing with more than the usual number of lights and gadgets.

While Mitchegai computer hardware was comparatively primitive, their programmers had had over a million years to catch up with their hardware. Their programs were very efficient, and they could accomplish a great deal despite small memories and slow circuits. When one of their computers crashed, it was *always* a hardware problem.

"I've gotten prices in on various forms of fencing, ranging from glazed brick, through stainless steel, and down to some galvanized steel mesh temporary stuff that's only guaranteed for six dozen years. It's only a twelfth the price of good brick, though."

"Since we don't really know if my design will work yet, and we don't know if there will be legal objections to what we have in mind, we might as well go with the cheap stuff."

"My thought exactly, sir. Then, I've gotten in a set of

standard survey maps for the area, but the most recent are over nine thousand years old. The Space Mitchegai had some satellite photos that are less than a year old, and I've been comparing the two. There were three new houses built lately, or in the last nine millennia, anyway, and an additional underground winter housing unit for juvenals, but that's about it, that I can see, anyway."

"How many of these wintering centers are there, and what's their capacity?"

"There are a dozen and nine units, with an average capacity of just over a million juvenals each. I have all of that compiled here for you, sir," Dol said, handing him a stack of fan folded computer printouts.

"You have been very efficient."

"I don't have to study my homework anymore, and I want to make myself indispensable to you, sir, so that I won't be dispensed with. I think that this project could make you a world power, and I like the idea of being close to a world power."

"Thank you. How is everything else going?"

"The gambling situation is not so good. We'd planned on having you win the épée tournament on Saturday morning, but the odds on you have dropped to a payout of only three for two! Someone has apparently bet a huge fortune on you. I suggest that we change the plan, and have you win the javelin distance competition instead."

"Ordinarily, that would be a good idea. But the person who placed the huge bet is probably Duke Dennon. The fool must have bet everything he got yesterday on the tip I gave him. No, I'll have to win with the épée, or I might turn a friendly, wealthy neighbor with a big army into an angry, impoverished neighbor, with a big army."

"I see your point, sir."

"Right. But don't bet any of our money on fencing. I have another idea. Maybe I can win at javelin tennis."

"The odds against you there are a dozen and one to one. You have never won a match, but due to your popularity, well, there are two dozen and eight players competing, and if you were only average, the odds on you should be two dozen and five to one, when in fact they are less than half that. But how will you plan to win at a game that is mostly luck?"

"Pole-vaulting, and taking the luck out of it. I'll let you know for sure, Friday afternoon."

"As you wish, sir. I've been doing a statistical study on the betting patterns for your events. Your fame is causing gamblers to bet on you in an irrational fashion. It really is a pity that you won both the fencing tournament and made a world record at the javelin accuracy event on your first time out. It was very profitable at the time, but it's costing us money now. So many are betting so much on you that they are bending the odds. They are losing more than they are winning by a factor of fully one-third."

"You mean to say that on the average, betting on me is a bad idea?" Kren said.

"Exactly. Since the second meet of the year, they have lost more money when they bet on the events that you lose than they have won when you win. And I'm including the wagers made by the *In Crowd*, who are making huge profits, along with everybody else, who aren't. Winning one event in three, the odds on you should be three to one, or a little less than that, after the house takes its cut. But they're not. They're more often two to one, or even less. It's a quirk of pari-mutuel betting. Your fame is driving down the odds on you, which reduces our winnings. When they bet *against* you, and we decide to win, we get their money. When they bet *on* you, they share in what we take. But I don't see what we can do about it."

"I do," Kren said. "Write up two versions of your study. Do one in Keno, or maybe Leno, the scientific language, and make it a properly formatted scientific paper. We'll get it out in one of the scientific journals. Then write up a simplified, popular version in Deno, and send it to all the newspapers and sporting magazines on the planet. Maybe if the gamblers learn that what they are doing is stupid, we can get the odds on me back up."

"I'll get right on it, sir. Getting a paper published as an undergraduate will be a boost to my academic career."

"You'll get it published, all right, even if we have to pay them to do it."

"That *is* the usual procedure, sir."

"Oh."

*   *   *

On Tuesday, Kren dutifully reported to the director, telling him that he hadn't seen Kodo, and that he would win the fencing meet on Saturday.

The director nodded and dismissed him, seeming distracted. He left his impressive office early, and was not seen again until the morning of the game.

The temporary coach in charge of javelins had been told to just let Kren do whatever he wanted to do, and Kren spent all of his time on the tennis singles courts, with a series of hapless opponents.

Kren's thought was that the reason why he always lost at the sport was that he couldn't know where his opponent was. There was a tall brick wall cutting the court in half, and any sort of signaling between the players and anyone else was strictly forbidden.

The wall was too tall for him to jump up and see over it, but a standard javelin was three and a half yards long, with blunted ends. It was lightweight, slightly flexible, and very strong. Kren thought that he might be able to use it to pole-vault himself high enough to see over the wall, and then, while he was flying up there, to whip the same javelin around fast and throw it downward at someplace where his opponent wasn't.

What made this maneuver even more difficult was the fact that the rules required him to return the throw in under two seconds.

By Tuesday evening, he had established that the thing was possible, but only if everything was perfect. He had to be near the wall, moving in the right direction, and on his left foot when he caught the javelin very close to the end, but it was possible.

The Mitchegai have a six-day week. They don't do Wednesday.

By Thursday night, he knew the strategy he had to use. This was to continue lobbing high, easy throws into the middle of the opposing court until just the right one came back to him. Then he would pole-vault, and nail the javelin into the ground.

On Friday, he sequentially beat every single member of the Dren University javelin team three times each. They all swore themselves to secrecy and went out to place their bets. So did Kren, Bronki and Dol.

Also, by this point, Kren and Dol had the plans for the outer fence completed, and had put it out for bids, telling the contractors that the strange shape had been decided on strictly for aesthetic reasons.

They were about to sign a deal with the low bidder when Bronki then got into the act, and within an hour managed to get the price reduced by one fourth, and got a sizeable kickback for herself from the contractor.

Kren suggested that Bronki use that kickback, when she got it, to buy more stock in the corporation. She said that she had been planning to.

Dol and Kren nodded to each other and signed the new contract.

On Saturday morning, Kren dutifully went to the opening ceremonies, and then participated in the fencing tournament. He won without great difficulty. Actually, losing was more work than winning, since he had to make losing look realistic. The crowds cheered, but no one came up and hugged him. The payoff was too small. But Duke Dennon would be happy, or at least not furious with him.

He did nothing unusual at the team tennis game, and for a change they won.

All of his cash, a gross, a dozen and four million, had been bet on the singles javelin tournament, which naturally made him nervous. There were many things that could go wrong.

It took three points to win a game, and he had to win five times in a row. One of his opponents could figure out his strategy, and counter it simply by always playing to the back court. Or, the judges could rule pole-vaulting to be illegal. Or, he could simply screw up, and lose before he had a chance to pole-vault. A single loss would wipe out everything that he had won since he got to the university.

He was beginning to think that betting everything on a single contest wasn't the best way to go. He swore that from this point forward, he would never bet more than half of his fortune. But for now, his money was already down, and he couldn't change that.

Kren won the first game surprisingly easily, before he got a chance to try his pole-vaulting stunt. He just kept throwing the javelins into the center of his opponent's court, and three of them didn't come back.

The second went well for the first two points, but then he lost two, and was beginning to worry before his opponent lobbed one high and near the barrier. Kren went into pole-vaulting mode and nailed it into the center of his opponent's field, to win the match. The crowd went wild, and the judges allowed the point, to Kren's considerable relief.

The third game went as easy as the first one, but on the fourth, he was up against some real competition. He stayed with the program, lobbing them back high and easy, and after over two dozen returns, the right one came in. Kren pole-vaulted for the point.

Someone told him later that it was one of the longest games on record, but all he could do was stick with his strategy, and eventually he pole-vaulted twice more and won the game.

The long game was starting to tell on him. Kren was beginning to tire as the last game started, and when he finally got a chance to pole-vault, there was his opponent, right in plain view, and making an obscene gesture at him.

This involved pointing the two upper fingers of the right hand upward with the other four closed, while moving the hand up and down. It signified "Up your cloaca!"

Something told him to get it over with, so instead of nailing the blunt javelin into the field, for the point, he threw it hard and straight at his gesturing opponent!

He was behind the wall before he could see it hit, but there was no doubt in Kren's mind. It was a perfect head shot.

Just to be on the safe side, Kren was ready to return the javelin, but it never came. He had won. The crowd was cheering enthusiastically, beating their left hands on their chests.

Injuries happened often enough in the game, so the rules were both well defined and well known. If the javelin was not out of bounds, it must be returned. And if a player was not able to continue, she lost.

Kren had expected the javelin to bounce off, rendering the girl unconscious. When he walked around the wall, he found her sitting there with the blunt javelin having gone into the skull, just above the eyes. A yard of it was sticking out the back of her head, stuck in the grass. It was propping her unconscious body up as the stretcher bearers arrived.

The next day, at the awards ceremonies, someone announced that she had lived, and was expected to be playing again in a few weeks.

Motile brain cells have several advantages. Among them was the ability to repair major brain damage. A human would probably have died on the spot.

The sportscasters said that Kren must have been very shaken up about the accident, since he did so poorly at the last two events of the day, the javelin distance and accuracy throws.

The director of athletics was furious at not having been informed of Kren's intention of winning the javelin tennis competition.

Kren said that he hadn't been sure that he could win it, that he wasn't sure that using a javelin to pole-vault with would be allowed by the judges, and that the director had been gone for most of the week, and out of touch, so he couldn't be consulted.

The director walked away grumbling.

Kren didn't really care. Not when his net worth was now one billion, two gross seven dozen and six million Ke. Plus a small duchy, of course.

The memory of the stunned look on his opponent's face as the javelin came at her was a very nice, lingering satisfaction.

CHAPTER THIRTY-FIVE

FROM CAPTURED HISTORY TAPES,
FILE 1846583A ca. 1832 A.D.
BUT CONCERNING EVENTS OF UP TO
2000 YEARS EARLIER

Kren's Kiddy Hotel—
They Check In but They Don't Check Out

The contractors started work promptly on Monday morning, putting up the first twelve miles of fencing around the new property. If it worked, they would get the go-ahead to complete the project, but they wouldn't have the whole job done for twelve weeks.

With Bronki working on the sales end of things, Kren and Dol started getting production going.

"We have to have an efficient method of gathering up the juvenals, getting them on the train, getting them to market," Kren said. "I think that the best way to do it would be to drug them, put them in boxes, and use material handling equipment from then on. There is a chemical called piperphentamone that is not on the illegal list, because it has no effect on adults. Injected into a juvenal in the proper dosage, it will knock her unconscious for a week. Also, there is an antidote, brantadiatol, which can bring them around in a few minutes, and it too is legal. I want you to find a manufacturer who can produce these for us."

"I'll get on it in the morning, sir."

"Right. Next, we'll need some shipping boxes for them.

Find out what the standard sizes are, and what they cost. Collecting the juvenals up won't be a problem at first, because winter is coming on, and they will be collecting themselves at the wintering centers. I note that each of these centers is near a train terminal."

Lacking the human urge for creativity, all Mitchegai train terminals were built the same. Once they had an efficient design, they stuck with it. Rarely used terminals in the countryside were just as large and well equipped as those in the cities, although more of them had been added as the cities grew. Since they were expected to last forever, and had been built before many of the current cities existed, there was a certain logic to this way of doing things.

"I'm sure that it was simply easier to build the centers where the materials could be easily delivered," Dol said.

"I expect that you are right, but it is still very convenient for us. I want you to work on some method of efficiently taking contented children from the center and turning them into boxes of product loaded on a hovercraft that can deliver them to the train station. Bear in mind that this will have to be done mostly outdoors, in the wintertime."

"Right, sir. Then there were the buildings you mentioned earlier?"

"That's what I'll be doing, drawing up some rough sketches of what we need. Later, you can do up some finished drawings on that fancy computer of yours."

"Very well, and I already have a plotter on order, to do proper technical drawings. It should get here in a week. You really should learn to use a computer, sir."

"Later, maybe. Just now, I don't have time. We'll need the packaging center, to gather juvenals from the fields and prepare them for shipment. I'll want it built and running by spring, and I'm very eager to start in on the breeding projects we talked about."

"Not to mention the grass-mowing machines and the business of growing grass under artificial lights."

"Right. The grass mowing is your project. We'll need it by next summer, I expect. Keep me posted. As to the artificial lights, I need some research done there. All of the artificial lights I've seen have imitated the spectrum of sunlight.

But plants are most efficient under a particular wave length of monochromatic red light. Any photons with less energy simply do the plant no good at all. Any energy above a certain level is wasted, and just goes into waste heat, which has to be gotten rid of. I want you to find me some inexpensive, monochromatic light sources."

"I'll see what I can do, sir. Do you know the precise wave length we need?"

"No, that slips my memory. I only remember that it was red. Vampire memories are not perfect."

"Or maybe Kodo forgot it."

"That too is possible. Well, you know what to do."

The next weekend was an away game, and the opposing javelin tennis team had been studying tapes of Kren's last performance. They all showed up to the meet wearing protective headgear, and they made all of their shots to the rear of the court, from which Kren could not effectively pole-vault. This made for some long and boring games. One of them was indeed a world record setter for both length and dullness, but they didn't give away any platinum medals for that. Kren didn't come close to winning.

Kren had suspected that something like this would happen, and hadn't bet on the tennis tournament. The odds were too low, anyway.

Instead, he won the javelin distance event, without setting any records. The payoff was only two to one, and Kren, in keeping with his earlier vows, had only bet half of his purse on the outcome. Bronki had always been a bit secretive about her betting, but Dol said that she would continue betting everything she had, since a girl never could tell when she might need another billion Ke.

"Dol, I've been invited back to Duke Dennon's palace for the weekend. Would you like to come along?" Kren asked.

"A visit to a ducal palace? Most definitely, sir!"

"Then book us a cabin on an express train on Friday afternoon, and find out from Bronki who we should contact at the palace to tell them we're coming. Tell her that she's invited along, if she wants, but if she's too busy, that's okay, too."

✳   ✳   ✳

As he and Dol walked into the ducal palace, Kren noted that many small changes had taken place. The carpeting was new, and of the very best quality, as were the drapes. Minor repairs had been made where necessary, and the servants all sported new uniforms. Only the very professional guards were unchanged, although Kren was sure that by now they'd all gotten their back pay.

They were immediately escorted to Duke Dennon's private quarters, which had been lavishly redecorated. They made the proper bow to His Grace, who stood up to greet them.

The duke said, "Kren! Welcome back! All the more so since you have made me a half gross billion Ke richer!"

"I thought that it might have been you who bet a gross billion Ke on that fencing match! Your wager drove the odds down so low that we almost decided to win the javelin accuracy throw instead!"

"I'm glad that you didn't! But the gross billion Ke you paid me for my land barely covered my debts. The additional money I made on that wager has given me financial security and permitted me to make some very needed repairs to my estate. Who is your friend?"

"Your Grace, this is Dol. She's nominally my servant, but she's also on my board of directors, and she has been acting as my chief engineer, so I suppose that makes her my friend as well."

"Your friends are always welcome," the duke said.

They had been speaking in Meno, the military language, which Dol was completely ignorant of, but the duke's smile was all that she really needed to go on.

Mitchegai do smile to express pleasure. Like humans, they do this by looking at the person they are addressing and exposing their fangs.

"I thank you, Your Grace," Dol said in Deno, the common language.

"I am almost completely ignorant of Reno, the engineering language, so I guess Deno it is," the duke said in fluent Deno. "It is difficult to express anything but the simplest things in the common tongue, though. I'm sure that you'd be far more comfortable talking with my chief engineer, Dako. In fact, I want you to meet her. Among other things, I am now the owner of a huge supply of mining machinery that is completely useless to me. It occurs to me that a conveyor belt designed to haul ore might prove useful in hauling grass clippings. I could give Kren here a very good price on it."

"That is a very interesting idea, Your Grace. Yes, Dol, by all means, find out what they have available," Kren said.

A servant was assigned to escort Dol to Dako's office.

"Just be sure and come to the party tonight," the duke said as they left. Turning to Kren, he said, "Now then, have you been thinking more about your fascinating plans for your new lands?"

"More than thinking, Your Grace. We've already started doing. For a week now, I've had a crew putting up fences around my land."

"First, you have now used up your allotment of 'Your Graces' for the entire weekend. Just call me Dennon. Second, you have been putting up your fences on the boundary with my lands, and the reports I've been getting are strange. You are building these curving things that have to be costing you half again more than a straight fence would. Your workers have told my men that you are doing this for aesthetic reasons, but that does not fit with my judgment of your character. Please explain this to me."

Kren said, "Very well, but you must agree to keep this a secret."

The Mitchegai never had anything remotely like a patent office. The only way they had to make a profit off of an idea was to keep it secret. This could be another reason for their general lack of creativity.

Kren then explained his new idea, the fish weir, drawing sketches on a pad of paper that the duke provided.

"And this strange device actually works?" the duke asked.

"In fact, it does. Dol found a standard industrial product, a long armed mechanical switch that operates a mechanical counter when something goes by in one direction. Putting two of them on one of the openings gave us the ratio of juvenals going one way as opposed to those going the other. More of them are going in the wrong direction than I thought they would, but it is still much better than a gross to one. My fence is an effective valve. I also intend to use something similar to make collection paths, where juvenals in the fields are collected up and sent to my packaging facility. They'll come to us, we'll select the ones we want and send the rest back out to the fields," Kren said.

"Remarkable. But all of this means that you will be denuding my lands of the juvenals that my subjects need to survive."

"That remains to be seen. Many will be entering my lands, but many more will be drifting into yours from the other directions. I do, however, promise that none of your subjects will starve because of what I am doing."

"I'll take your word on that, and hold you to it," Duke Dennon said. "Now, what of your other thoughts?"

Kren explained about how grass only absorbed red light, and how any artificial lights should be monochromatic.

"Now that is odd," Dennon said. "Somehow, I'd always thought of grass as being the perfect energy converter, changing sunlight into food for the children."

"If it was a perfect converter, it would absorb all of the light and look black. Grass is green because it doesn't need the green light, and reflects it back to our eyes."

"Interesting. But can you buy monochromatic lights?"

"I was surprised to find out that they are the *only* sort that you can buy," Kren said. "The white lighting panels that are used everywhere are made up of seven different sorts of tiny light emitting diodes, each of which is monochromatic, but of a different color. The numbers of each sort is such that together they appear to us as being white. Making a panel with only a single sort of LED actually cuts the cost in half, assuming that you are buying in large quantities, which of course I will be."

"I didn't know that."

"Neither did I until Dol did some research on it."

"And what about that business of breeding more efficient juvenals?" the duke asked.

"That will be a long-term project, of course. I have designed a research building with three dozen large complexes that will let us test three dozen types of juvenals simultaneously, keeping each type separate from the grub stage, through the pollywog stage, and then as juvenals and even a few brainless adults to make more eggs. We can have three dozen selective breeding projects going at the same time. Also, I will have a complete genetics laboratory, so that we can know exactly what we are dealing with in every experiment."

"But I thought that the DNA experiments had wound down, well, many millennia ago, when everything that could be learned had been learned."

"You are right, they did," Kren said. "The equipment I'm buying has been in storage for over twelve thousand years. I've put a clause in the contract whereby I won't have to pay for it if it doesn't work, but I'm more than a little worried about it. Having to build all new equipment from ancient plans would be expensive! Also, I've got seven biochemists on the payroll trying to learn what the ancients knew about DNA analysis."

"I wish you well! But now, it's Friday Night and Party Time! Come with me to the great hall, and we'll get the festivities started!"

CHAPTER THIRTY-SIX

Politics and My Boys
New Yugoslavia, 2212 A.D.

The Tellefontu normally carried an organic version of the Disappearing Gun in one of their front claws. This was necessary, since they lived in an ocean filled with large, small-brained carnivores like bluefinned tuna, who sometimes mistook them for a tasty treat. But while killing your attacker eliminated the immediate problem, it didn't teach him anything. It only killed him, leaving the others with no change in their behavior. Therefore, the Tellefontu had developed a weapon that caused intense pain, but no physical damage. It was a beam that really rattled the pain centers of the brain.

The pain-generating weapon had proved ineffective against the Earthly lobsters the early inhabitants had tried to grow in New Yugoslavia's oceans, as these crustaceans lacked enough of a brain to feel pain, apparently. And since the lobsters had developed a taste for young Tellefontu, our new allies had made a point of eradicating them.

I had been unaware of this, but with demand and no supply, it looked to be profitable to grow lobsters in tanks on my land, especially since as carnivores, they would give me something to do with that half of a cow (eyeballs, lungs, etc.) that people didn't want to eat.

The first eating-sized lobsters were finally coming out of the tanks, and Kasia and I ate the first two with gusto!

Bellor declined to join us.

✳   ✳   ✳

My annoying uncle, Wlodzimierz Derdowski, the President of New Kashubia, was now lording it over the Interplanetary Council of the Union of Human Planets. The new constitution was still being haggled over, and we still didn't have anything like a single individual in charge, but my uncle was currently the closest thing we had to it.

He'd written me that my "discovery" of the Tellefontu had been tremendously important, politically. The fact that I hadn't discovered anything, and that they had come to me didn't faze him in the least. Politicians are never very concerned with actual facts.

While the governments of the various planets were still behind the huge defense budgets that were required to prepare us to face the Mitchegai, the people were getting increasingly restless about the taxation and the dearth of civilian goods available.

Now, however, there was a race of intelligent beings who had witnessed and suffered through an invasion by the Mitchegai, and this forced people to take the whole thing seriously. While it would have been better if they could have been furry, cute, and cuddly, instead of looking like crabs, they nonetheless were instrumental in keeping the war effort going.

And the Tellefontu were cooperating very nicely, giving lots of press interviews and showing up regularly on talk shows.

In addition to the psychological boost, it was expected that as the new technology that the Tellefontu were giving us worked its way into the market, the economic boost would be considerable, and that would help the political situation a lot. What we had been able to learn from the Mitchegai scout ship wouldn't hurt, either.

My uncle invited me to come to New Kashubia, so he could pin a few more medals on my chest. I respectfully declined, claiming the press of things to be done.

Actually, I still hated the bastard. I never have forgiven him for letting the courts give Kasia and me the choice of death or joining the army, all those years ago, not when they had aborted our first child in the process.

My boys were now my great joy in life. The oldest were getting to the point where I could teach them to fish, to ride horses, and to play ball. They were spending more and more of their time in the golden castle that I'd had built, but couldn't sell, and that was good. The spirit of true knighthood was starting to grow in them.

Our machine tool industry was expanding with surprising rapidity. Our intelligent computers were keeping everything working twenty-four hours a day, seven days a week, and without holidays. There was very little downtime. A great deal was being done very quickly.

The engineers computed that with the Disappearing Guns, and the other things that Bellor had suggested, we could produce the fallout shelters at a quarter of the price originally estimated. We would want the Guns as weapons anyway, so we built a production line to mass produce them. We also built lines to make the self-powered lighting fixtures and the power-generating air conditioners.

Kasia never mentioned these savings in her dealings with the local governments, and got full prices out of them. I took much of the extra money, and spent it on better food supplies. We would now be able to serve something a little bit better than gruel. But we didn't tell them about that, either. It might have hurt sales on the luxury apartments.

As these new factories started to come on line, the shelters started to be dug in a hurry. One of our standard tanks, usually with a young soldier in training inside and oblivious to what his tank was really doing, could cut a tunnel eight meters across and ten meters high while traveling at eighty kilometers an hour!

It was a fast way to make floor space!

CHAPTER THIRTY-SEVEN

FROM CAPTURED HISTORY TAPES,
FILE 1846583A ca. 1832 A.D.
BUT CONCERNING EVENTS OF UP TO
2000 YEARS EARLIER

For War and Profit!

After the duke started things out by cutting off a pretty little girl's finger with a dull knife, and eating it to the applause of all present, Dol made a hit at the party by borrowing a large soldering iron from one of the repair shops in the engineering wing, putting it up one of the party snack's cloaca, and plugging it in. It was something she had learned at one of Bronki's parties, but it was a new innovation here. The resulting screams were outstanding!

Later, Dol told Kren that she would spend all day Saturday going over the mining machinery with Dako, but it looked as if most of it could be extremely useful. Besides the conveyor belts, there were eleven major power stations in storage here. These were high efficiency muon-exchange fusion units, capable of running for a thousand years at peak output before they needed refueling.

Dol said, "They have a massive amount of lighting fixtures, wires and cabling, and seven big tunneling machines. With them, it might prove feasible to connect the wintering centers directly to the train stations, which would greatly ease the job of collecting juvenals in the winter time. We could just run the children we want down underground tunnels to the train station and box them up there."

Also, the duke's engineers didn't have nearly enough to do, and Dol expected to get a lot of free engineering help from them.

The duke came up to them and said, "Now, now, you two. No discussion of business at a party! Anyway, the entertainment is about to begin in the arena, so come along, both of you."

They went to a small circular stadium surrounding a patch of synthetic grass two dozen yards across. At first, Kren thought that they would be in for some sort of gladiatorial event, but no, no one was killed. The duke thought too much of his troops to waste them on mere entertainment.

It was a tournament between two platoons of combat troops from two rival regiments. It was fought with weapons of full weight, but without sharp edges. The troops wore full, head-to-toe armor of a sort Kren had never seen before. The helmets were similar to what most of Dennon's soldiers wore, except that the face was also protected. The body armor was obviously of a more advanced technology, with many dozens of intricately fitting, overlapping plates that permitted complete freedom of motion.

The first event was one-on-one fighting with sword and spear between members of the two platoons. What with the armor and the blunted weapons, no one was seriously injured, but these troops were really fighting.

Kren found it good to watch real professionals go at it, and not the stupid buffoons on *Big Time Gladiators*. The rules were anything goes, and the fighting continued until the slain warrior declared herself to be dead. Honor was very important to these warriors, and the thought of cheating was abhorrent to them. Once a warrior took a blow that would have killed her, had the weapon been real and she without her armor, she fell over "dead" and the crowd applauded.

They even gave an award for the "Best Death of the Evening."

Most of the three dozen bouts lasted less than a minute.

"I've never seen anything like the armor they're wearing," Kren said.

"Actually, those are old space suits," the duke said. "New

ones would be hideously expensive, but these all had to be scrapped because they leaked air. But that's not a problem down here, and I always buy them, when they come on the market. I've got eleven gross of them now, and my best units have them."

"Those are space suits?" Kren said.

"They were. The Space Mitchegai all clip their claws very short, so we have to open up the gloves and boots to let ours out. We've taken the fittings for the breathing packs off, along with the heating and cooling apparatus, which wouldn't be allowed by the rules of war, and I never bought the space helmets in the first place. After that, well, a coat of paint in my colors, and there you are."

"I didn't know that any of the armies were using full armor."

"I might be the only duke with any large number of armored troops. Most of them find it cheaper to hire new troops than to armor the old ones. And in fact, I've never committed my armored division to combat. They've always been my strategic reserve, and so far, I've always won before they were committed to battle. But someday, I will need some real shock troops, and when that day happens, I'll have them."

"Conventional wisdom is that armor slows you down more than it is worth."

"To a certain extent, it does slow a soldier down. Also, the extra weight upsets your coordination and balance. To get good in it, you pretty much have to live in the stuff, full time, which is precisely what all of these troops do. They even sleep in it, usually."

"I'd like to try sparring in armor, sometime."

"We can do that tomorrow, if you'd like. I just bought four new suits that haven't been assigned to individuals yet. I think that two of them should be ready."

"I'll look forward to it."

When the individual matches were over, the two platoons formed up a battle line and fought a general mêlée, which left three troops standing from one side, and none from the other. The points were tallied up, and the losing side went back to their barracks. The winners got to join the party, and hobnob with the aristocracy, still in their armor, but with their helmets off so that they could eat.

The next day, a palace servant escorted Kren back to the arena, where he found Duke Dennon already putting on a suit of armor, with the help of some armored soldiers.

"Ah, there you are, Kren! Well, get suited up, and we'll try each other's mettle."

"As you wish, Dennon, but I hadn't expected to be fighting *you.*"

"Well, it would hardly be fair to put you up against someone who had been living in armor for years. I'm not a novice to fighting, of course, so I expect that I'll give you a bit of a challenge. Just be sure that you give me your best effort as well. I would be seriously offended if I thought you were faking it just to make me look good."

"Again, as you wish."

It took two soldiers twelve minutes to get Kren's armor installed and fitted properly, and he spent another two dozen minutes moving around, getting used to the feel of it. The weight of the tail armor was particularly bothersome. It threw his balance off considerably.

Finally, Kren said, "I think that I've got the feel of it now. I'm ready if you are."

"You are doing better than most," the duke said. "Many troops spend most of their first week getting up again, after they've fallen down, again. *On guard!*"

They started slow, feeling each other out the way professional fighters always do. Then the duke launched a fast attack, feinting with his spear while attacking with his sword on the other side. Kren was just able to parry both weapons, but his riposte didn't get through, and he had to leap backward to avoid the counter. After a short breather, Kren attacked, and after six counters, he doubled under the duke's sword, fencing style, and caught him in the chest with a thrust.

"Well done, Kren! I should have known to guard better against your point, having seen you fight at an épée tournament. Well then, do you want to have a go at one of my troops?"

Kren agreed to it, after a few minutes to catch his breath. The armor around his waist interfered with his lung exhausts.

In the course of the morning, Kren beat six of the duke's warriors, without losing a match.

"Wow, but your troops are good!" Kren said, "That last one in particular almost had me at least six times there! I hope that I never have to go to war against this bunch!"

"That last one was my weapons' master, Kren, and you are the first one to defeat him in his last three lifetimes! We are all astonished at your prowess, and to fight this well on your first day in armor, well, it is simply astounding!"

"Thank you. I think that I've had enough of a workout for today, though. I'll be happier when I get this armor off. My tail is protesting more than anything else. If this armor were mine, I think I'd have the tail armor removed, and just let my tail take its chances."

"Most novices to armor say that for the first two weeks. They get used to it in time, though, and an armored tail is sometimes useful. Once the strength in it builds up, the tail is useful for blocking with."

"Yes, I noticed two of your soldiers using it that way. But for now, get me out of this stuff!"

They spent the rest of the day strolling around the palace and its grounds. Most of the conversation revolved around Duke Dennon's problems in managing his estate.

To the duke, managerial details were simply a nuisance. His true and only intrest was in war, and in further developing his army. All else was trivia. In the late afternoon, the duke was called away to settle a minor emergency. He and Kren agreed to meet again in the morning.

Kren spent the evening reading a novel from the duke's small library.

In the morning, Dol came to Kren's room and started waxing enthusiastically about all of the machinery that she had spent the day before examining.

"I said that there were seven big tunneling machines, sir, but from the drawings, I didn't realize just *how* big they are," Dol said. "They each break up into eleven pieces so that they can be transported by rail! Can you imagine something eleven times as big as a rail car? Those things are built to dig a tunnel twelve yards in diameter through solid rock, loose sand, and everything in between. The cutters in the front can take on anything natural, even granite, chew it up, and spit it down a vibratory conveyor line that it drags behind it. They can move at a yard a minute through granite, and three times that fast through dirt. Actually, it's the conveyors that slow them down, just hauling the stuff away. And if the material is too soft to hold itself up, the tunnelers are equipped to build a metal tube to line the tunnel with. They take a coil of stainless metal, form corrugations in it, and then weld it in a spiral around the inside, all automatically. They've each got their own fusion power supply, too, and can run for a thousand years without refueling."

"That sounds impressive. It also sounds a little big, just to have juvenals running down it a few times a year."

"Right, sir. But there is also an eighth tunneler, intended for exploratory work. It cuts a tunnel three yards in diameter, dragging an extendable conveyor line behind itself, just like the big ones do. Through dirt, it can do twelve yards a minute, since it uses the same conveyors as the big ones do."

Kren said, "And does it put in the metal lining, like the big ones do? I think that most of the tunnels from the train stations to the wintering centers will be shallow, and through dirt, not rock."

"Oh, yes, sir. It does everything that the big ones do, except break up for shipment. It doesn't have to, since it will fit on a flatcar."

"Then that solves one of our problems."

Duke Dennon walked in through the open doorway.

"You were having problems, Kren?" The duke said in stilted Keno, which Dol and Kren had been using.

"Just the minor problem of getting the juvenals from the wintering centers to the train stations in the wintertime. If we had the use of your small tunneler, we could put in an underground connection to each of them, and thus avoid the inevitable losses that would occur if we took the children outside during bad weather."

"Oh. Yes, I can see where many of them might freeze to death, doing such a thing, and that would cut into your profits. Well, I'm sure that we can arrange something, one way or another. I've found a surplus equipment buyer who has offered to pay me one sixth of what I had to pay for all of that stuff, but that's the best offer I've had."

"Just how much did you pay for it, if I may ask," Kren said.

"You may. Including transportation charges, but not counting legal fees and the atrocious penalties I had to pay for late payment, it came to just over eight dozen billion Ke."

"Hmmm. It is possible that I could better the offer that the scrap dealer made you, but there would have to be a number of stipulations."

"I am interested. Just what stipulations did you have in mind?" The duke unconsciously slipped over to Meno, which he was more comfortable with.

Kren said in Meno, leaving Dol out of it for a while, "First off, I don't have anyplace to store so much equipment. Could I leave it here until I need it?"

"I don't see why not. We have plenty of room. I could let you store it here for, say, twelve years, before I start charging you rent on it."

"That would be adequate. Next, I'm a little low on ready cash just now. Would you be willing to take stock in my corporation in return for your equipment?"

"Now that would take some mulling over. How much were you thinking of offering me?" the duke asked.

"I offer to take it all for one quarter of what you paid, two dozen billion Ke."

"That sounds reasonable, and more than anyone else has offered. But this stock of yours, what sort of dividends do you intend to pay?"

"I intend for my company to continue reinvesting all of our considerable profits back into the business for the foreseeable future. There won't be any dividends for a very long time," Kren said.

"Well, what bloody good is an investment that doesn't make me any money? I'd be better off working with the used equipment dealer. There at least, I'd get *something* for my machinery! Why should I accept your strange offer?"

"You should accept my offer because it will make your army invincible, and you a world conqueror!"

The duke closed the door and sat down. "That is a remarkable statement. Would you care to expand on it?"

"I'd be happy to. You have admired my athletic abilities, and yesterday, you were impressed with my prowess as a warrior, yes?"

"Certainly. You are the perfect athlete. I've been saying so since I saw you win that first fencing tournament."

Kren said, "Would you like to have every soldier in your army be as good an athlete, as good a warrior as I am?"

"By the Great First Egg, I certainly would! Are you saying that this is possible?"

"I think that it is. But first, I must tell you that before I got this body, I was not a particularly adept soldier, and I wasn't any sort of an athlete at all. I was in fact physically very ordinary. Then I was badly injured in a field exercise, and didn't stand a chance of living half a day. It was night, and we were out of touch with our commander. There wasn't a normal metamorphosed youngster available to eat my brain, but a friend of mine found an ordinary slave, without much of a brain of his own. It could have worked out badly, but I urged my squad to give it a try, and they did. You have seen the result. There is something very special about this body, and I think perhaps it has something to do with the nerves. I think that with proper breeding and a lot of work, we can get it to breed true. It will probably take three or four generations to do it, but I am confident that in the end it can be done before this body is worn out. Then, we will have a breed of Mitchegai that can be the finest warriors the universe has ever seen! You were willing to bet a gross billion Ke on the outcome of a fencing tournament. I'm willing to bet that you would wager some useless machinery on the hope of building the finest army in this world, or any other!"

"You would win that bet, Kren! I'm with you!"

"Excellent, Duke Dennon! I see a long and mutually profitable partnership before us."

"Partnership?"

"Well, this is premature, and it will be many years before it brings fruit, but think on this. My interest is in business and management. Your interest is in armies and war. If we had a trusting relationship, together we could, in time, rule this entire planet!"

"That is a very interesting thought, Kren, but as you say, it is for the future. For now, I will have what we have agreed to today properly written up, and sent to you in a few days for your signature."

"Excellent, Dennon. You'll be hearing from us soon. For now, there's a train to catch."

"Very well, Kren. For war and profit!"

"Yes! For war and profit!" Kren switched to Keno. "Come along, Dol. It's time to go."

CHAPTER THIRTY-EIGHT

FROM CAPTURED HISTORY TAPES,
FILE 1846583A ca. 1832 A.D.
BUT CONCERNING EVENTS OF UP TO
2000 YEARS EARLIER

Billions for Building

Again, Duke Kren satisfied the needs of nature, with the pain in his head pulsing. Yet, as he reviewed his memories, he couldn't help but think that those were the great old days! The days of joy and fulfillment!

He lay down, and put the recording helmet back on.

Once they were in their private cabin on the train, Dol said, "Kren, just what was all that about?"

"Sorry, but the duke's Keno isn't very good. I just made a deal whereby Duke Dennon will give us all of the machinery that you inspected yesterday, in return for two dozen billion Ke worth of our corporation's shares, which he doesn't expect to make any money off of!"

"How wonderful, sir."

"You don't seem to be very enthusiastic about it," Kren said.

"I'm not! Don't you see that you've just blown me off the board of directors?"

"Perhaps, but not necessarily. The corporation only elects a new board once a year. You have plenty of time to come up with a few dozen billion Ke, and invest it properly in your favorite corporation. Then you can blow Bronki off the board."

"There is that, yes," Dol said.

"And anyway, the corporation is going to need a lot of spending cash."

"I expect that it will get it, since Bronki won't like being pushed out, either. She'll be buying more stock, too. Watch her!"

"Right, she will. Have fun, you two. If you both get really enthusiastic with the competition, maybe you can blow Duke Dennon off the board," Kren said. "Next, I want you to hire a crew who knows how to use our sort of mining machinery, and start them digging three-yard tunnels from the train stations to the wintering centers."

"Oh, we've already got them, sir."

"We do?"

"Duke Dennon's engineers have all been through an extensive course in how to use all the machinery they bought. The original plan was to have them set it up in that old copper mine themselves. They spent a year in mining school, came back eager to work, and the bottom promptly fell out of the copper market. They've all been sitting around for a year now with nothing to do, and getting very frustrated about it. I've already discussed the project with Chief Engineer Dako, and she wants to start immediately," Dol said.

"Then as soon as we get home, phone her and tell them to start on it! Do you think that they would be willing to take company stock for their work, instead of cash?"

"So far, there has been no mention of money. I tell you, sir, these girls really want to get going on *something*! But *if* the subject comes up, I'll relay your suggestion to them."

"I suppose that we can take the dirt we remove and load it directly on to railroad hopper cars," Kren said.

"That is the plan, yes. Dako suggested that the best thing would be to just dump it in the Borako Ocean Trench. There's a railroad station built on the grass mat right above it, and everybody within a thousand miles uses it for a dump. That trench is so big that at present usage, it will take three dozen million years to fill it up."

The Mitchegai tend to worry about ecological things in the long term, but not *that* long.

Dol continued, "That's what they were planning to do with the waste material from the Senta Copper Mine. I'll have to make arrangements with the MagFloat Corporation, for cutting holes in the walls of their loading docks, shipping in and out our equipment, and using their floor space to package the children. And hauling away the dirt, of course. I think that once we get the lighting strung up in the tunnels, we'll be able to buy the electricity for them from the railroad as well. It should be a lot cheaper than putting in our own power supplies."

"So you're way ahead of me on this thing. Good. Do it!"

"Thank you, sir," Dol said. "I'll get on it, directly."

"Right. Next subject. I'd been planning on building conventional buildings, big buildings, for growing grass in, and for feeding the juvenals until they are big enough to eat. I wonder if it wouldn't be cheaper to use the big tunneling machines to make underground buildings. We could take these big, metal-lined tunnels and weld floors in them. We could put lights and water sprinklers on the ceilings, and grass on the floors. Then we could have mowing machines running along rails mounted on the side walls. It has the nice advantage of keeping everybody else from knowing what we are doing."

"That's interesting, sir. I'll do some cost analyses in a few days, once I get the tunnels to the wintering centers going."

"Fine," Kren said. "But talk to Bronki about dealing with the MagFloat Corporation. She probably knows somebody on their board of directors, and can cut us a better deal."

"And get herself a kickback in the process."

"Which she'd better invest in company stock. I'm going to take a nap. Fighting in armor is a real pain in the tail, and I think I'll be sore for days. Wake me when we get home."

Kren felt perfectly safe, sleeping in the same room when Dol was awake there. If he was killed, she wouldn't have a sure thing to bet on.

When they returned home, Dol filled Bronki in, and she agreed to talk to several old friends on the MagFloat board of directors.

"You know, Dol, after five thousand years, one gets to know just about everybody who is really important."

By Monday afternoon, she had struck a deal whereby the Superior Food Corporation had permission to cut tunnels into a dozen and nine of their largely unused stations, provided that they placed a secure and attractive door over the opening when it was not in use. They could use the currently underutilized loading docks to package the children at no cost, provided that they cleaned up after themselves.

Superior Food would then pay normal rates to ship the dirt to the Borako Ocean Trench, to transport their machinery and personnel, and to get the juvenals to market, but these fees would be paid in packaged juvenals at a price of two dozen Ke each. The MagFloat Corporation would then sell these kids at a modest profit to their employees.

MagFloat also had plans to use the juvenals to promote long distance "Party Trips," in the hope of cutting into the long-distance trade, currently dominated by the airlines. The longest possible rail trip took five days. If a customer could enjoy a good party, and then eat a really big meal, she could sleep it off, and would be ready to do whatever she had to do at her destination, without the problems of jet lag.

"But Bronki," Dol said, "how are you going to make your usual kickback on all of this? There isn't any money involved!"

"Well, no, but a certain small number of the packaged children they receive will be delivered to my store. I'll get two per gross of what we pay them. There's always a way."

On Tuesday, Duke Dennon telephoned Kren, and asked him why all of his engineers were working on getting Kren's equipment ready for shipment.

"Your Grace, I think that Dol and Dako decided that your technical sorts needed something to do, and your engineers all offered to help out. I mean, I never agreed to pay them to do this."

"Well, don't you think that you should have asked me before you made use of my army?"

"I never intended to offend you, sir. Are you offended?"

"Well, not really, but you and I have a business arrangement." The duke said, "If you wanted something else, you should have discussed it with me, and not just let our subordinates go off on their own!"

"You are absolutely right, and I apologize. I'll see that this never happens again. However, it can't be good for morale to have troops who are absolutely bored, and I still could use their services. May they lend Dol a hand?"

"But I am paying each of those engineers a salary. If you want them, you should pay for them."

"Very well. The nature of having an army during peace-time is that you must pay for something that you aren't currently using. What if I were to pay you one third of their salaries, with the understanding that if they were ever needed by you, I would release them to you instantly. You would then still have your engineers when you needed them, but would be cutting your expenses by one third."

"And you would feed them while they were working for you?"

"Assuredly."

"Then make it half their salaries, and we have a deal."

"Excellent. I will of course be paying you for them in corporation stock, since you've already gotten most of my money."

"Humph. Okay, tell me which event you will be winning at this coming weekend, and we have a deal."

"I'll take the distance throw. But please, don't go betting another gross billion."

"I don't have a gross billion free anymore. My wager will be under a dozen billion."

"That won't depress the odds too badly."

"Very well, we have a deal. I'll write it up, and send it along with the deal we made last weekend. My courier will get there tomorrow evening."

"Excellent, Your Grace. Another thing. I'm going to be needing a fair number of unskilled workers, to herd and box up the juvenals for market. Would you be interested in renting me some of your ordinary soldiers, at the same rates?"

"Very well. But in a week's time, I'll expect to know about your next win in advance."

"We have an agreement."

On Thursday morning, the small tunneler was working on the first connection to a wintering center, which was projected to be completed within the week, being the shortest one.

On Friday afternoon, Kren had completed his sketches of the Research Center, to be placed near a railroad station in the center of his lands, and which had a wintering center near by. Besides the separate growing chambers for the various lines of juvenals, there was the genetic research building, an administration building, and very pleasant housing for twice as many workers as he could imagine needing.

These rather tall apartment buildings were to be equipped with "freight elevators," which were allowed by law, provided they each had a key-operated lock distributed only to certified movers. But since Kren was the law, and he was not averse to some illegal keys being distributed, he thought that the upper floors would soon be thought of as the most desirable. His own apartment would take up the entire top floor of the tallest building, and would be three times as big as Bronki's.

He gave his rough sketches to Dol, to have formal drawings made.

"Do it all to the standard building codes," Kren said, "But we don't have to bother with anybody's approval, since *we* are the law, hereabouts."

"Yes sir. But I've just completed my analysis of the costs of tunneling out floor space versus conventional construction, and you know? Once we have the tunneling machines, building underground is four times cheaper!"

"Now, that's good to hear. But our research workers are all going to be high-quality, well-educated individuals, and I think that they will prefer living and working aboveground. The shop rats can live and work in the tunnels, but the Research Center really ought to be aboveground."

"As you wish, sir."

"Good. Now, get all of the big tunneling machines working. And then start working on growing a lot of grass, underground."

The next weekend, Kren won at the distance throw for the second time in a row, on the theory that since they hadn't done this before, the odds should be higher. They weren't. The payoff was only two to one, and following his new policy, he only bet half of his ready cash on it. Nonetheless, he still made a billion Ke on the match. Dol, who was betting everything she had, made much more.

* * *

The week after saw their first shipments of children go out, a thousand to fill Bronki's new store, and three thousand as their payment to the MagFloat Corporation. The cold winter weather was closing in, but the wintering centers were still far from full, and they only had access to one of them. Next week the take would be much better.

They also broke ground on the Research Center. Construction would go on through the winter, with the workers in electrically heated suits. The first isolated breeding unit was to be completed by spring, and the whole complex was to be finished by midsummer.

Below ground, two of the big tunneling machines were in operation, filling hopper car after hopper car with dirt. MagFloat personnel connected them into gross-car-long unit trains, and sent them out at night when the shipping rates were lower.

Two more of the big tunnelers would be brought online each week. Fortunately, the equipment purchased from the duke had included a six-year supply of the metal coils used for making the tunnel linings, as well as the welding wire, and bottled argon used in the MIG welders that put them together, so this would not be a financial burden for a while.

Besides Duke Dennon's two gross of engineers, Kren now had six gross of regular troops on his payroll, in addition to almost two gross of workers that he had inherited from the duke when he had bought the land. In fact some three quarters of the native population on Kren's new lands were workers on his payroll. These workers maintained the wintering centers and the long grass fields above them, and they had to be paid in cash, not with company stock. The same was true for the genetics scientists Kren had hired. By Friday, Kren had to hire an accountant to keep tract of things, and she had to be paid in money, too.

The crews putting in the fencing had to have regular progress payments, as well, and soon they would be paying for the huge number of monochromatic lighting panels that they had on order.

And the Research Center had to be paid for in cash progress payments.

When the buildings that you are putting up are expected to last for many thousands of years without serious maintenance, construction costs are high. Kren was forced to buy stock in his own company with his own cash, to keep it liquid.

Neither Bronki nor Dol was the least bit interested in making any cash investments. Any money spent now on stock was that much less that they could use to bet with next weekend. They were both still saving everything they could, and betting it all on Kren's athletic prowess, in preparation for what they both knew would be a stock fight for membership on the board of directors of the Superior Food Corporation next year. Once that happened, the corporation would be rolling in cash, but until then, Kren saw some lean times ahead.

The next meet was an away game, and Kren won the accuracy throw, not quite breaking his old record. The odds only paid three for two.

Dol said that a billion here, a billion there, hey, it all added up. She now had more than twice the cash that he did.

Kren decided that, computing his projected expenses, he couldn't afford to play it safe any more. He'd have to go back to betting it all on every event, just to break even.

CHAPTER THIRTY-NINE

The Last War and Planetary Defenses
New Yugoslavia, 2213 A.D

Toward the end of the last war, our enemy, a renegade computer, as it turned out, had developed a method of destroying all of the Hassan-Smith transmitters and receivers on an entire planet. He had managed to do this to four of our colonized planets. He was too dangerous to leave alive, so I had fried him without finding out his secret.

Attempts to figure out how this had been accomplished had so far ended in failure. We even tried to duplicate the computer, and had tried to get it to develop the same technology, but no go.

The receivers had been placed in each solar system by a fleet of robot ships as they spread out from Earth. These ships never stopped at the solar system in question, they simply passed through at almost light speed, dropped a probe equipped with transceivers, and headed toward the next possible solar system.

But with *all* of the transmitters and receivers gone, the only way to get in contact with the cut-off planets was by ships moving at less than light speed.

Soon after the war, six new ships had been launched from the planets closest to each of our missing friends, each bringing transceivers with them.

Before their ships got to them, the inhabitants of New Erie had managed to build transceivers from scratch, and

261

reestablish contact with the rest of Human Space. The inhabitants and the Earthly invaders had worked out a truce, figuring to let the outcome of the war be settled somewhere else, as it probably already had been.

Now the first ship had gotten to New Israel. The Israelis had fought a six-year-long slugfest with Earth's abandoned forces, with things escalating until their population was down to one tenth of what it had been before the war. Earth's forces had been completely obliterated. Their once beautiful planet had been reduced to radioactive craters and scar tissue.

With hindsight, they would have been so much better off surrendering, since they would have ended up winning in any event. But some people just don't know *how* to quit.

Massive amounts of aid was now pouring into their planet, and what was left of them was being invited to join in the new political order.

The fate of the other two planets remains to be seen.

Our general staff had now seen to it that every inhabited planet had at least two disassembled transceivers hidden on it, along with assembly instructions. With them powered down, it was felt unlikely that any detection scheme could find and destroy them. If ever this transceiver-destroying technology was invented again by another enemy, we were ready for it. But it was much like locking the barn door after all the horses had escaped.

Ships were being launched very regularly from the New Yugoslavia system as well. Picket ships for our planetary defense system. Now that a duplicate set of production lines had been built, we were launching two a week.

The sixty ships for the Distant Early Warning Sphere were now all on their way, although it would be a few years before they got to their destinations. Once on station, they would each place over a thousand sensor clusters in their sector, to watch for incoming Mitchegai ships. These sensors also each contained a full-sized receiver, so that a counterattack could be launched through any one of them.

Also, every one of the ships and sensors would contain one of the microtransceivers that permitted small memory chips to be sent quickly to anywhere in Human Space. Up until now, these expensive items had been restricted to

Combat Control Computers, but in the future, I intended every one of our fighting machines to have one.

Every one of our ships and sensors would have an artificial intelligence aboard. Years ago, when the computers in all military machines had been upgraded from silicon chips to diamond ones, I'd bought up over a million of the old computers. There was no great need for cybernetic speed on either the ships or the sensors, and so when the silicon ladies volunteered for this duty, I gave them my blessings, and my thanks.

Our ships did not use the hydrogen-oxygen rockets that the old Earth ships still used. Cesium ion engines were cheaper to build and to keep supplied. New Kashubia had vast amounts of cesium available that nobody had ever figured a good use for. Now, they were mining it in great quantities.

At one light-year out from our sun, another sixty ships were being sent to make up the Comet Belt Sphere. It would have the same number of sensors as the DEW Sphere, but they would be planted four times more densely.

Additional spheres would be set up at a half light-year, a quarter light-year, and an eighth light-year.

Inside that, there would be a diffuse cloud of sensors throughout the solar system.

Then the planet itself would have three spheres of orbital defense, plus many other sensors in a loose cloud.

None of these ships and sensors would be armed, exactly, except for a massive self-destruct mechanism. They were there to detect the enemy, and to function as gateways where our fighting forces could exit into a wide variety of points. The plan was to let our forces go almost instantaneously to any point in the system where they were needed.

Getting those fighting forces together was another problem entirely.

Plans for our planetary defensive system were sent free to every planet in Human Space. We also offered a "Starter Kit" of basic machinery, so that they could do as we had done, using the fighting machines that they already had. We charged full price for that, but gave them credit on it.

More than half of the planets were building their own systems. As for the rest, well, we had done our best.

CHAPTER FORTY

FROM CAPTURED HISTORY TAPES,
FILE 1846583A ca. 1832 A.D.
BUT CONCERNING EVENTS OF UP TO
2000 YEARS EARLIER

Offers You Can't Refuse

Things started to settle down to a routine.

Dol made an inspection trip to the building and packaging site twice a week. Since his academic grades were now outstanding, sometimes Kren cut classes and went with her in the mornings, but not too often.

The design of the City of Dren was such that you could go almost everywhere by tunnel, and not have to expose yourself to the winter weather. Construction sites were something different. They had to wear heavy winter clothing and electrically heated underwear to go outside and inspect the progress of the construction work.

Kren found it almost as annoying as wearing armor. He vowed that when circumstances permitted, he would move to the tropics, where it was always warm, even if it was more expensive to live there.

Construction workers wore form-fitting, electrically heated garments in the wintertime, with safety helmets. Like most Mitchegai garments, these were color coded according to their specific trade. Heavy equipment operators wore black, plumbers wore brown, electricians red, and so forth. Their status and skill levels were displayed by the colors of their equipment belts.

In the summer, they might work nearly naked, but they still wore their belts and their color-coded safety helmets.

There was a separate construction language, Geno, but there were over a dozen dialects within this language that were almost languages in their own right.

There was an intricate cross-referencing between the various Mitchegai languages. An electrician, for example, could talk with an electrical engineer with little difficulty, but had trouble conversing with a hydraulics engineer, even though these two engineers could easily communicate with each other, and an electrician could always speak to a plumber.

There was no possibility of Kren's cutting his physical training classes, or his obligations to the director, so he always had to leave early in order to be back in Dren by seven, in the early afternoon.

Bronki ran the sales end of things fairly well, and sales increased, about one part in six, every week, and with very little spent on advertising. There was nothing on television, and only a few posters in the underground walkways.

One said, "The Superior Food Corporation now has a store in Dren! We have the best children at the best prices! Check us out! We're right under Bronki's Place! Or phone 24B9-129A3."

Soon, she was opening a second, larger store, on the other side of town.

"Have you heard the news?" Bronki said one evening.

When Kren said that he didn't usually pay any attention to that sort of thing, Bronki said, "The KUL and the PPG have just fought out a major war! When the KUL had the PPG down to a quarter of its original size, the PPG launched a poison gas attack on the KUL headquarters, effectively wiping them out! Now, the planetary police are attacking the PPG for their use of illegal weapons, and the PPG don't have a chance. It is expected that the City of Dren will be peaceful for a while, until some other gang moves in."

"Remarkable," Kren said. "And all of this for just a few Ke placed in the right places. You have much to be proud of, Bronki!"

"Oh, I am, but I don't dare brag about it. There are probably lots of survivors hiding in the basements, looking for someone to get even with!"

⁂   ⁂   ⁂

They found that one of Duke Dennon's captains, Yor, was very proficient at logistics, and a good manager besides. She was put in charge of production, and costs went down as production went up. Kren was afraid that before the year was out, he'd have to give her a hefty bonus, just in order to keep her.

And remarkably, under the efficient direction of Chief Engineer Dako, construction proceeded on schedule, and at, or even sometimes slightly under, budget.

Still, sales didn't begin to meet costs. And the betting odds on Kren continued to go down.

Dol's study of the statistical anomalies of the betting on an excellent, but erratic, athlete named Kren was published in *The Journal of Statistical Anomalies.* They charged two thousand Ke for this service, which Dol paid for herself to boost her academic career. Over six dozen popular magazines picked up on the story, including some of the majors, three of whom actually paid Dol a total of three thousand Ke for the privilege.

The written language of the Mitchegai was standardized, and absolutely phonetic. If you could speak it, you could read it.

It used three gross and six phonemes, each with its own symbol, a huge number by human standards. While humans, with all of their thousands of languages, use over six gross phonemes, the largest number used by any one language is less than a gross, and English uses only four dozen and four, and only half that number of symbols.

But since there were several dozen Mitchegai languages and many more dialects of them, most popular magazines were written in Deno, the common tongue.

Dol appeared on eight television talk shows, two of which were broadcast planet-wide, telling about her findings, but none of them paid her. Nonetheless, any publicity was good for one's career.

It did Kren no good at all. If anything, the publicity enhanced Kren's fame far more than Dol's. He had become too popular. Apparently, gamblers didn't care about studies or logic. They bet on their gut feelings. They kept on betting on Kren. The odds kept going down.

Kren knew that the thing to do was to lose for three or four weeks straight, to disillusion his fans. But he couldn't afford to do that. Building expenses were too high.

Betting his entire purse every weekend, he was not quite able to keep up with the spending that his building plans required. His purse started shrinking.

Then he got a letter from the City of Dren Internal Revenue Command. They had been watching his gambling income, and demanded that he pay them two billion Ke in taxes. Failure to do so immediately would result in his Death by Fire.

At this point, Kren didn't have two billion Ke, not in ready cash, anyway.

He promptly called a meeting of the board of directors of the Superior Food Corporation.

When Bronki and Dol were gathered in Kren's sitting room, surrounded by display cases of athletic medals and strange weapons, he explained the situation to them, and then said, "I take it that the IRC really is as ruthless as they claim to be?"

"I'm afraid so," Bronki said. "What's more, they like to make an example of high profile individuals. They feel it is good advertising, the better to intimidate the ordinary Mitchegai. And you, Kren, are about as high profile as you can get."

"I see. I'm sure that you will both agree that without me here and alive to run it, this corporation is not likely to be successful. It desperately needs cash, to meet current and future expenses, and to loan to me, interest free, so that I can satisfy the IRC. Neither of you has put any significant amount of cash into the company account, even though you have both made fabulous sums betting on me. This is because you both anticipate a stock fight just before the next board elections. What I propose is that you each buy four billion Ke worth of company stock today. This will rescue both me and the company, and still keep your race fair."

Bronki said, "It's really all your fault, Kren. Your building plans were entirely too ambitious. You should have done things spread out over several years."

"I had assumed that the betting odds would stay at least at the two to one level. Also, you both agreed with me on the building plans. Now, I need you each to contribute four billion Ke," Kren said.

"That's a lot of money, sir," Dol said.

"Yes, surely you can think of some other alternative," Bronki said.

"I have, but my only obvious alternative would be disadvantageous to me since it would result in my loss of the valuable services provided by both of you. To put it simply, I could kill you both, and by eating certain portions of your brains, I could obtain the information needed to gain access to all of your accounts. Thus, I would have all of the money that both of you possess, satisfying both the corporation's needs and the IRC demands. However, I think that my original proposal is superior from all of our viewpoints."

"I think that you are absolutely correct, sir," Dol said quickly. "After all, there is no point in being a director of a nonexistent corporation, and I really prefer being alive to the alternative. Would a check suffice, or do you really need cash?"

"A check would be fine, and there's still time to get it to the bank today."

"My check will be there at the same time, Kren, to help you in this time of need. After all, what else are *good friends* for?" Bronki said.

Kren said, "I was sure that you would both see the wisdom of my suggestions."

"Most assuredly, sir."

They wrote up the checks and deposit slips right there, plus a check for two billion Ke from the corporation to Kren's private account, signed by all three of them.

As Dol prepared to run it all to the bank before it closed, Kren said, "I have one other announcement. The payoff on our winnings has gotten extremely low, and Dol's excellent campaign to educate my fans has proved to be unsuccessful. Therefore, with the director's permission, I intend to have a losing streak. I will not be winning anything for the next three or four weeks. Let's see if that gets the odds up to where they should be."

"Yes, I think that in the long run, that might be the most profitable thing to do," Bronki said. "If the odds get back up to five to one, we could recoup our losses at a single meet."

Early the next morning, Kren verified that the checks had all cleared, and then personally paid the IRC their demanded taxes, being careful to get a receipt. With some organizations, even a warrior must tread carefully.

But by this time next year, Kren vowed to himself, *I will be officially living on my own lands, and not subject to City of Dren taxes. Surely, a residence there, and a year-long commuter's ticket, both costing infinitely less than two billion Ke, will satisfy the judges.*

That evening, Bronki reminded him, politely, that he also had to pay the taxes and utilities on the two country houses that she had given him.

Kren grumbled, but paid.

"Ah, Kren," the director said, "I take it you have your 'prediction' for next weekend?"

"Yes, sir. With your permission, I won't win anything."

"Indeed?"

"Sir, the payoffs on my wins have gotten so bad that it isn't worth betting on me any more. When you are only getting five for four, and there is always a chance of something going wrong, well, why bother? I mean, what if some gang of muggers breaks my arm? Why take the risk? I figure if I have a losing streak for three or four weeks, my idiot fans will stop driving the odds down, and maybe we can make some decent money."

"You know, I've been thinking the same thing. I saw Dool on the television, with that study of hers. That was your idea?"

"Yes, sir, but it didn't work."

"I knew it wouldn't. If there's anything stupider than athletes, it's the trash who bet on them. Okay, take a break, but keep an eye on the odds. You still have to show up for the games, of course, so you can lose in public, but if you want to cut a few training sessions, feel free."

"Thank you sir. I appreciate that. I need a rest."

"You're welcome. Have you heard anything about Kodo?"

"No sir. I've asked a few discreet questions about him, when I could work it into a conversation, but Kodo seems to have left the planet."

"I doubt it. Even the Sky Pilots wouldn't take that pile of burning trash. Dismissed."

* * *

Kren left the athletic center early, thinking about a good meal and a long sleep. Dol and Bronki were not home when he got there, so he phoned Bronki's store to order up a child to eat.

"Yes, sir! And what size did you want?" a pleasant voice on the phone answered back.

This was actually Kren's first contact with the store. Normally, Dol handled this sort of thing for him.

"Well, what sizes do you have?"

"The standard size is our 'Perfect Party Snack' series, which run from five dozen to seven dozen pounds. They go for two pounds per Ke. If you have a larger group, or are really, *really* hungry, the 'Belly Busters' go up to a gross pounds or even more at three pounds per Ke. Or for a more intimate party, you can buy a 'Munchkin' as small as two dozen pounds, at a pound and a half per Ke," the cheerful voice said. "There is also our 'Special Selection' series, but you have to come down here personally and make your selection. They run as high as a pound per Ke."

"That's interesting. I think I'll come down there."

"I'll be waiting for you!"

Since the outlet was directly below him, he was in the store in a few minutes. He was the only customer there, and with only a single shop girl in attendance.

"It's rather quiet here," Kren said.

"Well, this is early on a Tuesday afternoon, sir. Come here on a Friday night, and you'll find a long line of customers and two dozen shop girls worn to a frazzle! Oh my! You're Kren, aren't you! The famous athlete!"

"I'm guilty of that, yes. It's a rough job, but somebody has to do it." Kren found his fans to be annoying, and tried to avoid them. "You were going to show me this 'Special Selection' thing?"

"Yes, sir. You know, I always bet on you!"

"Yes, and you lose money doing it, just like everybody else."

"Yes, I suppose that I do. But it's so much fun, cheering you on, that I can't help myself. There's a gang of us who get together every Saturday, at the arenas or around a television set, on the away games. And sometimes I win."

"You can have no idea how depressing it is to cost my supporters money. But so many of you are betting so much on me that it drives the odds down!"

"Yes, I read something about that in a magazine. But you shouldn't let it bother you. It's our money, after all."

"It bothers me anyway, and I wish you'd all stop doing it. Now, show me these 'Specials.'"

The shop girl led Kren into a large room with about two dozen youngsters on display. About half were in attractive cages, some were clamped down on party tables, and the rest were held vertically, standing with their feet fastened on top of short pedestals, and with their arms clamped to the wall.

All sizes were represented, and these particularly attractive children had all been carefully washed and then coated with a light layer of oil, which made them glisten nicely. The spotlights on them glowed warmly.

A smaller one caught his eye. She was a lovely little thing, looking eagerly at him as she stood on her pedestal with her back to the wall.

He ran his hand gently down her side, and checked the flesh on her buttocks. She actually smiled at him.

"How much is this one?" Kren asked.

"She weighs five dozen and three pounds, and goes for a pound and a half per Ke. That's three dozen and six Ke, sir."

"I'll take her."

"Very good, sir. Did you want a box to put her in?"

"Does that cost extra?"

"No, but there's an eight Ke deposit on the box. You will get that back when you return it."

That was twice what they were paying for the things new, and Kren thought that to be proper.

The Mitchegai, with their long-term outlook on things, do not go in for disposable packaging, as a rule. Everything is carefully recycled.

"Well, I live just upstairs from here, and this one seems pretty gentle, so I'll forego the box." Kren gave her his credit card.

"Oh! You live at Bronki's address! I'd better check something." She checked quickly at a list behind the counter. "Yes, you are listed as a 'Friend of Bronki's.'"

"How much extra do I have to pay for that privilege?"

"Nothing, silly! Excuse me. I mean, sir. No, you get a dozen per gross discount," she said.

She deducted the proper amount from his card and returned it, along with a receipt. "Before you go, could I have your autograph?"

"Are you going to stop betting on me?"

"No, sir."

"Then you won't get an autograph. Unlock the child I just bought," Kren said.

As she did so, he petted his purchase to make sure that she was calm. He lifted her off the pedestal and put his hand gently around her neck, his claws almost touching, to be certain that the naked little child wouldn't try to run away. She walked obediently with him back up to Bronki's apartment, sometimes looking up at him and smiling. She even waited trustingly while he let go of her to get his card out to unlock the door.

Once inside, he let her take a long drink of water from the fountain, and once again, she smiled at him.

A fine, gentle child, Kren thought.

A human might have considered keeping her as a pet, but Kren, of course, wasn't human.

A few hours later, he expanded his earlier thought to, *A fine, gentle, and delicious child!*

And she had screamed so nicely when he ate her alive. When alone, Kren preferred to dispense with the civilized niceties like knives and branding irons, and to just chew his meat right off the bone, the way he did when he was a slave in the mines.

CHAPTER FORTY-ONE

FROM CAPTURED HISTORY TAPES,
FILE 1846583A ca. 1832 A.D.
BUT CONCERNING EVENTS OF UP TO
2000 YEARS EARLIER

Tunneling to War

Losing a match didn't bother Kren, since he got no joy from winning one. If anything, it was a bonus, since he didn't have to show up at the awards ceremonies, and thus he had his Sundays free.

After five weeks of relaxing, and paying more attention to the business than to his academic and athletic duties, the odds on Kren's winning an event had gone up to between five and seven to one.

The posted odds were always just rough approximations. The actual payoffs were computed to six duodecimal places.

Kren told the director that he would win at the accuracy event.

He also planned to win at the distance event immediately afterward, but kept this a secret, except for telling Bronki and Dol. The close spacing between the events meant that very few betters would be able to wager on the second event, based on Kren's performance in the first. The odds were not likely to go down much.

He made special arrangements with his bookie to have his winnings on accuracy to be bet automatically on distance, and since he was a very good customer, who had made the bookie a considerable fortune, this was readily agreed to.

The bookies did not care whether their customers won or lost. All bookies were tied into a planet-wide, computerized syndicate that shared out the wins and losses. The bookies took a nine per gross cut of all bets, wired the rest to the syndicate, which kept three per gross, and then distributed the pot, which was automatically wired back to the winners. The central syndicate didn't know who bet what, but of course, the bookies did, and they all placed side bets of their own. However, they didn't normally pass tips out for fear of reducing their own winnings.

Kren's bookie had learned that it was wise to bet the way Kren was betting.

By delaying payment on his debts to the construction contractors, Kren was also able to bet over four billion of the corporation's money on the double win.

Bronki and Dol used the same deal with the same bookie, betting such money as they had left over after paying their own taxes.

, The javelin accuracy event paid five to one, and distance paid seven. The result was that Kren's personal account increased to over three dozen billion, and the corporation's account to over four times that amount.

Afterward, Kren met with his bookie, and suggested that she invest a dozen billion Ke in Kren's corporation.

"But I don't have anything like a dozen billion Ke!" the bookie protested.

"That is unfortunate, because if you don't make this excellent, but long-term investment, I will be forced to take my future business elsewhere," Kren explained.

The bookie made the investment, though she was not happy about it.

The director of athletics was also unhappy.

"Burn you, Kren! You never said that you would win at *two* events on Saturday!"

"I didn't intend to, sir. But at the distance event, just when I was letting fly, my foot slipped on something, maybe some juvenal droppings, and I had to throw too hard to keep myself from falling on my face! It was an accident! Surely, the tapes of my performance will prove that!"

Kren had indeed faked slipping on that throw, but the director said that he needed more practice, and insisted that until further notice, he would attend all physical training sessions.

Kren thought that for well over a gross billion Ke, he could put up with a lot, and making the payments with the late penalties to his contractors didn't hurt him at all.

The next day, since the odds on him were down to typically two to one, Kren proposed that they slough off for at least three weeks, and the director agreed.

The rest of the year went that way. It was more profitable to win big once every three to five weeks than it was to win small every week.

Bronki completed her first paper on chaos theory, and it was enthusiastically accepted by their world's mathematical community. She was soon attending conventions around the planet as an Honored Guest Speaker, and was giving a course on chaos theory at the College of Mathematics to a large, packed auditorium, three days a week. Of course, all of this paid well.

And she did this while she kept the sales of children well above their ambitious early projections. She soon had six stores scattered around the City of Dren.

The early experiments with growing grass under artificial, monochromatic light had turned out extremely well. The lights used were actually twice as bright as normal sunlight at the wavelength useful to plants, but the total amount of energy radiated was only one-sixth that of sunlight. The result was that it was more than twice as productive as it would have been in a well-watered field at noon in the tropics, and without heat stress.

Grass had no difficulty adopting to a two-dozen-hour day, since it sometimes did that already in high latitudes, near the poles. There were always just the right amounts of water and nutrients available to it. The light was directly overhead, from a diffused area all the time, so the leaves did not have to waste energy turning to the sun. There were no cloudy days, no evenings, no nights. There were no juvenals walking on it, hurting the roots. There were no winters, when nothing grew.

The net result was that the annual production was a dozen and a half times higher per square yard than it was in the average field. It had to be mowed twice daily, or it would turn rank. Also, some research studies indicated that if the carbon dioxide content of the air could be quadrupled, production might be doubled once again.

Kren was pleased. Especially so since the underground grass-growing project was already well under way. Had growing grass in tunnels proved to be inefficient, a huge fortune would have been lost.

The MagFloat railroad system cut Kren's lands into vaguely hexagonal areas an average of six dozen miles across. This was so that they could meet their ancient political mandate of having a station within a brisk day's walk of every point on the planet.

Since it was convenient to have the production tunnels at the same level as the railroad tracks, and since, in theory, the MagFloat Corporation owned the subsurface soil under their tracks, Kren and Dol had picked a hexagon in the center of their property. They started to bore a tunnel from a station at the east of it to one at the west, a distance of six dozen and eleven miles.

The tunneling machines were not capable of starting a new tunnel at right angles to the one they were in, but the cutters were capable of pivoting enough to start a tunnel at half of that angle. As additional tunnelers were brought on line, this resulted in an array of tunnels that a human would have called a herringbone pattern, or perhaps something that looked like the shaft and veins of a feather.

Since the Mitchegai had never heard of a herringbone or a bird's feather, they just called it Dol's Design.

They bought roll-forming machinery to take a coil of the almost immortal metal alloy the Mitchegai used and shape it into a flooring panel. This was followed by a punch press to cut the floors to length and shape the ends to be welded to the tunnel walls. Lighting panels were then welded on the bottoms of all but the lowest ones, and wired up.

Once a tunnel was dug, a large assembly machine went in and welded in floors, attached side rails for the mowers, covered the floors with dirt, and spread grass seed. Water pipes, air ducts, and power conduits were installed.

The rail to the right that supported the mower was also a high-pressure water line that doubled as the electrical power common wire. The rail to the left doubled as the high-tension electrical conduit, and the rest of the structure was also a ground line. Kren thought that Dol had come up with an efficient design.

In a few months, there were two dozen of these assembly machines working, manned by Duke Dennon's soldiers, and supervised by his engineers.

The twelve-yard-high tunnels had ten floors in them, with only a half a yard between them for the mower to work in. If maintenance was ever required, the workers would have to be dragged in on a sled, lying on their backs, behind the mower working at that level.

The first few gross yards of each tunnel had fewer floors, and would be used to house the juvenals who ate the grass.

Using all seven big tunnelers, they figured to have one layer of tunnels, over ten thousand miles of them, completed in four years, and the whole thing in full production a year after that. Completed, it should produce over three and a half million large juvenals per year for market. It would produce more than that if indeed juvenals were more efficient at growing when they didn't have to spend most of their time and energy hunting for food and water. And much more than that if their selective breeding program bore fruit.

Dol said, "You know, sir, three and a half million a year at two dozen Ke each is really not a very good return on our investment. The bank would pay us better interest."

"Right now, yes," Kren agreed. "But I'm thinking long-term. Right now, the price of children is very low, because so many of them are available, free for the taking, in the countryside. But as we start producing more, the population of this planet will grow, and those available free won't be enough to feed it. At that point, we will be able to raise our prices, considerably."

"I see. But is our population actually limited by the food supply? Will the addition of more food really cause the population to grow?"

"If the population doesn't grow, we will have to take steps to make it grow. I can think of many ways to do this. We might become righteous warriors who will eliminate the criminal elements in the cities. They seem to be currently doing a lot to keep the population down. However, from this point on, it will be company policy to do whatever we can to increase the planetary population."

"Very well, sir. Then again, this one hexagon would feed an army of almost a quarter of a million warriors," Dol said.

"True. If we can't take this planet economically, we can always do it militarily."

"Still, there is a lot more money to be made gambling, sir. The citizens of this planet spend more than seven times as much on gambling as they do on food."

"Just now, there is, and this will continue so long as I am an undergraduate, another five years at most. After that, well, the betting on professional sports is not nearly as good as that on collegiate sports. I'll get involved with them only if I have to. I understand that on some planets, it is different, but not here. We must see to it that we make our fortune at gambling now, and then that we have a sustainable income that allows for considerable expansion later. The current profits on food might be low, but they are dependable. And in time, the food to gambling ratio just might reverse."

"I suppose that you are right, sir."

"I am."

The collector path stretched for half the length of Kren's property. This was like a double fish-weir fence that allowed juvenals to enter in between them, but not to go out. Additional sections of fish weir between them forced the children to walk to a central processing station, where some were selected for packaging, and the rest were released to grow bigger. Watering troughs were placed along both sides of both fences to keep the youngsters fresh and the losses down.

By early spring, about the time when both the outer fence and the collector path had been completed and paid for, the last tunnel from a train station to a wintering center was completed. The plans were to mothball the small tunneler.

At this point, Duke Dennon called and said that he wanted to borrow it.

"Of course, Your Grace. I'm sure we can work something out. How long would you be needing it for?"

"Oh, probably for several years, actually."

"Hmmm. Then you would probably be better off buying it than renting it. I could sell it to you at two dozen per gross off list price."

"Kren, that price is atrocious! You just bought it from me for nine dozen per gross off list!"

"Well, if you needed it, why did you sell it to me in the first place?"

"Because I didn't need it then, but I do need it now."

"Oh. What are you planning to do with it anyway?"

"I don't want to talk about that over the phone, and anyway, I'll be needing your help on this. Can you visit me in the near future?"

"Certainly. If I took an express train right after physical training tomorrow, I could be there by twelve in the evening. I wouldn't have to leave until five, an hour before noon, the next morning."

"I'll have a servant waiting at the station when you arrive."

"That would be excellent, Your Grace."

Kren booked a private cabin because he didn't want to risk having to sit next to one of his fans for two hours. Anyway, he billed it to the corporation, which was currently flush.

"So, Your Grace, what is this secret thing that you are planning on doing with the small tunneler?" Kren asked as they sat down privately to share a small snack. He was proudly wearing the sword that the duke had given him.

"War, of course. What else?"

"You are planning to take a tunneler to a war? Wouldn't that be against the Laws of War?" These laws strictly forbade the use of powered vehicles of any sort in warfare, either for fighting or for transportation.

"It certainly would, but I don't plan to use it directly, of course. But what if I were to discover that an ancient, forgotten tunnel just happened to go from beneath my palace to beneath Duke Tendi's castle? If I were to then march my men through this tunnel, and break through to his basement, would I bring down the bombs of the Space Mitchegai on me? I think not."

"So you need me to make this tunnel for you. Well, I presume that you have a map around here? Then let's take a look at what we're talking about."

In a few hours it was decided that Kren would run a big tunnel across one of the hexagons of his property that was closest to the duke's palace. A small tunnel would be run from this large one, and the dirt from both would be shipped out together by the railroad. This was to cover the fact that they were digging the small tunnel at all, if anybody checked the MagFloat Corporation's records.

A total of eight gross miles of small tunnel would be required, going entirely across the Dennon's lands, under Duke Tendi's castle, and considerably beyond that. There would be a maze at both ends of the tunnel with a series of deadly traps to discourage further exploration.

It would then be cleaned, all equipment would be removed, and it would be sealed up at Kren's end, beyond the maze. A mixture of corrosive gasses would be injected into the system to give the tunnel's metal walls the patina of great age.

Kren estimated that they could have the work completed within thirty weeks, if there were no hitches. If they ran into unusual soil conditions, hard rock, or underground water, it would take longer and cost more. At worst case, the battle might have to be delayed until the following winter.

Then, in a few months, when the gas had time to dissipate, some of Duke Dennon's workers would just happen to be digging a well, and accidentally find the ancient tunnel system. Naturally, he would have it explored and mapped, regretfully losing a few soldiers in the wicked traps in the mazes.

And in the coming winter, when most armies were standing down, Dennon would use it to attack his old enemy, Duke Tendi.

"Kren, I like it! Now, what would you want to dig this tunnel for me?"

"Well, first, I would expect to be reimbursed, in cash, not check or an electronic transfer, but actual cash money, for all of my expenses, the largest of which will be for paying the MagFloat Corporation for hauling away all of the dirt."

"That would be acceptable."

"Then, in the fall, I will owe you a gross million Ke, my annual payment for your military protection," Kren said. "I will want you to take that payment in my company's stock, instead of cash, and I will want you to continue doing so for the next two dozen years."

"If you'll tell me when you next intend to win at an athletic event, you have a deal."

"Very good, but there's one more thing that I want."

"Indeed? And what is that?" Dennon asked.

"I want to come along when you attack Duke Tendi! I enjoy a good fight."

"Your aid would be most welcome! Okay, we have a deal, but we'd better not put this one in writing!"

"Excellent! Now, let's finish off this party snack. The poor thing must be feeling very neglected," Kern said.

CHAPTER FORTY-TWO

The Weapons of War
New Yugoslavia, 2214 A.D.

Things progressed, but the important thing that happened this year was that my loving wife, Kasia, gave birth to a magnificent baby boy, our fifth. She also said that enough was enough, and that if I couldn't give her at least one girl, she was going to give up on it.

I said that I would have loved to have had a little girl, but I didn't have much say in the matter. She was just going to have to take it up with God.

She said that she would do just that, and until He answered, she was going on the pill.

Well, I loved her, and five really was a houseful.

Another of our lost planets had been found. New Palestine. Our ship got there to find everyone, both on our side and theirs, dead. Somebody had made a deadly virus and let it loose. Our intelligent machines were working on resurrecting the planet, but until the virus was eliminated, people dared not return, nor could we permit the electronic people to return to us. Repopulating the planet was being debated.

The basic weapon of the Human Army was the tank. This was essentially a well-armored box that contained a muon-exchange fusion power supply, a series of computers, one of which was intelligent enough to pass for a human being, and was smarter in some ways. It had a coffin that contained a real human, together with a life-support system capable of keeping him or her alive indefinitely. The human floated in an aqueous liquid that protected him from shocks and accelerations of up to fifty Gs.

This observer was linked through cranial and spinal inductors to the tank's computers, which could keep him in Dream World, living at thirty times the speed that he could live at in the world outside.

There was also a combat mode, where he became essentially a single entity with his tank, and lived at typically fifty-five times as fast as normal, depending on the individual.

On a planet surface, the tank used a track-laying MagLev system that laid magnetic bars before it, floated over them, and then pulled them in to lay them in front again. On a metallic surface, it could magnetize the metal under it, dispense with the bars, and travel much faster. On a real MagLev track, and in a vacuum, it could hit three thousand kilometers an hour.

A wide variety of weapon and propulsion systems could be magnetically bonded to the tank, depending on the mission. A tank could function as a land weapon, a machine for tunneling beneath the earth, an aircraft, a submarine, or a space ship.

As I saw it, the next war, or at least the early phases of it, would be fought in space. Some new strap-ons were in order.

Up until now, traveling in space in a tank involved using a hydrogen-oxygen rocket capable of giving you a thrust of forty Gs. It was fed through a pair of Hassan-Smith transporters from a fuel dump somewhere nearby. The transmitters were expensive, which means that you couldn't have very many of them. Also, the rockets were very bright and very noticable.

The captured Mitchegai ship had taught us a few things about ion drives, and New Kashubia had a major surplus of cesium available, a metal that was easily ionized, and very massive.

The new engines required less than three percent of the fuel of the old ones, and a single transmitter could keep thirty-five of them fed.

The old tanks had only speed-of-light communications available. An expensive microtransceiver that sent tiny memory chips had been invented, and I resolved that every one of my tanks would have one. I had a production line of our own built to insure this, and damn the bureaucrats in New Kashubia. Now, every single fighting unit could communicate with headquarters.

Our main weapon, the rail gun, had proved to be completely ineffective against the Mitchegai. Our secondary weapon, the X-ray laser, had worked, but only when used in mass firings. We now had the Disappearing Gun, a gift from the Tellefontu, and I planned to have ninety percent of my people equipped with it. Eight percent would have X-ray lasers, and the rest, rail guns. You never can tell.

And there was a wide variety of rockets, drones, mines, and antipersonnel weapons that we had in stock that might prove useful.

Everything military now was deep below the ground. Using the Hassan-Smith transporters, we could get to any point in Human Space in a hurry, but they'd have a hell of a time getting to us.

When the Mitchegai came, I hoped that we would be ready.

CHAPTER FORTY-THREE

FROM CAPTURED HISTORY TAPES,
FILE 1846583A ca. 1832 A.D.
BUT CONCERNING EVENTS OF UP TO
2000 YEARS EARLIER

A Cunning Scheme

The next morning, Duke Dennon mentioned that he had been able to purchase six more armored, but defective, space suits, and bemoaned the fact that there were so few of them on the market.

"Well then, why don't you make your own?" Kren asked.

"Make a space suit? Do you realize the level of technology that requires?"

"A space suit, yes. But all *you* need is a suit of armor! It doesn't have to be airtight. It doesn't have to provide the wearer with air to breathe. It doesn't have to be heated to bear the cold of dark space, or cooled to take the heat of the naked sun. All it has to do is to keep your soldiers from being cut by your enemy's weapons! Look, you already have a perfect pattern for what you need. You have some old space suits. Take one of them apart, give the three dozen or so pieces to some of your excellent engineers . . ."

"There are six dozen major pieces in a space suit, not counting the fasteners, Kren."

"Whatever! That means that they will have to make up six dozen sets of stamping dies, at a few thousand Ke each, unless they decide that they can do it themselves. Then, you buy a few stamping presses, and have your soldiers operate them. You'll have enough armor for your whole army in a dozen weeks or so."

"Do you really think that this is possible?"

"You've got the money, you've got the workers, and you have a product sample! What more do you need?"

"Would you handle this for me?"

"If you want to give me your money, I'll take it. But I'll just turn the whole project over to your chief engineer, who is currently working for me. You've already got the talent. Use it!"

"Somehow, I'd feel better if you handled this."

"As you wish, Your Grace. We'll set up your armor factory in your huge basement here, since I've emptied much of the machinery out of it. My price will be cost plus one third, to be paid to me personally in money, cash or check."

"That would be adequate," the duke said.

Kren left to catch his train, shaking his head. How such an excellent leader could have so little confidence in his own troops was beyond imagination. But since he insisted, Kren would take his money.

Kren filled Dol in on the two new projects.

"For the armor, just give the project to Kren's chief engineer, and let her run with it. See to it that the book-keeping on this project is kept separate from everything else."

"Easily done, sir."

"For the tunnel, well, we'll just call it the 'Exploratory Tunnel,' and tell the few workers involved that it's company confidential. Nothing super secret, but we're just examining soil conditions for future grass-growing tunnels. Also, there just might be some valuable minerals out there, and if we find any, we don't want anybody else to know about it. Even the workers operating the small tunneler shouldn't know what they are really doing, or even where they are. Don't give them any maps. Just give them short charts of angles and distances, enough to keep them busy for a week or so. And get the old charts back as you give them the new ones. Also, I'll want separate book-keeping on this project as well, with nothing concerning the exploratory tunnel to ever be put on any computer. Just one book for expenses, something that can be destroyed easily. No side notes may be written. All of your sketches must be destroyed immediately. You and I and Duke Dennon will know what is really going on here. Nobody else!"

"I understand, since I don't want to be bombed from space, either! But, sir, is this project really worth the risk?"

"I think that it is, both financially, and because Duke Dennon is very important to our entire endeavor."

"Very well. You are the boss. I'll get right on it, sir."

Kren's scientists got the ancient DNA lab set up, and to the wonderment of all, they managed to get most of the equipment working. Only two small pieces of gear had to be built anew from ancient plans. The first project he gave them was himself.

"I don't know why I am such an outstanding athlete, but I want to find out. I am positive that it has something to do with this body, and not my brain. Take some tissue samples, and see what you can learn," Kren said to them.

For the six weeks prior to the Planetary Collegiate Championships, Kren won nothing at all, not even a copper third place medal. For the championships, where the amount of money bet would be vastly greater than at any ordinary meet, he made arrangements with his bookie to win sequentially at fencing, accuracy, and distance, and bet half of his considerable personal fortune and most of his corporation's ready cash on the outcome.

He won all three events, setting new planetary records in javelin distance and accuracy. More importantly, he walked away with enough money to keep his corporation well funded for the next five years.

Kren promptly authorized the purchase of the machinery required to make their own monochromatic lighting panels, cutting their marginal costs by three quarters on this expensive item.

Saying that a victory celebration was in order, Kren invited three dozen of the university's best female athletes to a week-long party. Kren's prestige being what it was, every one of them was happy to attend.

The party started with a chartered MagFloat train consisting of an engine and three club cars to take them and a few carefully selected party snacks on the two-hour trip to Kren's Research Center. They were all laughing hilariously when the train pulled up, not to the passenger station, but to the loading docks, where there was an entrance to the Research Center.

On the loading docks, over a gross of workers were injecting children with knockout drugs, putting them into boxes, and loading the boxes into railroad box cars for shipment to Bronki's stores. It was an efficient process, and Kren proudly showed his slightly tipsy guests through the operation, quoting statistics about the huge numbers of youngsters that he had shipped out to date.

They then went through a series of huge, noisy, metal-lined tunnels where conveyor belts whizzed by full of dirt that was on its way to hopper cars that would be dumped into an ocean trench. From there, they went through a door that Kren unlocked with both his credit card and a mechanical key, and then up a freight elevator to what Kren privately called his "Breeding Room."

"Here we are, ladies! Our own private party room, but one big enough to hunt in!"

The room was huge. It measured two gross yards to the side, the ceiling was six yards above the grass, and it was covered with growing lights. The monochromatic lights were turned off now, but enough normal, solar spectrum lights were on to provide adequate lighting.

Six dozen children of various ages were grazing, foolishly unconcerned by their arrival.

Six party tables were clustered at one side of the room, complete with knives and a few electric irons.

"The floor is bouncy!" one of the athletes shouted, running across the room.

"Yes," Kren said. "That's real grass, growing on top of a tank of water that's six yards deep. I was afraid that it wouldn't be solid enough to walk on in time, but there it is!"

"I thought that this would be a more formal affair," another athlete said.

"No, I wanted to do something really unusual. Something fun! So, the party has begun! Pick a snack that suits you, and run her down! Strap the child to one of the party tables available, and we'll all chow down! And if we eat all of these, I can order up some more! Now let's see who gets the first scream, and who gets the best one!"

It was pleasantly warm in the big room, and when Kren doffed his clothing, the others did so as well, as he had planned, all the better to ensure that all of their eggs dropped on the grass.

Most of the party guests took off running after the children, and over two dozen were caught. Most of them were soon released, to be caught again later, when the first six occupied all of the party tables. Soon, six children were screaming in pain, to the applause of the party goers.

Kren circulated, spreading his sperm around. This room and this party were a refinement of his earlier plans for breeding more bodies like the one he wore. Here, inside of this fairly natural environment, their eggs and his sperm could interact, and a large number of grubs would be the result.

When the grubs were ready to become pollywogs, they had only to eat through the grass to get to the pool below. And when the pollywogs were ready to become juvenals, it would be a simple matter for them to eat their way back up to the air.

In a natural environment, on dry land, very few of them would have made it, but here, Kren reasonably expected to get a large number of them for testing.

The whole room had been built under stringent conditions, in the dead of winter, with every worker having her sexual organs carefully covered. Kren himself had filled the tank with distilled water and chemical fertilizers. He had spread the grass seed on the surface personally, and since that time, no one else had been permitted in the "Breeding Room."

Nonetheless, a certain amount of contamination was inevitable. Also, many of his own kids would doubtless prove to be unsuitable. Therefore, every single juvenal would be carefully genetically tested, and only the best would be allowed to live.

As the party became more boisterous, some of Kren's athletic guests began jumping up and down on the grass-covered water, generating waves that spilled the party tables and knocked some of the other ladies down. They were trying to figure out the right timing to bounce themselves ever higher in the air, trying to touch the ceiling.

Soon over a dozen of them were jumping up and down in the same spot, and the grass below them gave way. They went right through, and ended up below the water.

Their fellow party mates, who were more than slightly annoyed at their antics, laughed at them, literally rolling on the ground. No one was worried about them, since Mitchegai are naturally aquatic. Their webbed toes help to make them natural swimmers, and when necessary, a Mitchegai can go without air for a long time.

Kren laughed along with the rest of his fellow athletes. Nonetheless, rather than risk losing a third of the eggs he wanted to fertilize, he ran back to where he had dumped his clothes and retrieved the sword that Duke Dennon had given him.

He cut the hole in the grass much bigger, so that enough light would get through for his guests to find their way to the surface, and threw the mats of grass to the juvenals who eagerly started to eat them.

"Come on in, Kren!" the first one said as she bobbed to the surface. "The water is just the right temperature!"

"I will! Right after we're sure that none of you idiots have killed yourselves!"

A head count soon proved that they were all alive and happy, even the one whom Kren had accidentally cut while chopping the hole in the grass. They decided the wound wasn't serious enough to need stitching up, so the party went on. Infections didn't happen on a Mitchegai planet.

Kren jumped in, followed by the rest of the guests. Again, Kren wasn't worried. Eggs floated, and so did grubs.

This was actually the first time in his life that Kren had been in the water, but swimming came naturally to a Mitchegai. He loved it, with the breathing exhaust vents bubbling around his waist. He vowed to himself that in his new apartment, being built two dozen stories above them, he would have a big swimming pool in the main living room.

Hours later, with the party snacks mostly eaten, with only one who was still alive and whimpering pleasantly, Kren and his guests fell asleep, scattered on the warm grass.

The next afternoon, half of his guests were still asleep, but a few, including Kren, had been more moderate in their eating.

One of the athletes said to Kren, "So just what is it that you are really doing here?"

"Would you believe that I am relaxing in the presence of good friends after almost a year's hard work?"

"No. You are obviously plotting something."

"Is that necessarily bad?" Kren asked.

"Not necessarily. Tell me about it."

"Well, first off, I'd have to swear you to secrecy, and you would have to agree that if you ever broke this oath, you would permit me to kill you. I mean, I'd kill you anyway, but it's so much nicer to have the victim's permission, don't you think?"

She said, "And what's in it for me if I do take this risk?"

"First, you get to satisfy your curiosity. Second, there is a very good chance that you could become fabulously rich."

"I like the second part best. Okay, I will take your oath of secrecy. Now tell me about it."

"Very well," Kren said. "Do you realize that I could have taken the gold at every single event I played in last year?"

"A lot of us are of that opinion, yes. You only lose so that the betting odds get better."

"Correct. Now, before I got this body, I wasn't much of an athlete at all. When it gets so old that I have to replace it, it is likely that I won't be nearly as fit as I am now. This is a very superior body, and I want my next one to be just as good. What we are doing here is trying to breed some more of this sort of body. I think that I can do it in three or four generations, maybe four dozen years or so."

"Interesting. Yes, it makes sense," she said. "One male, three dozen physically fit females, and a place where grubs, pollywogs and juvenals can grow up in seclusion. If it can be done at all, this is the way to do it. But how does this make me rich?"

"Well, you can't breed just one of anything. I'll have to breed many of them, and do a great deal of careful selecting. In the end, there will be lots of extras, and you could have one, if you work with my program."

"I like that idea. What's the program?"

"When you change bodies here, we will also change your ID. I'll then send you to one of the universities on the planet, and pay all of your expenses there. You will enroll in the school's athletic program, and you will stay just good enough so that they don't drop you. Then, twice a year, *when I tell you to,* you win the gold at your event," Kren said. "You will do that for four years, multiplying your bankroll by maybe a gross each time, eight times in a row. Of course, I'll be betting on you, too, and that's where I'll make my money. But nobody else gets in on this, *understood?* If they did, it would drive the odds down, and we'd both lose money. Then, in your fifth year, you can go ahead and win everything, if you want to, and rake in all the glory that you need, but for the first four years, you will do it exactly my way, or I will kill you."

"So if I started with a thousand, after four years I'd be worth, uh, *By the Great Egg, there isn't that much money!*"

"Consider that my first gold, when nobody had heard of me, paid well over a gross two dozen to one. I can't promise what the odds on you will be. But however much money there is on this planet, you'll have a lot of it. Are you interested?"

"Most definitely, sir! When this body starts to get slow, I'll come a calling, and be your most obedient servant!"

That's one recruit, Kren thought. *Two dozen and eleven to go.*

CHAPTER FORTY-FOUR

FROM CAPTURED HISTORY TAPES,
FILE 1846583A ca. 1832 A.D.
BUT CONCERNING EVENTS OF UP TO
2000 YEARS EARLIER

The Death of the Faithful

Having nothing better to do, some of the party goers stayed on for weeks after the party officially ended, and four were there for the entire summer. Kren spent most of his summer in the breeding room, trying to manage his corporation from a computer that he had brought in. He was starting to learn how to use it, and he was swearing much of the time. Some of his braver guests tried to help him out, but most of them wisely avoided him when the thing was turned on.

But mostly, he was trying to make sure that every egg was fertilized. He moved his work station every day, pulling long wires behind him, to cover the whole area.

A group of sociologists that Kren had hired to observe the juvenals on his land reported that the children spent over half of their day walking to and from the watering holes on his property.

Kren ordered that a system of wells, pipelines, and watering troughs be set up so that it was never more than a half-mile walk to get a drink. The sociologists predicted a four per dozen improvement in juvenal weight gain. Kren hoped that they were right.

✳   ✳   ✳

A group of grass biologists found that over large areas of his land, the growth of grass was reduced because of the lack of sufficient water and nutrients. To a certain extent, the grass acted like a single plant, sending water and nutrients sideways to other plants when there was a local surplus. But this sharing was not perfect.

Kren ordered the planned watering system to be enlarged to include sprinklers in some areas, and chemical fertilizers to be added where needed. With proper watering and nutrients, the land's productivity was predicted to almost double.

Bronki turned the sales department over to a manager that she'd hired and trained, and spent the summer writing at Kren's country cottage, keeping her promise to Sava and Zoda.

As long as sales kept on increasing, Kren had no objections. And increase they did, despite the temporary drop in population as many students went elsewhere for the summer.

At midsummer, the College of Mathematics created a new chair for Chaos Theory, and invited Bronki to fill that position as a department head. She graciously accepted the promotion, with its higher status and pay, and resigned her former post as senior professor at the College of Literature.

Kren asked Dol how the big mowing machines were coming.

"It turns out that we already had a dozen and nine of them, sir. They came with the property."

"They did?"

"Yes," Dol said. "Each of the juvenal wintering centers had one. Huge things, they ride on rails set into the grass above the caverns below. Usually, they only use them once a year, for the fall harvest, but this year, I'm having them mow the lawns up there every week, on half of them. The total yearly production looks like it will be about the same, but the biologists tell me that the weekly clipped grass is much richer in protein, and has less cellulose. We're just dumping it into the same silos they've always used, and will feed it to the kids next winter. I want to see if there is any difference in weight gain."

"Is it cost effective?"

"To do it over the wintering centers, yes, by all means, since we already have the machinery and legal permission to fence the land. To do it over the rest of your estate, I doubt it. Let's give it a few years, and get some solid data before we try getting any legislative approval, though."

Dol worked on, managing the day-to-day operation of the corporation completely without pay, but becoming very wealthy even so. There was much that she had learned from Bronki.

Duke Dennon prepared for war, training his best soldiers, his shock troops, in the fine points of fighting indoors, and doing considerable damage to his newly refurbished palace in the process.

Entering into Tendi's castle through a single, small opening, it was vital that they enlarge their beach head quickly, so as not to get stuck in the bottleneck of the tunnel entrance. His troops had to be trained in a manner that humans would associate with marines, specialized troops willing to take casualties in order to push forward quickly.

Besides the special training, Duke Dennon planned to use certain illegal drugs that he had purchased from some of the assassin organizations that existed in most of the larger cities. These would encourage his soldiers to take reckless chances during the initial assault.

By late summer, the machinery for the armor-building project was completed, and mass production had begun. Soon, thousands of sets of nicely painted red and lavender armor were being issued to all of Duke Dennon's soldiers, starting with the officers so that the troops would think that it was a privilege, and not a punishment. They were required to wear this armor constantly, and most of the soldiers soon hated it, considering it to be a pain in the tail. Which, of course, it was.

Also, at this time, the "exploratory tunnel" was approaching Duke Tendi's land, ahead of schedule. For secrecy, Dol had kept the same six-worker team constantly at the small tunneler, sending food, water, and instructions

to them on the same specially designed truck that delivered the metal coils. They were paid triple time for this
arduous duty, but they complained constantly anyway. The
only possible security leak was the truck driver, a trusted
old sergeant who had been with Duke Dennon for many
regenerations.

Kren held another party at the end of the summer, and
two more in the fall and early winter. His theory was that
there's never enough unless there's too much.

Bronki and Dol had each managed to make enough money
on their gambling to buy more stock than Duke Dennon
had in the corporation, despite all of the stock he had
received for his machinery, for the use of his army, and the
stock he had taken in place of his payment for his military protection.

This stopped Dennon from being made a member of the
board of directors, which made Kren uncomfortable. The
duke was too important to offend.

He phoned the duke and explained that his two fellow
board members had gotten into a stock fight so severe that
Kren had had to buy more stock himself, just to maintain
his majority.

"Your Grace, would you like me to enlarge the board of
directors to four, so you can have a seat, too?"

"Now, why would I want a thing like that, Kren? I am
only interested in war, and in my army. I thought that I'd
made that clear to you. Everything else is a nuisance! As
far as I can see, the three of you are handling this commercial venture just fine. If I become unhappy with your
management, you will certainly be the first to know of it.
At that point, I will expect you to take such actions as are
required to make me happy again. Until then, I don't want
to be bothered."

"Yes, Your Grace."

Kren decided not to tell Bronki or Dol about this conversation. And the corporation could always use the money
that they had effectively donated.

The new school year started, and Kren changed the white
belt of a freshman to the yellow belt of a sophomore, even

though most of the classes he took were for freshmen. At least, he was no longer confined to remedial classes.

With the director's permission, Kren dropped the javelin tennis games, and only won at one of his other three major sports once every three to five weeks or so. However, he trained in one of the other three dozen collegiate sports for typically three weeks each, and when he had become sufficiently proficient at the sport, he was brought in at the last moment as an "emergency replacement." He invariably won the gold, whenever he competed in a new sport, and then he never repeated the performance.

This meant that most of the gamblers on the planet never had a chance to bet on him, and the odds were fairly high, often a dozen to one. They were that low because the small *In Crowd* was now in a position to bet fabulous sums. The money rolled in, and Kren gouged his bookie twice more during the year, forcing her to buy more stock that never paid any dividends.

By winter, the exploratory tunnel had been finished, the corrosive gasses had been released to give the tunnel an ancient-looking patina, and enough time had passed for these deadly gasses to react with the tunnel walls and be safe.

When the tired group of small tunneler workers finally came home, Kren made a point of being there to greet them and the sergeant who drove them their supplies.

Dol, along with Bronki, who of course had figured out what they were up to, encouraged Kren to kill these soldier-workers for security reasons, but Kren had decided that one of his major long-term goals was to increase the planetary population. Unnecessary killing was therefore to be avoided.

Also, the duke was very attached to his soldiers, and Kren thought that killing some of them might offend His Grace.

Kren told the workers, "I wanted to personally thank you for the long and arduous job that you have done for my corporation. I have your pay envelopes here, three times what it would normally be, and in cash money, so that you won't have trouble with the income tax goons. We carefully examined the dirt you sent out, and since you are interested, yes, you did find some very valuable mineral deposits. However, these deposits are such that the corporation won't be in a position to exploit them for many years. It is therefore vitally important that word of this does not get out, ever! Some have suggested that the most expedient course would be to kill all of you immediately, but you know that I am a soldier myself. Know that *I know* of the honor and the integrity of Duke Dennon's warriors! However, you all have doubtless heard of my prowess as a warrior, and I promise you that if any word of what we have done does leak out, I will find all of you, and I will kill you."

The soldiers looked at each other apprehensively.

Kren continued, "That's the down side. There's an up side, and it too is a secret. I have a bonus for you. This coming Saturday, I will win at the pole-vaulting competition at the University of Dren, even though I'm not presently listed as being entered in it. If you bet on me, you will make a lot of money."

"This is a sweet deal," the old sergeant said. "Triple pay and a tip on a bet that will make us at least a dozen times more than that! You guys ain't been watching the news lately, but Kren's wins really has been paying that much! And all we got to do is keep our stupid mouths shut!"

"Yes sir," the senior corporal said. "But what if he loses?"

"Soldier, if I lose, I will personally reimburse all of your losses three fold," Kren said.

"Then we are your silent but obedient servants, sir!" the corporal said.

Without Kren's knowledge, Bronki and Dol had visited the duke two days before. They had told him very privately about Kren's intentions of releasing the tunnelers, and that they both felt that it was an unnecessary breach of security.

Duke Dennon thanked them, and said that he would think on it, but warned them that they should remain silent on this matter. He secretly considered killing both of them for the very same breach of security.

A few minutes after Kren left the tunneling team, a lieutenant with six soldiers behind him stopped the workers.

The officer told them that the duke was granting them an extended leave, with full pay, but that he wanted to talk with them before they left to enjoy it.

The lieutenant and his troops escorted the workers back to the duke's palace and waited with them in a certain small room as he had been instructed. The duke was to call when he was ready.

The door locked after they went in, and could not be opened. The same corrosive gas that had been used to give the secret tunnel an ancient patina was released inside of the "waiting room." The old sergeant, six tunneler workers, the young lieutenant, and his guards all died quickly, and then the room was permanently sealed.

A palace repairman had secretly fixed the room's door lock for the duke, released the gas, and then plastered over the door.

This repairman died in an unfortunate accident the next morning.

It turned out that the amount of gas used was sufficient to kill the soldiers in the room, but not enough to kill the eggs that the Mitchegai always spread about them. And one of them was a male. The resulting grubs soon ate the dead bodies of their parents, and then each other, when that food supply ran out. Eventually, nothing was left but a single mummified pollywog who was never able to get to water, along with some scattered weapons, and seven well-filled pouches of currency.

Duke Dennon would have been happier if he could have killed Kren, Bronki, and Dol along with his own troops, but on consideration he decided that he had entirely too big an investment in the Superior Food Corporation to let it collapse without its management team. But he would keep an eye on them. Perhaps forcing Bronki and Dol to accompany Kren to the battle would increase their commitment. . . .

And anyway, the duke said to himself, *Kren is entirely too softhearted to worry about.*

CHAPTER FORTY-FIVE

The Tellefontu
New Yugoslavia, 2215 A.D.

The last of the lost planets, New Gambia, had been found. In this case, Earth's forces had won early and easily. They were running the place as a fairly benevolent dictatorship until our ship arrived and told them that despite everything, they had lost the war. It took months before our diplomats, and Earth's, could convince them to just go home. Even then, many of the occupying troops decided to stay where they were, especially those who had married local girls.

The Tellefontu were extremely reticent to talk about themselves, their customs, and their history. Still, over the years, a great deal was learned about them from casual remarks that they made privately, in conversations, in formal interviews, and on talk shows.

They were an ancient race, far older than even the Mitchegai. Their recorded history went back more than thirty-five million years, and their legends went back even farther.

They had a wide variety of art forms, including music, dance, the graphic arts, drama, literature, poetry, architecture, and at least nine others that were completely incomprehensible to humans.

They were capable of redesigning their own bodies, and indeed their own equivalent of DNA, to make themselves into whatever they wanted to be. They did this without the use of external machinery. Yet such was the extreme conservative streak in their nature that they were not at all interested in looking like anything else than what they were.

"Well, yes, of course," one of their representatives said to a talk show hostess. "I could, with considerable time and effort, make myself look like a human being. Even a very attractive human being like yourself. But, why would I want to do that? I am contented to be myself. Also, ask yourself, *Would you want to make yourself look like me?* I am, you know, a very attractive member of my own species. At least my spouses have always said so. I think that it is best if humans remain looking like humans, and Tellefontu remain looking like Tellefontu."

While by no means immortal, they did not have a definite life span. They could rebuild their bodies as necessary, and they had conquered all possible diseases. Many of them were thousands of years old. Death, when it came, was normally by accident, or other misadventure.

They were hermaphrodites, with each individual being simultaneously male and female. During mating, both partners were impregnated. The partners produced a single clutch of typically twenty eggs, one half of which was produced by each of them.

They then alternated, taking turns caring for the children and making a living. Once the children were raised and educated, a process that took several hundred years, the parents departed in a friendly fashion, and rarely saw either their former spouses or their children again.

As one of them put it, "After three hundred years, you get very much sick of them."

They did remain close to their siblings, however, and said that when the Mitchegai invasion finally came, they would fight in small platoons made up of siblings.

While they were perfectly capable of building and using machines, they generally preferred not to. They liked their existence to be as natural as possible.

While they were capable of living on land indefinitely, they felt most comfortable living an aquatic existence. "You humans go swimming on occasion, and you are enjoying the experience certainly very much. Yet you soon are wanting to get out of the water. We Tellefontu are just the same, but quite the opposite, you see. I think that we can definitely share this planet very nicely, without interfering with each other, but lending each other a hand when it is thought to be appropriate."

Laws had been passed on New Yugoslavia, giving them the oceans, although we were allowed to fish commercially at certain times and places, and to engage in sport fishing provided that we restricted it to hook and line. Also, they were given ownership of those islands that had been declared primitive nature preserves, provided that the original fauna and flora were actually preserved.

They were familiar with all aspects of space flight, but after some early experiments with it for scientific purposes, they had decided that it wasn't for them. They had been prepared to stay on their own planet for all time, having none of the outward-driving instincts that both humans and Mitchegai possess.

On their home planet, their astronomers had seen the Mitchegai invasion fleet approaching, and had been able to give their people a few months' warning. In that short time, they had been able to build weapons enough to give the invaders a stiff fight, but not enough to win. Scarcely a thousand of them had been able to escape, and make it to New Yugoslavia, over twelve hundred years ago.

They were searching the other planets in Human Space, looking for other possible refugee groups, but hadn't found any yet. There was some discussion about possibly colonizing other planets, to insure their racial continuity in the event that New Yugoslavia fell to the enemy, but nothing had been done, yet.

Once on New Yugoslavia, they had dedicated themselves to rebuilding their civilization, and replenishing their numbers. There were now over eight million adult Tellefontu living here, and seven times that number of children.

They had resolved that they would not again suffer what they had before. The next time the Mitchegai came, they would be better prepared, and they would be victorious.

They saw the humans as a way to help them do that.

CHAPTER FORTY-SIX

FROM CAPTURED HISTORY TAPES,
FILE 1846583A ca. 1832 A.D.
BUT CONCERNING EVENTS OF UP TO
2000 YEARS EARLIER

The Start of a Pleasant Little War

The duke's well diggers had made their fascinating discovery, the tunnel had been surveyed, and Dennon's army was secretly mobilized.

As a favor to Kren, the duke scheduled the attack to coincide with the two-week-long midwinter break. The scheduled date of the attack would be on Warrior's Day, a major winter holiday among the Mitchegai military.

Bronki's sales representatives arranged for a major giveaway program designed to encourage sales to the countryside outside of the cities. Duke Tendi was to receive two thousand selected children a week before Warriors' Day, as would eleven other dukes in the area.

This program had been designed to encourage Duke Tendi's forces to eat well and go into a stupor just before Duke Dennon's attack, and to have all of the other duchies around in no position to immediately counterattack Dennon.

At least that was the hope. Maybe it would work. And sales were such that there was a surplus of children just now, anyway.

Kren arrived the evening before the attack was to be launched, and he brought with him an entire trainload of supplies, along with Bronki and Dol.

"Welcome, Kren!" Duke Dennon said in high spirits while gesticulating with his sword, "But what is all of this stuff?"

"It's a present for you, Your Grace! First, there are a few thousand baggage carts, with room in each one for the armor of more than four dozen troops, water enough for the trip to Tendi's place and back, and room for two dozen warriors to sleep on top of it while another two dozen pull them along. With half sleeping and half pulling, you can keep going day and night! You've got a five-gross-mile-long march ahead of you, and with these carts you can do it in a week and a half, not the three weeks it would otherwise take you. Also, you will notice that they have lights on them, so you won't have to walk in the dark."

"You had these made especially for this attack? That must have been expensive! And I can't imagine ever needing them again. Wheels aren't permitted for overland transport over the grass, although they would be allowed in a tunnel. But, I mean, we will probably get away with pulling this 'discovered tunnel' stunt once, but I wouldn't dare try it again!"

"The carts were costly, Your Grace, but once you are through with them, I'll take them back, install electric motors in the wheels and new control panels for the operators, and use them for delivering children from the train stations to my underground stores. But as they are right now, they are perfectly legal for use in war."

"Well, thank you, Kren, although you really should have informed me of this in advance. If your scheme works, it will be a wonderful aid to our advance on the enemy. But if it doesn't, don't be offended if I abandon them all and do it the hard way. And those cages back there?" Dennon asked, pointing with his sword, "The signs on them say that those are young carnivores!"

"That's exactly what they are, two thousand of them! Please consider that you are inevitably going to take some losses in this attack. With all of these new bodies, you won't have to permanently lose any of your well-trained troops."

"That's very thoughtful of you, but all of my men have armor now," Dennon said. "We won't be taking that many casualties."

"Then perhaps we will be able to find some other use for the rest of these young adults. What do you do with captured troops, anyway?"

"Well, most dukes just kill them as a security risk, but my policy has always been to give them a choice. Once I've killed the opposing duke, his soldiers may either die with him, or they may give their oath to me. They lose two grade levels, and they have to go through *my* basic training system when coming into my army. We watch them very carefully for the first two years or so, but we treat them very well, otherwise. The great majority of them turn into loyal soldiers. If they don't, well, they still have that death sentence hanging over them."

"A practical policy. Do any of them prefer death?" Kren asked.

"One did, a few gross years ago, so we killed her. But you don't often see that sort of loyalty, not once they know that their leader is dead."

"And what do you do with the enemy dead?"

"The same thing that everybody else does. We burn their brains and eat their bodies," the duke said.

"Well, wouldn't it make more sense to rejuvenate them? I mean, why waste good troops? Once you conquer Duke Tendi's duchy, you will have to enlarge your army to guard it properly. Why not feed each of them to a young carnivore? Once those dead soldiers wake up in new bodies, you can give them the same choice that you gave the ones who weren't killed."

"Well, normally, there aren't that many young carnivores handy, and we need the food, anyway."

"But now there are, and I can provide all the food that your troops need," Kren said.

"Very well, once my own men are taken care of, we will try out your idea."

"Could I have half of the resurrected enemy soldiers? I could use some guards for my own lands."

"If you wish," Dennon said. "But I still think that you have too many carnivores out there. This battle will be mostly a matter of sneaking up inside of Tendi's castle, killing a few guards, and then killing the duke. It's not as though we will be fighting a full field battle. There just won't be all that many dead soldiers in need of ressurection."

"Perhaps. I imagine that you don't kill enemy civilians."

"Not normally. They are part of the wealth of the land, and after I reduce the taxes a bit at first, few if any of them will feel the least bit of loyalty to their old nobility. The noble leaders are all killed, of course."

"That makes sense," Kren said. "They have every reason to hate you, and it would be dangerous to have them around. Still, it seems such a waste, all those years of education, experience, and training, just dumped into the fire."

"I feel certain that another one of your wild ideas is coming up."

"One is, Your Grace. I would like to try feeding *most* of each of them to a young carnivore. Everything but the central portion of the brain, which contains the basic personality and personal memories. I think that what we would end up with would be a very well-educated idiot."

"The world does not need any more well-educated idiots, Kren," Dennon said. "The universities are full of them!"

Ignoring the duke's joke, Kren said, "But I also think that in time, a new personality will grow in there. It would be a personality that we would have a hand in molding, and I think that we could make it into a very loyal personality! I think that this might happen much quicker— and much more cheaply!—than it would if we had to start from scratch with a young carnivore. Anyway, I'd like to try it. I'll keep them all safely caged until we know for sure what happens."

"It smacks of vampirism, Kren, but actually, it is really the exact opposite of that, isn't it? Well, I won't stop you. Run your experiment if you wish. But not on Duke Tendi! He *must* die, or my rights to his lands will always be in doubt. Furthermore, I have a spot on the wall of my Trophy Room all picked out on which to hang his mummified head!"

Due to the complete lack of microbes, any Mitchegai body part naturally mummified and was preserved indefinitely provided that grubs and juvenals were kept away from it. For trophy heads, this was accomplished by smearing them with a bad tasting poison.

Adults, on the other hand, found mummified body parts to be particularly foul tasting, so bad that some Mitchegai would consider death by starvation to be preferable to eating them.

Some time later, the duke said, "But how are you going to get all of those young carnivores to Duke Tendi's castle?"

"I have a thousand large juvenals in the last three cars

there to pull them along in the tunnel. We've come up with a harness that keeps three dozen juvenals facing in the same direction. With some encouragement, and confined in a narrow tunnel, well, it worked when we tried it out. They'll have to be rested each day, so they won't be as fast as your army will be moving, but we'll get them there by the time the rest of you dig your way up into Tendi's castle. And of course, those same children will act as a mobile food source for your army."

"And you are doing all of this at your own expense?"

"Yes, although the loan of four dozen of your soldiers to act as drivers would be greatly appreciated," Kren said. "I could bring in some of my own men, but most of them are newly hired, to replace the soldiers who used to do the work, before you recalled them. I worry about their dependability and loyalty."

"Oh, very well, I'll tell the staff to assign the necessary warriors to your command. We'll let them ride to battle instead of walk. They'll still be there for the attack, after all."

The duke's staff officers got no sleep that night, reorganizing their army on the eve of embarkation so that they could work with the carts. They swore at Kren for pulling this surprise on them, but only after he had finished briefing them, had handed out three gross sets of written instructions on how the resurrection process would be arranged down in the narrow tunnel, and had left. Kren wasn't someone whom any of them would want to have for a personal enemy.

And they had to admit that at least now, once they started to roll, they could catch up on their sleep, while their troops pulled them into battle.

Duke Dennon's soldiers were delighted with the carts. The original plan had them walking the entire distance, and in armor! This way they only had to walk half the distance, they could do it naked, and they could sleep for the rest of the time. Pulling the pneumatic-tired carts on a smooth, level, metal floor, wasn't all that hard.

Four gross of engineers led the column, their twelve carts filled with cutting tools, tunnel liners, shovels, buckets, and surveying equipment. These carts were to their own design, and were not part of Kren's gift. However, in order to keep marching twenty-four hours a day, they were augmented by four gross of standard troops, whose armor and weapons were spread out throught the column.

Four divisions of the duke's best troops followed them, pulling carts with several dozen children chained to the back of each to feed the soldiers on the way. The chains were needed because the kids could generally chew their way through a rope, given time.

Kren's four dozen carts filled with young carnivores brought up the rear. These were boxed in large juvenal shipping crates and drugged with illegal substances to keep them lethargic, although they still grumbled and snarled a bit.

When the other dukes learned that Duke Dennon was attacking Duke Tendi, there was a strong possibility that one or many of them would attack Dennon, or Tendi, or both. The fact that it was winter might dissuade many of them, which is why Dennon chose this time of year for his attack.

Throughout Mitchegai history, many invading armies had won through to their objectives, only to find that they had lost their own lands behind them.

Thus, even though it was winter, and not the usual season for fighting, most of Dennon's army was prepared to go on alert in his palace and in his outlying fortifications, as soon as the attack started.

At that point, all civilian communications would be stopped. All railroad terminals would be guarded to stop word of the attack from getting out. Travelers would be allowed in, but not out. Everything of value that the duke owned had already been safely hidden away.

Whole towns would be evacuated and the citizens would be permitted to enter into the huge dungeons below the fortifications. The food supplies available to them were meager, but they would soon discover that they could order packaged juvenals from the Superior Food Corporation, at expensive wartime rates, of course.

Bronki was not happy.

"So here I am! I'm underground in a dark, stuffy, claustrophobic tunnel, I don't know how many miles from the nearest fresh air! I'm lying above a cage full of snarling, mindless young carnivores, with the roof inches above my nose! And I'm doing this so that I can perform a tediously large number of probably illegal operations on the nobility of a duchy that is about to be conquered in a highly illegal manner, so illegal that we will all likely be *nuked to shit* for participating in it! Why do I let myself be talked into doing such stupid things?"

"Because Kren wanted us here," Dol said. "And we have both made a lot of money off of Kren."

"I think that all of this is madness!"

"You should look at the brighter side of things."

"This insane mess has a bright side?" Bronki said.

"Well, they could have made us walk the whole way."

CHAPTER FORTY-SEVEN

FROM CAPTURED HISTORY TAPES,
FILE 1846583A ca. 1832 A.D.
BUT CONCERNING EVENTS OF UP TO
2000 YEARS EARLIER

Into the Breach!

Keeping four dozen carloads of young carnivores moving was more work than Kren had expected. Most of the problems centered around the large juvenals that were doing the towing.

When they had tested this idea out, they quickly found that they couldn't use whips to keep the kids moving. The tunnel was simply too small to swing a whip long enough to reach the lead pair. Eventually, it had been found that electrical wires fastened to the buttocks of the children, and connected to the same capacitors that ran the headlights, and would one day power the wheels of the carts, seemed to do the trick. The operator was equipped with a control panel that let him encourage individual children, or to give all of them a poke when the whole group was moving too slowly.

A more serious problem occurred when Kren found that he had underestimated the amount of food that the juvenals required. The difference in food requirements between a cold-blooded juvenal who was simply staying alive, and one who was being energetically exercised was huge, a factor of eight or more.

After a week on the road, they ran out of the compressed grass blocks they'd brought along to feed the draft teams.

Two days later, the first child died. Kren chopped the kid up and fed her to the rest of the team. This seemed to make them all a bit more energetic. When another died a few hours later, on one of the other carts, he had all of his drivers slaughter the weakest member of each team, hack it up, and feed it to the others.

The smaller juvenals that were brought along to feed the drivers were slaughtered next, and the adults went hungry for a few days.

On the eleventh day, when they finally caught up to the tail end of Duke Dennon's column, they were down to only a dozen children pulling each cart, with the drivers, Kren, Bronki and Dol pulling as well.

Bronki was particularly unhappy about this situation. "Look at the bright side!" she complained to Dol, "They might have made us walk! Dammit! They might have made us haul cargo, too! And they did!"

Dol didn't respond.

"I'm five thousand years old, I have two dozen and four doctorates, and they have me hauling mindless carnivores down an illegal tunnel to an illegal war for immoral purposes!"

Dol still didn't respond.

No one had ever suggested trying to use the mindless young carnivores for the task. The brainless but basically docile juvenals were hard enough to control. Trying to use the brainless but ferocious carnivores was unthinkable.

Kren resisted the suggestion that they use some of the young carnivores for food. He had a use for those bodies, and the juvenals were just food, anyway.

On arrival, Kren trotted forward and reported to Duke Dennon.

"You are late, Kren. Did you have difficulties?"

"Yes, Your Grace, but we still managed to get here. I was worried that the attack would be over before I could take part in it."

"No such luck. I still don't know how it happened, but when my engineers finally tunneled up to the surface, they found that they were not in Tendi's basement. They were in the middle of a snowy field! They had missed Tendi's castle by over two gross yards! Either your tunnel was out of position or my engineer's measurements were way off! And when I find out who was at fault, I will not be lenient!"

"Yes, Your Grace. Although a third possibility could be that the castle isn't where it's shown to be on the maps. It wasn't as though we could go out to Tendi's castle and survey it, the way we did with your palace. Once we'd done that, we were spot on with the tunnel there. I'll solve the riddle for you eventually, but there's nothing that I can do about it right now. I assume that a new tunnel is being dug?"

"Yes, of course. With any luck, no one in the castle was looking out over that snow-covered field when my engineer's head stuck up out of it. Just maybe, we still have the element of surprise on our side. We expect to be through to the proper position in a few hours, so you'd better get your armor on. I've saved you a place right behind me, leading the second company into the breach."

"We won't be in the front of the line? I'd had visions of being the first one up and out of the hole!"

"No, I've got some specially trained shock troops ready for that job. A leader must be visible, Kren, but that doesn't mean that he should be stupid."

Kren's trip to the rear of the column was slow. The carts had been pulled fairly close together, and many thousands of soldiers were trying to get their armor on in very cramped quarters.

Young, boxed carnivores were being handed overhead, and each was placed in a cart as soon as the armor was emptied out of it. Soon, the carts would become resurrection cages.

Eventually, Kren stood in his armor at Dennon's side. Dennon had made him a temporary colonel for the battle, and without that insignia on his shoulders, Kren might not have made his way through the crowd in time.

Combat engineers were still passing buckets of dirt out from the tunnel, and metal hoops into it that would hold up the roof. Soon, the sound of pickaxes attacking concrete could be heard. The duke went down the line of the first assault company and personally handed each soldier a small white pill.

Kren kept his thoughts on that one to himself.

In practice sessions, it had been proved that the spear was not an effective weapon for fighting indoors. It was too

cumbersome. All of Duke Dennon's men were armed only
with a sword, although one in six also carried an axe, and
one in twelve a pickaxe, for chopping through doors and
other barriers.

There was a shout, and the engineers slid down out of
the tunnel and got out of the way, their part of this operation
completed.

The first company ran gleefully up the steep incline, with
the duke and then Kren right behind them. Dennon had
stressed to his men, dozens of times over, that success in
this operation depended on moving fast, hitting hard, and
not stopping for any reason.

The tunnel came up, not through the floor, but through
a wall in a disused lower basement that wasn't shown on
the maps. This hadn't bothered the drugged troops of the
first company. They had found a light switch, a stairway
up, and had charged!

Kren and Dennon ran after the soldier in front of them,
having trouble keeping up with the drug-crazed idiot. On
the floor above they found six bodies, five of them
apparently unarmed, but in the livery of Duke Tendi.
Dennon's single casualty seemed not to have been wounded
by a weapon, but to have run into a wall and injured
her silly head.

Kren glanced at the dead or unconscious soldier and
thought, *I knew it, I knew it! Drugs in combat are a* stupid *stunt!*

They left her where she was and ran on.

The job of the first two companies was to go up, and
the third was to guard the landings. Later arrivals would
worry about making sure that each floor was secure, but
the way up had to be taken first.

They went up through five basements, and were on what
had to be the ground floor before Kren saw his first living enemy soldier. Small, high, heavily barred windows
showed that it was dark outside, the troop seemed to have
just awakened from a stupor, and she was holding her
sword in a languid manner. Kren took her head off with
a single swing and ran on without bothering to watch her
body fall.

Alarm gongs were sounding throughout the castle, Mitchegai were shouting to each other in a dozen languages, and

pouring out into the hallways. Some of them were armed, but most were not. But anyone who got in the way of the silent, panting invaders was cut down without a thought. They had no time for talking, and very little breath left for it, either.

Someone in a very expensive robe stepped in front of Kren, and died for her foolishness. Most of her would soon be revived, and it was all grist for Kren's mill.

The first assault companies were working their way to Duke Tendi's private chambers. Once Tendi was killed, preferably by Dennon himself, the rest of the castle's defenses could be depended upon to collapse. Loyalty among the Mitchegai was always on a personal basis, and never on a territorial one.

Kren and Dennon, who was having a hard time keeping up with his temporary colonel, found a pitched battle going on in a very large room between their armored troops and four times as many enemies who were pouring out of a guard room at the base of Duke Tendi's private tower.

Kren never slowed down, and when he got to the battle line, *he went right over it!*

He vaulted off the hip of one of Dennon's soldiers in front of him, propelling the warrior right through the enemy's ranks. This startled warrior could have easily been killed, but much to her surprise, she lived. At the time, Kren himself didn't much care. He wanted to be behind the enemy line, and he got there!

He stepped on another soldier's shoulder, and then on the head of an enemy troop, knocking her unconscious, after which another of Dennon's soldiers took her head off.

He killed two enemy soldiers on the way down with his sword, crushed a third beneath his armored feet, then bounced off a wall and took five more of them out from behind with three fast swipes of his sword before most of them even knew that he was there.

"I love this war!" Kren shouted, as the warrior that he had kicked through the lines started fighting at his side.

Then he started fighting in earnest.

During all of this mayhem, Kren was very careful to kill his opponents with clean neck cuts, and leaving their brains undamaged. One day soon, half of them would be his own troops, after all, and waste not, want not.

When Tendi's soldiers noticed that their rear rank was gone, some of them made the mistake of turning to meet this new threat, at which point they were cut down from behind by Dennon's drug-crazed troops. Fighting fair just wasn't the Mitchegai way of doing things.

In under a minute, all of the enemy troops were dead, and over a dozen of Dennon's were lying on the floor, dead or wounded. No armor is perfect.

The dead and wounded were left behind them. Later, there would be time for them. Not now.

The survivors, led by Kren and Dennon, continued to push upward.

By this time, most of the members of the first, drugged company were either dead, wounded, or lost, with some of them wandering aimlessly through deserted corridors, looking for someone to kill.

The soldiers who followed Kren and Dennon were mostly from the second company through the tunnel.

Two dozen of Duke Tendi's soldiers were armed and waiting for them in the narrow hallway, the staircase, and the landing leading to Tendi's private chamber.

The narrowness of the hallway stopped the attackers from using their superior numbers to advantage, but the first fighter to get there was Kren, so their lack of effective numbers didn't make much difference. It was one-on-one for the whole distance, and when one of them was Kren, the outcome was not in doubt.

Kren just plowed through, trusting that his armor would protect him, while killing an enemy soldier with almost every blow and thrust. The hardest part was watching his footing as he went over the bodies of those he had slaughtered.

One particularly aggressive guard, having been decapitated, managed to bite Kren's ankle as he went by. The leg armor stopped Kren from being hurt, but the head was a serious encumbrance. With some regret, Kren stamped on it with his other foot, squashing the brain to pulp on the floor. A pity, since the warrior had been a very good fighter. Kren would have wanted him for his future army. He fought on.

The open-centered spiral staircase turned properly to the right, to give the advantage to the warrior at the top, the vast majority of Mitchegai being left handed. For the fun of it, with

Dik, his fencing instructor, Kren had practiced with the épée right handed on occasion, and had become fairly ambidextrous. He switched hands and cut his way upward.

After almost tripping a few times over dead bodies, Kren made a point of always killing his opponents such that they went over the handrail and out of the way. Often, he had to take a moment and give them an extra shove.

Dennon and his soldiers got to loudly counting them as they fell to the floor below.

The four troops on the upper landing only lasted a few seconds before they went spinning, headless, downward.

During all of this, there wasn't much for the soldiers behind Kren to do, so they simply watched him. When the last enemy soldier was killed, they took their swords into their right hands and applauded him, with their left hands beating their chest armor!

Kren turned and looked down at them, surprised. Then, as was his usual custom when the crowd applauded him on the playing field, he bowed.

The rest was anticlimactic. The sturdy door was barred from the inside, and it took two axe swingers six minutes to chop their way in, while Duke Dennon fretted about the possibility of Tendi having some sort of secret escape route.

He needn't have worried. When they finally got into the large chamber, Duke Tendi was in a very deep stupor, along with three dozen of his top officials. Parts of children lay about, mostly dead. The duke had apparently decided to start celebrating Warrior's Day a bit early this year.

Duke Dennon went over and chopped off his opponent's head.

"I've been waiting to do that for over a thousand years, and when I finally got the chance, the bloody trash wasn't even awake to watch me do it!"

"You could have waited for him to wake up," Kren said.

"I'm not an absolute idiot, Kren. Stunts like that are for storybook fools! When you get a chance to kill an enemy, you do so *right now!* If you give them time, they will figure out a way to kill *you* instead! Okay. You wanted the rest of these nobles for your little experiment," Dennon said, pointing with his sword. "Should we kill them as well?"

"I'd just as soon wait with that until we have the rest of the dead fed to their new bodies. I'm not sure how long it will take for Bronki to perform the operations, and I don't want any of them to go stale."

"As you wish. You've certainly earned many privileges this day. Your fighting prowess is amazing! But I find it hard to believe that Tendi would be foolish enough to let so many of his leaders go into a stupor at the same time. And these boxes! They are the same sort that you use to ship children in, aren't they?"

"Yes, and I suppose that that's the answer to your first question, too. It would appear that the Superior Food Corporation has had a sales promotion in which it gave Duke Tendi two thousand of their finest children for his dining enjoyment. I wouldn't be surprised if half of his army is also in a stupor, somewhere around here."

"Ha! He fell for a stunt like that? When he alone was given such a gift of such largess? What a fool!"

"Perhaps, but everybody else got the same gift. I sent two thousand kids to each of the ten other dukes in the area as well. And who knows? Maybe it *will* stimulate sales."

"I almost feel jealous, since you didn't do the same for me!"

"Oh, but I did! To do anything else would have pointed you out as the aggressor! Only, you weren't home to receive your present, so my agent put them in storage, under your palace. By now, I expect that your dungeons are filled with refugees from your towns, and that my agent is selling the children to them at wartime rates. At least she'd better be, if she wants to keep her job. I really don't like waste, you see."

"Make all the profit you wish, Kren. But all of this means that I'm not likely to suffer a counterattack soon, doesn't it?"

"That is my hope, Your Grace. Come, let's make sure that the castle is secure, and that the proper individuals are all being properly resurrected. Captain," Kren said to the commander of the second company, "make sure that this room is well guarded. I'll be back for this bunch later."

Dennon picked up the head of his former rival.

"We might need this to convince some of the enemy troops that there is nothing more to fight over. Captain Zem, three dozen warriors will be sufficient to guard this area. Send the rest of your soldiers out as runners to every part of the castle, telling everyone that Duke Tendi is dead, and that Duke Dennon now rules here! Every former enemy who wishes to die may continue fighting. Those who wish to live may surrender. Their lives will be spared, and they will be offered positions in my army. *This duchy is now mine!*"

Kren was working on his armor.

"Are you coming, Kren?"

"In a moment, Your Grace. First I want to take off this bloody be damned tail armor!"

"I wish we was allowed to do that," one of Duke Dennon's sergeants mumbled.

CHAPTER FORTY-EIGHT

Drinking Buddies
New Yugoslavia, 2216 A.D.

I'm really not an alcoholic. I like my beer, but I only touch the hard stuff once every month or two. Yet those seem to be the times when things happen.

I was sitting in my den, enjoying my first glass of Jim Beam when Agnieshka said that Bellor had something that he wanted to show me, and could he please come up?

"Certainly," I said. "What's he got?"

"He has the first production model of the new Tellefontu Fighting Machine."

"I want to see that! Tell him to hurry up!"

This thing had been talked about for years. It was supposed to be a marriage between human and Tellefontu technology, and something that they could use to help us fight the Mitchegai. It had been designed by all three races working on New Kashubia, and I had been out of the loop on it. Tellefontu help was vital to the defense of New Yugoslavia.

In a few minutes, the door dilated to allow in a small, flat black, sleek-looking ovoid . . . thing. It was about two meters long, a meter wide and twenty centimeters thick. Every cross section of it seemed to be a perfect ellipse. It had no projections of any sort, and it glided in about ten centimeters above the floor.

"Well, it's pretty enough," I said. "Are you in there, old friend?"

"Most assuredly, sir. But certainly you must understand that this vehicle was not created for aesthetic purposes."

"That doesn't stop it from being beautiful. Climb out of it, have a drink, and tell me all about it."

"I would like that, since the last time I was here, I had only sampled halfway through your excellent collection of potables," my crabby friend said.

I hadn't noticed any seams in the craft, but a section to the left of center flipped open, and Bellor climbed out of a small pool of water. Soon, he was on the tabletop, across from where Agnieshka had placed a small soup bowl.

I started to fill the bowl with Jim Beam, but Agnieshka reminded me that last time he had stopped in the rums, and filled the bowl with 151 proof Bacardi.

"I have always been surprised at your love of alcohol," I said. "Was there a lot of it on your home planet?"

"Oh, most definitely, Mickolai. On your native planet, the animals store their excess, emergency energy supplies as fats, for the most part, and your plants usually use carbohydrates. On my beloved home world, both types used ethanol for this purpose. It was our major source of chemical energy. I wish that I could offer you some Jaga berries from the garden I once maintained! They had a magnificent flavor which I am sure that you would have enjoyed, but, Alas! They were all destroyed along with the rest of my planet."

Agnieshka refilled his bowl with something blue that I didn't recognize.

He continued, "Then, when we escaped to New Yugoslavia, we found an ecology here that was primitive, but in many ways similar to what we were used to, including the prevalence of ethanol. Many of the starches and proteins were different, of course, and we were hard pressed for the first few decades to modify our metabolisms, but there was at least enough ethanol to keep us alive until we had adapted."

Next, he was on something bright orange. Hell, I don't know what it was. I'd just told them to stock the bar with everything that anybody might want. I stuck to my sour mash bourbon.

"But when you humans got here, you perforce modified the environment to suit your own metabolisms. At first, it was not at all clear to us what was happening, and there were still plenty of the old plants and animals around. We were a bit slow in realizing the ecological change happening around us. It started slowly, but finished quickly, in the oceans, at least."

Agnieshka filled his bowl with some sort of a thick, yellowish green syrup called Chartreuse. Bellor drank it dry without a comment.

"I was out exploring, and far away from my people when the last of the change happened. I was quite unprepared for it. I had foolishly pressed onward, assuming that I would soon find something to eat. Thus it was that I found myself on an unfamiliar sea coast, starving to death, barely able even to walk. And then you came along, instantly deduced my problems, and put me into a large container of magnificent food. I shall always be grateful for that!"

I said, "I'm glad that I could be of help. You said that the old ecology here was similar to that of your home planet. You know, when I first saw you, I took you for one of the original inhabitants here. I suppose that it was mostly because of those push-pull muscles that work your legs. Many of the local fauna use the same thing."

"Well, it is a far more efficient system than the pull-only arrangement that your people use." Bellor was sucking up something dark brown called Old Navy rum.

"I suppose that it might be," I said. "But you came here to show me this black blob of a fighting machine here."

"True. Its almost absolute blackness continues across most of the electromagnetic spectrum, incidentally. The enemy will be able to see us clearly only if one of us happens to pass in front of a star. If we have to fight on land, we will use the Squid Skins that you have developed, but for deep space, this is superior."

"Can I get that covering for my tanks?"

"It will be available to you soon, yes," he said. "This was the very first Fighting Machine off the line, but we expect to build eight million of them in the next two years, enough so that every adult Tellefontu will be able to join in the defense of our new home."

"That's quite a production rate!"

"Many of our little technological tricks were used on the production lines, as well as on the product."

I said, "I see. I hope that they are applicable to our production lines as well. But if all of your adults go off to war, who will take care of your children?"

"Our older children will do this service, of course. By our definitions, you have to be at least two hundred years old before you can qualify for adulthood, and many take half again longer than that, to be sure. But they are no stupider than your people are of the same age. It is simply that our standards of adulthood are somewhat . . . different, shall we say. In any case, they are quite capable of letting their educations slide for a bit, during an emergency."

"My own sons will be ready for war when they are eighteen."

"We would consider that to be immoral," Bellor said. "But your race must set its own standards."

"We do what we have to," I said. "By your standards, my race is very short lived. But tell me, your machine floated in here. This is some sort of antigravity?"

"Oh, no," he laughed. "Such a thing would be surely impossible! No, we are using the same magnetic technology that your people use, taking advantage of the magnetic surface that you have placed under your floors. There are magnetic cylinders that I can carry to act as treads, when necessary."

"Okay, but why the three-dimensional ellipse, or whatever you call that shape."

"Because it is obviously desirable to have a minimal frontal area with respect to one's volume. This shape permits that from a wide range of angles."

"I won't argue with you," I said. "What's your power supply?"

"A muon-exchange fusion bottle, much as you use, but considerably smaller and somewhat more powerful. Alas, it is not as compact as the one on the Mitchegai ship you captured. This was the best that we could do."

"I see. And the space drive?"

Agnieshka was pouring something milky-looking into his bowl.

"A simple cesium ion engine, much like yours, but smaller and more efficient. It enables a thrust of forty-two Gs, and is quite comparable to those in your tanks. It runs down the center of the vehicle," he said.

"And your weaponry?"

"The same Disappearing Gun that we gave you plans for. It is mounted internally to the right. We are capable of mounting a wide variety of weapons externally, but for space combat, one gun should be sufficient."

"Perhaps. Your craft doesn't appear to have much armor," I said.

"This is indeed true. But armor is not effective against the Disappearing Gun, or indeed against the rail guns that your people have used in the past. Surely, the only purpose for the armor on your vehicles was to protect the inhabitants of your craft from their own weapons. The Disappearing Gun is safe for everyone except those that it is aimed at, so we dispensed with the armor."

"Interesting." I asked, "Will your people be working with an artificial intelligence?"

"Most definitely. Your people are masters at that art form. We have been able to tailor the package to fit into the confines of the hull, but no other improvements were possible, that we could see. We also have full Dream World capability and are able to operate at combat speed, when needed. The electronic people will increase our fighting efficiency considerably. Also, they are so very pleasant to talk with. We enjoy being around them. Oh my! I do believe that I have made a social error! Mickolai, I would like to introduce you to my friend and my ship, Belladonna. Belladonna, this is our planetary commander, General Mickolai Derdowski."

Belladonna and I said the usual formal words to each other. Then I said, "But as to enjoying our metal ladies' company, I expect that the feeling is mutual. So what you have here is something approximately equivalent to one of our tanks, but much smaller."

"Yes, but being much smaller, we will be much harder to hit," he said. " 'We're pressing on with each new ship, less weight and larger power. We'll have the Loco Engine soon, and thirty miles an hour!' "

"You are quoting Kipling, one of my favorite poets!"

"Indeed, I have been making a very thorough study of your human culture, and Rudyard Kipling is certainly one of my favorites, also."

"I'll drink to that. And to him!"

Agnieshka poured him another bowlful of something. I wish that I knew where he put it all.

When it was time for Bellor to go, he started to return to his small space ship, but his coordination was way off. At one point, he tried to move all three of his right legs at the same time, and fell over.

"Well, my friend," I said. "It seems that I finally know what your limit is in alcohol!"

"It is indeed true that I have overindulged, to my considerable embarrassment, but it was not the alcohol that subverted the control of my legs. Ethanol is only a healthy food to people of my sort. It was rather the inordinate amount of various sugars in some of your potables, some of which have a certain physiological effect on those of my race. Fructose in particular. Without stepping over the bounds of good taste, may I ask if you could you perhaps assist me to my vehicle?"

"Are you sure that you can drive?"

"I am sure that I cannot," Bellor admitted. "However, Belladonna is fully functional, and she will take me home quite safely."

"As you wish." I picked him up, swearing that he weighed less than all the booze that he had drunk, and put him back in the small pool of water in his tank. Once he managed to get all of his legs inside, the lid closed, and the little black ship went home.

Agnieshka, who always seemed to know what I was thinking, said, "Remarkable creatures!"

CHAPTER FORTY-NINE

FROM CAPTURED HISTORY TAPES,
FILE 1846583A ca. 1832 A.D.
BUT CONCERNING EVENTS OF UP TO
2000 YEARS EARLIER

Wrapping It Up

Kren spent the rest of the day collecting up heads and decapitated bodies and sending them down into the tunnel for resurrection, that is to say, to be eaten alive by young carnivores who would soon have their brains taken over by the person that they had just eaten.

The colonel's insignia on his shoulders was a great help in getting the troops to obey him. Never once did he have to kill one of them to encourage the others.

Bronki and Dol were wearing armor with captain's insignia that Kren had arranged for. They set up a surgery in one of the basements, and with the help of a dozen shanghaied soldiers, performed well over a thousand questionably legal operations on slaughtered civilians. Many of them were members of the former nobility hereabouts, but some of them were merely servants who had gotten in the way. Kren decided that he might as well have them all. There were plenty of young carnivores. With the right conditioning, he was sure that he could make most of them into willing slaves.

When they ran out of heads and decapitated bodies, the duke's men started slaughtering the nobility who had been captured, but not yet killed. Many of them were still in their eating stupors, and never did wake up.

Bronki ran into over a dozen of the nobility who had once been friends of hers, since in five thousand years, you meet a lot of individuals. With a bit of trickery, and some help from Dol, she managed to send these down for resurrection with their brains intact, having quietly cautioned them to act as if they were brainless when they woke up, and reminding them that one day, they would owe her some really big favors.

Duke Dennon spent his time negotiating with groups of Tendi's soldiers who had yet to surrender, and accepting their oaths of allegiance, once they did.

"Kren, I think that this might be written up as one of the most successful campaigns in history," the duke said. "We have taken a major duchy, killed almost a thousand of their soldiers, and captured nine entire divisions of their troops, thus far. And we did it with an assault force of only two divisions, and the loss of barely two dozen of our own warriors! And I owe much of this success to you! I thank you, Kren, and somehow, in the future, I will find a way to reward you properly."

"Thank you, Your Grace. I would say that ours was a mutually profitable relationship. But for now, I have only one favor to ask."

"Ask it!"

"I understand that you will be needing all of your regular troops, controlling this new duchy, at least until your new recruits go through basic training and get settled in to your army," Kren said. "But could I please have your engineers back? The construction and tunneling projects on my land have come to a dead stop without them. Also, there is one of your captains, Yor, who is a remarkably good administrator. I would like you to transfer her to me permanently."

"Absolutely! I'll release them to you immediately! And you are right about my needing the rest of my army for the foreseeable future, but look. You seemed to want half of the enemy soldiers that you had resurrected. Would you like them all? I have plenty of new recruits for the time being, and I'll be getting many more once I've had a chance to talk to Tendi's other divisions in all of his outlying fortifications. After all, I have more land now, but one fewer border to guard!"

"Thank you! I'll take them! I'll have to figure out a way to get them, the old nobility, and my carts back to my lands. There's no way that we can get the carts up that small tunnel that your engineers built into the basement here, but it's a three week march back to your palace by the old tunnel."

"Don't worry about it," the duke said. "I'll be marching all of these new recruits back to my old palace by way of that tunnel. That's the program, you know. You fill your new lands with your old troops, and then take the new ones, retrain them, distribute them around your old lands, being careful to break up all of their old platoons and squads. Left as individuals, they rarely cause trouble."

Dennon continued, "Anyway, they might as well haul your prisoners and property back to the palace while they're at it. From there, I'll have a MagFloat train take it all back to your Research Center. I'll be staying here, of course, and I'll be bringing most of my leaders here as well. You have to do that with newly conquered land, for a few years at least, until the populace is used to your rule. My old estates are secure enough to get along without me."

"Again, thank you, Your Grace. Well then, Bronki has finished slicing up all of the brains that needed it, so with your permission, we'll be going home."

"Must you leave so soon? I thought that you'd want to stay for dinner. We're serving Tendi!"

"I hate to give up on a chance to eat a real duke, but I'm still a schoolboy, Your Grace. Tomorrow is a school day!"

After a quick talk with Dennon's chief engineer, Kren, Bronki, and Dol changed into their usual academic garb, walked to the train station, and bought tickets for home.

A team from the Battle Confirmation Authority soon arrived at Tendi's old castle. Their job, among other things, was to confirm that the Laws of War had been properly adhered to.

They were particularly fascinated by the ancient tunnel that Duke Dennon had found, and even though he repeatedly warned them that he had lost seven soldiers trying to explore the mazes at each end, the inspectors insisted on investigating it personally, using electrically powered motorcycles that they had shipped in.

When two of their members were permanently killed in a cave-in at the east end of the tunnel, they gave up on this portion of the investigation.

They spent three weeks interviewing everyone concerned, and even talked to Kren, at Bronki's apartment.

In the end, they declared that everything had been done in a legal manner, and congratulated Duke Dennon on his remarkable victory.

The duke had a thousand sets of arms and armor sent to Kren for use by his new guards. They were identical to those worn by the duke's soldiers, except that he had them painted in red and black, to match Kren's academic garb.

Kren thanked him profusely, and then quietly had all of the tail armor removed and put in storage.

Kren returned to school, got good grades, and stayed with his program of making huge winnings at his betting on collegiate sports.

Bronki stayed angry at Kren, refusing to speak to him for weeks, but betting on him nonetheless.

Dol remained philosophical about the entire affair, knowing when she had a good thing going.

About the time that Kren's first, well-fed offspring were eating their way up to the top of the grass as juvenals, his biochemists reported that they thought they knew which genes were responsible for Kren's athletic prowess.

They weren't positive about their findings. There were still many unknowns. What they told him about were simply their best guesses at the present state of their investigation.

But certainly, it wasn't just one gene. It seemed to be several dozen of them working together. Also, several of them were located on the "J" chromosome, which in the Mitchegai determined the sex of an individual. This suggested that it was unlikely that a female would have all of his athletic and military prowess.

Kren's comment was, "Well, it's sure going to make for some stinky locker rooms!" A heavy concentration of male aerosol sperm was considered offensive by a Mitchegai.

Kren put his scientists to selecting several gross of the

female children who had a maximal number of the genes that they thought might be making him so good. In a dozen years, they would be mature and he would go into another round of breeding.

Kren decided that it wasn't necessary to preserve any of the males, since he was still there to do the male side of the breeding.

Some of his scientists secretly objected, and preserved a few promising-looking males just in case Kren came to an early death. Also, it would be interesting to run some tests and comparisons on them, and a vivisection now and then always provided some comic relief.

All of the rest of Kren's offspring were eventually eaten in house.

Meanwhile, every juvenal brought in from the surface to the underground feed lots was branded with an ID number and weighed periodically. Those who put on the most weight were placed in a special group to be raised to adulthood for use as breeders.

Once they found some that were particularly productive, the scientists could get busy at finding out why this was so, and productivity could be increased even further.

Four weeks passed before Kren's new slaves, military and civilian, were delivered to him. Duke Dennon had lent him a dozen trained drill instructors to train the thousand or so resurrected soldiers in the duke's way of doing things.

Kren told them, "It is very simple. You were all killed in combat. I killed a fair number of you myself. It is traditional for dead enemy soldiers to have their brains thrown into the fire, and their bodies eaten by the victors. You were lucky. Duke Dennon permitted me to resurrect you because I needed soldiers willing to work and willing to fight. If you do not want to do this, let us know, and we will happily kill you again, permanently, this time. If you want to live a fairly decent life, you must work very hard at staying with the program. But remember that for the next twelve years or so, your legal status will be that of slaves. You have no rights at all. You must prove to me that you are valuable enough to be worth feeding. After those twelve years, if you keep your teeth clean, you will be granted the full privileges of an adult citizen. Sergeants, take command!"

✳   ✳   ✳

To Kren's surprise, Bronki got over her anger at being dragged off to battle, and volunteered to set up the training program to educate the thousand or so young vampires that their use of Duke Tendi's nobles had resulted in.

"We're alone now," Bronki said to the supposedly mindless student across from her. "Do you know me?"

"Yes, of course. You are Bronki. You saved my life. I'm Seba. We studied art together."

"Well, I'm glad I've found you again, Seba. I'll be putting you in a class along with the dozen or so others I managed to save. While in class, you will be able to talk with the others, but outside of it, you must continue to pretend to be stupid. It will probably be a few years before I can get you out of this, but if you want to live, and if you want *me* to live, play the role very well at all times!"

"I will, Bronki. But tell me, why did you risk your life to save me and the others?"

"You know, I'm not entirely sure. On the one hand, being a friend of Bronki has always meant something. Or maybe, I was just so mad at Kren at the time that I wanted to disobey him. But once having done it, I am now forced to protect you as best as I can, and to complete the job, for my own security. Just remember that someday, I might need some serious favors and when that happens, I will expect your bunch to be obliging."

"Oh, we will be. You can count on it!"

Kren's surveyors managed to prove, with a bit of fudging, that Duke Tendi's castle was in fact over two gross yards away from the position shown on the ancient maps. Whether this was caused by an error in transcription, some time in the last three dozen thousand years since the castle had been built, or if it had been a deliberate error on the part of the architects to confuse future aggressors, was a question on which they could not offer an opinion. Duke Dennon grumbled, but was eventually satisfied.

Actually, the error had to have been made by one of the engineers, since no one else worked on the project. But Kren needed all of the technical troops to keep his building projects going, and he didn't want Duke Dennon to kill any of them.

✳   ✳   ✳

In the spring, Duke Dennon was confronted with two half-hearted attempts at counterinvasions, but when he faced them each with many divisions of fully armored soldiers, the enemy soon ran away, or rather the survivors did. It would be several years before Duke Dennon would have things organized well enough to dare making another attack himself.

One of these invasions happened to coincide with the spring break, and Kren was able to participate in the battle, to Duke Dennon's delight.

At Bronki's suggestion, Duke Dennon hired a friend of hers as a ghost writer, and came up with a book called *Three Battles*. It sold remarkably well, adding to Dennon's fortune and fame. More importantly, it made other dukes deadly afraid of attacking him, for now they considered him to be a master of the warrior's art.

At the end of the book, Dennon said, "It will therefore be obvious that anyone who attacks me will encounter large numbers of very well-trained warriors who are all well armed and armored. On the battlefield, we regularly kill four of our enemy for every soldier we lose.

"Furthermore, I have the wealth to see to it that every one of my troops who dies in combat is properly resurrected. When you attack me, you do not reduce the size of my army! I also see to it that all enemy soldiers killed are resurrected as well. Then, both these resurrected soldiers and those whom my warriors have captured are given the option to either die, or join my army.

"Very few choose to die! Among other things, I feed, treat, and pay my warriors very well. I give them the finest arms and armor that money can buy. They live in sumptuous private rooms, and when they are not rigorously training, their time and money are their own. Sometimes, our enemies seem to *want* to be captured!

"When you attack the lands of Duke Dennon, you reduce the size of your army, and increase the size of mine!

"You might also make me angry enough to attack you in return!"

Dennon's success with the use of armored troops caused many dukes to consider the use of armor with their own armies. At Kren's suggestion, Dennon sold it to them, painted in their own colors, at very good prices. After all, if they didn't buy it from Duke Dennon, someone else would eventually start producing it, and Dennon would lose the profit.

Bronki was given the contract to handle these sales on a commission basis, and she soon hired Brandee to come up with attractive coloring schemes for the armor.

At Kren's suggestion, the weight of the tail armor sold to other dukes was doubled, and the design was changed to make it difficult to remove. Also the armor around the neck was made of an inferior metal. They might one day have to fight an army wearing this armor, and there was no point in making an enemy more comfortable, or that much better protected.

Based on the casualties sustained at the taking of Tendi's castle, and the two field battles that followed, a number of subtle but very effective modifications were made in the armor worn by Dennon's troops.

The original space armor had been intended to protect the wearer against abrasion to the inner fabric, and not to be effective against swords and spears.

Innovations were in order. By making those edges of the plates that were on the inside curve outward, to snag the enemy's blade, and those edges on the outside curve inwards, to deflect it, it became much more difficult to slide a sword between two armor plates and injure the wearer. Also, the neck protectors became stronger, the tail pieces became lighter, and the sensitive Mitchegai skull was better protected.

These modifications were kept secret, and were not available to the public. If anyone noticed the difference, they were told that they were looking at the old style armor, and what was sold to cash customers was the new stuff.

At the Planetary Championships, Kren was entered in eleven events. He again won three gold medals, and set two collegiate planetary records. But they were in swimming, all three of them, and the outside betting on Kren was low, since no one had seen Kren swim before.

The money rolled in.

Dol graduated with honors, and promptly enrolled in a doctoral program, studying aerodynamics. She had decided that there was no need to rush things, she had plenty of other things to occupy herself, and why risk any possibility of being charged with vampirism, anyway.

That summer, Kren officially moved into his lavish apartment above his research center, mostly for tax reasons. He was virtually a duke in his own right, so why should he have to pay taxes to anyone? Taxes, after all, existed for the benefit of the rulers, and not for those who are taxed!

Nonetheless, he often visited Bronki, and happened to stay the night, about three times a week, when there wasn't a home game. When there was, he stayed over six times a week.

An inexpensive worker was hired to travel back and forth from the Research Center to the university every day, always getting Kren's season ticket punched, again for tax reasons.

She also acted as a courier for messages between the Research Center and Kren's interests in Dren, those that were best not trusted to the phone lines.

The next several years went very smoothly. Growth was as projected, and all concerned were content.

CHAPTER FIFTY

FROM CAPTURED HISTORY TAPES,
FILE 1846583A ca. 1832 A.D.

Progress, Boredom, and Something Kren
Can Sink His Teeth Into

On Earth, it was 1832 A.D. Americans were crossing the Appalachian Mountains and sometimes finding their way into the Great Plains, flintlock rifles in hand. Europe had finally recovered from the Napoleonic Wars, and a private British company was conquering India without quite intending to. The Mitchegai could not possibly have cared less.

At the same time, Duke Kren was waking up again from the long stupor of resurrection. He stumbled once again to the toilet and to the drinking fountain. Then once more he lay down and put on the recording helmet.

Every time he got a new body, it seemed to take longer. And to hurt more. Still, the pain was starting to abate. Perhaps in a day or so, it would be time to leave the resurrection chamber and get back to work.

He glanced at the recorder. He had three thousand years of personal history to record, and most of what he had gotten down in his two weeks of recovery time had covered a period of barely two years.

At that rate, this body would be middle-aged before he was through, and the colonizing fleet would be long gone without him.

Bronki, his academic advisor, would not be pleased.

Still, the two years covered were his formative years, when

most of his basic plans had been well laid down. For the rest, Bronki would have to be satisfied with a summary. He remembered . . .

Kren had resorted to vampirism only one more time in his long life. He had been forced to kill a scholar with doctorates in over three dozen different languages, the circumstances were such that he could not permit the academician to be resurrected, and it was just too tempting to pass up. Now, he could talk with almost everybody who might be important to him, including the Space Mitchegai, who had many languages of their own, quite different from those used by the Planetary Mitchegai, although everyone spoke Deno, the common tongue.

In sports, Kren had continued to perform at collegiate events until he was forced to graduate, and was no longer qualified to play. He declined to get involved with professional sports, since he found the whole thing to be profitable, but boring. The cheers of the crowds meant nothing to him. In fact, he was never sure why they did this strange thing.

Business was far more interesting, especially when it was spiced up with the occasional battle, assisting in Duke Dennon's conquests.

Kren liked fighting in battles. Here was something that he could understand, the joy of pitting himself against another warrior in the ultimate contest, and the fierce pleasure of taking her head off when he won!

He and the duke had indeed become very good friends, learning over the years to trust each other implicitly. For over a thousand years, Dennon built his army, and periodically conquered another duchy until most of the Southern Continent was under his command. He spent most of his time working with his army, and taming each new duchy until it was loyal to him, and to his partner, Kren.

Kren spent his time making sure that they both always had a surplus of money.

Each newly conquered duchy was soon converted to the efficient production of children for food. Watering troughs, sprinklers, and the use of chemical fertilizers spread across the land. The grass above the wintering centers was mowed weekly, but additional mowing machines were not installed, as they were not cost effective.

The small tunneler stayed busy, connecting wintering centers to the train stations, providing children for winter meals.

In time, Kren's corporation bought an additional three dozen large tunneling machines, and kept them all working constantly. The ground under the land of the entire continent was eventually filled with a layer of twelve-yard tunnels, as was the land under the surface of the uninhabited South Polar Continent, which Kren bought for a relatively small price.

The South Polar Continent already had a complete, but unused, MagFloat rail system, built thousands of years before to satisfy the MagFloat Corporation's original political mandate. This corporation was delighted to finally have something to ship out of the South Polar Continent, and gave Kren very attractive shipping rates.

Vast tracts of North Polar lands on the two northern continents were purchased as well, and put to use. The advantage of polar lands was that the dirt from the tunneling machines did not have to be shipped by rail to the nearest ocean trench, but could be simply piled on the grassless snow above. Keeping the tunnels warm when they were beneath many yards of dirt and snow was not a problem.

Each underground tunnel system was vast, but most Mitchegai did not know that they existed. The system was largely automated, and Kren's fanatically loyal workers lived apart from the rest of the population, with neither group really being aware of the other.

Kren's workers were all vampires of a sort, though they didn't know it. Their knowledge was taken from others, the old nobility of the continent, and criminals who ran afoul of Kren's justice.

Their personalities were formed in the rigid, authoritarian schools that Kren and Bronki had set up. These workers did as they were told, and took an almost religious joy in performing their duty. Those few who did not were soon reprocessed, with most of their brains being fed to a new young carnivore. This was followed by another careful education. But, three times and you were out.

It was eventually found that the most profitable method of food production was to use carefully selected stock, raised to the midsized juvenal stage indoors on artificially grown grass. Then they were taken outside for a year, to toughen them up, and to develop a proper amount of muscle tissue, meat. This was followed by a dozen weeks of heavy, indoor feeding, to soften the meat and build up the right amount of body fat.

By Mitchegai standards, they were delicious!

Soon, eating natural children was something for those primitives in the countryside to do. Civilized individuals ate the fine products of the Superior Food Corporation. The prices of food rose, slowly, by a factor of six.

Many companies were formed to compete with them, but without the SFC's vast industrial plant, they could compete in neither price nor quality. All of them eventually dropped by the wayside.

Over the years, the planetary population had tripled. Most of them chose to live in the cities, where there were jobs, entertainments, and interesting things to do. Kren's construction teams enlarged many cities, and built dozens of huge, new ones.

Building new cities became a particular interest for Kren, and he played with dozens of innovative designs. With Bronki's influence, and some help from Brandee, beauty became more important than economic efficiency. Surprisingly, the most beautiful cities soon became the most profitable, since citizens were willing to pay more to live in them.

In order to make the towers taller and more slender, Kren passed a law stating that buildings on his lands more than a dozen stories tall were permitted to have elevators. The Planetary Council, fearing to offend him, made no objection.

Each new city became more beautiful than the last. Some boasted buildings with spires over a mile high, and with more than three gross stories. Many spires had great, arching bridges connecting them. Some were built entirely of structural glass, and not covered with grass at all, to the scandal of the critics.

Kren didn't care about critics. His cities were beautiful, and the apartments and commercial spaces were often purchased before they were even built.

Each new city had a university, often founded as an offshoot of the University of Dren. Kren simply thought that a city should be built around a university. Anything else seemed unnatural to him.

The cities that Kren owned had efficient police departments, staffed by absolutely honest officers, the products of his authoritarian schools. The criminal classes never got a foothold in them. Murder became a rare event, and the population grew.

When it came time for Brandee to get a new body, she branded it in a manner similar to what Kren had done to her, although she had done the branding herself weeks before she was eaten by the young carnivore. She had no desire to suffer the pain, personally, however pleasant it might be to force another to endure it.

In time, full body branding became the standard for professional artists, so that they could display their talents wherever they went.

The certainty of Duke Dennon's conquests eventually got to the point that he was able to send a letter to a fellow duke, saying that he had decided to conquer that duke's lands, but that if Dennon were to promptly receive a notarized deed for the property, he would spare his opponent's life, provided that the former duke left the planet within one week, along with his nobles.

And most dukes took him up on his offer!

Those who didn't, died.

Unfortunately, Dennon had long ago developed a habit of using his sword as a pointer, and gesticulating with it when talking. While touring one of Kren's factories, he asked a question about a high-tension electrical cable while his helmet happened to be touching a grounded metal surface. Death was instantaneous and permanent.

By Mitchegai law, when a stockholder like Duke Dennon died, his stock ceased to exist, and his share of ownership was effectively distributed to the other stockholders. To those of their race, inheritance was a null concept.

Kren actually had nothing to do with the duke's death, although many didn't believe it. He had been very pleased with his arrangement with Duke Dennon as it stood. He had actually *liked* Dennon, at least as much as a Mitchegai can like anybody.

Such had become their partnership, that when Duke

Dennon died, there was no question in anyone's mind but that Kren should succeed him.

Oh, there were a few minor rebellions at the start of his reign, but Kren put them down without difficulty. He was more brutal than Dennon had been in his conquests, since it was necessary to establish himself as a leader, and not just a business man.

At one point, he burned over eleven thousand rebels at the stake over a two-week period, with planet-wide news cameras recording the whole thing.

The show increased Kren's popularity immensely. It went into reruns, and was used for filler material for a thousand years.

There were no further rebellions.

Kren retained the red and lavender uniforms that Dennon had used, and adopted Dennon's use of a military uniform for his everyday wear. He felt that continuity was important, and he intended no changes in policy, anyway.

After that, Kren completed Dennon's plan of conquering the entire southern continent, but further conquest did not appeal to him. He could always buy whatever he wanted, and nobody wanted to fight him anymore, anyway.

Biologically, the grass resisted all attempts to genetically improve it.

Kren's scientists determined the precise conditions for optimal productivity under controlled, underground conditions, with the result that a square yard of grass in the tunnel system produced just under two dozen times as much food per year as the average square yard of uncontrolled surface grass. With the tunnel system, there were eventually six times as many square yards below that surface as on it.

With an optimal watering and fertilizing schedule for surface grass, productivity was typically doubled.

However, the basic genome of grass remained unchanged. It was already as good as it could get.

This was not true of the Mitchegai themselves. After two thousand years of careful, selective breeding, and a bit of genetic engineering, children were now normally raised from the egg to eating size in under five years, and they required only half of the food to accomplish this that they had before.

For adult bodies, Kren's physical descendants had largely taken over the planet, to his considerable regret. Once everyone had a superior body, Kren lost his huge advantage on both the playing field and the battle field.

For almost a thousand years, he had been able to keep his descendants "in house," making his soldiers astoundingly effective in combat, his workers efficient, and his athletes amazingly profitable.

The Mitchegai spend more on gambling than they do on food and housing combined. After a thousand years of being able to occasionally predict the winners of sporting events, more than half of the wealth of the entire planet was in Kren's hands. Mostly because he enjoyed doing it, he continued to gouge his bookie, usually twice a year, forcing her to buy more stock that *still* didn't pay any dividends.

At one point, he had so much of the planet's wealth that he was forced to loan money to banks at excellent rates, just to keep the planetary economy going. Later, when they could not repay him, he simply foreclosed. He then bought out the entire banking system, added it to his vast holdings, and increased the rates.

Once Kren's personal breeding program bore fruit, for the first gross years only males could be bred that had Kren's athletic prowess, to the dismay of anyone who had to walk into a locker room or barracks. Dol and Bronki were particularly unhappy about this, but finally became males for a while.

Eventually, the biochemists were able to transfer the requisite genes to other chromosomes than those that specified sex, so that females could again be as physically fit as males, and the Mitchegai world returned to normal.

Kren remained male.

But such a thing as a superior body could not be kept under wraps forever. Adults had to occasionally go out into the fields. Natural breeding took place, and each Mitchegai normally sought the best possible body for her next resurrection. The secret was out, but oddly, it was considered to be an entirely natural development. No one attributed the advance to Kren, or his scientists.

This was just as well, since there was a very

conservative streak in many Mitchegai. Very long life does that to you. There was even some talk of sterilizing the entire planet, as would be done with any new world about to be colonized, just to preserve the "Purity of the Mitchegai Genome."

After many years, messages were received at light speed from the nearer inhabited planets, through the huge, interstellar lasers and telescopes, requesting that ships be sent to them with fertilized eggs of these new Mitchegai. This interstellar approval was sufficient to make the new bodies socially acceptable, and in a gross years, everybody had one.

Usually, they paid considerably extra, and bought the very best bodies from the Superior Food Corporation. When the price of an eating child had gone up to over a gross Ke, the price of a purebred young carnivore, guaranteed to be genetically perfect, had gone up to over twelve thousand, and there was a waiting list.

Bronki was very successful as head of the Department of Chaos Theory at the College of Mathematics. Her department was soon the most profitable one at her college, and remained so for the next dozen years. Bronki herself became very popular among the other department heads, doing many personal favors, and often providing the very best party snacks.

Then, the director of the college had a fatal accident, falling from the balcony of his apartment late one winter night, and freezing solid before anyone noticed his body. Freezing destroyed the cells of the brain, and made resurrection impossible.

It was soon found that he had large doses of recreational drugs in his system, and the university hushed the whole thing up.

Kren was sure that Bronki had arranged the affair, but didn't think that it would be polite to ask about it.

The other department heads elected Bronki to be their next director, and within a few years, the College of Mathematics was the most profitable academic college in the university, not counting athletics and drama, of course.

This continued for five dozen years, at which time the chancellor of the University of Dren simply went missing.

Eight weeks went by while a massive, planet-wide search went on for him, but nothing was found. There wasn't a clue as to his whereabouts, or his fate.

A joke went around suggesting that Director Kodo had eaten him.

The other directors elected Bronki to the chancellorship of the University of Dren on the first ballot. This cost her well over a billion Ke in bribes, a great deal of money for most, but a trivial amount for her.

Bronki was pleased.

One of her first actions was to invite Kren to come into her city and to clean out the criminal elements. For a modest fee, he agreed to do this, and over a one-year period, the job was done. With Bronki cracking into their computers, and providing him with times, names, and places, the population of the city fell by one sixth. Only half of these were killed by Kren and his warriors, who by now had bodies genetically identical to his own. The rest were criminals who were smart enough to get out of town.

The director of athletics was among those quietly eliminated, and Kren performed this task personally, for vengeance and the pure fun of it.

Dik, Kren's old fencing instructor, was elected to take his place. The university's athletic program prospered.

There were over a dozen pitched battles between Kren's professional soldiers and the various criminal gangs that had infested the city. Kren's troops won every one of them, despite their use of legal weapons while the criminals used everything from guns to poison gas.

The fighting spirit is always more important than the weapon used. Numbers help, too.

Once the heavy battles were over with, the underground corridors and the surface walkways were well patrolled by honest policemen, and the independent trash were slowly swept up. Citizens could walk late at night without fear, shopkeepers no longer had to pay out most of their profits for protection money, and very few individuals paid to have new, three-inch-thick steel doors put on their apartments.

Now they could spend their money on better quality food, happily provided by the Superior Food Corporation.

Bronki became a very popular politician, and let her academic career slide.

She had many disagreements with Kren over the years, but both of them were very pragmatic. They both knew that the profits were much better when the other was around. Their "friendship" continued.

Mostly because Kren enjoyed a good battle, and because, eventually, very few dukes were willing to fight him, Kren took on many more, not very profitable, contracts to clean the criminal elements out of other cities. He and his men became very proficient at it, and the planetary drug trade dwindled to nothing.

Eventually, with success, even that source of fun began to run dry.

The population, and the profits on selling them food and housing, increased. But Kren felt that things were getting dull.

Kren's wealth and power were such that he had an automatic place on the Planetary Council. He spent a week there and left, totally bored. To him, the council was nothing but a gross of fools who thought that they could solve all of their problems by talking about them!

Finally, he said to one idiot, "Very well, then. We will put the question to the scientific method. When next it happens that you and I have a disagreement, you will resort to talk and what you are pleased to call reason. I will bring in my army and we will attack. We shall see who has the superior technique!"

Kren's opponent left the room and wasn't seen again.

Kren offered his chair to Bronki, but she declined it. It wasn't because it bored her, but because she felt that it was too dangerous. The number of political assassinations was large.

Kren had noticed a few killings, but hadn't thought it anything out of the ordinary. Certainly, no one had tried to kill him. He would have found that refreshing.

Eventually, Kren just hired an observer to look after his interests at the council, and generally ignored the whole thing. If anyone gave him difficulties, Kren resolved that he would simply kill them. Politics was not for the likes of Kren.

*   *   *

Dol continued with her program of running the day-to-day operations of the Superior Food Corporation, and continued her academic work on her doctorate in aerodynamic engineering. She remained absolutely loyal to Kren during all of this, but made a lot of money on the side, anyway.

The education that she had gotten from Bronki had served her well.

Eventually, over the next two thousand years, Dol obtained a total of three dozen and two earned doctorates, surpassing Bronki and all but three of the senior academics at the university. If any of this academic achievement was the result of additional vampirism, well, Dol never said, and Kren never asked.

Kren had been deadly bored for a gross of years, when, twelve years ago, the word came that a suitable new planet had been discovered on the outer periphery of Mitchegai Space, and that his planet had won the sector lottery. The most powerful individual on his planet would be selected to take his subordinates, and to conquer this new world.

There was no doubt anywhere on the planet but that this most powerful individual was Duke Kren!

An entire new planet was to be his to tame! *This* was something that he could sink his teeth into!

CHAPTER FIFTY-ONE

Wealth, Power, and Danger
New Yugoslavia, 2217 A.D.

Two more of the small, spherical Mitchegai ships were found in Human Space.

Both had been single-pilot exploration ships exactly like the first that Abdul had come across.

Both had had opened fire on us, ignoring our attempts at communication. All they seemed to understand was raw violence.

Both had been destroyed, one with a bank of X-ray lasers, and the other with a Disappearing Gun.

While the second ship was simply gone, the first was yielding more data about our enemy. It had contained many more books than the original one had, and with these our intelligent computers were starting to decipher the enemy's language, habits and thought patterns.

Everything that we could learn about them said that they were absolutely evil. They had no concept of God. They had no concept of Family. They had no concept of Justice. They were rapacious carnivores that simply didn't care about anything or anyone but themselves.

And they really did eat their own children, to the exclusion of everything else.

One other disquieting thing was that both of these new ships had been coming from the same direction as the original one, and that both of them were on a beeline for New Yugoslavia.

∗   ∗   ∗

With our metal ladies running the factories, our industrial strength on New Yugoslavia grew at a remarkable rate. We now had a sufficient number of picket ships built to adequately guard New Yugoslavia, and we were selling eight ships a week to the government in New Kashubia. Those mistaken individuals were still doggedly trying to defend the entirety of Human Space, and not the planets where humans actually lived.

Fortunately, well over half of the planets were disregarding the Union of Human Planets, following the lead of New Yugoslavia, and setting up their own defenses.

In another year, we would have enough sensors built to fill in the gaps between our ships, and we already had orders to sell all that we could make after that. In five years, so would a lot of other planets.

All of our picket ships and sensors were now equipped with Disappearing Guns. I'm not sure that this made much sense from a military standpoint, but our silicon ladies felt more comfortable, being armed.

We had expanded into civilian products as well, including household appliances that used the Tellefontu ambient temperature power generators, and vehicles that could use the Loway transportation network. The demand for these cars and trucks was very high, with good profits and a considerable waiting list. Kasia became richer than ever, but she didn't seem to care about that as much anymore. Maybe, she was finally growing up.

The social drone factory was going at full capacity, and within a few months every artificial intelligence on the planet would have a drone of her own. They would each be able to go out and pass for human if they wanted to.

Soon, we would be selling social drones at cost to the ladies in the rest of the army. They could afford it, since they were getting paid, now. Often, their human observers chipped in on the cost. There was much to be said for having your beautiful friend with you in the real world. Among other things, she could do the housework.

There was talk of a social drone that looked like a Tellefontu, for use by the AI who were in the crabs' fighting machines, but nothing had come of it yet. Their AIs were all entitled to a free humanoid social drone, but many of them had not taken advantage of this. Time would tell.

The Parliament of New Yugoslavia had passed laws making both AIs and the Tellefontu human in the eyes of the law. Both groups here now had full and equal rights with human beings. New Kashubia had already done the same thing, a little ahead of us.

It was expected that this equalization would eventually be expanded across all of Human Space, but again, time was needed.

My ranch was now finally at full production, with dozens of agricultural products not only feeding the people who lived in my valley, but being shipped across most of Human Space. The "Derdowski" brand name was being recognized everywhere as meaning that this was a first-quality product.

My industrial factories, all deep below ground, were now bringing in far more money than my land, but still, the ranch was my first love, and I was taking steps to protect it. Everything that could be moved down to three kilometers below the surface had been so moved. This included the grain elevators, the chicken, turkey, pig, and egg factories, and the feed lots. All of the processing plants were down there now, too, as were the lobster ponds.

Provisions had been made below to remove the dairy cows, the beef cattle, and all of the other animals living on the surface, once the Mitchegai got within a few months of us. We were stockpiling food to feed them.

We also had stockpiled grass seed and soil microorganisms, so we could restart the fields if the enemy destroyed them, and had grown scions from every tree in the valley under artificial light far below ground.

Many of the other farmers on New Yugoslavia were doing similar things. The new Disappearing Guns made floor space down there very cheap.

It was *so* cheap that a fair percentage of the population was moving down as well, living permanently in apartments that had been intended as emergency shelters. They were really very nice, and they cost much less than anything on the surface. I began to wonder if we would become a race of troglodytes!

My wife Kasia was making her plans as well. Most of her assets had been transferred to New Kashubia, since everything we were able to learn about the Mitchegai said that they only wanted planets like Earth, or New Yugoslavia. They wouldn't touch a metal ball like New Kashubia, circling its deadly Neutron Star!

She was planning to send the boys there as well, as soon as we made contact with the enemy, to live with her parents until the emergency was over.

This was fine with me. Once the danger was real, there was no point in keeping any noncombatants here, and I liked her family better than I liked mine, anyway.

But Kasia herself would spend the war fighting at my side in our CCC, she said, to make sure that I kept out of trouble.

I loved her.

Kasia and I had long ago resolved that one day a week we would have dinner alone, without the boys around. I mean, we loved them, but we loved each other, too, and sometimes five boys, aged three to thirteen, sort of got in the way.

Sometimes this meant going out to a nice restaurant, but often we just sat and ate out on one of the balconies, looking out on our land.

The boys were happy to be able to order pizza once more, and the drones were delighted to join them.

Kasia had been silent through the champagne, the appetizer, and the salad. When our T-bone steaks and lobsters arrived, I knew that she was ready to talk.

"They'll be coming soon," Kasia said. "I can feel it."

"Yes, I've been having those premonitions, too."

"They'll destroy everything that we've done here, won't they."

"Not if *I* have anything to say about it!" I said firmly. "And I *am* the military commander of this planet! We have done everything that I or anybody else can think of to make sure that our defenses are as strong as they can possibly be. If they attack us, they will die, every last damned one of them!"

"But they are older than we are, more experienced, and perhaps wiser."

"They are a bunch of damned cannibals who eat their own children! I don't know what kind of military forces they can throw against us, but we definitely have the moral high ground! God willing, we will be *victorious*!" I almost shouted.

"God willing," Kasia said, quietly.

CHAPTER FIFTY-TWO

FROM CAPTURED HISTORY TAPES, FILE 1846583A ca. 1832 A.D.

Kren Prepares for War

It had been twelve years since Kren had received notice of his new prize. This was barely enough time to do all that needed to be done.

The Eleventh Colonizing Fleet could take only two dozen million Planetary Mitchegai to the new world, and Kren had more than six gross that number of subordinates. He had to be sure that he took only his very best along. He decided on taking a dozen million of his most proficient warriors, six million of his most competent scientists and technical people, and six million others, including his most astute administrators, businessmen, and the finest academics from all of his universities. He even planned to take along a few artists, poets, and writers.

Most of these selected people had been in space for years, training for their mission in new, first-quality bodies.

Kren had spent most of his vast personal fortune equipping his subordinates for this venture.

His engineers and builders needed the generalized machines necessary to build the specialized machines that made all of the myriad products that his new planet would need. They had to be prepared to be able to start with nothing but the rawest of materials, and to turn out the finest of end products.

Kren insisted that everything that they took with them must be of the very best quality.

The Mitchegai had millions of years of technology behind them, but if they did not have drawings of every possible thing that they might ever need with them, they would have to invent it afresh, something that they were not very good at. The technical plans alone for all that would be needed filled an entire large cargo ship. This was because their computers were so primitive, by human standards, that they had to take all of their plans printed on thin sheets of their immortal plastic.

They had to have enough food and supplies to last them at least two dozen years, when they should start to become self-sufficient in many matters. If anything was forgotten, they simply wouldn't have it. The success of the entire colonization program could depend on some trivial item, and when it did, they must have it with them.

His academics insisted on having a complete library of more than twelve million books, and Kren gave them permission to loot every library in every university on his lands, if need be, to get everything that they could possibly need.

Every person going was permitted to bring two tons of personal goods along, with the understanding that they would have to live with that for at least two dozen years before much of it could be replenished.

At his own considerable expense, Kren purchased an armored space suit for every one of the Planetary Mitchegai who was accompanying him. The Space Mitchegai told him that this was a silly way to waste money, and that they would never be needed, but they took his cash, delivered the products, and trained his subordinates in how to use them.

His best soldiers and officers, twelve million of them, were also equipped with every high-tech weapon that the Space Mitchegai could provide. They had been spending the last nine years in space, learning how to use them. This, too, was laughed at, but they took his money. His warriors got the weapons and training.

Kren also bought one million additional single seat fighters, and had a million of his warriors trained to use them, at a price that almost cleaned out his bank accounts. Indeed, he had to borrow money from his own banks, on zero interest, indefinite loans, before the production run was over. They called him crazy once more, but as always, he got his way.

His banks knew that they would never be repaid, and computed that it would be over a thousand years before they recovered. Yet none dared dispute the wishes of Kren.

Kren also had to purchase five additional cargo ships of the largest standard size to transport them all, and all at his own expense.

To Kren's mind, he had the money, and he was going to see to it that absolutely nothing got in the way of his smooth takeover of his personal planet.

"Madness," everyone else said.

Privately, Kren allowed that they might be right. It was probably wasted money. The cost of all of these precautionary expenditures was large but finite, and he could afford it. But the cost of failure was infinite! His life. And that, he could *not* afford!

What else could he spent his money on, anyway? Should he leave it in the bank on a planet four gross light-years away?

In addition to all of this, Kren was obligated to provide food for his own people, for the Space Mitchegai who would be accompanying him, and for the operators and fighters of the entire Eleventh Colonizing Fleet. They had to be fed for the duration of the trip, and for the next two dozen years thereafter, until the grass was growing and the juvenals were prospering. He also had to feed the fleet personnel, during their return trip.

Most of these children could be provided cryogenically frozen, to be thawed in microwave ovens before eating. This provided food that was barely acceptable to an adult Mitchegai. But fully a quarter of it was expected to be delivered live, for the culinary enjoyment of the upper ranks.

The ships were equipped with compartments that kept a child dormant at a few degrees above freezing, while surrounding her with monochromatic growing lights virtually identical to those Kren had developed to grow grass underground.

Since the Mitchegai skin could convert light to food almost

as well as the grass could, these compartments could keep a juvenal dormant but alive for many years, ready to eat.

Kren had been very proud of those monochromatic lights that he had developed for his tunnels, and here, the Space Mitchegai had had the technology all along!

Kren just turned the problem of supplying enough children to feed the expedition over to Dol, and told her that the Superior Food Corporation would do it at its own expense.

Dol said, "Yes, sir."

Those he was leaving behind would have to be organized to survive without him. He did not want his lands to be overrun by other dukes, or his investments to go sour in his absence. There wasn't a really rational reason why he should care, but somehow he felt a certain attachment to what he had spent a long lifetime building.

General Yor had proved to be unfailingly competent and loyal for thousands of years. He had chosen her as his successor.

Kren awoke once more and stretched. He didn't feel *totally* miserable, and that would have to suffice. There wasn't much time left, and there was much yet to do.

He pulled off the recording helmet, relieved and refreshed himself. He dressed, removed the tape from the recorder, and put it in his pouch.

He went to the combination lock at the door, remembered the twelve number combination, and dialed it in. This was important, because ancient tradition required that if a duke forgot the combination, he would be left in the chamber, to die there. There was no way to open the door from the outside without causing the entire complex to self-destruct, violently.

This system protected him while he was in his stupor, but also there was always the possibility that something could go wrong in the resurrection process, and no one wanted to be ruled by an incompetent duke. Better a civil war than to have only half of your old master on the throne.

Kren opened the door to find Dol and Bronki waiting for him.

"It's good to see you well," Dol said.

"Yes, we were beginning to worry about you, my friend," Bronki added.

"Every time, it seems to take longer and hurt more," Kren said.

"You could always give up on this stupid *traditional* way of doing things, take an anesthetic, and wake up feeling good, the way sensible people do," Dol said.

"A leader who did that wouldn't be a leader for long," Kren said. He handed the personal history tape to Bronki. "I am still a bit worried about telling the truth about all that has happened. I know that your background as a historian makes you want what really happened to come out eventually, but it is still a very dangerous thing to do."

"Kren, despite everything, besides being individuals, we are also members of a great civilization. Without our history, we are nothing," Bronki said.

"Just be sure that this stays secret until long after I'm dead."

"Until long after all three of us are dead, if it contains everything that I think it does! I've already made arrangements with the Bonding Authority to keep it until one thousand years after the last of us has been registered as certainly and sincerely deceased. Then they will send it to the College of History at Dren."

"I suppose that the Bonding Authority can be trusted, if anybody can," Kren said. "I don't suppose that either of you has changed your minds? You are both intent on staying here on this planet when I leave?"

"Yes, sir," Dol said. "We're both really city girls, you know. We wouldn't fit in well on the wild frontiers. And anyway, you have set things up such that this entire solar system will starve if the Superior Food Corporation isn't managed properly. What's the point of conquering a new planet while leaving the old one to destroy itself? And who can say? Maybe you will need something from here once you are out there. It might take eight gross years to get there, but that's better than nothing."

Bronki said, "Also, there is always the chance that things will not work out on the new planet. It has happened a few times before in history, you know, where a promising-looking planet has had to be totally destroyed. If that were to happen to you, wouldn't you want to have a nice, safe place to come home to? We'll just put your stock in escrow, put the next largest stockholder on the board of directors, and carry on until you return, however many thousand years that takes."

"And who is this fourth largest stockholder?"

"Your bookie, of course!" Bronki said.

The Eleventh Colonizing Fleet was built, operated, and maintained by the Space Mitchegai. It was crewed by a very special group, since they spent most of their time traveling at nearly light speed. The time dilations involved were such that once they left, there wasn't much point in going home again. And indeed, their mission was such that they rarely went to the same solar system twice. Their lives, which from the outside seemed to be millions of years long, were spent in, with, and for The Fleet.

This consisted of over three thousand large cargo and passenger ships, and many times that number of smaller, auxiliary vessels. The local Space Mitchegai were contributing an additional gross of ships, and refurbishing the rest as needed, as their contribution to the coming venture.

The fleet also had three gross of truly massive battle ships, plus many thousands of small, single-seat fighters. This military arm had never seen action in its millions of years of existence, but military force had proved to be very useful to some of the other colonizing fleets in the past.

Of the seven thousand planets sent colony fleets to date, a dozen and ten had had indigenous populations capable of putting up a ferocious fight. Indeed, nine of those planets had had to be completely destroyed, since otherwise they could have become a threat to the entire Mitchegai civilization.

And anyway, the Mitchegai always felt more comfortable when they were well armed.

CHAPTER FIFTY-THREE

FROM CAPTURED HISTORY TAPES,
FILE 1846583A ca. 1832 A.D.

The Space Mitchegai

Besides the Planetary Mitchegai, the fleet would be transporting an additional two dozen million Spacers from Kren's solar system to the new system as well. As Kren and his subordinates were taming the new planet, these Spacers would be taking on the rest of the new solar system.

The Space Mitchegai were racially identical to the Planetary Mitchegai, but culturally very different. They had originated in the asteroid belt of their home system, long before interstellar transportation was developed.

While the Planetary Mitchegai preferred a placid, traditional lifestyle, with a minimum of technology, the Space Mitchegai lived in relatively small, high-tech habitats, scattered throughout the solar system, but especially in planetary orbits and the asteroid belt. The Space Mitchegai lived more regimented lives, and more active ones.

It was the Space Mitchegai who had developed what humans would call the slow, multigeneration ships that first got to the nearer stars. This effort was greatly aided by the very long effective lifetimes that the Mitchegai enjoyed. Even traveling at one part in a gross of the speed of light, with a typical trip length of two dozen light-years, they still could make the journey in a sixth of their expected lifespan, if they were careful. A ship's crew member might make several round trip voyages before she happened to die.

The situation became much better once the Inertialess Field was developed, based on the technology of a race that they had conquered. This device put a field around almost the entire ship that temporarily canceled inertia. When the field was disconnected, inertia returned, and the ship proceeded on a vector identical to what it had had in the beginning.

Mitchegai ships were powered by their muon-exchange fusion reactors, very much like those used by humans, but smaller, more refined, and much more powerful. These converted hydrogen into helium and electrical power with almost perfect efficiency.

The Intertialess Field was used in conjuction with a pair of ion engines that each fired positive or negative ions, atoms with either more or less electrons in their outer shells than was normal. Sodium and flourine were the preferred elements for this purpose. These two beams of ions came out of the back of the ship at close to light speed. Once they recombined, there was quite a fireworks display behind the ship, but this was far enough behind to cause no damage, to the ship at least. It was however a formidable weapon.

The exhaust ports and drive coils of the ion engine were the only parts of the ship that were outside of the Inertialess Field. Their mass was typically less than one thousandth of the entire mass of the ship. The ship was therefore capable of accelerating to nearly light speed in less than a week, while the occupants felt no acceleration at all. The effects of time dilation were such that a long interstellar trip usually took place in only a few years of subjective time.

A valuable side effect of the Inertialess Field was that it also acted as a shield. Anything that the ship encountered while traveling at close to the speed of light became inertialess just before it collided with the ship. Particles, dust, and even fair-sized rocks caused the ship no harm. They became inertialess, lightly bounced off and eventually drifted out of the field.

At that point, their inertia returned, and they continued on their way, once the ship had passed. Sometimes, when the angles happened to be right, a single rock had been known to hit a ship a dozen times without causing harm.

Encountering a star, a planet, or even an asteroid was something else, of course. Even if the surface was inertialess, the mass farther out could cause a very deadly spray of radiation as it rammed the normal matter in front of it. Often the energy generated was on the order of an extremely large nuclear weapon.

Fortunately, such encounters were rare, and a ship's watch officers could generally avoid such situations, usually by turning off the field, which immediately sent them on the low speed vector that they'd had when they started.

On reaching their destination, it was necessary to turn off the field, and run the drive in the proper direction for the required time to bring the ship to the same direction and speed as the planet they were going to. Much of the science of navigation revolved around doing this efficiently.

The Space and Planetary Mitchegai interacted constantly. Economically, socially, and culturally, they needed each other.

Economically, the Space Mitchegai, in any inhabited solar system, handled most of the heavy industry. They mined the asteroid belts for metals and other useful materials. They mined the outer planets and moons for water, ammonia, and carbon dioxide.

They used these things in efficient space-born factories, powered by their ubiquitous muon-exchange fusion generators. They didn't have to worry about polluting their environment, or destroying their fragile planetary ecology. They produced most of the durable goods used both on the planets and in space.

They also provided several services to the planetbound. They built and repaired the communication satellites that augmented the fiber communication cables used on the planet. They made and serviced the huge lasers and telescopes that maintained contact with the nearer solar systems, and through them, with the rest of the Mitchegai civilization.

And they provided the security system that insured that planetary wars would not get out of hand. They created and commanded the neutron bombs that were in low orbit, ready to destroy any duchy that violated the Laws of War.

Limited wars with primitive weapons were good for the planetbound. High-tech wars were not, and for a fee, paid by the Planetary Council, they ensured that this system would continue.

Among the Space Mitchegai, the airless environment they lived in was sufficiently dangerous as to cause a regular depletion of those individuals who were not sufficiently intelligent as to be of benefit to the race. Wars were therefore not necessary, and were not tolerated.

However, they loved watching panetary wars on television, just as much as the planetbound did. The volume of gambling was often greater on the wars than it was on athletics.

They got most of their other entertainments from the local planet as well, and they felt that planets were great places to visit and vacation on, although they didn't want to live there. Hunting expeditions on the grass covering the ancient oceans were particularly popular.

The Planetary Mitchegai made most of the food produced in the system, along with most of the textiles, paper, and other minor items. They sent it out, much of the food still alive, by way of the two planetary geosynchronous cables, that humans would call beanstalks. These were sufficiently long so that at the platforms at the ends, a full planetary gravity was felt. By releasing or capturing a ship or capsule at the right time and place along the cables, a cargo could be sent to, or received from, any point in the solar system with very little additional energy added.

Ships were faster, and more desirable for use with passengers, but even ships equipped with the inertialess field used the cables, so that when they arrived at their destination, they would have the right speed and direction to dock quickly.

To keep the cable system in dynamic balance, and to insure that the planet stayed in chemical balance, additional cargos of lighter elements were sent in to the planet to match those sent out as food, and cargoes of useless rock and dirt were sometimes sent out and into the sun, to match the mass of the durable goods brought in.

Other spinning cables throughout the system were used in a transportation system that efficiently distributed goods to all of the heavily populated regions.

In the long run, it was far less expensive than using cargo ships, and the Mitchegai always thought long term.

The Space Mitchegai had a vast array of weapons available to them. There were dozens of various sorts of lasers, and at least as many sorts of particle beam generators. There were chemical explosives, rockets and bombs. There were rail guns, accelerators, and even cannons in their extensive arsenals.

There were ships of all sizes, from seven-mile-long dreadnaughts to tiny kamikaze craft, piloted by surgically stunted pilots who were convinced that wonderful things would happen to them if only they could put their bomb-laden ship into the enemy.

Many of these weapons had originally been the property of races who had had the silly gall to try to defend themselves against the all-powerful Mitchegai.

And the Eleventh Invasion Fleet had the pleasant advantage of being one of the first to be equipped with the Disappearing Guns. These had been used by a race of blue crustaceans who had actually managed to delay one conquest for a dozen weeks or so.

They had improved on it, of course. It was now thousands of times more powerful, and had been linked in with each ship's sensors such that if they happened to inadvertently be about to strike some massive object, the gun fired automatically. Calculations indicated that if they were about to strike a fair-sized planet while the ship was traveling at near light speed, the gun could actually cut a hole all the way through the planet, and let the ship pass through unharmed!

No one had actually put this ability to the test, yet, but time would tell.

CHAPTER FIFTY-FOUR

They Are Coming
New Yugoslavia, 2218 A.D.

My lands were now dotted with magnificent fountains.

Early on, we had installed simple, utilitarian drinking troughs for the cattle. Then, the AI people had discovered that the controls on the Disappearing Guns they had been issued were sufficiently fine to sculpture with. The beam width could be turned down to less than a millimeter, and the depth of cut could be controlled even finer.

And since we were cutting out all of these rooms in the granite anyway, they got to slicing out huge blocks of the stuff, and getting artistic with them.

Once the city started to have really too many statues, the electronic ladies hit on the idea of making fountains in their off hours, and putting them out here. I suppose that you'd have to call it a hobby.

Out riding my land, I'd stopped to water my horse at a Renaissance-looking thing that was at least fifty feet across. It had hundreds of naked sea nymphs and gods in a two-story pile in the middle, all squirting water out of various orifices. The dozen cows and two camels drinking around it didn't seem to mind, and neither did my horse.

My communicator buzzed.

"Boss, they're coming! Stay where you are. I've sent a helicopter to pick you up," Agnieshka said.

"The DEW Sphere found them?" I asked.

"Yes, they're more than two years out."

"Then what's the rush?" I said, trying to act cool, "Why the helicopter? When the Spanish Armada was sighted, they let Sir Walter Raleigh finish his bowling game."

"Because if I didn't, you'd probably kill your horse racing back. Sir Walter Raleigh you ain't."

I took the helicopter back.

When I got to my CCC, my colonels, including my wife, were already inside.

"There are a lot of them," Kasia said. "And they are very big."

CHAPTER FIFTY-FIVE

FROM CAPTURED HISTORY TAPES,
FILE 1846583A ca. 1832 A.D.

Kren's Departure

The ceremony whereby Kren enlarged General Yor up to Duke Yor had taken half a day. It had been so long since a duke had voluntarily given up his power that Kren had had to assign a historian to find out the proper procedure.

It was boring, but it had to be done.

The next day, Duke Kren walked from the train station to the side of the gross-thousand-mile-high geosynchronous cable that would take him to his waiting fleet. He had only three Mitchegai with him. Duke Yor, Dol, and Bronki. The crowds and the news cameras had been kept far away.

Kren stopped at the doorway.

"Duke Yor, I think that I have taught you everything that I can about successfully running my old duchy. You are as prepared as you possibly can be. But one last word of advice. You must rule with a firm hand. If you encounter the slightest opposition from anyone on anything, you must be absolutely ruthless. This is especially important in the first few dozen years. Perhaps after that, you can let up a bit if you wish. But at first, until they fear you as much as they fear me, when in doubt, burn them publicly at the stake, and in large numbers. It is far better to kill the innocent than to let anyone think that you are soft."

"I will act on your advice, Your Grace," Duke Yor said.

"And you two," Kren said to Bronki and Dol, "My advice

375

to you is to keep expanding. Keep building underground fields of grass, keep increasing the food supply, keep the population expanding. Nothing stays the same in this universe. You must continue to grow, or you will start to die!"

"Yes, sir," Dol said. "There will be no change in your basic policy. It has worked well for two thousand years, and it will continue to do so."

Bronki said, "We will be sending you messages every few years, just to let you know what is happening. In a few gross years, once you have an interstellar laser built in your new solar system, drop us a line, and tell us of your new life there. Remember that we will always be your good friends. One last thing. I have gone over the history tape that you gave me. I've annotated it, and made you a copy. I think that you should take it with you, for reference, if nothing else."

Bronki gave the tape to Kren, who put the tape in his pouch.

He had nothing more to say. Feeling much as he had the day when he had first stepped out of the Senta Copper Mine, he stepped into the elevator, looking forward to his next exciting new adventure.

INTERLUDE TWO

Agnieshka's Plea
THE RIGELLIAN INSTITUTE OF ARCHEOLOGY,
EARTH, 3783 A.D.

The audience loved the performance. They clapped and barked enthusiastically.

Sir Rupert stepped up to the podium and raised his hands to the crowd.

"Thank you! Thank you my friends! But before we retire to the dining room, where suitable refreshments are waiting for us, Agnieshka would like to say a few closing words to you!"

Again, Agnieshka was applauded up onto the stage.

"My good friends," she said. "From what you have just seen, it should be obvious to you that the War Against the Mitchegai still goes on! The Tellefontu and the artificial intelligences are continuing to press against the enemy, even though our Human friends are no more. Because of the vast size of the Mitchegai domain, it would be at least four thousand more years before this vile race can be properly exterminated, even if we were always successful against them, which we have not been.

"Your Canine civilization has had the time to develop because the allies have shielded you from the Mitchegai. Have no doubt that without the Tellefontu and the AI, the Mitchegai would have long ago killed every one of you, destroyed all life on this planet, and taken this world for their own!

"The Tellefontu and the AI need all the help that they can get, and now that you Canines have proven yourselves

377

to be a civilization worthy of taking the place of the Humans, I think that it is fitting that you should take their place, fighting against our common ancient enemy!

"This will take great effort and sacrifice on your part, and many years of diligent labor. I know that we can get the artificial intelligences to help. If nothing else, together we can build more people like me. Together we can get our proper revenge on the unspeakable race that destroyed our first friends, the Humans!

"I beg you to think on this, to discuss it among yourselves, and with your leaders.

"Together, we can take our proper place in history!"

TO BE CONTINUED . . .